fro...

HEAVENLY LAND

Eliza's Story

A NOVEL

Cathy Slusser

Blessings!
Cathy Slusser

To Mom and Dad,
with love and thanks.
Who knew when you took me to
St. Simon's where it would lead?
... and to Glen,
with love and thanks as well.
You knew where it would lead,
but took me back to St. Simon's anyway.

Introduction

Caveat:
warning, caution, admonition, qualification, limitation

Writing historical fiction is a lot like being a forensic anthropologist. The writer, like the anthropologist takes a skeleton and creates a life from it. An anthropologist interprets a person's existence by looking at their bones. Broken, worn or misshapen limbs all tell a life's tale. While spreading hipbones indicate a woman gave birth, they do not convey the pain and agony of those moments or whether the child lived or died. A shattered nose cannot communicate the wrenching force of another human being's hand smashing it in such heated anger that the bone snaps like a fragile twig. A third finger of a left hand is worn from the rub of a wedding ring over a long period of time. Was the marriage a happy one? Bones do not tell that story. So it is with the writer of historical fiction. We investigate the facts, when humans die, where they live, who they marry. We do not know what they felt, how deeply they loved or the hurt they endured. The story told here is partly real, partly fiction. Elizabeth Margaret Atzeroth Dickens Fogarty was a real woman who spent the majority of her life on Terra Ceia Island on the central west coast of Florida in the nineteenth century. From historical records, I know much about her, but little about who she really was inside. The facts you will read are true. For the most part, I have taken liberty with her thoughts and words. If I am wrong, I hope Eliza will forgive me. I can't help but imagine that she was a woman just like you or me and that the events she experienced shaped the person she became. I must note that I am indebted to other authors and historians who came before me recording the history of the Atzeroth and Fogarty families, especially Ollie Zipperer Fogarty. They provided the skeleton; the rest of the body is my own.

Beginnings

Yellow sky. Dead calm. Low clouds. Animals huddle in their burrows. No birds in sight. Over time, I learned the signs, the clues in the sky and air that forecast a hurricane bearing down upon us. In the early days, newly arrived from Germany to the tropical wilderness, predicting the weather wasn't easy. Papa always said that Florida, like a woman, never could make up her mind. That kind of talk earned him a sour look from Mama, but he was right. A day might start clear and beautiful, but by nightfall, the howling wind threatened to steal everything from you. That's how it was, one fall morning, just after breakfast when I was six and watched my father walk down to the bay to look for clams. He promised Mama he would bring her some in time for dinner, but before I could finish washing the dishes, Papa reentered the cabin.

"Joseph? Did you find the clams so soon?" Mama asked.

"Julia, I'm worried about the weather. Something is not right. The air is so still. The sun is out, but the sky is very dark in the west. You and the girls stay close to the cabin. It looks like we are in for a storm. Clear the porch of anything that might blow. I'm going to check on the animals."

With that word of warning, Papa left again. My cousin, Mary, and I followed Mama to the porch. Trees blocked our view of the sky, but it was hard to breath the air was so humid and oppressive. Mary, sensing Mama's anxiety began to whine.

"Crybaby," I thought, even though I, too, felt uneasy.

For the next few hours, we worked to bring inside all the wash basins, chairs, tubs and crocks from the cabin's porches. As usual, Mary was no help, clinging to Mama's skirts and getting in the way. Mama said I should be more patient with her. After all, she was an orphan with no mother or father of her own, but how I hated sharing my parents with her and resented her incessant demands. How nice it was when it was just the three of us in our snug little log cabin near the shore of Terra Ceia Bay on Florida's west coast. Papa chose to homestead this land because it was halfway between Fort Brooke and the Village of Manatee. He envisioned the island as a trading post between the two larger communities. Back then, we had the island to ourselves, and I liked it that way. The other settlers laughed at us for our German accents and ostracized us because of our Lutheran faith. Southerners and Methodists. German and Lutheran. Northerners and Catholics. I saw no difference. But, they did. As long as I had Mama and Papa, who needed anyone else?

During the morning, the weather changed quickly. The wind began to howl. Trees around the cabin turned and twisted in its grasp. While clouds blocked out the sun, eerie yellow light filtered all around the cabin. When the rain began, it came in torrents. No gradual, gentle start but a deluge. Papa raced back into the cabin, soaked to the skin. Before coming inside, he latched the shutters over the windows and bolted the doors shut. Mama lit the candles, and everyone gathered in the kitchen. The light did not reach to its far corners. Sitting at the table, I could barely see their faces. The edges of the room remained black. My chest constricted. I tried not to panic. It would be alright. Papa would keep us safe. What was happening outside? Not knowing was almost as bad as knowing.

For the next few hours, the thud of falling tree limbs echoed around the cabin. The wind ripped shingles off the roof and whipped them into the trees. Rain seeped inside the chimney, extinguishing the coals from the morning's fire. It washed the sides of the logs, poured through the cracks and ran in streams down the interior walls. Puddles accumulated on the kitchen floor. Mary cried herself to sleep, still sitting in Mama's lap. How could she rest at such a time? Excitement mixed with fear propelled me from my seat. I thought I would go mad if I couldn't look outside. Before I took my first step, a great crash came from the direction of the front porch. Then, as if a giant hand turned off a spigot, the rain and wind stopped. It was so quiet! I rubbed my ears thinking the noise of the storm made me deaf. But, listen! I could hear the trickle of water dripping. Somewhere, the cow was calling for its calf. The storm must be over!

Excited, I ran to the front door. Shut tightly, I could not open it. Papa reached around me and undid the latch. Just as I stepped onto the porch, Papa pulled me back. The porch was gone! I couldn't believe what I saw. No match for the wind, one of the largest oak trees lay on its side in front of the house. The water soaked ground softened, and with no support, the tree fell. Its branches pulled the porch away from the house. It lay in ruins under the limbs. Despite the chaos, I had to laugh. The tree looked funny on its side. I could look right into a bird's nest.

The sun peeked through the clouds. Everything was still.

"May I play on the tree, Papa?"

"No, Eliza, not just yet. Do you remember that storm that I sailed through on the way to get Mary?"

"Yes, the one that was so terrible. When you thought you were going to drown?" Papa placed his hand on my head and gently rubbed my hair.

"Eliza, that storm came in two parts. In the midst of the storm was a time just like this. We thought the worst was over. Then, it came back with greater force than before. I don't think we are finished with this one yet. Go back inside." He turned to Mama and said, "Julia, I'm going to check on the animals."

"Joseph, stay here. If the storm should come back, you could get caught out there. Besides, there is nothing you can do. If they are gone, they are already lost."

"The water may rise in the second half of the storm. If I can lead them to higher ground, they will be safe. I have to try." With those words, Papa bolted the front door closed again, walked quickly down the hall and exited through the back door.

I followed him as far as the porch.

"Eliza, stay here. Don't come any farther. I mean what I say." Though I desperately wanted to go with him, I dared not disobey.

"Yes, Papa," I replied. I grasped the railing of the porch with both hands and leaned as far out as I could to watch Papa until he was out of sight.

Not long after my father left, the wind began to build again. This time, it came from the back of the house. Its strength pushed me away from the edge of the porch towards the wall and slammed the back door shut. *What if I can't get back inside?* I pounded on its wooden frame. Immediately, Mama reopened the door, reached outside and pulled me into her embrace. I buried my face into Mama's apron.

"Where is Papa, Mama? Will he get back before the storm does?"

"Of course. We must pray, Eliza. God will bring him back to us. Perhaps that is him now!"

Mama's prayers answered, Papa rushed into the doorway. Resisting the wind, he leaned into the stout door, closed and bolted it.

Breathless, he wheezed, "Most of the animals are alright. There is no sign of the chickens, but the hen house still stands. It's coming back from a different direction. I think we better stay here in the hallway. I am not sure what this second half will bring."

Papa moved some chairs to the hall. As the wind continued to rise and rain beat against the cabin, each of us coped as best we could. Taking out his knife and a stick of kindling, Papa whittled. As he worked, he whistled. I paced back and forth. Always a copycat, Mary trailed behind me.

Mama watched us for a time. Then, she snapped.

"Girls, sit down! You are making me insane. Joseph, let's sing something."

Mama began in her clear alto voice, "A Mighty Fortress Is Our God."

Papa joined in and their voices blended together:

A mighty fortress is our God, a bulwark never failing;
Our helper He, amid the flood of mortal ills prevailing:
For still our ancient foe doth seek to work us woe;
His craft and power are great, and, armed with cruel hate,
On earth is not his equal.

As their voices rose above the wind, it sounded like an act of defiance against the storm. Just as they reached the final chorus, a high pitched wailing from outside joined their song. It reached a crescendo as it came closer to the cabin.

"Julia, get Mary! Follow me!" Papa shouted over the wind as he scooped me into his arms and ran towards the front door.

Bursting through it, Papa lost his balance and knocked me into the doorframe. The rough wood scrapped the skin off my hand. It stung, but I was too afraid to pay it much mind. Outside, the wind took my breath away. Papa crawled under the fallen tree where the porch once stood. Setting me among the leaves, he reached back to take Mary from Mama. She slipped under the wide limbs beside him. Pushing us back under the tree's trunk, Papa shielded us with his body. I felt the oak's rough bark pressing into my back and rain soaked my hair. I closed my eyes against the blowing sand and debris. We huddled there together, wet and muddy as the wind whistled through the branches above. Moments later, Mama screamed, and I opened my eyes just as a tornado demolished the cabin.

Six Years Later

Chapter One

"Daughter, why are you so quiet? When you begged to come along, you promised to keep me company."

From atop the broad high back of Papa's mule, Dan, I look down on my father as he walks ahead of me. Papa swings his machete in even strokes clearing a path though the saw palmettos. Traveling overland means more work for him. He complains that the brush grows so fast a man could be surrounded in the time it took him to blink. Ordinarily, Papa would sail from our house and store on the northern bank of the Manatee River to the farm on Terra Ceia. Today, he needs the mule's help to prepare the fields for planting. So we must walk. Rather Dan and Papa do. I ride, but I smile as I imagine the mule loaded into the bow of Papa's ketch. *No, that will never happen.*

Papa glances back over his shoulder. "Ah, a smile. I was beginning to wonder if you regretted your choice to come with me. What are you thinking about that makes you so solemn?"

I squirm in the saddle. How to tell Papa my true thoughts? If there is one thing I've learned in my twelve years, keeping a secret from Papa is nearly impossible. How to say that the stillness of the air and the heat of the sun remind me of the hurricane? Six years gone by, but not one day passes that I don't think about it. The storm destroyed more than my home. That day marked the moment I set aside my reliance on Mama's God. More than the many moves to find a better home, more than school and the torments suffered there because of my heritage, if a single event could shape a person, I blame the storm for emptying my heart of any trust in a good and loving God. Even as I helped rebuild the log cabin, I wondered, "Where was Mama's

God while the storm raged about us?" While Mama sang of God's greatness and compassion, He let the wind have its way with our home. In the end, God abandoned us.

I remember the first time I voiced my growing disbelief in Mama's God aloud. After the storm, we moved into the henhouse while Papa went to Fort Brooke to get supplies to rebuild our home. One day at dinner, Mama asked me to say the blessing. I felt out of sorts. In the thick and still summer air, I could hardly breathe. The monotony of the long summer days wore thin. I missed Papa.

Instead of bowing my head, I complained. "Why should I say a blessing? Did you thank me for weeding around these carrots or Papa for raising this hog? You cooked these nice biscuits. Shouldn't I be thanking you? Where is God anyway? I don't see him, so why should I be talking to him?" As soon the words escaped, I regretted them. Surely God would strike me with lightening for being so wicked. That is if Mama does not beat Him to it.

Instead of becoming angry, Mama was quiet. Then, she said, "It is too hot to eat. Let's take a walk, Eliza. Mary, come."

Leaving dinner on the table, we left the cabin. Before stepping off the porch, Mama tied my sunbonnet under my chin. We walked towards the bay, and I wondered where we are going and why. I was afraid to ask. *Was Mama angry? She didn't act angry, just sad. Why did we leave the table? Was I being punished in some strange new way?*

Mama asked me questions. "What do you see, Eliza?"

"I see flowers."

"Tell me about them."

"I see blue spiderwort and yellow tickseed."

"Did you plant them?"

"No, they just grew."

"What else do you see?"

"I see lots of trees, big ones and little ones."

"Did you plan where they would sprout to give us lumber and shade?"

"No, they have always been there."

"What else do you see?"

"I see a beautiful red cardinal."

"Do you feed him his dinner every day?"

"No," I replied. *Why did she ask me all these questions? They didn't make sense. I felt unsettled.*

"What is over there?"

"Our spring."

Walking closer to its edge, Mama asked, "Do you tell the water to come up out of the ground each morning?"

"No, it just flows."

"Look down into the water, Eliza. What do you see there?"

I looked closely and saw my reflection in the water. "I see myself!"

"Eliza, God makes the flowers and trees grow. He cares for the birds and gives us water to drink and food to eat. Yes, we work hard, but we have nothing that God does not give us. He could take it all away at a moment's notice. That is why we must be grateful and give thanks. He made you too, Eliza. He made you just like you are. Is Papa still your father even though he is gone and you don't know exactly where he is?"

My heart hurt to think about Papa. I wanted him to come home, but I nodded my head.

"Eliza, God is your Father, too. And even though you can't see Him or hear Him, He gives you good things and takes care of you."

I thought about what Mama said. What did she mean? Then, my stomach knotted as I thought about God watching me and disapproving of me. *Did he see my ungrateful heart? Was He waiting for me to appreciate what He had given me? If I didn't say thank you, would He take them away? Papa was gone. When was the last time I thanked God for Papa? Oh, I was grateful, truly I was!*

For a time, I asked more questions. I wanted to believe, but God seemed distant and unreal. A stern taskmaster watching from afar. Mama held me close and smiled. "You just have to learn to trust that God is in control and knows what's best."

What kind of answer was that? For six years, I wondered and watched, but it didn't seem to me that God was in control. In fact, the world grew more unpredictable and uncertain every day. How do you learn to trust someone that you can't see or know?

I can't tell Papa any of that so I keep my peace. As we cross through the pine forests and along the south shore of Terra Ceia Bay, I fan my face with my hand. Dan's shoulders glisten with sweat. His feet kick up dust that turns to mud on his flank. I hold tightly to his mane to keep from slipping off. *No, better not to bother Papa with questions.*

"I think perhaps you are disappointed with my mule," Papa teases. "Dan is not like those fancy ponies of Chief Billy." *Now that is something we can talk about.*

"Oh, no, Papa, Dan is fine. I love riding him very much."

"Now, Eliza, it can't be nearly as fun as Chief Billy's ponies."

Papa is right, but I don't want to hurt his feelings. I first met the Seminole Indian leader, Hollatta Micco or Chief Billy Bowlegs as the other settlers call him, while we lived in Fort Brooke. After the hurricane, Mama took a job working for Colonel Belknap the commander of the small regiment of soldiers stationed there. Chief Billy loved Mama's cooking and often came to visit.

I cannot help but smile when I think of Chief Billy. He saved my life once. I have always been fascinated with horses and Colonel Belknap owned a fine pair. Once, I slipped away from the house and climbed into the corral. From the ground, they looked a lot bigger. I eased closer to the one nearest the fence. With his nose to the ground, he nibbled at the grass. I thought the horse was ignoring me and reached out to touch his shiny black mane, but he spun quickly, turning his back and raising his hind leg to kick me. It seemed to happen in slow motion. I saw the danger, but my legs would not work.

Just as the black hoof came within inches of my face, I felt myself lifted into the air and swung around out of harm's way. Twisting to see my rescuer, I was face to face with a dark skinned man dressed in an odd costume. Over a shirt made of many bright colored fabrics, he wore around his neck many strings of beads. A band, like a large crown, encircled his forehead and from it were six tall plumes of soft feathers. His black piercing eyes gazed into mine, and I realized that I was in the arms of Billy Bowlegs himself.

"Little girls should not go near big horses," he said in rhythmic tones so heavily accented that I had to think carefully about their meaning. Then, he set me on the other side of the fence away from the horses. "Someday, I give you ride on my horse. Today, you stay away from these."

Not knowing whether to stay or to run, I stood my ground. *This was a real Indian!* People said Indians were bad, but Billy Bowlegs said he would give me a ride on a horse. From this angle, I saw why he had earned his nickname for his legs were in the shape of a bow.

"What happened to your legs?"

Grinning, he replied. "Not afraid, little miss? Don't you run away?"

"I want a ride on your horse. You promised."

"Even if your legs turn crooked like mine?"

I hadn't thought of that. But, maybe just one ride wouldn't hurt. I nodded.

"Brave girl."

And so, I took my first horseback ride upon Billy Bowlegs' very own horse. The pretty brown horse was smaller than the ones who pulled Colonel Belknap's wagon. He was lovely. As the chief led him by the reins, I sat upon a soft blanket placed on

15

his back. Not even having to share that glorious moment with Mary could rob my joy. She screamed and cried for a chance to ride the horsie as well. With one hand, I held onto Mary's dress to keep her from falling off, but with the other, I rubbed the thick muscles of the horse's shoulders. I loved the way his head bobbed up and down as he walked. I could hear the jingle of his bridle.

Someday, I will have a horse of my own.

But, for now, I settle for a ride on Papa's mule.

I break my silence. "Where do you think Chief Billy is to-day?"

"Life cannot be easy for him, I am afraid," Papa sighs.

He tells me that just recently Florida's governor authorized the establishment of a group of mounted volunteers to begin removing the Indians from Florida and that the federal survey-ors push farther and farther south in an effort to prepare those lands for settlement.

"Just last month, three Indians were hanged at the Tampa jail."

"Oh, no!" *I cannot bear to think of my friend in danger.* "What about Chief Billy?"

"I expect your friend is hiding in the Everglades. He is a smart man. He knows that the surveyors and soldiers don't know how to survive in the swamps much less track an Indian who has lived there his whole life. I am sure he is safe and sound."

Seeing my distress, Papa changes the subject and gestures towards his left.

"See that herd of cattle over there? Those are ours, too."

Cattle? I know about our small herd on Terra Ceia, but this is still the mainland.

"We own cows on this side of the bay?"

"Our herd multiplied over the years. There are now too many for the island to support, so I forded some over here. See

16

they all have the letter A marked on them for a brand."

As the shore of the bay turned north, we pass the Petersen brothers' boat landing.

"Do Christian and Henry still live here?" I ask.

"Yes, and also some new settlers as well. The Boyles and the Mitchells." Papa frowns as he says their names. He starts to speak again and then, stops.

Changing the subject again, he says, "Look Eliza. See the spoonbills?"

We pause for a moment. Hundreds of pink birds bend and scoop their spoon shaped beaks into the mud at the edge of the bay.

I laugh when Papa says, "They are having mud soup for dinner!"

On the east side of the bay, we come to the Terra Ceia River.

"How will we get across, Papa?"

"Well, you and I will take the boat, and Dan will swim across."

Papa lifts me off Dan and pulls the pack from the mule's back throwing it into a small rowboat which he drags from its resting place at the river's edge. Untying it from the mangroves that serve as its tether, Papa motions for me to step into the boat. Then, he hands me the mules' reins.

"Hold them tight and don't let go until I tell you to," he orders. "He has done this before so he should be alright, but if something frightens him and he starts to thrash around in the water, turn him loose or he will capsize us."

Papa starts to row and clicks with his tongue for the mule to follow.

At first, Dan does not want to get his feet wet, but with some coaxing, Papa lures him into the water. Then, he rows hard to keep up with Dan's quick pace. Dan is in a hurry to get to the other side. Once there, Papa hollers for me to drop the reins.

"Let him get out of the water on his own or he will drag you and the boat right onto shore," he calls over the sound of the mule's splashing. I do as he says and watch Dan wade out of the water and shake himself dry. I am surprised that he stands still and waits for Papa to tie the rowboat to a palm tree and stow the oars under the seat.

"Do you want to ride some more or walk until he dries?" Papa asks.

Looking at the dripping mule, I think how wet I will be if I sit atop Dan once more. I decide to walk. Taking Dan's reins, I lead him along a trail behind Papa.

"Keep your eyes on the path, Eliza and watch for snakes," Papa warns. "Mules are good about spotting them before we do, but you don't want to be caught unawares."

I shudder. *I don't like snakes. Maybe I should ride after all.* We walk along the bay's north shore through the thick mangroves and some hidden oyster beds. I cut my feet and cry out.

"I'm ready to ride again, Papa."

"Eliza, we must get you some shoes."

"No thank you, Papa. I'm fine. I'm just tired is all."

The path soon leaves the edge of the bay and winds through the oak hammock. I begin to recognize our surroundings. After an hour later, we emerge from the forest and approach our farm. Papa rebuilt our cabin after the hurricane. Though we now live farther south on the Manatee River closer to the other settlers, I still think of this as home.

"I know you are eager to look around," Papa says, "but first we must take care of Dan and pay him for the ride."

I twist around until my belly is flat against Dan's back. With my feet dangling in the air, I let go and dropped to the ground. I walk beside Dan as he follows Papa to the small paddock behind our log cabin. Dan heads straight for the water trough and drinks. Then, he lies down in the soft dirt of the corral and turns over on his back wiggling and rolling in the warm sand. It blows in puffs around him as he gyrates. I laugh and clap my hands at the show.

"What is he doing?" I ask.

"Scratching his back," Papa replies. "And the sand covers his skin to protect him from the bugs."

I could stay all day watching Dan as he grazes on the grass, but Papa reminds me there are other things to see.

"You can go exploring if you like. I need to get a fire started, so when we want to cook supper, it will be hot. Then, I must check to see if the fields are ready to plow. I don't know how I will manage to get all the work done, but somehow, I will. Go on, now. Have a look around."

Oh, how I have missed my island. When Mama decided to open a store on the north side of the Manatee River, we moved from the Terra Ceia farm. Mama likes being closer to the Village of Manatee, but Papa and I miss the isolation and peace of the island. I breathe deeply. *Home!* It even smells differently. I walk to the spring and watch it flow from the ground creating a large bubble out from which ripples drift across the small pool. I kneel down in the damp earth beside it and peered into the water. Though small for my age, my face no longer has the chubby roundness of a little girl. I rub the slim wedge of my chin and feel the hollows of my cheeks. *I wish my hair were a more exotic color. Plain brown makes my features look pale and my dark eyes too recessed. If only my eyelashes were longer.* Suddenly, I hear a loud grunt in my ear. I jump and start to scream, but a brown hand clasps my mouth shut. I struggle against whoever holds me tight, but their grasp is too powerful.

Then, beside my own face in the water, I see the smiling face of Chief Billy. He removes his hand and steps away from me. Though my knees tremble, I stand. Furious, I rise on my tiptoes to be as tall as I can be.

"Chief Billy, don't ever do that to me again. I could have hurt you. How do you know I don't carry a knife? I might have stabbed you before I knew who you were!"

The Indian tilts back his head and roars with laughter. "Little Miss would need a big knife and thrust deep to pierce this thick old skin. But, you are a mighty brave little girl so Billy Bowlegs will be more careful next time."

How good it is to see my old friend. I set aside my indignation and reach up to hug Chief Billy.

Wrapping my arms around his waist, I press my cheek against his brightly colored shirt and ask, "Where have you been? I've been so worried about you. All this time, I did not know where you were."

"Ah, but Chief Billy sees you on your travels. I know your cabin on the river's edge. You leave many traces and are easy to track. I follow you all the way here. I watch to make sure you are safe and see you ride so tall and bold upon that mule. You cross the river without fear. You don't know where I am, but I know where you are all the time."

Despite my excitement, I feel a stab of fear. *He watches me, but I don't know he's near?*

Then, Chief Billy offers his hand. "Come, let's find your father. I must talk with him."

Papa is pleased to see Chief Billy. He invites the Indian to stay for supper.

"It will be simple fare," Papa warns. "My wife is not here so you will have to put up with my cooking."

"I know you left her and the other little one behind," the Chief concurs. "We did not disturb them, but followed you here instead."

Again, I feel uneasy knowing that the Chief noticed everything we do. *How long did he spy on us? Was Papa uncomfortable as well?* I cannot tell as he busies himself frying bacon and eggs over the fire.

"Eliza, slice some of the bread your mother sent and we will have some toast." While we work, I feel Billy Bowlegs' eyes upon me and wonder why he is here.

After a hastily prepared meal, Papa and the chief move to the porch to smoke. I admire the silver medallions that Chief Billy wears around his neck.

"Where did you get them?" I ask.

"I hammer them from silver coins I get in Washington when I see the President a long time ago."

He lets me feel the raised images on the coins and the smooth edges worn down from their beating. Once my curiosity is satisfied, I sit on the steps and listen to them talk. Papa offers Billy Bowlegs some of his tobacco.

"You grow?" he asks.

"Yes," says Papa. I can hear the pride in his voice. "This land will grow anything you put in it. The east portion of my property is just the right soil for tobacco. When John Jackson made his map of the island, he noticed it, too and called that area Tobacco Bluffs. I chose well when I selected this place. I just wish my homestead papers would come from the government."

The Indian grunts in agreement. "This is fine land. Once my people were happy here. Do not get too comfortable," he warns. "Some day, someone else will want this land and will take it from you just as they did to us."

"I fear they already are. I can't help but think that there is more than meets the eye in the difficulties I have over settling my claim. Despite the good men who stand up for me, I still do not have proof that this is my homestead."

The Indian nods.

"Yes, I understand this problem. I come to you because you seem an honest man. My friend, Colonel Belknap, called you his friend. He never lied to me. Will you tell me the truth as well?"

Papa extends his hand to the Indian. "I promise."

Billy Bowlegs continues, "General Twiggs will not rest until the last of my people are driven from this land. At first, they promise us the river of grass. We agree to go, even though we miss the rolling hills of our homeland and the vast forests full of game. As long as we can stay here, we will share this land. Tell me, what have you heard about my people in the settlements?"

"There are many tales of your brutality. They say six teamsters died on the route from Fort Mellon to Fort Frazer on the Kissimmee. When we ask why the mail does not come, we are told that the mail riders cannot get through because of your strength. The settlers in Manatee are begging for more troops. They build their fortifications sure that there will be war soon. General Twiggs plans a series of forts from Manatee across the state. He wants one every ten miles with two companies at each post. While he requests a mounted company of three hundred men, he is also gathering boats as the navy does not have the equipment it needs to follow you up every shallow creek and river in south Florida. They are making plans. They will not rest until there is war. You must be alert and ready."

Chief Billy looks towards the bay. The light fades as the sun sets and twilight settles upon the island. His voice is steady and strong.

"The settlers are greedy. They do not share. They want what was promised to us. They will get it by telling falsehoods about us. We do not kill unless we are provoked. Just ask the surveyors. Ask your friend John Jackson. They do their work and move throughout our land freely. It is only the soldiers and settlers who take what is ours that we resent."

Turning to Papa, he extends his hand as well. "But I thank you for your honesty. Now, I have one more favor to ask of you."

He stands. His swiftness catches me by surprise. He waves his hand in the air. Like lightening, in front of the cabin, five more Indians emerge from the trees. I gasp, not out of fear, but delight for each one sits upon an Indian pony. Two of the braves lead riderless ponies behind them.

"Come, you are safe here," the Chief calls.

From the darkness of the woods, a black man stumbles toward the house. The chief stands waiting for him to make his way forward, but Papa hurries to help him onto the porch and into an empty chair. The man wears clothes so old that they are mostly rags. Through them, I can see his bones sticking out at odd angles.

"Eliza! Get some water and slice some bread. Our guest is hungry."

I hurry to do as I am told. Bringing the food, I offer it to the man who hesitates to take it.

"Go on," Papa urges. "It is alright. Eat."

The speed at which he devours the bread and drinks the water is alarming, as is the way his eyes dart back and forth from me to Papa to the Chief and back. I make two more trips to the kitchen for bread and water and a little bit of leftover bacon. The stranger eats it all.

When the food is gone, Chief Billy speaks again.

"This is Henry. He is a runaway. He wants to go with me to my people, but he is not strong enough to make the journey. I ask of you a great favor, but I do so knowing your heart. Will you take him? When he is able, he will be of great help to you. I see the size of your farm. You cannot do this work alone. May he stay?"

Papa is quiet, then, replies, "I do not believe in slavery, Chief Billy. I will hold ownership over no man."

"I am not asking you to take him as your slave, but as your hired worker," the Indian states. Then, he repeats, "He will be of help to you."

"But, he is someone's property. It is against the law to harbor him. I am already in a precarious position with no legitimate claim to my land. You are asking me to risk it all," Papa argues.

"I only ask you to lend aid to a man in trouble. You would do it for me, would you not?" Papa nods and beside him, I nod as well. "Then, do it for Henry."

With that, the matter is settled. The Chief steps off the front porch and into the grass.

"To thank you for your kindness, I have a gift for your daughter."

Once again, he waves his arms and one of his men rides forward leading a small grey pony. On the mare's forehead is a white diamond and her rear left leg appears to have a white stocking upon it. Chief Billy reaches back and beckons to me. I run forward, and he lifts me on her back.

"A brave little miss like you should not be riding a stubborn old mule. She is more suitable for your skill and courage. Her name is Niihaasi which means Moon. Treat her well and she will take you to the stars and back."

Then, the other man brings the remaining horse forward. Chief Billy jumps upon its back, and the group disappears as quickly as they came. If not for the feel of the little mare beneath me and the gaunt runaway slave sitting on the porch, I might have imagined the whole affair.

That night, I cannot sleep. So, many thoughts whirl around in my head. *Finally, a horse of my own! Niihaasi, what a beautiful name. And doesn't she look all silver and beautiful just like the full moon on a winter night! Mama won't say no, now. Not to a gift from Chief Billy himself.* I tremble with excitement and roll over onto my side. I tuck my hands up under my chin. *Was it all a dream?* Oh, smell. My hands hold the faint scent of Niihaasi's hide. *She must be real! Won't I be able to fly across the island on her back? If only daylight will come so we can ride. I want to go downstairs for one more glimpse of her. She is just out back. Not far from the house.*

Just as I roll off the bed and start for the stairs, I remember the other surprise of the day. Henry. The runaway sleeps on a pallet on the back porch. Earlier, Papa urged him to come inside the house, but he refused.

"No, Mr. Joe. I been sleeping outside so long now I can't rest with a roof over my head. I be fine out here."

"Henry, I don't feel right making you stay outside," Papa

argues as he cleans the skillet after frying eggs for Henry. "There's plenty of room here."

"You ain't making me, Mr. Joe. I choose to sleep out here. It been a long time since I free to decide for myself. I be fine," he repeated. "Thank you for the meal. Good night."

Will Henry still be here in the morning? Will he really stay to help Papa run the farm? As much as I want to visit Niihaasi, I do not want to face Henry in the dark so I crawl back under the covers. *What has his life been like? It must have been awful if he was willing to risk the consequences of running away.* The <u>Florida Peninsular</u> newspaper often runs the ads of slave owners seeking their runaway slaves. They offer rewards for their capture. *What if Henry's owner comes looking for him? What will Papa do?* I have heard Papa and Mama discuss the ads, but Papa never expressed his feelings against slavery so clearly until today.

Once, I saw slaves sold at the auction in Tampa. Just like a horse or a piece of land. No concern for their thoughts or feelings. *How could a person enslave another?* Mama says the United States is a better place to live than Germany. She says it is a land of opportunity and freedom. But, not for men like Henry. Or Billy Bowlegs either. *Was Papa right? Will the other settlers agitate until there is war and the Indians are driven from their land? Why do they tell such lies? Poor Chief Billy. Poor Henry.*

I toss and turn for a long time, thinking of all I have heard and seen today. *What can I do?* Then, I remember what Mama would do. *God probably does not care, but what could it hurt to ask?* I kneel on the wooden floor. The planks dig into my knees as I think of words to say. Mama says just talk to God like he is a friend. *How to start?* Then, I remember Niihaasi.

"Thank you, thank you for my horse. She is just perfect. Thank you for her beautiful color. Please let Papa say I can ride her tomorrow. And let Mama say yes to keeping her." Thinking of more pressing concerns, I add, "Don't let there be war with Chief Billy and keep Henry's owner from finding him."

Tired, I climb into bed once more. Finally, I drift off to sleep and dream of Chief Billy riding through the Everglades on Niihaasi with Henry hanging on behind him.

Chapter Two

The next morning, Papa frowns as he rummages in the cupboard for some of Mama's special herbs to make a tea for Henry. Despite the heat, Henry shivers on his pallet.

"Swamp fever," Papa says. His voice is grave as he sends me outside to make sure the animals have water. Glad for an excuse to check on Niihaasi, I avoid the sick man by leaving through the front door and run around the house towards the pen. There she is. My own horse! Dan towers over her, already protective of the addition to his herd. It wasn't a dream. Oh, if only I can her ride today. I take the halter and reins that Chief Billy left from where they hang on the side of the gate. Outside the pen, I stoop to pull a handful of grass, and then duck through the rails and into the paddock.

I coax Niihaasi to come to me. She is shy, but the offer of grass begins our friendship. I place the bridle around her soft nose. I think she's small enough that I can get on her myself. Leading her to the edge of the pen, I position her left side against the fence. Holding the rope, I climb up on the rails and lean forward. Carefully, slowly, I ease onto Niihaasi with my stomach laying flat across her back. Though she accepted me when Chief Billy placed me upon her back yesterday, Papa led her to the pen.

Will I be able to ride her alone? Away from her Indian trainers and in a strange place, Niihaasi does not cooperate. As I swing my leg over to sit upright, she twists sharply to the right. I am no longer against the edge of the fence but facing it. The thrust of her sudden motion forces me head first to the ground. I land hard on my shoulder. Shooting pain radiates down to my elbow, but I cannot cry. If Papa hears, he will forbid me to try again. Besides, I don't want to take him from his care of Henry.

I try again. Now that she knows what I want and how to keep me from it, she refuses to stand still next to the pen. Short of leaping onto her back like an Indian warrior, I waste precious time positioning her and climbing back onto the rails. Over and over again, I try to mount. Sometimes, I can catch myself and slide off to safety, but many times, I fall. Now, angry at my predicament and the mare's stubbornness, I no longer feel the pain. I also have Dan to contend with. Not content to simply watch, he gets between Niihaasi and me or bumps into her making her even more skittish.

Finally, Niihaasi either gives up or understands what I want her to do. Victorious, I sit upon her back. I'm tempted to take that ride around the island I was dreaming of, but decide it is safer to stay within the pen for today. I urge Niihaasi forward, and we make several circles. Then, exhausted, I slip off her back and remove the halter.

Oh, I can't believe how stiff I am. Every muscle hurts. Still, my horse must be rewarded for choosing to let me on her back. I give her some scraggily carrots pulled from the garden. While she eats, I stroke her neck and chest. She is sweaty from the workout. Remembering something Chief Billy told me once, I blow into Niihaasi's nostrils. He said that horses remembered people by scent. If you blow your breath into theirs, they never forget you.

"You are my horse, now Niihaasi. You will be forever. Someday, we will ride around the island and swim across Terra Ceia River. I know you miss Chief Billy, but I will take good care of you."

Returning to the cabin, embers glow in the fireplace, and Henry still sleeps on the porch. Where is Papa? Is he down by the bay? I look towards the water and see Papa standing on the bank with his cast net.

Tiptoeing, I approach quietly, so not to disturb his concentration or the fish. Out of the corner of his eye, he sees me coming and motions for me to stop. Holding a corner of the net in his teeth, his other hands grasp the string. Suddenly, he spins flinging the net out in front of him as it opens in a perfect circle and hovers in the air before dropping down in the water. Papa pulls it up on shore full of broad silver mullet that flap and arch in an effort to free themselves from their restraints.

"There's dinner, my girl! Help me untangle them."

I hesitate. I don't like touching the slimy fish. Tentatively, I reach for the net only to squeal and jump back when one waves its tail in my direction. Tripping on a root, I fall. I try to catch myself with my hand, but, my arm, strained and tender from the morning's activity, fails to support me. I land on my side as pain explodes in my ribcage.

"Eliza, are you alright?" Papa sets down the net and reaches for me. I can't help but flinch when he touches my elbow.

He looks closer at me and exclaims, "Eliza! Where did you get all these bruises?"

I look down at the ground. *Will he be angry with me?*

"Eliza?"

I must answer, and I cannot lie to my father. Looking up, I confess. "I was trying to ride Niihaasi. I did ride her, too. But, only in the pen."

"Did you fall?" Papa asks gently.

I hold my side and nod my head. Even that movement hurts.

"More than once, it appears," Papa concludes.

I nod again. More gently this time.

"It is not safe to ride a new horse alone, Eliza. I know you want to ride, but please wait until I can help you. Tomorrow we will try again. Unless you are too sore. Sit here and wait for me."

I rest on a stump while Papa picks the mullet from his net. I cringe and turn my head away when he breaks their necks to bleed them.

"Your mama likes the mullet better when they do not have such a strong taste," he explains. "Bleeding them when they are first caught helps."

Papa carries the fish back to the cabin to clean them. Saving a few out for dinner, he salts the rest to keep them fresh. When the meal is ready, Henry finally wakes. He says he is better, but still refuses to join us at the table for our meal of fried mullet and corn mush. He eats his alone on the porch. After our dinner, we join him there.

"Mr. Joe, you gots to treat me like a slave. Iffn the other settlers see me, you cain't act like I'm same as you. They'll know your feelings and come after us both."

"How long have you been ill?" Papa asks.

"A few months. It come and go. Chief Billy know the damp, it'd make me worse. I think I gonna die, but God, He spare me. I still weak, but gettin' stronger. I promise I work hard."

"I am not worried about that," Papa explains, "but I will need to get back to my family on the river. I don't feel right leaving you here by yourself."

"You can trust me, Mr. Joe. I do right by you."

"Oh, no Henry, I didn't mean that I could not trust you. I don't want to leave you alone in case you get sick again."

"I figure God brung me this far, he not gonna watch me die now."

I wonder about the man's simple faith. *How can he speak of God's provision with all that he has endured?*

"We'll see how you are tomorrow," Papa replies. "Besides, my daughter here will not rest until she can ride that horse all the way back to her mama." With that, Papa stands and stretches. "And I better get started on what brought me to the island. Those fields won't plant themselves."

Henry stands as well.

"I go, too, Mr. Joe."

"No, you rest for now. There will be plenty of work for you to do after I leave. Eliza, come along. I can use your help though."

By the end of the day, my muscles scream from the bruises and the planting. All afternoon, I follow behind Papa and Dan stooping and bending placing seed into the freshly plowed earth. Three seeds go into each hole.

"One for the birds, one for the ants and one to grow," Papa says.

Too tired to eat my supper, I rest my head upon the table. I don't protest when Papa sends me to bed early.

Our time on the island slips by as the days run one into another. Papa is true to his word. Each day, he carves out some time from the planting for horseback riding lessons. Soon, I can ride Niihaasi with assurance outside of the pen. Henry improves as well. It is not long before he works with us. Skilled with animals, he joins Papa in helping me train Niihaasi. By the time the crops are in the ground, Papa is also confident that Henry will be alright alone on the island.

Papa and I take to eating our meals on the porch with Henry. One night at supper, Papa announces that we will be returning to the river house tomorrow.

"I had not planned to be gone this long," he explains. "I am sure my wife is worried by now. Niihaasi is ready for the journey. Henry, will you be all right? I think you know what to do around here."

"Yes, sir, Mr. Joe. Plenty to do here."

"You take it slow until you are feeling completely well. I will be along every few weeks to check on you. I just hope that the fever does not come back."

"I be alright, Mr. Joe. You and Miss Liza needs to be goin'. I be grateful for this chance. I do right by you."

"I know you will Henry." Papa extends his hand to Henry. For a moment, Henry just stares at the gesture of good will. Then, slowly, he raises his and smiles as the two men shake hands in agreement.

The next morning, I wave good bye to Henry from atop

Niihaasi. Papa walks at her side but I insist that he not lead us. Leaving the mule behind on the island for Henry means that Papa will walk to the river house. The river house is how I prefer to think of it. My real home will always be the Terra Ceia cabin, but having Niihaasi to ride means I am not quite as sad about leaving.

When we arrive at the Terra Ceia River, Papa asks, "Are you worried about how Niihaasi will get across?"

Yes, I am nervous. That must be why I have an ache in my stomach.

"Papa, what will I do if she gets loose and runs away? I will never catch her again."

"Don't borrow trouble, Eliza. She has been across this river and countless others before. Chief Billy trained her well, I know. In fact, I think we are going to try a new way. Stay there for a minute."

Papa's words surprise me, but I stay where I am. Any minute he will ask me to dismount and climb into the rowboat. Instead, he unties the boat from its mangrove mooring and crawls over its side alone. Taking up the oars, he calls to me.

"Push her forward now. Right on into the water. Just hold on tight. If you should fall off, I will come and get you, but I think you will be alright." *What? Stay on Niihaasi for her swim across the river?*

"I'll get wet, Papa!"

"It's alright. You'll dry before we get home. Come on now. Don't let her feel you hesitate. If you are brave, she will be too."

Skeptical, I kick Niihaasi with my heel. At first, she stays on the shore, so, I kick her again. Just as she must have done many times before, Niihaasi plunges into the water following Papa and the boat to the other side. It happens so suddenly, I don't have time to be afraid. Even as the cold water surrounds me and my skirt floats around me, I hold on for dear life. With powerful strokes, Niihaasi propels us across the river. When she feels the ground underneath her once again, she climbs from the river onto the other bank.

"Hold on tight now, Eliza!" Papa calls.

In my excitement, I let go of Niihaasi's mane, but I grab it again just as she shakes the water off of her, just like a dog. I struggle to stay on her back and just barely manage to keep my seat. Still, I laugh aloud as water drops fill the air around me.

"Good job, Eliza!" Papa grins. Then, he stows the boat in the mangroves once more, and we begin our walk around the bay towards the Manatee River.

"Oh, Papa," I exclaim once I have regained my breath, "That was so much fun! Why didn't we ride Dan across, too?"

"I don't know if they are smarter or dumber than horses," Papa explains. "But, it's hard to get a mule into the water. We were better off leading him across. I was pretty sure a little creek like the Terra Ceia River would not be a problem for an Indian pony."

Continuing to walk beside Niihaasi, Papa clears his throat and says, "Eliza, don't tell Mama about Henry. Let me think of a way to tell her myself."

"But, how will I explain my horse?" I ask.

"We will tell Mama the truth. She is Chief Billy's gift, but not exactly why she was given. At least not just yet. And I must ask you not to tell anyone else about Henry as well. What I have done is a crime, but my conscience could not allow me to do otherwise. I must think of a way to keep Henry safe without bringing harm to our family."

"Papa would they arrest you? Or me?"

Though my dress is still damp, I wasn't cold until now. The thought of jail makes me shiver.

"Not you little one, but I must be careful. Just don't tell anyone why Chief Billy gave you Niihaasi or about who is working our farm. Mama and I will come up with a story to explain it all and will tell you what to say. In the meantime, don't say anything other than she is a gift from the Chief."

The rest of the way home, I fret. Biting my lip, I ponder if I can keep such a secret. *I know that Mary could not. Mary is a baby. But, surely, I can.* If I am grown up enough to have a horse of my own, I can do what it takes to keep both Papa and Henry safe. Really, I have no choice. My tongue must not betray me. As we near the river house, I see Mama hanging laundry on the line as Mary hands her the linens. My worries vanish. I cannot contain my excitement.

"Mama! Mary! Look at me! Look what Chief Billy brought me!"

Papa waves at the two and turns to me. Whispering, he reminds me, "Not a word about Henry, Eliza."

"I know Papa. I will be careful."

I will, but, now, I have to show off my new pony. So, I kick Niihaasi and gallop to the house, leaving Papa behind in a cloud of dust.

After giving Mary a ride behind me on Niihaasi, I take my horse to the pen and give her some water to drink. My horse! That thought thrills me still.

"Papa says that once you know this is your home, I can turn you loose to graze. But, I don't want you to run away and go back to the island, so you have to stay here for now." I wish we could turn around and go back for Mama is not pleased about Chief Billy's gift. She scolds Papa for letting me ride so fast and astride.

"Joseph, I am trying to teach Eliza to be a lady and you have undone everything," she fumes.

I dawdle at the pen running my fingers through Niihaasi's mane. The dried salt left it tangled. Perhaps when she isn't so angry, Mama will give me a comb to brush it out. Even though living on the Terra Ceia farm is hard work, it was nice not being under Mama's watchful gaze all the time. I run my fingers through my own hair and try to neaten it as well. Mama will not be happy with me at all.

Dinner is tense. When we are done, Mama sends Mary with me to take the laundry off the line. Even from that distance, I can hear snippets of conversation as my parents discuss my horse and behavior as well as the length of Papa's absence. Mary wanders over to a clump of wildflowers and begins to pick some so I can leave the clothes basket at the line and move closer to the house to hear their conversation. It is not rare that Mama raises her voice to Papa, but still I am surprised at the intensity of her words.

"I was worried. You said you would be gone a day or two and here it is over a week later. What was I to think?"

"I'm sorry. When I got there, I decided to go ahead and plant. The weather was right and I did not want to miss the opportunity. If I could have sent you word, I would have."

"You always do this! You get to that farm and lose all track of time. I needed you here. We must buy supplies and get this store operating. People already came by with their requests. I know we can make a good living here, but I cannot do it alone."

For a time, Papa lets her expound on her fears, about what might have happened to her and Mary alone with no protection, and her loneliness.

"I'm sorry, Julia," Papa says. "Come here."

Mama is quiet. *Now what?* I peek around the door opening. Mama stands in Papa's embrace as they kiss. Ah, that is the real reason Mama is mad. She missed Papa. They really do love each other despite all the shouting. I feel good inside at the thought. *One day, will I have a man to love me like that?*

I turn to resume my laundry duty, but hear my name mentioned so wait to hear what is said.

"Please do not encourage Eliza to gallop that horse all over creation. You know how strong willed she is. Before long, she will be riding all over the settlement. What will people say?"

With his arms still around Mama, Papa says, "They will

think we have raised a smart, strong and healthy girl who can take care of herself in this wilderness. Isn't that what they say about her Mama?"

Mama smiles. "But, did Chief Billy really give her that gift?" At Papa's nod, she asks, "Whatever for? I know he favored her at Fort Brooke, but to seek her out with such a fine animal as that? What does that Indian have up his sleeve, Joseph?" Mama gasps. "Oh, no. You don't think he wants her for his wife, do you?"

I never considered such a thing. *What would it be like to live with the Indians? Would I get to ride my horse every day?*

But, Papa laughs, "No. Chief Billy does not need another mouth to feed. He has enough troubles already." His tone grows serious. "Julia, sit down. I have a story to tell you. I need your help figuring out what to do."

Papa tells of Chief Billy's arrival, thankfully leaving out how badly he scared me. He quotes the Indian's instructions and describes Henry's condition, improvement and subsequent help with the plowing.

Finally, he concludes, "I am not sure what to do. I could not turn down the Chief's request for help, and you know how I feel about slavery. But, how can we keep him hidden from the other settlers?"

"Joseph, this concerns me greatly. I understand why you did what you did, but you are risking us all for this one man. Give me time to think. We must come up with a plan."

Suddenly, I remember Mary. *Where is she?* If something happens to her, Mama will blame me. Fortunately, Mary is standing on the railing of the pen feeding Niihaasi flowers. I finish taking down the laundry keeping one eye on her. But, I don't really see Mary or even Niihaasi. In my mind, I remember my father and Henry smiling and shaking hands.

That evening, Mama sends Mary on to bed without me. When she fusses and begs to stay, Mama swats her on her behind. Mary cries and stomps from the room.

"Eliza, sit down, we need to talk."

"Yes, ma'am."

Oh, no. Will Mama tell me that I must give up my horse? I will not do it. I will run away and go live with Chief Billy!

"First, about that horse."

My eyes water. *No, please Mama, not Niihaasi.*

"Don't look at me so sadly. I am not going to make you give her up. But, there will be some rules."

My heart lifts. I can keep her! Whatever Mama wants, I will do, as long as I can keep Chief Billy's gift. "First, no riding astride."

Not at all? I hate riding side saddle. How can I go fast with both legs hanging off the side? I consider arguing, but bite my tongue. *Sidesaddle will be better than nothing, I suppose.*

Mama knows me so well and senses my struggle. She smiles and continues, "No riding astride as long as others are around. If you are alone or with Papa, it is okay. But, if you get any-where near a settlement or a house, I want you looking like a lady. We will make you a pair of pants to wear under your skirt so your underwear doesn't show!"

Hooray! I can't sit still and jump up to hug Mama. Mama hugs me back, but then, holds me away from her as she contin-ues. Her face is somber as she looks into mine.

"Papa says he has talked to you about the danger to Henry and to all of us if word gets out that we are harboring a runa-way slave." I nod. "As far as anyone is concerned, he is our hired man. We will just have to hope that no one asks to see his papers. If they do, we will try to tell them that they are lost. I am not sure that it will work, but that is the best we can do for right now. Hopefully, no one will go near the farm to see him and we can keep him hidden at least for a while."

I can't speak. Such joy and sorrow mixed. This tale is risky, but maybe the story will be believed. Papa does need the help so hiring a man to work the farm is true enough.

Chapter Three

I can hardly believe my good fortune to finally have a horse of my own. The pleasure of horseback riding and the freedom it brings balance the hardships of my life. I don't mind the chores or housework. Even taking care of Mary is not as bad as what I feel when I have to mix with the rest of the Manatee River community. I loathe school. Days spent at Mistress Lee's academy in Manatee are long and confining, partly because I am indoors, but mostly because of the other students. I love my father and mother and in a way, even Mary. But, my family is different. Our many German customs and beliefs along with my parents' accents make us stand out from the other settlers who are mostly southern and from states such as South Carolina, Georgia and Virginia.

In public, Mama always calls Papa, Mr. Joe. She says it is a sign of respect, but the other settlers think it quaint and call Mama, Madam Joe, instead of her real name, Julia. Religion also causes a rift between us and the established settlement farther down the river. Though I am skeptical about God's role in the world, I recognize that membership in the church at Manatee might open doors to friendships and help us to fit in. Mama refuses to attend the Union Congregation despite my pleadings.

"We can worship God here. I can teach you girls about Him just as my own mother did. I pray to him as well. I do not need someone telling me what to think or how to live."

It makes me laugh to think that someone could tell my mother what to do. Papa rarely tries. Certainly those in the Manatee settlement wouldn't be able to change her mind. Would it hurt to go politely to church wearing a fine dress and mingle with the other ladies? The other girls' mothers are petite and feminine, so different from my tall, strong mother. They coo and talk so sweetly to each other, unlike Mama who says what she thinks without fear of consequence. Mama shoots and rides and works alongside Papa in the fields. She doesn't sit and serve tea with slaves waiting upon her. Perhaps that is the problem. It might not be Mama's appearance at all, but her opinions that keep us separate. Though almost everyone in the settlement shops at our store, culturally, most shut us out.

Our nearest neighbor is Robert Gamble. Mr. Gamble's house is the biggest one I have ever seen. Two stories high, even though it stands a half mile from the river, it can clearly be seen from the water. The two foot thick walls are made of tabby, a mixture of sand, shell and lime and gleam a sparkling white. The material and a double layer of porches on three sides keep the house cool, even in the summertime. On the few occasions I have been there, I feel like tiptoeing as I walk the narrow hall along the east side of the house past the parlor where a large piano sits near the fireplace and into the dining room. The beautiful walnut table shines with layers of wax and is always set with china and silver. Even Papa maintains a respectful distance from our neighbor and prefers to call him Mr. Gamble. Mr. Gamble built a road from his house to our store. The river landing isn't as deep at his place as it is at ours. Papa doesn't mind letting Mr. Gamble dock his boats at our shore. It just means more customers for Mama.

As far as I am concerned, Mr. Gamble did me a favor, too. It was through him that I met Nannie Hunter who is a second cousin of Mr. Gamble. Though Nannie lives in Manatee, she stays at Mr. Gamble's sometimes. Now that I have a horse, I can ride Niihaasi over to visit Nannie when she is there.

Nannie is my best and only friend. I do not know why she thought to take me under her wing, but she did. I try to tell myself that one friend is all I need to make me happy. The other students at school talk of parties and dances, but I am never invited. Not that it matters anyway. Even if they included me,

Mama would not let me go. Mama thinks I am too young for such frivolity. I wouldn't have anything to wear anyway. My plain everyday clothes would not suit for the kind of events I long to enjoy.

"No, Eliza," Mama says leaving no room for argument. "That is not for you. That crowd is fast and rich. They are not our type."

When I venture to beg, Mama sends me to the garden to weed.

"Go remember whose daughter you are," she commands. "We are not of the planter class with slaves to do our work."

I know that I am the daughter of a store keeper and a farmer, just as I know that as Nannie's sixteenth birthday approaches, I will not be allowed to attend her birthday party. With the help of her mother, Charlotte, and her twenty year old sister, Susan, Nannie is planning a dinner and dance to be held at the Gamble Plantation. Charlotte Hunter is the exact opposite of my mother. Small and thin, she speaks with a Kentucky drawl and calls everyone she meets by some sweet sounding name. Simply crooning "Sugar, honey, or dear" to whomever she addresses brings an immediate desire to please her. I, too, am mesmerized by her spell. In fact, I long for a mother like Charlotte. Especially when she assumes that I will also be attending Nannie's celebration and includes me in the discussions about dresses and table decorations.

"Cousin Robert's cook will take care of the food," she explains. "We will have a real dinner to keep the men happy, not a lot of party and finger foods like we ladies would prefer."

I have no idea what those kinds of delicacies might be, but find it satisfying that Charlotte includes me in the description of ladies.

"But, we must have cake. After all it is a birthday party!" she continues.

Later, alone with Nannie, I confess. "I can't come to the party. My mother will not let me, I am sure."

"What? You are my best friend. You have to be there. Just don't tell your mother. Tell her that we are spending the night at the plantation. You don't have to tell her that there will be a party as well."

I consider my friend's words. I learned a long time ago not to lie to my mother. Then again, what Nannie is suggesting is not really a lie, is it? I could spend the night at the plantation. I just wouldn't tell the whole truth. But, what could I wear?

"Nannie, I can't. I don't have anything to wear."

"Oh, we can take care of that. You can wear something of mine."

"You are so much taller than me. I couldn't wear anything of yours. It would drag on the ground."

I cannot discourage Nannie. Taking her sister into our confidence, we tear apart a dress of Susan's and another of Nannie's and remake them to fit me.

"It wouldn't do for you to appear in something that we have worn. I think we can make a dress for you that is different enough that no one will notice." Susan chatters. "Eliza, you have such a tiny waist, doesn't she Nannie? I wish mine was as small. And your hair is beautiful. It will look so pretty with this white muslin. I can't wait to style it for you. Aren't the little pink flowers in the fabric sweet? We will have to find some real flowers that match to put in your hair."

At home, I stare into the mirror. Susan is so lovely. Does she really think that I am, too? I do not have to ask permission to spend the night at Gamble Plantation. Nannie does it for me.

"Please, Mrs. Atzeroth. It would mean so much to me. It is my birthday, you see. We are going to have dinner with Cousin Robert, and I do so want my best friend to be there. But, it may be late when we are done dining, and I would not feel right about Eliza riding home alone. If she spends the night, we will make sure she gets home safely the next day."

Nannie sounds so much like Charlotte, that if I close my eyes, I would think it her instead; so sweetly and charmingly does Nannie ask. It is no wonder Mama agrees. Even *I* feel as though Nannie has cast a spell over me. I feel guilty that Mama does not know the whole story, but I am thrilled to be allowed to go, I am willing to keep the secret from my mother.

Finally, the day of the party arrives. I prepare to leave fitting the bridle around Niihaasi's head and throwing the saddle over her back. My thoughts whirl as I wrestled with my trickery. How to conceal my excitement?

"Eliza."

I jump causing Niihaasi to snort and spin away. Pulling the mare back to me, I fumble with the buckle on the girth. Mama is behind me.

"Girl, why are you so nervous? Here let me do it."

Oh, Mama, I think. *I am worried because of my deceit.* Instead, I lie. Really, isn't that what I have been doing all along?

"I am a little nervous about spending the night away from home. I have never done something like this before."

Or lied to you in this way, I do not add.

"I've seen the table at Mr. Gamble's There are a lot of different forks by the places. What if I make a mistake?"

Mama sighs. "That is why I came out here to talk to you. It will just be Nannie's family and Mr. Gamble there."

My stomach clenches. *Oh, Mama, if you only knew how many were coming.*

She continues, "Just watch Nannie's mother and do what she does. Eliza, I know that Mrs. Hunter and her daughters have been kind to you. Mr. Gamble as well. But, you must remember, they are different from us. They have lived a life of privilege that your father and I can not give you. Don't set your heart on being like them."

Mama smooths my hair off my forehead and looks into my eyes. I adjust Niihaasi's bridle and refuse to meet hers. *What if she can see the lies in mine?*

"Eliza, remember, you are smart and strong. They are no better than you are. I'm not saying that they are bad. It takes all kinds to settle this country and make it a good place for all of us to live. Like I said, they are different from us. Don't try to be something you are not." Giving a final warning, she adds, "And Eliza, be careful about what you say."

Taking Niihaasi's bridle, she hands me the reins. "Get on up there."

I hop on one leg and swing the other over Niihaasi's back. I settle a small pack containing my night gown and other necessities behind me.

"Have a good time. I love you."

When was the last time Mama told me that? Why did it have to be today when I am being so wicked? I want to fling myself off my horse and tell Mama the truth, but Mary chooses that moment to run from the house.

"Are you going? Oh, Mama, please make Liza take me with her. I want to go to dinner at the Gamble's too."

"No. Only Eliza was invited this time."

Thinking of the guest list, I want to confess, "I'm not the only one invited," but the opportunity passes. *What if Mary heard something at school? What if she tells Mama?*

Anxious to leave, I spur Niihaasi forward and call back to Mary, "I'll bring you a piece of cake. Good bye!"

"See you tomorrow! Be careful!" Mama's voice follows me.

I try to drown out the nagging of my conscience by thinking of the beautiful flowered gown and the adventure that awaits me at Mr. Gamble's house.

Before dinner, I watch as Manda, one of Mr. Gamble's house slaves, helps Nannie and Susan dress. I put my hand on my stomach and try to settle my nerves. I have been decorated by Nannie and Susan who act like schoolgirls playing with a doll. The white gown floats around me and makes me think of the wisps of clouds in the winter sky. The tiny pink flowers embroidered into the printed white squares on the muslin are set off by bright green leaves. I tug at the gathered short sleeves dropping off my shoulders. I am not used to so much skin being exposed.

"Eliza, quit pulling on your dress," Nannie orders.

I put my hands down and smooth out the skirt. The borrowed hoop, underneath, feels odd when I walk. The hem of my dress bounces against my ankles.

"Look at you, Eliza! Didn't I tell you your waist was tiny?" Susan propels me to the mirror. More than two dozen small metal hooks fasten up the back of the dress. A green sash in the color of the leaves taken from an old dress of Nannie's accentuates my shape.

"Oh, that flower just won't stay in. Give me another pin, Manda."

As Susan fusses with my hair, I catch Manda's eye in the mirror.

"You look beautiful, Miss Liza. Mr. Joe would not recognize you I don't think."

At the mention of Papa, my heart begins to pound.

I try to stay calm. "You know my father?"

"Only of him," Manda replies. "I know Henry."

"Who is Henry?" Nannie interrupts.

I hesitate. Mama warned me to be careful of what I say. *How to explain Henry?*

"He is our hired man. You have never seen him. He stays at the farm on the island."

"Manda, you better not let Cousin Robert find out you have been fraternizing with a freedman. He will be angry with you," Susan warns.

"Henry ain't no freedman. Mr. Joe just treats him like he is. There, you girls are ready. I best be seeing to your mother." Manda leaves me to face my friends alone.

"Your family has a slave?" Nannie asks. "Father says your

parents came from Germany and that is why you don't have any slaves."

"No, no. He is our hired man. Manda doesn't know what she is talking about." *Will they believe me?*

My discomfort must show, so Susan changes the subject. "Nannie, come here. Let me fix your sash. Come girls. It is time we went downstairs. I wonder who has arrived. Maybe Edward will ask you to dance, Nannie."

Nannie reaches to pull her sister's hair. Everyone knows that Eddie Gates cannot dance He was injured as a child. The Manatee settlement did not have a doctor in those days and by the time his father rode horseback to Fort Brooke with little Eddie in front of him, the bone had already set. He still walks with a limp. I'm sorry that they made fun of Eddie, but am glad to have the focus off of me. I follow the two laughing girls downstairs.

Nannie's borrowed shoes are too big for my feet. They rub blisters on my heels as I walk behind the Hunter sisters down the narrow hallway to the dining room. Instead of place settings, food covers the long glossy table. Perhaps I worried about nothing. It will not matter which fork I use after all. Chairs and small tables line the outside porches. More guests have been invited than can be seated indoors.

Imitating Nannie, I fill my plate with sliced roast beef, tiny new potatoes and carrots then make my way outdoors to the east porch where Susan is already holding court among an admiring crowd of young men and women. I find a place at an empty table and quietly began to eat, listening and watching as the party swirls around me. Despite the jarring noise of a small group of musicians tuning their instruments on the other side of the house, I can hear many conversations taking place nearby in addition to Susan's banter.

Inside, a group of women discuss the latest gossip from the settlement, and Virginia Braden describes a recent trip to visit her family in Tallahassee. I can hear their talk through the window beside me.

"George's plantation is now 5,000 acres. I swear he made a good match when he married Sarah Jane. The fields of cotton are so white, it looks just like winter with snow draped on the bushes."

Charlotte replies, "If only it would snow here. I am so hot; I think I will melt in a puddle."

Virginia continues her recital of her brother's accomplishments.

"I just don't understand why George was not elected governor in the last election," she whines. "He manages over 160 slaves and many other workers. He could do a wonderful job running our state."

I hear Charlotte clear her throat and change the subject.

"Robert built this house for a bachelor. These rooms are really too small for entertaining. Let's go outside where there is a breeze."

Several other women agree, and their talk fades as they leave the room.

Behind me, masculine voices come from Mr. Gamble's office.

"You should have seen ole Billy in Washington." That sounds like Joab Griffin. "He thought he was something else. All dressed up in his feathers and beads talking to the President himself. He was sure stubborn. Luther Blake couldn't get him to agree to leave Florida, but President Fillmore must have known how to sweet talk him. Billy signed that agreement before leaving Washington. He sure did. Now he is obligated to get his people and move out of here."

"Did he really sign in at the hotel as Mr. William B. Legs?" Joseph Braden asks.

"That he did. It is as big as bold in the guest register of the American Hotel in New York City," Joab confirms. "I saw it with my own eyes. Cheeky devil."

The men laugh. I don't like how they make fun of my friend.

Imagine Chief Billy talking to the President.

Joseph adds, "It is about time. We told Governor Brown over two years ago that the economy will not grow until the threats of war pass. Who wants to move to the Indian lands and take a chance on this country?"

Then, Robert Gamble chuckles, "You mean besides us crazy fools?"

"Send the cowboys after those savages, I say," continues Joseph. "They aren't afraid of the regulars and the Army, but the volunteers, they will protect their land."

"Now, Joseph, remember our guest here," Nannie's father, Nathaniel Hunter interjects, "Captain Casey, what do you think of all this talk?"

Captain Casey is here? I've heard so much about Captain John Casey, the former Indian removal agent. Luther Blake took his place, but Papa says there is no man who knows the Indians better than Captain John Casey.

"The only way to bring peace to this land is to deal fairly and honesty with the red man. They have been treated with such hostility and deceit that they are reluctant to talk to even someone like me who has gained their respect. They are afraid to come to the bargaining table for fear of being snatched and sent west in chains. No Indian will advocate emigration without being denounced by the other men and scorned by the women. The women are very hostile to emigration." Captain Casey confides, "We must win the women over if we are to have any success. Blankets, fabric, thread and needles, as well as money, are the way to convince them to leave."

I should go into the room and correct Captain Casey. None of those things would convince me to leave my home in Florida. Why would the Indian women be any different? But, I can't move and continue my eavesdropping.

"There is already peace in the air, gentlemen. Why, any cracker cow driver can go across the line without fear. It is safe. I guarantee it. You can drive your cattle all the way to Fort Myers any day," Captain Casey declares. "Now, if you will excuse me, I must get a breath of fresh air. The Florida climate has been good to me, and I am much healthier than when I arrived in this state, but I still only have one lung. I won't ask you to quit your smoking, but I must step outside."

"Kind negotiation," mutters Joseph Braden. "I will show him what kind negotiation it takes to bring peace to this land. Get rid of the Indians. That is the only answer."

"It won't be long," Robert Gamble pronounces. "Roads are being built through the Indian lands as we speak. The surveyors are hard at work. The Indians won't stand for it much longer. I don't care what papers Billy Bowlegs signed. War is coming soon. The Indians will be forced out."

I shudder at the hatred in his tone. Joab Griffin adds, "There's a bounty on their heads even now. I heard they'll pay five hundred dollars to the one who brings in Chief Billy himself."

No! They will be after Billy Bowlegs for sure. *How can I warn my friend?*

"Gentlemen, why are you hiding in the office?" Charlotte interrupts the men's talk. "How can we have dancing if you stay all huddled up in here. Come, it is Nannie's birthday. No more talk of war and Indian removals. Let's enjoy ourselves, shall we?"

All the furniture, except the piano, has been moved from Mr. Gamble's small parlor; but even so, it is still not large enough for more than five or six couples to dance at a time. In the days leading up to the party, Susan teased her mother about wanting to waltz. Charlotte was horrified at the thought.

"Susan that is a vulgar dance. You know what Madame Celnart wrote about it in her book, 'The waltz is a dance of quite too loose a character, and unmarried ladies should refrain from it in public and private'."

"Oh, Mother, it is all the rage now. If the gentleman does not encircle a lady's waist until the dance begins and does not touch her waist with his bare hands, what harm is there in it?"

"Susan, absolutely not! This is a sixteenth birthday party, not a brothel."

So, instead of the waltz, the couples dance the Virginia Reel. Taking turns, five or six couples line up long ways in the small room. With all the men on the right and all the ladies on the left, they join hands in a long line. Moving forward, then backward to eight beats of the music, they turn first to the right and then, to the left. Taking two hands, the top couple sashays down the center of the set, then back to their place where they hook their right elbows together and turn one and a half times before switching partners and beginning again.

I sit in the windowsill of the hall, peek through the doorway at the happy couples and tap my foot against the thick tabby walls. This is a good seat to observe the fun. I am not so bold as to think someone might ask me to dance. Nannie cajoles one of the young men into dancing the next set with her. They make a nice couple. From outside, a female voice carries through the window over the sound of the music. Virginia again. *Is she still talking about her brother?*

"How can we be successful if we can't keep our people at their work? The men just slip away from the plantation. It is as though they disappear into the woods. I know that the Indians are hiding them. One of my brother's best men, Henry, disappeared a while back, and George is still angry about it. George loaned him to us and before we could return him to Tallahassee, he just walked away. George still posts ads. One day, George says he will find him and then, Henry will pay. Someone has to teach these darkies a lesson about running away."

Henry! Is that our Henry? Oh, I must warn him right away. Perhaps someone is looking for him now. Suddenly the party loses its glow. If I could leave now, I would, but I am too afraid to take off through the darkness on my own. Besides, the coachman would never let me have my horse at this time of night. *I long for morning. I just want to go home. Coming here was a bad idea.*

The party lasts late into the night, but despite my lack of sleep, I rise early and start for home. I drape the pretty muslin gown over a chair where Nannie can find it. She told me that she would ride home with me, but I cannot wait for her to dress. I slip out before my friend wakes. Mr. Gamble's cook left breakfast on the dining table for everyone to help themselves, so I snatch a biscuit and some bacon. Then, I run to saddle Niihaasi. As much as I want to go straight to Terra Ceia and warn Henry, Mama and Papa will worry if I don't go to the river house first. I must not call any more attention to myself than necessary. It will be hard to pretend that everything is normal, but I cannot let my parents know about the party. I will have to figure out a way to get to Henry myself.

Once home, I greet my family, casually taking care to keep a smile on my face. They are just finishing up their own breakfast.

"Well, look who is here," Papa smiles as I enter the kitchen. "The traveler has returned home." I remember the old days when Papa would swing me up on his shoulders. *Oh, how I wish I could go back to a simpler time.*

"Liza, Liza! How was it?" Mary asks as she balances plates to clear the table. "How was the party? Did you get to dance?"

She might as well have punched me in the stomach. *How did they know?* Stunned, I stare at Mary before slowly turning to face my parents. Mama nods.

"How was the party, Eliza? Did you enjoy yourself?"

"How did you know?" I stammer.

"It is a small community, Eliza. Did you think we would not find out? Mary told us about it days ago. Daughter, why did you lie?"

I burst into tears. All of the tension of the night and the worry over my deceit combined with the humiliation of being caught in a lie.

"You wouldn't let me go. I knew that you wouldn't let me go. But, all the other girls were going to be there. I am tired of being different. I want to be like them!"

Mama sighs. "You are right; I would not let you go. I think you are too young to be exposed to that environment. I want to keep you safe and innocent. But you are fourteen now. How did you find your company?"

Mama's eyes reveal her disappointment.

"I knew where you were headed before you left, but your father convinced me to let you go. He says it is time for me to realize that you are growing up. But, I did wonder how long it would take for you to tell me. Would you have kept your secret from me forever?" In frustration, she raises her hands in a pleading gesture. I rush into the safety of her arms.

"I'm sorry, Mama." I wipe my tears on her apron. "I was wrong. I should have told you. If it makes you feel any better, I did not have fun after all. There was so much talk of Indians and of war. It worries me. What will happen to Chief Billy?"

"War?" Papa asks. "What did they say about war?"

I tell them everything the men said. Papa and Mama exchange glances, and Mama nods.

Papa says, "Eliza, this confirms what your mother and I have been thinking. It is not safe anymore for you and Mary to travel alone to school each day. Your route is too predictable. While Chief Billy might offer you some protection, we cannot guarantee that the others would not kidnap you or bring you harm in another way."

Mama adds, "It is best for now if you stay home and help me in the store."

Papa continues, "I do not want you to go out alone on Niihaasi anymore, either. Some days, you may ride with me, but no more travels on your own."

No more school! This should be a day to celebrate. But to

stay close to home and no more rides unless accompanied by Papa?

"Am I being punished for going to the party?"

Papa replies solemnly, "No, daughter. Times are changing, and we all must be careful. You want to be grown up? Then, you must understand what the true cost of living in the wilderness can be."

Chapter Four

Even though I am now free of school, I can't be happy. It isn't just the confinement at home. Or even the fact that I must work in the store. Once more, I withhold the truth from Mama and Papa. I neglect to tell them that Susan and Nannie know about Henry or that he might be the runaway Virginia Braden described. I fret over Henry's safety as well as Chief Billy's. My fears eat at my conscience, but I cannot think of a way to tell Mama and Papa about what else I heard without confessing I betrayed Henry.

For several days, I look for an opportunity to travel to Terra Ceia and warn Henry. Papa seems in no hurry to visit the farm. *Will I have to tell him the need?* Then, Papa announces one evening that we will leave early the next morning to buy some cows from John Boyle and move them to the island.

"I need Eliza to come with me and check the bill of sale. It is a real handicap not being able to read. We are lucky that she got so much schooling. I will feel better to have her at my side to review any contracts before I sign."

The next day, I saddle Niihaasi, and ride with Papa north towards John Boyle's homestead on the south shore of Terra Ceia Bay. Papa's new horse, a little bay Morgan purchased in Manatee, prances beside Niihaasi swishing his long black tail in her direction.

"Prince, remember your manners," Papa laughs.

Nodding towards Niihaasi, he adds, "And don't forget that fine lady is an Indian princess. She's too fine for you, little boy."

Oh, it is good to be on horseback again.

"Let's trot, Papa!"

"My old bones won't take it, Eliza," Papa replies, but seeing my disappointment, he kicks Prince and bolts ahead of me. He calls back, "Let's just see if an Indian pony can outrun a racing horse from Vermont."

Despite Prince's head start, Niihaasi and I gallop past him and soon, we are far ahead of Papa. I know I should rein in my horse and wait for him, but it feels so good to run free, once more, that I don't stop until I see a large herd of cattle and some cow hunters ahead in the distance. As the group travels, swirls of dust rise about them in a cloud. I can hear the crack of the cow hunter's whips as they command the cattle to move forward. Then, remembering Mama's rule, I slow Niihaasi and swing one leg back over her saddle. We stop so Niihaasi can catch her breath. Papa and Prince can join us.

"I won. Fair and square!" I say when Papa pulls up beside us. I click my tongue to urge Niihaasi into a slow walk beside Prince.

"And my horse is prettier than that plain old brown horse of yours, too!"

"Don't listen to her, little boy. That's how all women are; sure they are the prettiest and the best. We know the truth don't we Prince? If they just gave us another half mile, we could come from behind. That Indian pony might be fast, but she isn't an endurance horse like you are. She might think she's better than you, but in the long run, a woman is nothing without her man."

"Papa! Don't tease!"

"Oh, Eliza, I pray that someday you will know the love of a good and kind man."

I feel my cheeks grow hot. "I only have to look for one just like my Papa. Does Mama know how lucky she is?"

"I hope so," Papa laughs. "If she doesn't, you be sure and tell her. Look, here comes Mr. Boyle. Let me do the talking now. Even if you do think you know best."

John Boyle gallops towards us and circled us like he would a herd of cattle. Prince and Niihaasi shy away and whinny as his tall black horse snorts, racing around them. I try to hold her in place, clinging to my saddle. It would not do to take a tumble in front of Mr. Boyle and his men. Like Niihaasi, I do not like the feeling of being confined.

Mr. Boyle enjoys the game, however, and smiles. In his thick Irish brogue, he says, "Atzeroth" and nods at Papa.

"Mr. Boyle," Papa replies in a steady voice. "I hoped to catch you today."

"What can I do for you?" Mr. Boyle calls over the horses' squeals.

"How about reining in your horse and let's stop under that grove of oaks over there to talk," Papa suggests.

Mr. Boyle spins his horse around and gallops away at full speed. Oh, how I would like to beat him in the chase, but Papa warns me with a look, as we work to calm our horses and proceed at a sedate walk. Niihaasi tosses her head. I struggle to hold her in check. By the time we arrive at the shaded glade, Mr. Boyle's mount is already tied to a low hanging branch. The black horse stomps and swings his tail, even as he twists his long thick neck high into the tree to feast on the Spanish moss that dangles there. We settle our horses a short distance away where they can graze on grass and approach Mr. Boyle who waits for us. Just the sight of Mr. Boyle makes me uneasy. He stands so tall and arrogant. He stares at me just like he can see right through me.

Wasting no time, Mr. Boyle quickly gets down to business. "So, Atzeroth. What is it you need from me?"

"I want to purchase some cattle. My stock needs some new blood. I admired some of your herd and would like to purchase from you."

Mr. Boyle puffs out his chest. "Yes, I've got some good stock. They would certainly raise the value of your cattle. What are you looking for?"

"A couple of cows, some with calves if you can spare them. Perhaps a yearling or two."

"Five total then? Two cows and some young. I've got some that might suit you, but I am reluctant to let them go. I am building my own herd, you know. But, for a price, I might be persuaded to sell. How about $12 for each of the cows and $5 each for the young ones? $39 might convince me to let them go."

"Hmm, that price is a little more than I am willing to pay," Papa replies.

I listen carefully as Papa and Mr. Boyle negotiate the sum. *How can Papa bargain when he didn't even know which cows Mr. Boyle is willing to sell?*

As though reading my mind, Papa asks, "Which cows are you speaking of?"

Mr. Boyle explains, "I have a black and white cow. It came from Harvey Lockwood's stock and is a fine producer. And another that's a brindle, almost mahogany color. It is marked with Captain Hooker's brand, but she is mine. I just haven't had time to mark her yet. Both have calves at their side. There's a yearling that I have not seen, but I hear it is a yellow brindle."

"Well, those do sound like what I am interested in, but $39 is still more than I can pay. I can give you $5 for each of the cows and $1.50 for each of the calves. I will let the yearling go this time. I don't want to buy what I cannot see." Mr. Boyle calls to his cow hunters to bring the two cows and their calves closer for inspection. Papa examines them. They are good quality, just as Mr. Boyle promises, but he holds firm to his original offer.

Finally, Mr. Boyle says, "Alright Atzeroth, I can see you have your mind made up. How about $8.00 for each cow, $2.00 for the calves and I will throw in the yearling for free if you can find it? $20.00 is a good price for five head."

Papa nods in agreement.

"Done," he replies. "Eliza, get your paper and pen from your saddle bag."

I cross to my horse. Again, I feel as though Mr. Boyle's eyes follow me closely.

When I return, Papa asks, "Mr. Boyle, will you draw up a bill of sale?"

"No, get your girl to do it," he says brusquely.

I stammer.

"I have never written a bill of sale before. I don't know how to do it."

Mr. Boyle looks at me with distain. "Just get your paper. I will tell you what to write."

As Mr. Boyle dictates the words, I write. "Manatee, Florida. October 24, 1854. I sold to Mr. J. Atzeroth 2 cows: 1 in the mark of Harvey Lockwood a black and white cow. The other is a brindle cow with Captain Hooker's brand on her. The mark not known and 2 calves belonging to the same cows and 1 yearling if it can be found. The whole amount $20.00."

I give the paper and pen to Mr. Boyle to sign, but I am surprised to see him simply put an X for his mark. The brash Irishman cannot even sign his own name! Feeling superior, for the first time, I finally see that an education is not to be taken lightly after all.

After marking the paper and accepting a $20 gold piece from Papa, Mr. Boyle says gruffly, "Atzeroth, you best get those cows out of here. Take them home and get them marked in your brand. Captain Hooker will be up soon to gather his cows and he might take her by accident. If you can find Mr. Gamble's cow driver, Jim, he can help you find that yearling. It's been mixed in with his stock, I think." Papa shakes Mr. Boyle's hand and turns to go, but before we leave, Mr. Boyle speaks.

"Atzeroth, I hear you got yourself a hired man." Papa stops in his tracks, but does not turn around. "Nate Hunter told me. Said your girl here told Nannie and Susan." *I wish the ground would open up and swallow me.* I dare not meet Papa's eyes.

"Henry's his name, isn't it? I was thinking someone ought to ride over and take a look at him. Check out his freedman's papers. You do have his papers don't you?"

Papa does not acknowledge his question. He continues walking towards Prince and says instead, "A pleasure doing business with you, Mr. Boyle."

Papa does not speak as we ride around the bay's south shore towards Terra Ceia River driving the cows before us. While Prince does not know how to act around the cattle, Niihaasi is a dependable cow horse. It is a good thing she knows her job, because I am too distracted by my guilt. Niihaasi pushes the two cows and their calves into the water and across the river onto the island. As we approach the farm, I see a new cabin on the shore of the bay.

Curiosity overcomes me, and I break the silence. "Whose house is that, Papa?"

"George Wilson and his family have joined us on the island. He claimed the land east of ours. His wife's name is Kate. They have three daughters about your age. Perhaps you can be friends."

Then, Papa grows quiet once more.

"Papa."

"Eliza." Both of us speak at once.

"Let me go first," I plunge in and feel just as I did the first time I crossed the river on Niihaasi as relief at finally spilling my secret frees me to speak.

"I'm sorry I told about Henry. I did not mean to. Manda, Mr. Gamble's house slave said something about Henry to me in front of Nannie and Susan when I was at the plantation. I did not know what to do. I told them he was our hired man, but I don't know if they believed me because Manda said he is not free. They said it was odd that our family would have a slave. Their father told them we did not believe in slavery so someone must have already known. I did the best I could, Papa. Please believe me!"

"I know you did not intend to harm Henry. This is what comes from mixing with people who are so different from you."

Papa's words, meant to comfort, only bring me more shame.

"Papa, that is not the worst. At the party, I heard Mrs. Braden talking. She says her brother, George loaned them a slave from his Tallahassee plantation. He ran away and hasn't been seen, but George still looks for him. Papa, that slave's name was Henry! What will we do if they come looking for him here? What will we do if Mr. Boyle wants to see his papers?"

"I do not know Eliza. He is in danger that is for sure. We will have to think of something. I am anxious to get to the cabin and find out if anyone has been snooping around. For all I know, Henry could already be gone."

Oh. I didn't think of that possibility. "Do you mean the slave catcher might have found him already?"

"Maybe, or Henry may have gotten word that they are looking for him. Perhaps he left to join Billy Bowlegs again."

I don't know what to wish for. Should I hope Henry will still be at the farm or that he will be far away safe in the Everglades with Billy Bowlegs to protect him? Following the edge of bay, I want to leave Papa to tend the cows and rush home ahead of him. I know he needs Niihaasi's skill to get them safely into the pen so I stay to help. Once home, they will wait to be branded with Papa's brand, an A. If released too soon, they will try to return back to their original herd. It will take them awhile until they will think of Terra Ceia as home. Someday, when they are marked properly so that everyone knows to whom they belong, they can be driven back to the mainland to mix with the rest of Papa's cows roaming free on the land between the Manatee River and Terra Ceia Bay.

Until then, Niihaasi and I have work to do. As we round a bend in the shore, I see smoke billowing from the cabin's chimney. *Henry must still be here!* Crossing behind the cabin to the cattle pens, there he is working in the fields tending the fall crops of peppers, tomatoes and onions. Bent over pulling weeds, Henry straightens when he hears the bellow of the cows as they approach. He waves and walks towards us setting his hoe to rest against a tree on the edge of the field. I let Niihaasi do her job, and soon, the cows and their calves are securely in the pen. Only then, can I jump from Niihaasi's back and run to meet Henry.

"Henry, Henry! You're still here! Oh, it's good to see you!" I dance around him like a frisky puppy. In fact, I am joined in my excitement by a medium sized dog and her six puppies. They come pouring out from underneath the log cabin at the sound of our voices.

"Oh, look, Papa, look at all the puppies. Where did they come from? Get down, get down!" Giggling with wonder, I sit down on the ground and am soon covered in puppies. Their sharp little teeth gnaw on my hands and pull my hair. A brown one with white fur on his belly puts his paws on my shoulders and looks straight in my eyes. Then, he licks my face with his rough tongue. As he gives my cheeks a good scrubbing, I laugh.

"Where did you come from, Brownie dog?"

"Ole Mama Dog just showed up here one day, big and fat she was. I knowed she were expectin', her belly draggin' the ground. Lookin' for a handout poor girl. I start feedin' her and look what she give me in return."

"Papa, can we keep them? Can I have one of my very own? Please?"

"Well, I don't know about keeping all of them," Papa replies. "But, I think that little brown one has already chosen you."

"Really? I can keep her?"

"Well, Miss Liza, sound like your Papa agreein', but you best be askin' if you can keep him. That's a boy dog you got there."

"I'll name you Brownie." I give him a hug and he nibbles on my ears.

"Stop it, Brownie." I stand and hold him in my arms. He

wiggles and squirms. I am afraid that I will drop him so I put him back down. "Can I take him back to the river house with me?"

Papa nods.

"Henry, what will you do with all the others?" I ask.

"Oh, if Mr. Joe say it alright, we can keep one or two here. Mr. Gamble's cowman, Jim, say he want a couple to train as cattle dogs. He think they be right smart dogs. We can use 'em ourselves, too. They be good watchdogs. Mama here don't let no one get by without lettin' me know."

"Speaking of Jim, we bought another yearling that's not in the pen yet. We need to round her up. Jim should know which one she is. Tomorrow, I'll go looking for him. Do you want to go with me?"

"Yeah. Mama's weaned them pups. We can take him two when we go." Henry nods at me.

"Those four cows you brung look good. And Miss Liza, that Indian pony is one fine cow horse. I see how you drive them here all by yourself."

I am proud of myself and of my horse.

"Yes, she is a good girl. It was a lucky day that Billy Bowlegs brought her to me and you, too, Henry."

That reminds me of the other reason we have come. Papa must have remembered, too.

"Henry, let us get these horses unsaddled and then, let's sit down and talk."

"I'll go inside, Mr. Joe. I got some beans cooking on the fire and some cornbread ready to bake. You and Miss Liza hungry?"

Suddenly, my stomach growls aloud. Embarrassed, I grab my waist.

"Thank you, Henry. I guess we are," Papa laughs while I blush. "Come on Eliza, let's get these horses settled and then, we'll eat."

After dinner, Papa and Henry sit on the porch while I play

with the puppies. I am glad that Brownie chose me, because it is hard picking a puppy for Mary. They are all so cute. Maybe I will just let Henry choose his cattle dogs and take what was left over to Mary. As I watch the squirming canines wrestle each other for a stick, I wonder what Papa will say to Henry. For a few minutes, Papa is quiet as he smokes his pipe. The yelping and whining of the puppies punctuate the silence, and behind the house, the cows low softly to their calves. Somewhere in a nearby tree, a woodpecker knocks on a trunk trying to find food. I hold my breath. Will Papa tell Henry that I gave away his secret?

Finally Papa speaks. "Henry, do you get lonely out here by yourself?"

"No sir, Mr. Joe. I thought I might. Always had people round. But, I like the quiet. Gives me time to think."

"Has anyone been around? Maybe asking about you or where you came from?"

"Mr. Wilson, he come by sometimes. He asks a lot of questions, but only bout crops and cattle. First, I think he checkin' on me, but now, I think he just want to know how we do things here in Florida. He from Alabama. Different there."

"How does Mr. Wilson treat you?"

"Treat me? Why do you want to know that?"

"You work for me. I expect him to treat you fairly."

"Mr. Joe, he treat me however he want don't you know."

Papa just looks at Henry. Then, he says quietly, "You know what I mean."

"He treat me alright. He ain't my best friend, but he don't abuse me none."

"What about others? Anyone else come by?"

"Just Jim, Mr. Gamble's man. He come by looking for some stray cattle. Least that what he say. I think he was lookin' at what kind of man I am."

"What do you mean by that, Henry?"

"You know, slave or free. Whose side I on? Black. White. Indian."

"What did you tell him?"

"I tell him I my own man, Mr. Joe. The only side I see be mine. And I look out for my friends. You been good to me, Mr. Joe. Right now, I be on your side, too."

"Fair enough," Papa says. "So no one by the name of John Boyle then. Tall, Irish, full of himself?"

"You mean the one who thinks he's god?"

Papa laughs. It sounds just like Mr. Boyle. I figure Henry must know him after all.

"No, he ain't been round. But, Jim, he tell me to watch out for Mr. Boyle. I'll stay away from him if I can help it. But, if not, I know what pleases his kind. I know how to act."

Papa hesitates, then asks, "Where's your home, Henry?"

"Mr. Joe, I ain't got a home. Not like you and Miss Liza. No place to put down roots and belong. Started in Virginia. A man there own me. Had some family, friends. But, then he give me to his son who move to Florida. And bring me with him. I could've made a home there, but he hire me out. Sends me round to other plantations. Some folks good to work for, others not so good. He got a notion to loan me to his sister. That's how I come to be here in Manatee. A man could make this place a home, if he were 'llowed. When it came time to go back to Tallahassee, I too tired of being tole where to go. So, I run away. You know how I tried Indian Territory. Too wet for me. This island now. It bout as close to heaven as I can imagine."

Henry stops, lost in thought. Then, he speaks again, but his voice sounds weary. "I guess you can say I'm a little like Abraham. In the good book. He a stranger and a pilgrim just like me, lookin' for the promised land. I don't see a chance of finding my little bit of heaven on earth, not as long as men like Mr. Boyle are bout, but I still keep lookin'. I don't have much, but I still got hope. Iffn I can't find it here, I still got my heavenly home to look to."

"Indeed you do, Henry," Papa nods. "Indeed you do. But, I give you my word, I will try to work towards your freedom if I can. Henry, was your master, George T. Ward?"

"That he were, Mr. Joe. The very man."

"He's still looking for you, Henry. You need to be very careful. I will see what I can do to contact him and raise the funds to pay him off. Try not to leave the island and should anyone come around, it might be best if you would lay low until they leave. Don't be talking to Mr. Wilson if you can help it. And whatever you do, stay away from Mr. Boyle!"

"Yes sir, Mr. Joe. You don't have to tell me twice."

I've stayed quiet as long as I can. "Oh, Papa, that is a wonderful idea. If you can buy Henry from Mr. Ward, then Henry will be free! Won't you be happy to be free, Henry?"

"Well, Miss Liza, your Papa give me a taste of freedom here and it sure be fine. As long as I stay here on this island, I do what I want when I want to. He don't stand over me like an overseer telling me what to do every minute. I guess you can say, I'm free, but not free. No one ever really free, Miss Liza. The big man make rules, we obey them. Jesus the only one who make any man or lady free, Miss Liza. His truth set us free. Even a man like me with a bounty on his head."

"Henry, how do you know so much about God? Who taught you?" I ask.

"I learn a little here, a little there. A wise woman, she teach me. In Virginia, we go to church. Mostly, I learn by listening. He speak to me when I be still and listen."

Then, Papa asks Henry about the crops, but my mind wanders. I ponder Henry's words. *How can you be free and yet, not free? What does that mean? If Jesus really can set Henry free, then why is Henry still a slave? If Henry can hear God talking to him, could I as well?* Even after the men leave the house and walk out to the field, I stay on the porch thinking. But, as the afternoon wears on, my eyes start to droop and I feel sleepy. The puppies sprawl out under a tree in the sandy front yard and go to sleep. *I wish I could join them.* Just about the time I start to go inside and lie down, Mama Dog jumps up and begins to bark. All six of her babies join her in frantic little yelps.

Men on horseback approach the house. One of the horses is big and black. Mr. Boyle! I must warn Henry. I race through the house and off the back porch missing a step and almost fall. I catch myself and keep running. I can see Papa and Henry talking near the cattle pen. I won't be able to reach them in time! I can't breath, but gather all my strength and holler at Papa. "Mr. Boyle's coming!"

Immediately, Henry runs for the woods behind the house while Papa calmly walks towards me. I put my hands on my knees and bend over panting. By the time Mr. Boyle and his men round the back of the house, Henry has disappeared. Mr. Boyle pulls his horse to a stop just in front of Papa. The horse sprays foam into Papa's face, but he does not flinch.

"Mr. Boyle, what brings you here? Is something wrong?"

Mr. Boyle looks beyond Papa, craning his neck in all directions.

"No, Atzeroth, nothing's wrong. I just wanted to check to make sure you got those cows home. I didn't know if you might need a hand since it was just you and your girl to drive them."

"Eliza and I managed just fine, but thank you for checking. As you can see, they are penned up nicely. We hope to brand tomorrow after finding Jim and the yearling." The two men with Mr. Boyle do not stop, but circle the yard and field on their horses.

"Are your men looking for something, Boyle?" Papa's voice is cold. "I'll thank you to pull them back out of my field. Those crops are almost ready for harvest, and I prefer to gather them rather than have them trampled."

"Just having a look around, Atzeroth. Even though we are

neighbors, this is the first time I've been to your place. Nice spot. Though remote. I bet very few people come this way. Any trouble with thieves or vandals? A man could be attacked clear out here and no one would ever even know about it." Mr. Boyle's tone makes me shiver. *Is that a threat?*

"No, we've had no trouble, nor are we looking for any. But, I appreciate your concern."

"You can't be doing this all alone, Atzeroth. Where's your help?"

"Gone to the other side of the island to get some fish for dinner. I expect he will be back soon."

"Got his papers on him?"

"What papers?"

"Don't play games with me, Atzeroth. You know he has to carry his papers with him wherever he goes. His freedman's papers or papers from his master giving him permission to travel? You are his master aren't you?"

"No, I am not his master. He's free, just like you and me."

Mr. Boyle frowns. I'm sure he doesn't like the thought of a black man being equal to him.

"Well, tell him to keep his papers on him, then. One of these days, I'll run into him and I'll want to see them."

Mr. Boyle whistles and spins his horse around. His men turn as well and come to join him, but not before riding straight through Henry's neatly plowed furrows. Their horses' hooves pull plants from the ground and scatter them in all directions.

"Good day, Atzeroth! I'll see you again soon."

My heart pounds with fear as I cross the yard to stand beside Papa. I reach to put my hand in his for comfort. I want to cry, but will not give Mr. Boyle the satisfaction of knowing he upset me. Mama Dog barks, her puppies yip in excitement and even Niihaasi calls after the departing horses, but Papa and I stand quietly as the men ride out of sight.

Chapter Five

The next morning, Henry assures Papa that he will be alright on the island alone.

"I don't like leaving you here, Henry," Papa says.

"I be fine, Mr. Joe. I wish I could go with you and Miss Liza, but best stay here. I keep one eye on my work and another eye out for Mr. Boyle. Tell Jim I say hello and hope to see him soon."

The October sky is a bright blue as we ride off the island. There is not a single cloud in the sky. I feel like I can see all the way to heaven. If there is such a place. Mama believes that there is. Henry does, too. I'm not so sure though. If I believe in heaven, then, I'll have to believe in God. Despite all that I've been taught, He still doesn't seem real. Even if He is real, what would He care about one girl like me, anyway?

I put it out of my mind so I can enjoy the day. I love fall the most of all the seasons. The air feels crisp and fresh. I'm glad to leave hot sultry summer behind. Tall purple paintbrush grows besides the trail and waves gently in the north wind. I don't even mind that we must spend the whole day looking for Jim. First riding southeast in the direction of the plantation, we see no sign of Mr. Gamble's herd. We stop under the shade of a large spreading oak to eat our lunch, biscuits and sausage left from breakfast washed down with tea Papa carries in a mason jar in his saddle pack. Small wasps buzz high above us in the moss that hangs from the tree. I reach up and pull some down for Niihaasi. She loves the sweet tasting treat.

"They are storing up some food for the winter," Papa says.

As we eat, Papa points out a red shouldered hawk circling above us.

"Winter's coming."

"How do you know that, Papa?"

"I've been seeing more and more hawks out hunting lately," he replies. "Fall is their breeding season. His mate should be coming back from her summer down south. He's taking advantage of the drier weather. The grass is starting to thin, and he can see the rabbits and mice a lot better now. Watch him."

My eyes follow the hawk as it spins and twists in the air. Then, suddenly, he dashes towards the ground slipping through the grass and emerges with a long black snake hanging from his talons. The reptile fights to be free, but the hawk holds it fast.

"I'm glad he got a snake." I say. "I wouldn't want him to eat a little rabbit."

"That snake probably just ate a rabbit and was moving slow after his meal," Papa laughs. "So, Mr. Hawk got two meals with one dive."

With lunch finished, we remount and set off to the north-east. All afternoon, Papa and I scan the horizon for Jim.

We almost reach Frog Creek where I start to suggest that we give up and head east towards home, when Papa says, "There."

I turn to the direction he nods and far off in the distance, I see the air is grey almost as though fog rolls in. Except this is not moisture, but dust scattered into the air by the milling cattle. Papa clicks to Prince and pushes the Morgan to a gallop. Niihaasi needs no urging. I hold on to my reins and enjoy the wind on my cheeks. *What joy!* This is the best way to ride.

We pull our mounts to a stop a short distance away so as not to scare the herd. Papa waves to Jim, and he leaves the cows in the charge of some other men and rides to where we wait.

"Jim, that's some fine looking head you have there. "

"Yes, Sir, Mr. Joe. Mr. Gamble will be right pleased, I think. He was just saying he had a hankering for some beef steaks. What brings you two out this way?"

"I bought a yearling from Mr. Boyle the other day. Yellow brindle color. Mr. Boyle said you would know where it is."

"Saw it just the other day up by Cockroach Bay. You need to

ride a little farther north. If it is still there. It took up with a group of wild cracker cows. There is a big strong bull with that group so watch your back when you find them."

Papa looks at the angle of the sun. "Thanks for the advice, Jim. We will heed it. Well, it looks like we don't have time to get up there and round 'er up today. We'll head on back and try again tomorrow."

"Henry still staying at your place?" Jim asks.

"Yes," Papa says. "We had a little run in with John Boyle the other day though. Know anything about it?"

"No, Mr. Joe, but you be real careful of him. He's a hard man with a grudge against us blacks. Are you staying on the island?"

"For a while, but not for long."

"Tell Henry to come and find me if he has any trouble. Even up the stakes a little should Mr. Boyle come calling with his men."

"I pray that doesn't happen, Jim."

"Even, so, Mr. Joe, you best give him the message."

"Thanks for your offer of help, Jim. I will. And thanks for the warning about the bull." Then, Papa turns and I follow.

"Good-bye Miss Liza," Jim calls. I wave back as we trot towards home.

The next day, we ride out again, this time turning north just before the Terra Ceia River. We wind along its bank until we came to the shore of a small bay that feeds into Tampa Bay. Mangroves replace saw palmettos where the footing grows soft and wet. As we ride, fiddler crabs scurry out of our way. I love watching them wave their oversized claws as they run. It does look like a fiddler sharpening his bow. In some places, there are so many it looks as if the whole earth is moving as they swarm in waves racing before us. I swat at sand gnats that swarm out of the mangroves and scratch my head.

"Ooh, Papa, I don't like these bugs. They are in my hair!" I rub my ears as the tiny black insects crawl around my face. They are no bigger than flakes of pepper, but sting as they bite me.

"Let's ride and get out of here," I call and start to trot along the beach.

"Eliza, wait. There are the cows. Look! Jim was right. That is a huge bull!"

Even from a distance, the mottled colored bull looks enormous. His rough grey horns stretch at least three feet on each side of his head before turning upright. Nearby, several cows graze on the saw grass that grows near the shore. In the middle of them is not one, but two yellow brindle yearlings.

"Which one is ours, Papa? And how will we get her out of there?"

"Now, that I don't know, Eliza. At least not yet. Give me a minute to think. First, I have to figure out which cow is ours. And I need to do it without catching the eye of that mean looking old cuss. Mr. Boyle said that the yearling was marked with Mr. Hooker's mark," Papa remembers. "Can you see an H on either one of those cows?"

I urge Niihaasi forward to see, but stop short when the bull swings his head in my direction.

"I don't know, Papa. Maybe the one on the right. It has a mark on it that could be an H, I guess."

"Well, we will just have to see if we can separate her from the rest of group, then. I'm going to push them away. You and Niihaasi cut the yearling off and move her towards home. Keep an eye on that bull, though. Don't let him charge you."

Papa and Prince cautiously move toward the herd. When he is about twenty yards from them, Papa raises his whip and flips it down striking the ground with a loud crack. The cows turn and run in the opposite direction. As they do, Niihaasi and I block the path of the yearling. At first, the bull runs alongside his herd, until he realizes that one has been left behind. The lone cow bellows with fear, and the bull stops and turns to face her. Papa cracks his whip again, and the bull hesitates, undecided whether to face the man with the whip for one cow or leave the entire herd. Then, he lowers his head, as though to charge.

"Papa!" I scream.

"Eliza, pay attention to your work! Keep that cow away from the others."

But, I can't move. *Who will win? Papa or the bull?* The bull begins to run towards Prince and Papa, but Papa stands his ground. Once more, he lifts his whip. This time, he aims at the bull instead of the ground. He hits the animal on the neck, but the bull continues to advance. Again, he strikes at the bull, this time catching him on the face. The bull roars in pain, tosses his head in bewilderment, and then, gives up the fight. He turns around to follow his cows to safety. The little yearling cries out again.

"Eliza, push her back away from the shore."

So, I urge Niihaasi forward. My horse gets behind the cow and forces her to move. Niihaasi loves the game and darts back and forth around and behind the cow driving her farther and father away from the others. I am glad she knows her job, for I can only fret and worry about Papa. Soon, I hear the thud of hoof beats behind me as Papa and Prince catch us.

"Good work, girls!" Papa shouts his approval, and we head toward home.

We are almost to the cabin before I speak aloud my fears.

"Papa? I think I made a mistake."

"About what, Eliza?"

"I am afraid we got the wrong cow. This one does not have the H mark as I thought."

"It will be alright. Considering the circumstances, we did the best we could. I am not inclined to go back and tell that bull, 'I'm sorry Mr. Bull, but we got the wrong one of your girls. May we please exchange her for the correct one?'"

I laugh. "No, I guess we can't do that, can we? But, what will we do if Mr. Boyle says we got the wrong one? "

"We'll just tell him what happen. He is sure to understand."

I hope so, but I am not convinced. Papa isn't describing the same Mr. Boyle that rode away so furiously from the cabin a few days ago.

After supper, Papa quietly smokes his pipe, while I tell Henry all about our escape from the bull.

"I knowed that little Indian pony of yours be a good cow horse," he exclaims. "And you right smart to stay on her like you do, Miss Liza. Chief Billy done a good job teaching you to ride." His compliments make me feel good.

Then, I ask Henry the question I have been thinking about for days.

"Henry, what did you mean when you said you are free, but not free?"

"Well, Miss Liza, we all got rules to live by. No one make their own rules, even most important men like Mister George T. Ward or Doc Braden. Then, they be rules ain't nobody on this earth control. Who tell the sun to rise and set? Who tell the seed to sprout from the ground? Storm comes. Season changes. Man ain't got no control over those. God do though. I figure, we all got some master or another. The good book say we are all slaves to somthin'."

"But, Henry, doesn't it make you mad that people are always telling you what to do. Don't you just want to be able to make your own choices? At least sometimes?"

"Ah, Miss Liza. That a good question, yes indeedy. You gotta ask yourself, 'Who'll I follow? How'll I act?' See there, little miss. I do have a choice. No man can make me feel what I don' want to feel. No sense gettin' riled up and fightin' 'gainst chains that bind me. They just serve to hold me close to my real Master. God knows where I be. He know my name. This ain't my real home, Miss Liza. I just be passing through. Things will be better by and by. God made me a promise. Me? I jes' follow Him on home. My body may be slave, but my soul be free."

Then, in a deep low voice, Henry begins to sing. The song's melody is nothing like anything I ever heard in church. The notes at times seem out of pitch, but the words, catch the essence of what Henry believes.

"Don't be weary, traveller,
Come along home to Jesus;
Don't be weary, traveller,
Come along home to Jesus.

My head got wet with the midnight dew,
Come along home to Jesus;
Angels bear me witness too,
Come along home to Jesus.

Where to go I did not know
Ever since he freed my soul.
My head got wet with the midnight dew,
Come along home to Jesus;
Angels bear me witness too,
Come along home to Jesus.

I look at de worl' and de worl' look new,
I look at de worl' and de worl' look new.
My head got wet with the midnight dew,
Come along home to Jesus;
Angels bear me witness too,
Come along home to Jesus."

That night in bed, Henry's song echoes in my head. *Oh, to be content with my life like Henry is.* To know that everything makes sense even when life doesn't seem fair. Henry believes in God and thinks of Him as a kind and gentle Master. *I wonder what it would be like to believe the same way.* My heart longs like Henry's for heaven. *But, what would it take for me to get there, too?*

Papa does not forget his promise to Henry. I hear him talking to Mama about it shortly after we arrive back at the river house. Mama irons in the kitchen while I wash dishes. Papa finishes his coffee. After explaining the situation, Papa grows silent. I can tell he is thinking about Henry's predicament. No one talks in order not to disturb him. The only sounds are the water splashing in the sink, the crackle of the fire on the hearth and the soft thump, thump of the iron hitting the wooden board as Mama smooths the cotton sheets. Finally, Papa clears his voice and speaks.

"Julia, I don't even know where to begin, but I must figure a way to purchase Henry. I hate to go directly to Dr. Braden and have him serve as intermediary. I am sure that there is some pride involved as Henry belongs to his brother in law and Dr. Braden was responsible for him."

Papa gets up from the table and places his cup in the dishwater. He pats me on the shoulder.

"By what Eliza overheard Virginia say, I expect that he would rather take Henry back and punish him than sell him to me."

"Not to mention that he might exact revenge upon you for giving Henry a safe haven," Mama replies. "We must proceed carefully. Are you sure that it is worth it, Joseph?"

"I gave the man my word, Julia," Papa exclaims. "Would you have me go back on my vow?"

"Calm down, Joseph. I know you are a man of honor and that you believe strongly he should be free. It is just that you need to think of your family and the impact on them. Do you have any idea how much this might cost both in dollars and in possible ill feelings with the crowd at Manatee? They have much power and could make our lives miserable. Think of the girls."

At that point, I can't hold back any longer. I have never

shouted at my mother, but I do now.

"Mama, you don't know Henry like Papa and I do. He is a good man. He deserves to be free. Don't worry about me. Do what is right, Mama."

Mama sets down her iron and frowns.

"So, daughter. You feel so passionately about this that you would talk rudely to your own mother? Watch your words and show more respect. I don't have to know the man to believe he should be free. But, my first responsibility is to you and Mary. If you and your Papa would jump into this fight, at least you should go into it with your eyes open. You must realize how much is at stake here. This is not a popular thing to do."

I feel flushed, but do not know if it is my passion or my embarrassment. I should not speak to Mama this way. Still, I refuse to look away from her gaze. Once more, I have angered her by speaking my mind. But, if I can help buy Henry's freedom, I will.

But, Mama says you draw more flies with honey than vinegar so I lower my voice and speak gently.

"I'm sorry Mama. It is just the evil in Mr. Boyle's face. He will not let this go until we can prove Henry's freedom. We must do whatever it takes, Mama. I have never been popular with the people in Manatee. None of us are, really, but Mary."

"So, what of your cousin, then? You would sacrifice her happiness for that of this slave?"

I would choose Henry's well being over Mary's any day, but how can I say that aloud? There is no love lost between us. Mary is a baby and everyone's pet. She thinks only of herself and her own comfort. She cannot possibly understand how important this decision could be. How to explain that to Mama?

"Why doesn't someone ask me what I think?"

Mary! *How long has she been listening?* Mary enters the kitchen. She sets down her laundry basket and stands with her hand on her hip.

"Doesn't anyone care what I think? No one ever asks me my opinion. You all treat me like a baby. But, I am twelve years old now. And I can think for myself. Don't you want to know what I think?"

Papa smiles at Mama, then, turns to face Mary.

"Yes, little one. What do you think?"

"See, there you go again. I am not a little one anymore, Papa. I have a right to help make decisions, too. Just like Liza. I can say what is on my mind as well."

I think that Mary has never been shy about speaking her mind. It is usually what is best for Mary. But, I have already spoken mine. I wait for what I am sure will come. Nothing is more important to Mary than Mary. But, when Mary speaks, it was not at all what I expect to hear.

"I agree with Liza. Don't worry about us, Mama. Do what is right. I know how you feel. You have taught both of us well. You don't believe in slavery. None of us do. It is time we took a stand against it, Mama. We need to make a difference even it is in the life of just one person."

"Well, Papa. It looks as if our girls have decided then. Come here, Mary, Eliza." We rush to Mama and she gathers us into a hug. "These are good girls, Papa."

"I agree Julia. They are good girls. Yes, they are," and Papa encircles the three of us in his arms.

I can hardly believe my ears. *Is this really my selfish little cousin who loves being doted on by everyone? When has she grown up and become wise?* Then, Mary pushes her way out of the group.

Stomping her foot, she says, "Now, maybe you will remember that I am all grown up and quit treating me like a baby!"

Papa and Mama laugh, but I think, perhaps, the old Mary is not completely gone after all.

"Somebody better come help me take down all this laundry. It's hot out there."

With a newfound respect for my cousin, I volunteer. "I'll

go!" and I follow Mary outside to the clothes line.

That evening, Mary and I help Papa write a letter to Senator Hamlin Snell. Senator Snell, who lives at Yellow Bluffs on Sarasota Bay to the south, represents the eighteenth district that makes up the counties of Hillsborough, Levy and Benton. Papa believes that if anyone can help us, it will be Senator Snell. Even though he was raised in Savannah, Georgia, the senator mixes with all different social classes and is well respected in the settlement. After Thanksgiving, Senator Snell will be traveling to Tallahassee for the legislative session. If any man can help negotiate the purchase of Henry, it will be the senator.

"Don't mention that you want to set him free," Mama advises. "Senator Snell's brother, William Wyatt is a slave owner. He might not take kindly to your abolitionist ideas."

With the letter mailed, there is nothing left to do but wait and pray. I don't often call upon God, but Henry trusts God to take care of him. I decide it won't hurt to remind God of what He needs to do for Henry. So, every night before I go to bed, I ask God to keep Mr. Boyle away from Terra Ceia, to protect Henry from the slave catchers and to help Papa buy the man's freedom. I never forget, even one night; but as the months drag by with no word from Senator Snell, I can't help but wonder if Henry isn't wrong. *Does God really listen and care?*

Then, one day, Dr. Branch sails across the river from Manatee. Though he serves as the community's doctor and postmaster, I think he probably has come to talk politics. He tells us that the state legislature just passed a law to establish a new county that will include the Manatee River settlements and some of the residents are not happy about the change. They don't believe there are enough people to keep a county government running. When Dr. Branch starts to leave, Papa asks him if he has any mail for us.

"Oh, I almost forget. You do have a letter. From Senator Snell himself." He hands Papa a thick packet. "Were you expecting something, Mr. Joe?"

"I wrote Senator Snell about another matter several months ago. I thought he would have responded before now. I had almost given up hope."

"Now, Mr. Joe, you know that I see you get your mail as soon as it comes through," Dr Branch eyes the letter suspiciously. "Got some troubles for the law to take care of?"

I hold my breath. *Will Papa tell?* What if Dr. Branch spreads the news? But, Papa is careful.

"No, just a question is all."

Dr. Branch persists. "You never got your claim settled now did you? Perhaps Snell can help you with that."

Papa does not bother to correct Dr. Branch's assumption. "No, I hope to hear. It has been a long time in coming."

I am relieved that Papa has distracted Dr. Branch. Though not the complete truth, I know that Papa is concerned about the land grant as well.

Dr. Branch responds. "Without title to your property, you can't run for office in the fall if we don't stop the establishment of the county. They say elections will be held in October. Gates, Green, and Hunter have already filed to become Justices of the Peace."

Nannie's father will run for office! What if Papa did, too? Then, perhaps he could have an influence over how the government will be run. But, Papa just shakes his head in embarrassment. He looks down and scrapes the toe of his boot in the sand.

"Oh, politics is not for me. I'm content with my store and my farm."

"Well, we'll need every citizen if they insist on a new county," Dr. Branch says as he turns to go.

As soon as Dr. Branch is gone, Papa hands me the letter to read aloud:

"Dear Mr. Atzeroth, I have diligently undertaken your request to locate the owner of a certain runaway slave named Henry located somewhere in the Manatee lands. As you noted, he was once owned by George T. Ward. However, Mr. Ward recently sold him to Benjamin Burgess. This particular slave whose ownership you seek is a highly skilled and valued man. So much so that Mr. Burgess was willing to take a risk on purchasing him sight unseen. Mr. Burgess now wishes information on his whereabouts. He requests that you advise him at your earliest convenience where he may claim his property. I am not clear on whether you have such knowledge, but if you do, I would advise you to be open and honest with me and with Mr. Burgess as harboring a slave is a great offense in this state. Should you still wish to purchase this man, Mr. Burgess is open to an offer. However, you should know that he paid $800 to Mr. Ward and wishes to make a profit on all his dealings.

Very Sincerely Yours,
Hamlin V. Snell, Esquire."

Everyone sits in stunned silence.

Then, Mama speaks, "Joseph, eight hundred dollars! So much money! How can we afford such an amount?"

"Julia how can we not? What price would you place on a man's freedom?"

Then, Papa dictates another letter to Senator Snell. Once more, we wait for the senator's reply.

Despite Dr. Branch's protests, elections are held that fall and county government begins. On the first Monday in October, Papa travels to Manatee to vote. While Papa says he is proud to be able to vote, he confides he does not relish the trip to Manatee. It has been one year since Papa sent his first letter to Senator Snell, but as yet nothing has been done to secure Henry's freedom. I continue to worry and pray. *I wonder why God does not answer.*

Then, a month later in December, something happens of such profound importance that I begin to think that God is busy with other matters.

Chapter Six

Thanksgiving Day brings another face to the table when Captain Sam Bishop arrives just in time for dinner. Captain Sam is one of the first people who made friends with Mama and Papa when they arrived in Florida.

As his sloop, the *Mary Nevis,* makes its way to the landing, Mama says, "That man has a knack for showing up just in time for a celebration. Set an extra place at the table, Mary."

With wild turkey and fresh oysters for stuffing, sweet potatoes cooked in the fire, green beans and squash make a delicious meal. Mama serves pudding for dessert. My mother makes a delicious pudding. To a pint of cream, a handful of flour, egg yolks, and almonds beaten together, she adds a little bread, sugar, lemon peel and butter. She pours the mix into custard cups and bakes them in the oven. When they are done, Mama turns them out onto a plate and pours syrup made of melted butter, wine, and sugar over them. When we finish eating, Captain Sam pushes himself back from the table and rubs his ample belly.

"Julia, once more you have outdone yourself! That was superb! You are an extraordinary cook!"

Mama smiles, "Thank you Captain. I'm glad you could join us. That is a compliment coming from someone who has traveled as much as you have. Now, you gentlemen go outside for your smoke while the girls and I clean up."

As soon I finish my chores, I skip across the lawn that separated the house from the kitchen and around to the front porch where Papa and Captain Sam talk.

"There is going to be trouble soon, mark my words, Joseph. There are some settlers who will not rest until they have removed all the Indians from Florida. They are putting more and more pressure on the army to force them out," Captain Sam says. "Billy Bowlegs vowed peace, but even he will break if they keep harassing him."

"What are they doing?" Papa asks.

"Sending troops into Indian territory. Just a show of force they say, but it won't be long before some sort of conflict will arise. Got a lot of young hotheads itching for battle. They think they are so powerful that they can wipe the Indians off the map in a matter of days. It won't be so easy."

"Yes. The natives know this land inside and out. They know where to hide and where to take their stand. I just hope Chief Billy can keep his temper in check. The last thing we need is a war right now," Papa agrees.

I hate this talk of war. Why can't they just leave Chief Billy alone? Isn't Florida big enough for everyone to live at peace? I rise from the steps, brush off my skirt and head down to the river. Maybe if I am lucky, I will see some manatees. I love lying on the dock and looking out over the backs of the big lumbering sea creatures. Sometimes, they swim so closely together, I imagine I can walk across the river on their backs.

I remember the first time I saw the animals who gave their name to the river we called home. It was the day we arrived at the site of our river home. As Papa prepared to anchor, I saw dark shadows floating below us. They were bigger than a man. Looking closer, I saw that they were some kind of animal. Two little flippers protruded from where their arms should be and a great flat tail arched and waved propelling them gracefully through the water. Periodically, they floated to the surface, took a breath and submerged below the water again. Their eyes looked like tiny black buttons in their wrinkled face, and fuzzy whiskers extended from their snouts. One miniature sea creature nuzzled close to its mother.

"What are they Papa?" I asked.

"Those are manatees, Eliza. Remember Captain Sam telling you about them? They gave their name to this river. Some say

84

the word means Big Beaver in the Indian tongue. Their tail does resemble the tail of a beaver. They are also called sea cows."

I thought they didn't look like cows, but they did have a beaver's tail. Papa said that they wouldn't hurt us. I learned that they were gentle creatures with no enemies except humans who killed them for their oil and blubber like whales. I can't help but think of Captain Sam's prediction about what will happen to us. Even the manatees are hunted. Now, so are we.

Just before Christmas, word spreads throughout the Manatee Settlement that Chief Billy and thirty of his men attacked a surveying party under the command of Lt. George Hartsuff. Four men died, and four others were wounded. Even Lt. Hartsuff suffered a grave injury.

Papa says it was their own fault.

"While the men state that they only took a bunch of bananas, others say that they trampled Chief Billy's prized banana patch. They did it on purpose to make the Indian mad. When he came to them and demanded an apology, the men taunted him and even tripped him."

I feel so sad. I know how it feels to be teased and taunted. No wonder the Chief fought back. How could he do otherwise and save face among his people?

"No matter what the reason," Mama says. "The people have their war now. I hope that they are still happy when none of us are safe in our own homes."

"Mama, what do you mean? Will the Indians come here and hurt us?" I ask.

Mary cries, "Isn't Chief Billy still our friend?"

"There are no friends in this kind of war, Mary."

"I don't believe you!" I say. "Chief Billy won't hurt us. He won't let his men come here. Mary is right. He is our friend."

"Believe what you want girls, but I am telling you. War has begun, and even if he wanted to, your friend Chief Billy cannot control his warriors now."

Everyone else thinks the same way. Many of the settlers rush to Dr. Branch's two large log homes near the mineral spring on the south side of the Manatee River. Dr. Branch built them to serve as a sanitarium, but the frightened settlers feel safer congregating together in one place for protection. Headlines of the Tampa newspaper delivered to Manatee fuel their fear. They proclaim, "Indian War Inevitable. Seven Men Massacred . . . 18 public animals shot down." I listen as Mary reads the story aloud to Papa and Mama.

"The time for negotiation has passed. The time for action has come! The ball has commenced rolling, and it is our hope, it may never cease until the race of the 'red-man' is extinct in Florida." The strong language is shocking to me. Why would anyone hate the Seminoles so much? I am glad Mama and Papa decide to stay at the river house. They are just as uncomfortable as I would be about mixing with the other settlers in such close quarters.

On Christmas Eve, all of the men in the settlement receive orders that they were to enlist in the militia. Mama complains about the timing.

"Couldn't they have waited two more days until after the holiday was over? Why spoil everyone's fun? Today of all days!"

I agree. I know how special Christmas is to Mama. Not only because of the religious holiday, but Christmas is also Mama's birthday. Such bad news. We all know that Papa will have to enlist. It is part of the requirements of the Armed Occupation Act that divided the land up for settlement. Even though Papa still has not received his homestead papers, he is obligated to go, but his term of service will not begin until after the spring planting. He will go sometime in April to serve under John Addison, a cattle rancher, now commander of one of the units.

We all work hard to get the crops into the ground before Papa has to leave. We plant a large garden at the river house as well as the usual fields of vegetables, sugar cane and tobacco at the Terra Ceia farm. I worry about Henry even more now with the war. I hope Mr. Boyle has other things on his mind than a runaway slave, but what if the Indians force Henry to join their side? I remember how easily Billy Bowlegs surprised me, and how he described keeping watch over us. I always wonder how close the Indians are. Whenever I work in the fields, I have a funny feeling I am being watched. I can't get the story about Mary Wyatt out of my mind. Mary is about my age, so it is easy to imagine the same thing happening to me.

According to the tale circulating throughout the community, one day when Billy Bowlegs visited her family, Mary asked him, "If there should be an uprising among your people, would you come back and kill us?"

Supposedly, Chief Billy replied, "Yes, we would kill you easy."

I hope that the Chief meant his words as a kindness to comfort poor Mary, but the thought that the friendly Indian I remember might do the same to me is unnerving.

In spite of the unrest, a surprise visitor arrives. Senator Hamlin Snell himself comes to call. The stout man with a thick gray beard moves slowly as Mama welcomes him into the parlor. He eases himself in Papa's favorite chair by the fireplace.

When he catches me staring at him, he smiles.

"Bad knees," he explains. "This cold does not do them any good."

While the men make small talk about the war, Mama brews tea. Mary arranges a plate of cookies, and I place cups on a tray. Senator Snell eats every cookie on the plate as we watch politely and wait to hear the reason for his call. I think I might burst with excitement and want to question him right away, but Mama warns me to be quiet and wait for the Senator to speak first.

Senator Snell compliments Mama on her baking. He adds, "Captain Sam told me what a good cook you are, Mrs. Atzeroth.

He was disappointed that he could not come inside, but had to sail on up the river to Manatee."

"I will fix a bag for him to take when he returns to pick you up, Sir." She paused.

When will the Senator tell us why he is here?

Papa must not be able to stand the suspense as well and finally, he asks, "So, Senator Snell, to what do we owe the pleasure of your company?"

"Mr. Atzeroth, you requested my assistance over a year ago, and I have finally been able to obtain an answer for you."

As he reaches into his coat and withdraws some papers, he says, "I have here in my pocket, a bill of sale for one runaway slave named Henry. Benjamin Burgess has accepted your offer of nine hundred dollars."

"Oh!" I shout. Mama and Papa both give me a warning look. I want to say that Henry will be so glad, but stop myself just in time.

Mama distracts me. "Eliza, please go and fix that bag of cookies for Captain Sam. I am sure he will be here shortly. Mary, go help her."

We race from the room and in the privacy of the kitchen and clasp hands. Trying to stay quiet, we smile and dance. Henry's freedom is finally here! When we can finally restrain our exuberance, we sedately return to the parlor to see Papa pulling on his coat. Mama comes from the bedroom with Papa's small bag.

"Girls, I am going with Senator Snell to Tampa to withdraw some money from the bank. We will go down to the landing to wait on Captain Sam. I need you to stay close to the house and don't give your mother any cause for concern."

"That is right, young ladies. Remember the dangerous times in which we live. This is no time to wander off and be kidnapped by the savages. Soon, they will be gone, but for now, follow your father's orders and obey."

Papa opens the front door and allows Senator Snell to exit

ahead of him. Before he leaves the house, Papa turns back, winks and smiles broadly. Henry is free!

I wish I could ride to Terra Ceia to give Henry the good news, but I stay close to home as Senator Snell commanded. I help Mama in the store, take care of the horses and work around the house. It is so hard to wait! Then, one day, I see the familiar shape of the *Mary Nevis* as it approaches the shore. Papa is home!

I run to the dock shouting, "Did you get the papers, Papa? Did you buy Henry?" I clap my hands over my mouth. I have to learn to be more careful. *Can Captain Sam be trusted?*

"It is alright Eliza. The captain knows how I feel. We have discussed the issue quite a bit. Yes, I got the papers. I'll tell you more about it when we see your mother. Now, help us unload the boat. I bought a lot of new items for sale in the store."

For the next two hours, we all carry parcels and crates of building materials, and supplies such as fabric, lanterns and crocks from the boat to the store. The men bring bundles of flour, apples and fine sugar, food items that can not be grown in Manatee. Common medicines and remedies for colds, cough and fever fill the shelves as well. When every item is put away, Mama stands back and claps her hands with pleasure.

"This is good merchandise, Joseph. You thought of every-thing. We should have enough to sell for several months now." We move to the kitchen where Mama bustles about setting out coffee and cake to reward all of us for our hard work.

As we enter the kitchen, Papa reaches into his coat pocket and hands Mama a long white envelope.

"Put this somewhere safe until I can get over to Manatee to file it with the court, Julia." "What is it?" Mama asks. "Is it the bill of sale for Henry?"

"Yes, we need to record it with the Clerk's Office so every-one will know he is bought and paid for," Papa replies as he stirs his coffee.

"Will you be setting him free then, Joseph?" Papa looks down at the table and then, says softly.

"Not I, but you."

"What do you mean?"

"Open the envelope." Mama pulls the papers from the envelope and hands them to me to read aloud.

"Why, that says that I purchased Henry! Why is it in my name, Joseph?" Mama exclaims when I am done.

"I couldn't do it. Even if it is just for a short while, I could not own any man. I had Senator Snell make the bill of sale to you."

Mama sits down in a chair still holding the paper in her hand. "So, you put him in my name?"

"I thought it best. Besides you are the property owner in this family. You own this place. I still do not have the deed to the farm on Terra Ceia." He stops, and then repeats, "I thought it best."

"Does it really matter, Papa?" I ask. "You will be setting Henry free now anyway, right?"

"Captain Sam and I talked a lot about that. He knows we do not believe in slavery, but he advised me not to free Henry right away. As long as he is owned by us, he is under our protection. If he is free, he is vulnerable to being taken from us and sold again. We think that perhaps, as far as the law is concerned, he should remain a slave. But, we can promise him his papers should he want them or decide to leave. I don't know what is best. What do you think, Julia?"

I don't wait for Mama to answer.

"I think he needs to be freed. You promised him Papa."

"Eliza, don't be so rude. Let me think about this. Captain Sam makes a good point. This is not something to be taken lightly," Mama states. "Besides, your father has spent nine hundred dollars. Perhaps if Henry is my property, I should keep him as such just as an investment."

"What? Mama, how could you even think that?" I jump from the table ready to argue.

"Sit down, daughter; I know the value of a promise. I was just teasing you."

"This is no joke," I grumble. "A man's life is at stake."

"Yes, daughter, that is exactly what we are saying. A man's life is at stake. And though that life has been purchased, at a high price might I add, is that life better spent in safety as a slave or in danger as a free man?" Mama questions. "That is not something we can decide today. We must travel to Terra Ceia and speak directly to Henry about his feelings."

The next day, Mama asks Captain Sam to take her to the island so she can talk to Henry. Though Mama rides a horse as well as any man, we only owned two horses. If all of us go, it is easier to travel by water rather than overland. Mama locks up the store, and we sail out of the mouth of the river. I realize that Mama has never met Henry. How will the two of them get along?

After sailing north through Tampa Bay and around the islands on the west side of the mainland, we enter Terra Ceia Bay. Papa helps Captain Sam adjust the sails to best catch the wind. I duck underneath the headsail and move to the port side of the boat in order to watch for our cabin. We pass a little cabin with smoke coming from its chimney. What would it be like to have a house of my own? Nannie giggles and longs for a suitor to court her. I am not sure that I am ready for that yet. Boys make me tongue tied. What would we find to talk about?

Distracted, I almost miss the landing, but soon, I see it as we round a bend in the bay. Home again. *Oh, how I love this island!*

After we disembark, Captain Sam sails farther up the bay to check on some of the other settlers to the east.

"I will be back soon," he calls as the wind catches his sails once more. We all go in search of Henry to tell him the good news. Between the log cabin and the garden, Henry has built a small one room cabin.

Papa stops abruptly. "Something is not right. Girls, go back to the cabin."

Then, he continues without us stepping onto the porch of Henry's cabin, peeking into the doorway. Mama and Mary do as Papa asks, but I struggle with Papa's command. I don't want to go back to the house. I want to see Henry. *Why does Papa always think he has to protect me? If something is wrong, I can help. Really I can.* Ignoring his order, I take a step forward to follow him.

"Eliza!" he calls. "Go get your mother. Now! Tell her to bring some rags and water and some ointment."

Henry must be hurt! Immediately, I follow his directions and soon, return with Mama and Mary. Mama rushes into the cabin. I start after her, but stop in the doorway. *What a mess!* Splintered chairs. The table tipped on its side. I hear the crack of broken dishes as Mama walks across the cabin to where Papa kneels beside Henry who is stretched across the floor face down. Deep gashes on his back ooze blood. What happened?

With one word, Papa answers the question. "Boyle."

"With what?" Mama whispers.

"A whip." Papa stands and balls up his fists.

I shrink back at the fury on Papa's face. His eyes narrow and his mouth turns down in a grimace. Papa looks as though he could kill someone. Mary whimpers and hides behind me. Papa realizes we are here.

His face softens a little. "Go outside, girls. Henry will be alright. Your Mama and I need to tend to him."

I take Mary by the hand and pull her from the cabin. Outside, things are not much better. The imprint of hooves fill the garden. Young plants just recently sprouted from seeds sown a few weeks earlier lie crushed on the ground. The gate to the livestock pen stands open. A short distance away, a calf bawls for its mother. As I survey the damage, I feel like crying. *Is this the work of Mr. Boyle? Where is God? Who will help us now?*

When Mama finishes bandaging Henry's wounds, she calls me inside his cabin to sweep the floor of cracked pottery. Then, she takes Mary back to the log cabin to cook dinner. As I clean, Papa rights the table and stacks the broken chairs on the porch until they can be repaired. His deep sighs reveal the distress he feels as do his frequent glances towards Henry now lying face down on his bed.

"I'm sorry, Mr. Joe," Henry's muffled voice can barely be heard. I stop sweeping. I don't want to miss what he says. Papa takes the one intact chair and pulls it to Henry's bedside.

"For what, Henry?"

"All the mess. Garden ruined. Cows loose."

"It can all be fixed. You have nothing to be sorry for. Do you feel like telling me what happened?"

I begin to sweep again. Perhaps if Papa thinks I am not listening, he will not send me away. I want to hear Henry's story. *Who could do such an awful thing?*

"Mr. Boyle come. And his men. I see them coming so run off to hide like you tole me to do. But, I didn't go too far. I feared what they was up to. Mr. Boyle tole them to make it look like it were Injuns. They push their cattle through our fields. Our mamas and babies got riled and busted down the pens and joined up with theirs. That weren't the end of their mischief though. They was goin' to torch the cabins. I just rose up, Mr. Joe. I didn't have it in me to stand back and watch them take everythin' from you. So I come outta the woods. Mr. Boyle, when he see me, he takes his whip to me. All the men gather round. Took bets on how many licks I could take."

Papa clears his throat. Henry's face is still buried in the bedding.

"Is Miss Liza still standing there with her big ears listening?"

"That she is Henry. Eliza run on now." I can't move. I stay frozen in my spot. How can anyone be so cruel? To beat Henry with the same long whip used to drive cattle. I shudder and imagine the cracking sound as it made contact with his back.

"I be careful what I say, Mr. Joe. Miss Liza needs to hear what happened next." Henry continues, "I couldn't stand up no more. Fell to the ground and closed my eyes. I hear the cock of a gun and know the end be near. Not afraid though. Such peace in my heart. I knowed when I open my eyes again I'd be lookin' in the face of Jesus. But, I guess I lay so still, Mr. Boyle, he thought I were dead already. He tole his man, 'Don' waste a bullet.' And they drug me on into the cabin. They were planning on burning it down with me layin' inside. If anyone see the marks on me, they know it weren't Indians who done this. You know, it were strange. I still alright. Don' matter none what they do to me. Just like Daniel, flames can't destroy me. I come out on the other side. But, I worry 'bout what will happen to your place. So, I pray and ask God to keep it safe. Mr. Joe, Miss Liza, He was listenin'. He spared your place. The Lord weren't ready for me to come on home yet, I reckon. What exactly going on in Mr. Boyle's mind, I don't know, but God's hand come down from Heaven and stopped his evil He never tole his men to start the burnin'. His men were eager, Mr. Joe, but Mr. Boyle, he just walk away and took them with him. It weren't my time to die, to see that Heavenly Land."

I feel faint, as though I haven't taken a breath the whole time Henry has been talking. Oh, how close he was to death, but, he was not afraid. He said God was with him and listening to his prayers. *If he is right, is God still here right now? Maybe He does still care.* I remember why we came.

"Henry, Henry! God did more than save your life. He set you free, too. Papa has your papers. He bought your freedom. But, everyone thinks you will be safer if you stay a slave."

Mama's hand rests on my shoulder. When did she come in the room?

"No, Eliza, we were wrong. Courage such as this cannot be purchased. Henry risked his life for our home. He deserves to be free."

Papa nods. "Eliza get some paper from the cabin. We will write Henry's freedman's papers right now."

"I thank you Mr. Joe, Mrs. Joe. But, member I tole you. Henry's already free. Not once, but twice. God save me again today. Give me a piece of paper that show man set me free if you want. But, God, He write his freedom on my heart a long time ago."

"I know, Henry. I know that for sure. But, let's make it official as well, shall we? Get some paper, Eliza."

I run to the log cabin and return with paper and a pen. Still breathless, I write what Papa tells me to say. I watch as Mama and Papa make their marks on the page and Henry receives in writing the freedom on earth that he long ago was given in heaven.

When we are done, Mama brings a plate of food for Henry. Then, she, Papa and Mary go back to eat their dinner at the log cabin. I volunteer to stay and help Henry with his meal. Gingerly, he rolls off the bed and sits to eat. I stand beside him ready to assist. Though the room is quiet, save for the sound of his chewing, Henry's words about God's rescue resonate as though he still speaks. Then, I ask him the question I really want answered.

"Henry, did you see God?"

"No, Miss Liza. Not with my eyes. But, He were there. I know. I felt Him." He looks up, and I can see tears running down his cheeks.

"Oh, Henry! Do you hurt? Should I call Mama?"

"No," Henry continues. "My back don' hurt. But, my heart do. Oh, Miss Liza, if only you'd believe. You gotta know. God protected me. But, He don't just watch out over me. He watches out for you, too. You can't see Him, but He's always there. Always lovin' you and always in charge. Not a sparrow falls that God don' know about it. God know what best for you. Even when you think He don't. Even when you think He don't care a lick. I want so bad for you to know this. If I could, I'd give up my freedom if it would help you to believe. I'd be a slave again to set you free, Miss Liza."

Stunned, I can barely comprehend the depth of Henry's faith, and the fact that he wants me to have it, too. *Can it be true? Is God really so concerned about me? Will He protect and keep me safe? There has to be a catch? What will He require of me?*

So, I ask. "What does God want from me, Henry?"

"He want nothin' but your heart, nothing but your love."

"But, I am not a very good girl. Why would he want me? He must want something from me. What do I have to do?"

"You don't do anything. He does it all. Takes you and makes you the girl he wants you to be."

"Mama says I have trouble with obedience. I am rebellious."

"Obeyn' come later. Iffn' you know how much He loves you, pleasin' Him just comes naturally."

"I'll think about it Henry. You make it sound so easy."

"It is Miss Liza. Don't be thinkin' too much. Folks try to make it harder than it has to be."

I think about Henry's testimony. I think about it over and over, but it just doesn't make sense that God would want me and love me when I am always doing the wrong thing. In fact, the more I contemplate the situation, I get angry. Why would God let something so awful happen to a man who is so good and who loves Him so much? It is easier to be angry with God than to believe He might really love me.

On the way home from the island, I listen to Mama and Papa talk to Captain Sam. He reports that the Wilson and the Petersen families are concerned about an Indian attack.

"They are thinking of banding together up at Frog Creek away from the island. At least until things settle down."

"Joseph, what do you think we should do? Should we take the girls and go to Manatee?"

Papa's face hardens.

"No, Julia. I don't think our problems will come from the

Indians. I think our enemy is closer to home."

While Mr. Boyle was still on Papa's mind, by the end of the month, the Seminoles begin their attacks on Manatee settlers. The first comes to the Braden family at suppertime one Monday evening. It does not take long for news of it to reach the other settlers. We hear the news from Mr. Gamble who rides over to tell us.

"I was there with the family at supper. No one suspected trouble was coming. The nurse was upstairs with the baby and when she looked out the window, she saw shadows creeping along the ground. She very casually rose and quietly walked down the stairs. She entered the dining room. When she reached the table, she blew out the candle and whispered to Dr. Braden, 'Indians'. By this time, the Indians had reached the porch. When the lights went out, we heard sounds of several men jumping from the porch. Dr. Braden still thought perhaps that someone from Manatee was playing a trick on him. So, he eased over to the window. You know those windows are twenty inches thick from where the tabby was formed. He called, 'Who's out there?' but no one responded. Instead, we heard the sound of shots being fired at the house. That is when we realized it was not a trick, but an Indian attack. Virginia and the girls hid under the dining table, but Dr. Braden and I began shooting back. I had a new gun of mine, a Cochran, nine shot turret rifle. I think it was that gun that drove the Indians away. With nine shots being fired in rapid succession, the Indians must have thought there were more men were in the house than just us. The Indians left the house, but stole seven slaves, mostly children and three mules that they used to carry the children away."

"Joseph, John Addison is organizing a party to track the Indians and bring those people home where they belong. A lot of the women and children are moving back in with Dr. Branch. Some are coming to my place. We thought it was safe to go home, but we were wrong. Madam Joe, you and the girls should move in with me."

"Will Nannie be there?" I ask.

"No Miss Eliza, Nat decided to take them to Bradens to help defend their house."

"Thank you, Mr. Gamble. We will certainly give it some consideration. For now, I need to stay here. We just stocked the store and must stand ready to defend it."

"Don't lose your life for a lot of merchandise, Ma'am. It is not worth it."

"Yes, I agree. But, for now, we will stay put."

A few days later, Captain Sam brings the rest of the story. John Addison's company followed the Indians into the Everglades and came upon them at sunrise on the second day of their search. The slaves ran to meet the soldiers, alerting the Indians to their approach. Most of the Seminoles got away by diving into a deep creek near their campsite, but two were shot and drowned in the water. The soldiers scalped them and put one scalp on display at the Braden Plantation and the other in Tampa.

Their actions generate much discussion in the Tampa newspaper, as some believe it was a cruel thing to do while others feel it a necessary part of the war. When Papa travels to Manatee to file the bill of sale for Henry's purchase, I am glad that he does not take me with him. The thought of seeing the scalp of a dead Indian makes me sick. All I can think about is Billy Bowlegs fine head of hair.

Chapter Seven

The attacks continue throughout the spring. A week after the attack on Dr. Braden's house, the Indians burn Senator Snell's. The Snells stayed with Dr. Branch, but the settlers needed food. Senator Snell traveled home to Yellow Bluffs to fetch some potatoes. He discovered his house gone, only a pile of charred wood and ash. A few weeks later, both Asa Goddard and John Boyle's homes suffer a similar fate. When I hear of Mr. Boyle's loss, I cannot not help but feel that somehow justice is served. I wonder if the Indians know of his cruelty towards Henry.

The day comes for Papa to join John Addison's company and leave on a mission to fight the Indians in the Everglades. I struggle with my concern for my father and my confusion over how he can go and fight against our friend, Billy Bowlegs.

"Eliza, I made a promise. When we settled on Terra Ceia and claimed our land, I swore that I would take up arms against the Indians if called. I cannot go back on my word. I did not start this war, and I have my doubts about its necessity. But, I still must go."

We watch him sail away. Mama, Mary and I are now alone to defend the river house, should attackers come. I still look over my shoulder every time I go outside. I imagine danger lurks behind every tree, but will it come from someone within the settlement or my friend, Chief Billy and his men?

My sixteenth birthday arrives, but no one feels like celebrating. Mama bakes a lemon cake and gives me a pretty pin to wear on my dress. I receive a beaded purse from Mary. The party only makes me long for Papa even more. I just feel out of sorts. Is it Papa's absence or my reticence about the war? Maybe it stems from my memories of the fancy party and the pretty dress that I wore at Nannie's sixteenth birthday party. Why can't I have a time where I am the center of attention? I want a party, too. I miss my friend, but she is now living on the other side of the river. We cannot ride our horses alone. Mary is lonely, too, and wants me to keep her company. She follows me around asking questions and chattering every minute. *I wish she would just leave me alone.*

Summer rainy season begins several months early. Day after day, grey clouds fill the sky, and the ground stays wet and muddy. I think I might explode if I can't go outside. Staying close to the safety of home, Mary's constant companionship, working every day in the store and the never ending dampness all combine to make me edgy and irritable. If I could just go for a ride. I could clear my head and chase away my ill temper. A good gallop on Niihaasi will cure me. That might be just what I need, but I know better than to bring it up to Mama. She will not understand or even consider such an idea. Everyone else is so afraid of the Indians, but I am convinced that they will not harm me if I am with the horse that Chief Billy once owned.

A week after my birthday, the sun finally returns. A gentle breeze pushes the musty smell of damp earth away, and the air feels crisp and clean. The weather change brings customers to the store. Settlers venture down the river in the daylight hours to purchase supplies or just escape from the confines of Dr. Branch's stockade or Mr. Gamble's house. They greet friends, exchange stories and dawdle over the shop's wares. Mama, Mary and I stay busy most of the morning helping customers. It is good to see some new faces, but I long to be out in the sunshine. At dinner, traffic through the store eases, so Mama asks me to go to the kitchen and fix a quick meal. I take them bowls of leftover stew and cornbread and then excuse myself to clean up.

I have a plan, but I don't share it with my mother. I rush through the dishes and hurry out to the pen where I keep Niihaasi. I have just one hour. *I have to get out of here for just a few minutes or I will go insane.* I don't bother with a saddle and just pull a bridle over Niihaasi's head and throw a blanket on her back. I climb onto the fence rail, straddle my mare and make a kissing noise to signal her to move out. Niihaasi must feel as frustrated as I do about being confined for she leaps forward and races away from the house. In an instant, we are out of sight, and I feel the burden of the past few days lift from my shoulders.

We ride north at a gallop. Though I have not planned it, I realize that we are heading for Terra Ceia. I don't have time to go all the way home. If I stay away too long, Mama will surely miss me and begin to worry. But, if we ride hard, perhaps I can just catch a glimpse of the island from the south shore of Terra Ceia Bay. Our quick pace continues until Niihaasi is covered in sweat, and I am tired of holding on so tightly. It is harder to ride bareback than in a saddle which offers stability. I slow her to a walk. There is no time to go as far as I hoped. I reach down to gather my reins and turn towards home.

With my head tucked near Niihaasi's neck, I hear a gunshot echoing from my left and feel the rush of a bullet just inches from me. If I hadn't being reaching for my reins, it would have hit me. The sun is in my eyes so I cannot clearly see the source, but I see its effects as cattle scatter in many directions. Staying low, I shade my eyes. That looks like Papa's herd! *What is happening? Who is shooting? Are they shooting at me?* I push Niihaasi to a gallop and ride towards the cows. In the distance, I see a large brown form still upon the ground. Someone has killed one of our bulls! Blood pours from a gunshot in his side. *Who did this? Where did the shots come from? Could it be the work of Indians?*

The impact of my predicament overwhelms me. I am on the wide open range. Niihaasi and I are unprotected targets. Mama was right. It is not safe to ride alone, but it is too late for regrets. I look for a place to seek shelter. Scrubby palmettos, stocky cabbage palms and tall pines surround me, but until I know where the gunman hides, I don't know the direction to ride. Before I can move, a gun explodes on my right and Niihaasi squeals in pain falling to her knees. I tumble off and hit the ground so hard it knocks the wind from me. *Have I been shot, too?* I gasp for air and struggle to control my panicked horse. If we can just lie still among the palmettos, perhaps whoever is shooting at us will go away.

Afraid and in pain, Niihaasi's first reaction is to bolt, but the injury to her leg keeps her on the ground. I wrap the reins around her head, hold her close and sooth her with my voice. She quiets. I still wear my apron. I was in such a hurry to leave the house, I did not remove it. *Oh, what I fool I was.* Now, I put it to good use and stanch the flow of my horse's blood. My hands grow sticky and red. The wound is deep. The bullet pierced Niihaasi's right shoulder. I cannot tell if it is still lodged inside or not. I am afraid to probe too much. She may pull away from me. Niihaasi groans in pain.

What now? Is the gunman still out there? Why is he shooting at us? Will he stay until I rise and then, shoot me too? I try to stay calm, but my hands shake as I push the cloth against Niihaasi's shoulder. My own side hurts from where I hit the ground. My fall. I remember Henry's words. Not even a sparrow falls that God does not know about it. Here, I am far away from home in the woods. *Can God see me?* Desperate, I turn to Henry's God.

God, if you are there. Send help. I'm sorry I disobeyed. Henry says you love me even when I am bad. *Please God, help me.* In the midst of my prayers, I hear a rustling in the palmettos. I looked up and see a mule's head poke through the bushes. *Is that Dan?* Then, I hear a voice.

"Miss Liza? That you? What you doin' out here, little miss? Are you hurt?" Henry! *Thank you, God. You sent help.*

I cry. "Henry, get down. Someone shot Niihaasi. And one of our bulls too. He is dead. I am afraid Niihaasi is going to die. She is bleeding a lot. Oh, Henry, be careful. Someone might shoot at you, too."

"I think they be gone, Miss Liza. Let me look at Niihaasi." Henry slides off Dan's back and drops to the ground beside me. He feels around her leg carefully.

"It don' 'pear broke. You done a good job stoppin' the bleedin'. In time, she'll heal." Relief floods over me.

"Henry, how did you know I needed you?"

"I felt somethin' weren't right. Somethin' kept telling me to saddle up Dan and go for a ride. When I hear the shots. I didn' know who might be shootin' so I came to look. I see now, God was a tuggin' at me to come and get you."

"I was praying, Henry," I confess.

"And He was listenin' to ya, little miss."

Henry urges Niihaasi to her feet. She stands on three legs holding her injured leg off the ground. Her head hangs down.

"Hurts don' it baby girl?" Henry croons.

"Miss Liza, I don' know what else there is to do but send you on home on Dan. Your Mama, she goin' to be terribly worried. You gotta get back to the river. Niihaasi, she go home with me. It'll be a long while. She'll havta walk slow. I take care of her. Soon as she well, I bring her to you."

"Henry, I want to go with you. I don't want to leave her."

"Miss Liza, you know how much I care 'bout you and this horse?"

I nod. "Yes, Henry. I know you are our friend.

"Then, you gotta trust me to care for her. Let her go with me. You do what's right and go home to your Mama. You got some splainin to do of your own. I take good care of her and I promise I bring her to you soon as she able to make the trip."

What Henry says makes sense. Still, I hesitate.

"Miss Liza. Have I ever fail you?"

"No, Henry."

"Then, listen to me and listen good. You gotta learn to trust. Not just me. But, God, too. Even if I can't heal her, God can.

Now, get up on Dan and ride as fast as he take you home."

I allow Henry to help me up on Dan's back. Then, Henry smacks the mule on his rear, and he takes off at a bouncing trot.

"Keep your head down low on his neck. Just in case," Henry calls.

I hold fast, feeling like a sack of potatoes at Dan's disjointed gait. Despite Henry's warning, I turn my head back and watch as he assists my little horse away in the opposite direction.

"Please God," I whisper. "Let her be alright. Keep her safe. Thank you for Henry."

As Henry predicted, my mother is frantic with worry. She and Mary run towards me as soon as they see me approach the house. Mama reaches up and pulls me off the mule hugging me close and cries with relief. Her relief turns to anger as she holds me away from her and shakes me in frustration. My legs are so weak, I don't think I can stand. Mama scolds me for causing such fear.

"What were you thinking? I guess you weren't thinking were you? Haven't you been paying attention to all the stories? We are at war, Eliza. You could have been killed."

Looking at my soiled dress, she exclaims, "Where did all this blood come from?"

Sobbing with sorrow over the pain I have caused not only to Mama but to Niihaasi, I choke on my words. Finally, I stammer the whole tale. When I finish, Mama stands still and sober.

Turning towards home, she simply says, "Come daughter. You need a bath. I don't expect I have to tell you what wrong you have done. It sounds as though you made your own punishment. Mary, put Dan away."

Then, she draws me under her arm and helps me back to the house.

After a warm bath, I dry my hair in front of the fire while Mama dictates a letter for Mary to write to the army officer stationed at Mr. Gamble's plantation. She asks the sergeant in command to assign a company of men to our house. She relays that two of our animals have been shot and that we do not know the source of the threats:

"I fear for my daughters' and my safety as my husband, Joseph, is serving under John Addison in the service of the militia. We have many enemies, and I would feel much better if two or three men could come and protect us."

Mama hesitates, thinks for a moment and then, continues:

"The reasons for our alienation are many. We have different beliefs than the main crowd in Manatee and do not attend their church. We will be grateful for your assistance. We will of course, make sure that they are properly housed and fed while they are here. They will be of great service not just to us, but to all of the settlers in this vicinity."

The sergeant in command, Captain Hart, pays us a visit to respond to Mama's request. He promises to write his superior, Colonel Monroe, and urge him to assign a company to our house. He said, "I do not know how long it will take, Madam Joe, but I will do my best to convince him of the urgency of your predicament. I do pray that your daughter will not go wandering off alone again, however. I hope that her horse will be alright."

I blush and look at the ground. No. No matter how much I long to know Niihaasi's condition, I will not be leaving the house again soon. *I have learned that lesson the hard way.* Though I do not believe that the gunfire came from Indian attack, stories of more Seminole atrocities reinforce my resolve to stay at home. Captain Hooker's men discover the trail of fifty to seventy-five Indians near the headwaters of the Manatee River and follow it all the way to the Little Manatee River. The Griffin family's house at Myakka is burned as is Captain Hooker's own home near the Manatee River. On June 14, near Fort Meade, Indians attack the Tillis family. They escape only because Mrs. Tillis was awake caring for a sick child and heard the Indians approach.

Even if I wasn't afraid to travel, rain continues to fall all summer long, keeping me at home. The season is referred to as the Flood of 1856. In the standing water, mosquitoes breed, forming clouds of insects. Every night before we go to sleep, Mama tucks us in bed beneath sheets of mosquito netting.

Finally, in August, several detachments arrive in Manatee to help defend the region. Captain Harvey Allen, commanding officer of the troops, assigns a corporal and eight privates to our house and store. The men erect tents along the river in front of the house. Mama ensures that they eat well as a reward for their protection. Despite the company and the distraction of the extra work that they bring, Mama continues to fret. Papa has been gone much longer than we expected. She does not say it aloud, but I know she worries that something has happened to him. I am anxious, too. So fearful that I resort to praying again. I add Papa to my pleas for the wellbeing of Niihaasi and Henry. Henry said I must learn to trust. It is hard, but I try. God knew where I was when I hid in the palmetto scrub with Niihaasi's blood covering me. Surely God knows where Papa is in the vast wet land of the Everglades.

One afternoon in late September, Mary and I sit on the kitchen steps shelling butter beans. As we work, Mary repeats a story she heard in the store, but I try not to listen. Pulling on the tough green strings that hold each pod together, I pop them open, and scrape the beans out with my thumb. My mind is not on the chore.

In rhythmic time with the split of each shell, the words, "Please keep Papa safe" echo round in my head. Where is he? The suspense is almost more than I can bear. Two weeks ago, one of the soldiers told me that he heard Papa's company would return to Manatee in about ten days. Four more days pass since everyone anticipated his return. Mama even baked a cake in hopes that Papa would arrive. While the soldiers appreciated the extra treat, my fears increase every day that Papa does not come home.

Though the calendar says it is fall, summer holds its grip on the Manatee lands. I fan my face and brush my hair from my eyes. *What I wouldn't give for a breath of air.* I set down my basket and stand to stretch. At sixteen, I am still about the size of most ten year olds. I've given up hope of growing taller. Some of the soldiers tease me and call me their little baby doll. It makes me uncomfortable not only the name, but to be singled out by the young men. Most of them are not much older than me. Lonely and far away from home, they seek our company.

Mary loves their attention. They call her "Mary Magpie" for her constant chatter. I prefer to be alone. A friend to talk to would be nice, but the soldiers are more interested in flirting than really getting to know me. Other girls my age think only of marriage and beaus, but I have too much on my mind to think about boys. Some girls my age are already married. Mary dreams of marriage, too, but I do not. I am not ready to settle down and have a home of my own. All I want is for things to be the way they once were. For the war to be over, for Papa to return and for a chance to ride Niihaasi freely once more.

"I'll be back in a minute. I need to stretch my legs," I tell Mary.

I walk out to the horse pen. Niihaasi grazes on thick grass, at least one good product of the long rainy summer. It is so good to have my horse home again. As promised, Henry brought her back from the island as soon as she was strong enough to travel. The sun makes her silver coat glow. She still has a scar and a bald patch on her right shoulder. Henry says it may never go away. I bend down and duck through the rails of the fence. When I scratch Niihaasi's neck, she wiggles with pleasure. I idly traced the scar with my finger.

"I'm sorry, girl. I will always be sorry." I am lucky, or blessed, as Henry prefers to say. God watched over us on that day that seems so long ago now.

"Eliza, Eliza!" Mary's call interrupts my thoughts. "Come quick."

Now, what? Mary is always getting excited over something. I leave the pen and walk back to the store where Mary stands waving frantically. Papa! It must be something about Papa. That thought quickens my steps, and I enter eagerly, but Papa is not there. A soldier towers over Mama as she rests in a chair near the counter. Mama never sits down while in the store. *Why is she seated? She looks pale. Is she crying?*

"I am sure that we will hear more news soon, Madam Joe. I have no confirmation that this rumor is true, but I thought you should hear it as soon as possible. Some of my men learned about the attack while in Sarasota. They came as quickly as they could to tell me."

"What is it? What's wrong?" I ask.

"Miss Eliza, I am sorry to tell you. The boat party with which your father served has met with disaster. We received word that they were all massacred by the Indians three days ago near Fort Myers."

"What? What did you say?" A million flies buzz in my ears. Surely I heard wrong.

Then, my legs give way, and I crumple to the ground. Mama reaches forward and pulls me close to her chair. She gestures for Mary to draw near as well. With one of us under each arm, she holds us fast.

"Girls, we have no proof that this is true. Sir, I thank you for letting us know, but until we have official word, I will not believe my husband is dead."

Mama stands and raises me beside her.

"Girls, this man must be famished. Are you finished shelling those beans? Let's get supper started."

As the days pass, I can hardly think for worry. I move from one chore to the next as though sleepwalking. *Is the rumor true?* After her initial shock, Mama behaves normally as though Papa will walk in the door any minute. *But, will he? And if he really is dead, what would happen to us all?*

Night after night, I do not sleep and lie awake begging God to bring him home. Sometimes, when I cannot think of any more words to say, I lie still under the crisp white sheets that smell of sunshine and sea and listen to the call of the Whip-poor-will as he cries for his mate. Mama says the arrival of the Whip-poor-will means cooler weather is on its way. He just sounds lonely and afraid. I know how he feels. I don't even want to go to bed at night. I know I face long hours of tossing and turning before I will finally sleep.

One night, Mama and Mary go to bed, but I chose to stay in the parlor. I say I want to finish sewing some buttons on a new dress but I know it is fruitless to try to sleep yet. As much as I hate sewing, I welcome even a few more minutes downstairs. Somewhere in the distance, the dogs bark a few short yips and then, quiet. Just as I finish my last stitch, I hear a thump on the front porch.

Immediately, I think of the Indian attack on the Braden Plantation when the Indians came as close as the front door. I should go for the gun, but I can't move from my seat. Surely, there, no one will get past the soldiers on guard right outside. *What is it?* Probably one of the men taking a rest from patrol duties on the front steps.

Then, I hear a voice. "There you go sir. It is good to meet you. I know your women will be glad you are home."

I shoot from my chair as though propelled by cannon fire. Papa! Papa is home! Racing to the front door, I fling it open. Papa's fist, just getting ready to knock on the door almost hits my nose as I dash into his arms. My cries of joy wake Mama and

Mary. Mary rushes downstairs two at a time. I don't think her feet even touched the last few steps as she embraces Papa. Mama, not the least bit concerned to stand on the front porch in her night dress, kisses Papa over and over again. Loudly talking and laughing, we pull Papa into the house for a private celebration. Mama settles him into his favorite chair with a cup of tea and a piece of pound cake.

"What else do you need, Joseph," she asks.

"Julia, I would dearly love a pan of hot water to soak my feet. They have not been clean and dry since I left here, and I think I may have picked up a disease."

I run for the basin from the back porch, and Mama fills it with water from the tea kettle. Mama kneels before Papa and takes off his boots and socks. She shakes her head at the condition of his worn and hole filled socks and cracked blistered feet.

"Oh, Joseph, your feet. They are so raw. How ever did you manage? They must be painful." Mama bathes Papa's feet and dries them carefully.

"That feels wonderful. I was not sure I could walk the distance home from where the boat dropped me at Hooker's Point."

He groans and rests his head against the chair, "It is so good to be home."

"Papa, we missed you so. They told us you were dead, but Mama didn't believe them, and she told us not to believe either," Mary exclaims.

"Your mama is a wise woman," Papa says with a little smile. "They tried, but they couldn't kill me." He sighs.

"Papa, what happened?" I ask softly. I hate to disturb him, but I must know.

"Oh, daughter. I can't even begin to tell you."

Mama interrupts. "Your Papa's tired. Let's all get some sleep. There will be time for stories tomorrow. Shoo, girls, get on upstairs. Come Joseph. Let me help you. Let's go to bed before you fall asleep in that chair."

I head for my bedroom, but turn back before leaving the room. My parents embrace as Mama's tears stain the back of Papa's shirt. Before I slip into bed, I kneel, thinking of Mama tenderly washing Papa's feet. I take a long time to thank God for bringing him home safe and sound.

After a good night's sleep, we gather around the breakfast table. Papa's mood is lighter as he teases Mary about all her beaus camped in the front yard and asks me if one of them is mine. He eats his fill of Mama's biscuits, bacon and eggs, then pushes back from the table and lights his pipe.

"Julia, it is true what they all say, you are the best cook in the world. And I am not just saying that because I haven't had anything but fish and crackers to eat for weeks." He laughs at Mama's frown.

"Joseph, where in the world have you been? They told us weeks ago to expect you home."

"We sailed down from Fort Myers eighty miles south of Punta Rassa to where the Shark River empties into the Gulf of Mexico. It took us two days to get to its headwater. From there, we could only go farther by getting out of the boat and pushing and shoving it through the deep mud and grass. At times, we could not even see where we were headed. The grass was so tall above our heads. The muck was so thick that it caught our boots and pulled them off our feet. Most of the time, my socks and boots were full of water."

I remember the poor condition of Papa's feet. No wonder they are raw.

"The worse part was the monotony. Day in and day out, everything looked the same. We never knew if the direction we headed was the right one. All around us we could hear the call of alligators, and at times, water moccasins swarmed around us. I was afraid to sleep at night."

I know how he felt, but my insomnia was caused by sorrow

rather than fear.

"I think the wild animals were more harmful than the Indians. We searched for them and often found signs of their camps, but always, they were invisible. They disappeared into the sea of grass, and we never saw even one of them."

I can't stay quiet. "Why did they tell us you were dead? It wasn't right to scare us so."

"The situation is a mess down there. No one knows what anyone else is doing. Rumors come and go. The army was not prepared for a war of this sort. Not even those of us who have lived here for a while know what to expect from the Seminoles."

"Did you see Chief Billy, Papa?" Mary asks.

"No, I didn't see him, but that reminds me. Get my pack, Eliza."

I pick up Papa's bag from where he dropped it by the front door. Handing it to him, I sit in front of him. Papa rummages around inside and pulls out something wrapped in one of his shirts.

"Eliza, I did not forget your birthday. I am sorry I missed it. Sixteen years! It is hard to believe. You are growing up so fast. I got this for you. I thought you would like it."

I pull away the cloth and inside it is a silver cup and spoon.

"That's pretty, Papa." I wonder where it came from. Surely there were no stores in the Everglades.

"Look at the words on it."

I turn the cup over and look closer. It reads, "Given to Chief Holata Micco with friendship from the United States of America."

I drop the cup in my lap as though I've been burned. Mary plays with the spoon and does not notice my reaction.

"Who's Holata Micco?" she asks.

"That is the Indian name of Billy Bowlegs, himself," Papa explains. "I found it in one of the villages. Don't you like it, Eliza? I thought you would want to have something from your friend."

No, I do not like it. I do not like it at all. But, how to explain to Papa? He might as well have stolen it. This is not his to give me. I rise with a calm I do not feel and set the cup with the spoon inside it on a shelf. I give my father a kiss on the cheek.

"Thank you for thinking of me, Papa. It is beautiful. May I be excused? I have chores to tend to."

I think I have surprised my family, but I do not care. I exit the room quickly. Once out of sight, I run to the horse pen and rest my head on Niihaasi's grey back. I just need a minute to compose myself. How could Papa even think I would want such a gift? Somewhere in the Everglades, Chief Billy is on the run. Strangers invade his home and give him no place to call his own. What other pieces of his belongings have strangers claimed and taken as theirs? How horrible it must be.

Sure. God answered my prayers. He protected me when I was in danger. He healed Niihaasi and brought Papa home. *But, where is God when Chief Billy needs him? Does God only love some people and not others? How can God stand by and watch him suffer?* My heart heavy with the sadness of it all, I weep.

For almost three weeks, the silver cup and spoon rest on the shelf where I placed them. Just a glimpse of Papa's gift causes my heart to constrict. I avoid looking their way. When it is my turn to dust the room, I simply wipe the cloth in the general vicinity of where they rest. I dare not handle them again. Then, one day, they disappear. I wonder, but do not ask where the mementos have gone. Perhaps Papa realized his mistake or Mama noticed my reluctance to touch them. At any rate, the cup and spoon are gone. I am relieved when no one in the family mentions them again.

Chapter Eight

Even though Billy Bowleg's cup is out of sight, it is impossible not to think about the Indian war and its impact on the chief and his people. Papa sails to Manatee to vote in the fall elections. When he returns, he grumbles that he might as well have stayed home. On the ballot are the names of the same men who always run for office and win. They simply trade positions. Hamlin Snell will represent our region in state government again. This time in the House of Representatives rather than the Senate.

I ask Papa why he continues to cast his ballot.

He replies, "In this country, every man gets a vote. I will continue to use mine simply because I can."

I overhear him say to Mama, "Many of the men are signing up to fight for another three months. John Parker is organizing another company."

Mama lowers her voice. I strain to hear.

"Will you be going, too, Joseph?"

"No, Julia. I completed my obligation to the land office, even though they have not fulfilled their promise to me. I will not take up arms against the Indians again."

Papa still does not have his homestead papers, even though fifteen years have passed since we first came to Florida. I wonder what other forces keep the government from issuing title to his land. Some of the other settlers question Papa's loyalty. Rumors that he is an abolitionist with strange religious beliefs circulate throughout the community.

In June, Mama finally talks Captain Sam into selling the *Mary Nevis*. She pays $250 for the sloop, and Papa begins a mail, freight and passenger service between the river and Tampa. I love sailing with him and often join him on his trips to Manatee and the other mail stops along the river. Sometimes, he drops me off to stay overnight at Gamble's plantation. Nannie's family moved there when Robert Gamble decided to return to his family home in Tallahassee. Nat Hunter operates the plantation while Mr. Gamble looks for a buyer for his land. Papa and Mr. Hunter agree that he will never find someone interested in it until the Indian war was over.

Mr. Hunter also delivers a warning to Papa.

"I hate to even bring it up, Joe. I don't like to spread rumors. Some of the other settlers are talking about you. No one knows why you set your man free. John Boyle is the worst of the lot. I do not know why that man has such a grudge against you, but watch your back."

Papa just nods. This is not news.

Henry seems a different man now that he is free. He is confident in his abilities and advises Papa on planting times and methods without being asked. He does not wait for Papa's approval but makes decisions on his own. The farm prospers under his care.

Henry grows bolder in his witness to me as well. Every time we meet, he reminds me of how much God loves me and cares for me. I question Henry about his faith. He knows I still struggle with the idea that God is in control, but does not help people like Henry and Billy Bowlegs. *Does God have favorites? How can He want the best for people and ignore them in their time of need?*

One afternoon, Henry arrives at the river house and asks to speak to Papa. As he approaches the house, I think he is taller and stronger than that man who stumbled onto our front porch so long ago.

"What is it Henry? Why do you need to talk to Papa?" I ask as we walk down to the river where Papa rigs the boat.

"Mr. Boyle been callin'," Henry says.

"Why? What did he want? Are you alright, Henry?"

"Always full of questions, Miss Liza. Just wait till I can tell your Papa."

Papa greets Henry with a handshake. The two men stand on the landing, but I climb into the bow of the boat where I hang over the side looking at the tiny minnows that hide in the grasses. I listen as Henry tells his story.

"Mr. Boyle come this morning. He 'long with Mr. Wilson went out markin' and brandin' calves. None of theirs, but Mr. Goddard's. Came to your place to see if any wandered in with yours."

"Asa Goddard recently died," Papa states. "I expect they are trying to do an inventory of his stock so they can settle the estate. Boyle is married to Goddard's daughter."

"Well, you know that dark yellow brindle cow you snatched out from under the nose of that big ole bull?"

"The one I bought from Mr. Boyle? The one that Jim told me where she would be?"

"That very one," continues Henry. "I thought for sure he come for that cow. You know we never knew for sure that she were the one he mean to sell you. But, he surprise me. That weren't the one he come for. Mr. Boyle, he claim that red brindle cow and her calf belong to Mr. Goddard. Even though she got your brand on her and the calf, too. He take it as his own. I'm sorry, Mr. Joe. Nothing I say convince him otherwise."

Though Papa's arms remain at his side, he balls up his fists. Then, he relaxes and sighs.

"Thank you for coming and telling me Henry. I don't blame you. I will have to think about how I want to handle this." He pats Henry on the back. "Come, let's go up to the house and see what my wife has for us to eat. I think she was mixing up a cake when I came down here."

I follow them wishing that Mr. Boyle had been inside his house when it burned down. *Why does the man plague us so? Why can't he mind his own business?* Papa must wonder the same thing.

As they walk, he asks Henry, "Did Boyle ask to see your papers?"

"Yes, sir, he did."

"What did he say?" Papa asked.

"Nothin'. One of his men read them. Mr. Boyle got a right mean look on his face, then, throw my papers on the ground, turn 'round and go."

"Be careful, Henry."

"I am Mr. Joe."

I am sure that Papa will go to Mr. Boyle's and get his cow and calf back, but he never does. It makes me angry, and I clinch my fists in frustration. I don't know why Papa decides to ignore Mr. Boyle's offense, but nothing more is said of it. Perhaps it is the weather. The summer rainy season begins again, and it is another unusually wet year. In nine days in July, ten and a half inches fall. An epidemic of yellow fever follows the deluge. Before I know it, fall arrives and with it, crops to plant, another round of political speeches and rallies prior to elections, and a renewed effort to win the war.

I listen in disbelief the day that Papa tells Mama the war is over. Chief Billy will move to the Indian Territory. I don't know what to think. *How can Chief Billy leave the land he loves? But, then, how can he not? Who would like to live where you are constantly on the run, and cannot live in peace to farm and hunt?* Despite my understanding, I am disappointed that he chooses to give in and angry that he is forced to do so.

One hundred and thirty eight Seminoles join him in agreeing to go. Captain Tresca, serving as lighthouse keeper on Egmont Key, tells Papa that he never has felt such pity as he does on the day when they sail away. I agree. No matter what people say, I can't believe that peace with the Indians was impossible. I am glad I was not there to see my friend leave Florida.

I can't get over my sorrow. I imagine what it must feel like to stand on a boat and watch your native land disappear from view. Mama urges me to give up my melancholy.

"The war was bad for us all. It is time to get back to the business of farming and earning a living. I will be glad to be able to go outside without looking over my shoulder all the time."

"Yes," Papa replies. "That is, if we can believe that our enemies were truly the Seminoles and not our fellow countrymen."

Late August brings confirmation of Papa's fears. Along with a wagon full of lumber to load on a barge at the landing for shipment to Key West, Nat Hunter delivers a warning. From inside, I listen through the window as the two men talk on the porch.

"Mr. Joe, John Boyle, and George Wilson are bringing charges against you to the Grand Jury. They say you are harboring a runaway slave and that you altered the brand on one of Asa Goddard's cows. Our daughters have long been friends, and I have always known you to be an honest man. Is it true what they say?"

Papa clears his throat. He looks beyond Mr. Hunter towards the river. Then, he faces his friend and replies, "No, Mr. Hunter, they are not true. I have only one man working for me, and I have a bill of sale for him. My wife purchased him a while back during the Indian War. We set him free, but he remains faithful and continues to work our place on Terra Ceia. As for the cow, I purchased some head from Mr. Boyle a long time back. I have the bill of sale for them as well. I expect there is just a misunderstanding is all."

"I don't know Mr. Joe. It sounds pretty serious. What is between you and Boyle anyway?"

"I cannot say. I really cannot say."

"Because you don't know or because you can't talk about it?"

"I don't know. I have contemplated it a great deal. I do not know what I have done to offend him. I can trace no reason for such a grudge. Yet, no matter where I turn, Boyle is there. Always watching me. Always looking for a reason to provoke me."

One by one other settlers stop by the store to repeat Mr. Hunter's message. I cannot figure out if they want to offer their support or just get more information from Papa about the rift between the two men. Papa simply states the same facts over and over. If he is not at home, Mama repeats the story. Each time, they are met with knowing looks and smirks. It seems everyone believes Mr. Boyle and no one believes Papa.

As the weeks go by, I sink deeper into my melancholy and burn with anger. At the same time, Papa grows more and more silent. When I would condemn the nosy customers for their inquiries, Mama shushes me.

"Not now, daughter. You are upsetting your father. Let it go."

But, I cannot let it go. It is not right. It is not fair. Papa did nothing wrong. In fact, Papa does everything right. *Why should he be punished when it is Mr. Boyle who is so wicked? I think I should pray, but why bother? If God really truly cares, Mr. Boyle would be under investigation and not Papa.* Finally, Mama excuses me from the task of waiting on customers in the store and sends me to the house to clean and prepare the meals. So, I fume alone.

One day, Mama invites Christian Petersen to stay for dinner. He and Papa served together in Addison's Company during the Indian War. Christian once was our nearest neighbor when we first arrived on the island. After dessert of sweet potato pie, Christian prepares to leave. As he stands, he offers his hand to Papa.

"Should you ever need a friend, Mr. Joe. You can count on me. Just send word. My brother or I will drop whatever we are doing and come to help."

He tips his hat at me. "Thank you for the dinner, Miss Eliza. I can tell you have been learning much from your Mama. Someday, you will make a young man a mighty fine wife."

I blush as he leaves the room. When he is gone, Papa says aloud what all of us know to be true.

"That is the kind of friend a man needs. No matter how many miles or years pass between their last meeting, he picks right up where you left off. He is the sort I know I can count on to watch my back. I knew it, but it is nice to hear it from him as well."

"May I be excused?" I ask.

Mama looks around the kitchen.

"Yes, you may. You did a good job with dinner. Thank you for cleaning up as well. Mr. Petersen was right. Someday, you will make a good wife."

I take a shawl off the hook by the door and leave the kitchen. Pulling the wrap around my shoulders, I walk down to the landing. In the full moon, I can see the mullet swimming in thick schools. Papa needs to bring his net, but I don't feel like calling him to come. I want to be alone. The fish ripple the water as they jump into the air. I wonder why they leap. Perhaps they are unhappy with their home and trying to fly like a bird instead.

Though the surface of the water is too disturbed to serve as a mirror, I do not need to see my face to know how I look. Men seek beauty and a woman who floats gracefully on their arm at a dance. Will someone ever take a second look at an ordinary girl like me? Plain brown eyes and hair. Though my hair is thick and wavy, I keep it pinned and out of the way. Why am I so short? What I wouldn't give to be tall and willowy.

None of it matters anyway. Even if a boy looks past my outside, even if he does come for a meal and think it delicious, he will find me too quiet and shy. How will he get to know me? I'm not a talker. Particularly around strangers. No, no matter what Mama says, or Mr. Petersen either, I will never make some man a good wife. Like the mullet, I wish I could fly away somewhere else.

Throughout the fall, I keep a list of my inadequacies. I watch Mary interact with the customers at the store and despair of ever being so carefree and outgoing. Instead of trying to compete with her bubbly personality, I withdraw even more. I like staying in the background, doing the cooking and cleaning. At least it gets me away from people and the store. When young men come to make their purchases, Mary is quick to wait on them. I pretend to be happy. Leave them to Mary. No sense in trying. Despite my effort to keep it from her, Mama notices my withdrawal and urges me to get out of the house more. I have no interest. I want to be alone. I just don't care.

In November, Papa received a letter in the mail telling him to appear before the judge.

"It says I neglected to serve jury duty in the fall term of court," he states.

"I'm surprised you missed," Mama says. "That is not like you Joseph. Did you forget?"

"I didn't know," Papa replies. "I never received word that I was to go." He stops lost in thought.

"I wonder what they are up to now?"

In January, while picking peas in the garden, I see two men in a boat tying up to the landing. They walk to the store. Soon, they come back out and sit down on the porch. I wonder what they are doing. It is not unusual for people to use our store as a meeting place, but in light of all the rumors about my father circulating through the community, I feel uneasy about their presence. The men look impatient. They sit down, then, stand back up. One man paces back and forth on the porch while the other talks to him and gestures wildly with his hands. Soon, Mama comes out of the back door of the store and walks to the kitchen. I pick up my basket and join her.

"What do they want, Mama?" Mama shakes her head slowly. "They are waiting for your father. Eliza, now don't get upset. Two days ago, the Grand Jury indicted him on charges of harboring a runaway slave and altering the brand on the cow of another."

"What? Who made that decision? How could they be so blind?"

"Eliza it will not help matters if you get angry and speak out of turn. We must stay calm. The sheriff has been ordered to arrest Papa. That is why they are here."

Arrest Papa? I place my hand against my heart. It beats wildly at the thought of Papa locked behind bars.

"Will he go to jail?"

"No, the order does not call for him to go to jail.'

Mama explains that Papa has one month to post a bond of five hundred dollars. I figure that the same people who are behind the charges know that Papa does not have that kind of money. Everything we own is tied up in land, the farm on Terra Ceia and the store on the Manatee River. According to the government, Papa does not even own any of those parcels. Mama owns the house and store on the river. Though more than sixteen years have passed since our arrival in the Manatee region, Papa still does not have his homestead papers though most of the other settlers received theirs long ago.

"So, what will we do? How can we get that much money?"

"I don't know Eliza. I need some time to think. Please go in the kitchen and take some tea to the men. Take them some slices of the chess pie you made yesterday as well."

"Mama, I cannot do that. These men are our enemies. How can you even ask me to be nice to them?"

"That is exactly what you must do, Eliza. You must be kind. Jesus told us to bless our enemies. Besides, we do not know that we will not have to ask them for their help today."

I want to argue, but Mama simply raises her hand to silence me.

"Take the pie, Eliza. Do it now."

The walk from the kitchen to the store is the longest distance

I have ever walked. Dutifully, I serve Sheriff Green and his companion, Joab Griffin, but my hands shake and hateful thoughts fill my mind the entire time. Sheriff Green lives far out east. *Did he even know the man he came to arrest?* Joab Griffin accompanied Billy Bowlegs to see the president. He was the one who had made fun of the chief.

Finally, Mama returns to the store.

"Gentleman, as I told you I do not know when my husband will be home. He has taken the mail run to Tampa. You are welcome to wait here for his return, but perhaps you would just as soon deal with me. I do not have the money to post as bond, but am willing to mortgage this property to obtain it. I just need to make some inquiries as to who will be interested in assisting me."

The two men look at each other. Joab Griffin strokes his long grey beard.

"Well, Madam Joe, that is exactly why I came along. When I heard that Sheriff Green would be serving his papers today, I thought to myself, while the Atzeroths are fine upstanding people, they are not likely to have that much cash around."

He smiles. *I think he looks like the devil himself.*

"I happen to have some money I would be more than happy to loan you, Madam Joe. In fact, I took the liberty to have the papers drawn up before leaving Manatee. If you will just sign here, I think I can assist you right away. No need to look for help anywhere else."

"Well, thank you so much, Mr. Griffin. That was very kind of you to think about us. If you will just give me those papers and a few minutes to read through them, I am sure that I can accept your offer."

"Oh, no need to read them, Madam Joe. It is a simple transaction. Should you not be able to pay back the loan in six months time, you forfeit the rights to this property including the house, store and its contents." His eyes glint with pleasure at the thought. "But, I am sure that will not happen. It is just a matter of one man helping another."

"I am sure it is very clear, Mr. Griffin. Still, I would be obliged if you would indulge me on this. Please give me the papers and a moment to absorb it all. Things are happening so fast, and I am in such distress about the prospect of my husband's arrest."

If I didn't know my mother, I would think there was an air of frailty and hopelessness to her voice. But, that was not the Mama I know. *What game is she playing?* Mama extends her hand once more. Mr. Griffin hesitates, then, slowly, places the papers there.

"Eliza and I will be back momentarily. Make yourselves at home, gentlemen. Come Eliza."

I follow her back to the house where I read every word aloud to Mama twice. She shakes her head.

"Five hundred dollars and at such a high rate of interest. I wonder how Mr. Griffin knew just what would be required?"

The edge in Mama's voice surprises me. Sarcasm is not usually part of her vocabulary. Perhaps she will not take this passively.

"Let's go, I plan on doing some negotiating. Pay close attention for when we are done, you will need to read the changed wording to make sure it accurately reflects what we have agreed upon."

For the next hour, I watch and learn as Mama slowly and steadily talks Mr. Griffin into a lower rate of interest and two years to repay the debt. I carefully check the revised agreement and nod my approval before handing the document to her for her mark. As he folds the signed papers and places them in his pocket, Mr. Griffin bows to Mama.

"You are a knowledgeable woman, Madam Joe. It was a pleasure doing business with you. I will make sure that these papers are filed with the court tomorrow." He turns to go.

"I believe you have forgotten one thing, Mr. Griffin. May I have the five hundred dollars, please?"

"Oh, I did not forget. I thought I would just file it with the court for you since I am returning to Manatee."

"No thank you Mr. Griffin. I will let my husband take that responsibility, thank you anyway."

Once again, Mama holds out her hand. Mr. Griffin reaches back into his pocket and pulls out a small pouch. He hands Mama ten fifty dollar coins which she recounts in front of him. Sheriff Green laughs.

"I don't think this woman trusts you, Joab."

"It is not a matter of trust, but good business principles, wouldn't you say, Mr. Green? Now, if you will excuse me, I must get back to work. I have a loan to repay now don't I?"

Mama turns and goes back into the store. With one backward glance, I follow her. Sheriff Green and Mr. Griffin stand watching us. Then, they too turn and leave to go down to their boat.

When Papa returns home that night, he is furious with Mama. I have never seen him so angry.

"I do not need you to protect me. How does it look for me in the village to have my wife negotiate for my freedom? Besides, Julia, this is your land. You need not sacrifice it on my account. I can get the money somewhere else. What if we cannot repay the debt? What if I am convicted and have even more fines to pay? We could lose all we have worked for!"

Despite Papa's temper, Mama responds calmly and evenly, "Joseph, there was nothing else to do. I do not plan on losing this land. I will not owe Mr. Griffin a debt for long. I will repay it before the two years is up. No matter what happens. He may think he will win, but this is our home. No one will take it from me. No one."

Mama is right. We are blessed with a good harvest and many customers in the store that year. It takes hard work and some scrimping, but she and Papa pay off the debt to Mr. Griffin in the six months that he originally offered. Papa's trial is set for the fall term of court, but by then, we are free and clear financially although the legal issues still hang over our heads.

Papa sails to Tampa to hire an attorney. The firm of Gettis and Magbee agree to represent him. Because Papa has a bill of sale for Henry, they expect the charges of harboring a slave to be dropped, however, both James Gettis and John Magbee warn Papa that despite his innocence, the brand altering case will be a difficult one to win.

"It will be the issue of who the jury will believe," Papa says upon his return from Tampa. "My bill of sale for the cattle should help, but Mr. Boyle has a lot of friends in the community. Mr. Gettis suggests and Mr. Magbee agrees that we should ask to have the trial held somewhere besides Manatee. It will be hard to get a fair trial there."

"They sound like wise men who understand your situation," Mama says.

Papa hesitates, then, adds, "Eliza, it is likely that you will be called to testify about what you heard and the bill of sale. I know it was five years ago and you were only fourteen at the time. How much do you recall about the day's events?"

My stomach knots. I remember it all. Everything from Mr. Boyle's haughty attitude to my determination to write the bill of sale exactly as I was told. I recall the talk with Mr. Gamble's cow man, Jim, and the search for the cow. But, most of all, I remember Mr. Boyle's cruelty towards Henry and the wounds upon his back after his beating with the whip. Papa needs me to speak up and tell all I have seen. *But, where will I find the courage to do so?* Mr. Boyle is an evil man. He deserves to be punished, and I can help set the record straight. *But, in front of the court?* Papa knows how I fear the people of Manatee.

"All you have to do is tell the truth, Eliza. Just let the truth be told. We will trust God to do the rest."

Mama folds her hands together and looks to heaven, but I think we will need more than God on our side. Maybe with the help of Mr. Gettis and Mr. Magbee.

Chapter Nine

The request for a change in trial locations is denied, and on the first Monday in November, we sail to Manatee for the fall session of court. Because court is only held twice a year, the session may take all week. Once we dock the boat, Papa leaves us to go on ahead and meet his lawyers. Mr. Magbee advised us that I should not arrive at the courthouse at the same time as Papa. to avoid any appearance of impropriety. *How silly.* When I testify, everyone will know we are family. Still, I do not want to take a chance and go against Mr. Magbee's counsel.

As we near the little wooden courthouse, my stomach twists in knots. I think I may be sick. I look for the nearest outhouse, but see none. *So many people! Will I vomit in front of them all?* The lawn in front of the courthouse is full of horses and wagons, and even though it is not yet nine o'clock, men sit in the windows of the courthouse and peek into the doorway; trying to find a place to view the proceedings. I halt. Perhaps I should stay out here. Perhaps they will not need me to testify. Maybe I could just stay outside and wait to see if I am called. Mama takes my hand and pulls me forward.

"Follow me, Eliza. Mary stay close, I don't want to lose you in this crowd."

"Eliza!"

Someone whispers my name. I turn and there stands Nannie. I tug on Mama's hand, and we stop. Nannie reaches out and hugs me.

"I just wanted you to know that I was here. Father says I may not go inside. There are too many people there already, and only room for the men. But, I will be thinking about you. I know you will do fine. Just tell the truth. It will be over before you know it, and your Papa will be free." I nod and give my friend a weak smile. Oh, how I wish the circumstances were different. I long for the days of childhood and long horseback rides with Nannie at my side.

"Come, Eliza. It is almost time for the court to start. We must go."

I turn, then, look back. Nannie still stands there watching us. She gives a small wave, and I wave back before starting again for the courthouse.

I climb the three steps into the building, but shrink back before going inside. Everyone turns to look at me, and the noisy room grows even louder. Mama takes my arm and propels me to a bench in the very back of the room. Two men get up from their seats, and we squeeze into the space. I try to breathe deeply and calm my rapidly beating heart. The room smells like sweat and tobacco. Mr. Magbee warned me that it is important for me to remain calm and not to appear afraid. I like Mr. Magbee. He is quiet and gentle, unlike Mr. Gettis who is loud and boastful. Mr. Magbee promised that he will be the one to question me. We practiced what I should say. As long as I only have to answer Mr. Magbee's questions, I will be alright, but Mr. Magbee warned me that the prosecuting attorney, Henry L. Mitchell, will probably cross examine me.

"He is getting ready to run for office, so he'll do everything he can to use this case to make a name for himself," Mr. Magbee stated. "Just answer his questions directly and carefully. Be factual. Don't let him trick you into saying anything that is not true."

Mr. Gettis added, "For all his bravado, he is still a gentleman and knows it will not look good for him to be rude to a lady. Don't be afraid of him, Miss Eliza."

I can't help but be afraid as I sit on the hard bench of the courthouse, anticipating my time to testify. Isn't it hot in the courtroom! With men filling every window of the building, there is no way for fresh air to come inside. My stomach rumbles. I could not eat breakfast. Now, I feel light headed and nauseous. I need to leave. *I am going to be sick any moment!*

Before I can get up, the bailiff, Josiah Gates, stands and calls loudly, "All Rise! The Southern Circuit Court of the State of Florida is now in session. The Honorable Judge Thomas F. King presiding."

Judge King enters the courtroom from a small room on the building's left front. He sits behind the large judge's bench and bangs his gavel onto the desk. My frayed nerves cause me to jump. Mama pats my shoulder to try and soothe me. *When will Papa appear?* All morning, I wait as one case after another comes before the judge. First on the docket are the cases of settlers suing one another for fraud, neglect or failure to pay debts. In all, ten lawsuits are settled or continued to the next term of court before dinner time.

At noon, Judge King orders a two hour recess. My legs feel weak as I rise. I stumble before regaining my balance and following Mama out the door. At the top of the steps, I feel faint. A hand reaches out to steady me.

"Madam Joe, I would be pleased if you and your daughters would come home with me for a meal and to freshen up. Charlotte would have my head if I left you standing here alone." Nannie's father has come to rescue us.

"Thank you, Mr. Hunter. I would be obliged. I am not sure that Eliza can make it for a moment longer."

"Follow me," Mr. Hunter says and keeps a hand on my arm in case I fall.

I feel like I am in a dream. Hunger, tension and exhaustion make my head fuzzy and dull. I gratefully accept a cool cloth from Susan to wipe my face and hands, eat what is placed before me and then, lie down on Nannie's bed for a few minutes. I might have dozed. I do not know. It seems like just minutes before Mama calls for me to come and walk back to the courthouse.

This time, I know what to expect. The crowd does not surprise me. I keep my eyes averted as I retake my seat in stuffy courtroom. Again, Josiah Gates announces the judge's arrival and eve-ryone stands. As I look at the Judge, I notice Papa is in the room as well. He sits between Mr. Gettis and Mr. Magbee near the front. Perhaps, his case will finally be heard. Things seem different. Judge King asks Edmund Lee, Clerk of Circuit Court if the jury is seated and ready. Reverend Lee stands to read a list of jurors. Who are these men? Do any of them know Papa? Can they be trusted to be fair and impartial? I do not know. On the judge's command, the clerk swears in the jury.

Then, Judge King asks, "Is the defendant, Joseph Atzeroth, of the County of Manatee, present?"

At once, Papa stands and replies, "Yes, Your Honor."

Then, he sits back down.

Judge King continues, "Will the State present the charges in this case?"

My first glimpse of Henry L. Mitchell is surprising, as he stands to state the complaint against my father. How young he looks. He cannot be much older than I am! But, when he speaks, he commands the attention of the entire courtroom.

"It is charged that on the first day of September, in the year of our Lord, one thousand eight hundred and fifty eight in the coun-ty aforesaid, Joseph Atzeroth fraudulently did alter the brand of an animal." He drones on giving the state's side of Papa's case.

Why that isn't how it had happened at all! I squirm in my seat. This is all lies! Who said such a thing? Mama pats me on my knee, and Mary holds my arm as if to keep me in my seat. But, they cannot stop the fury from boiling up within me. I do not think it will be so hard to tell the truth after all. The anger will make me bold.

Once again, Judge King addresses Papa, "Joseph Atzeroth, how do you plead?"

Again, Papa stands, "Not guilty, Your Honor."

A murmur rises within in the courtroom. Judge King raps his gavel on the bench to quiet the room.

Then, he says, "The Prosecution may call its first witness."

Henry Mitchell stands and says, "The prosecution calls J.G. Wilson." As Mr. Wilson walks to the witness chair on the left side of the judge's bench, I remember Papa and Mama praying that God will let only the truth be told. Even though my parents trust in God to protect them, I have little faith that Mr. Wilson will do as he had just promised.

Henry Mitchell begins his case asking Mr. Wilson to describe the cow and its brand. After a few more questions about whether Mr. Wilson knew who branded the cow and the color of the cow, it is Mr. Gettis' turn to question him. But, he declines to cross examine, and Mr. Wilson is sent back to his seat. Why does the attorney let him go? Isn't he going to prove that Mr. Wilson is lying? I feel my face turning red. This will not do. I must remain calm. It is important. My turn might be next.

Instead, Mr. Mitchell calls John Boyle to the witness stand. I shrink back into my seat, remembering Mr. Boyle's forcefulness in the past; but this is a different man than I have seen before. He is calm and subdued. There is no trace of the anger or arrogance I observed in him. Mr. Boyle carefully answers some of the same questions posed earlier, but elaborates on Mr. Wilson's testimony.

"What was the cow's value?" Mr. Mitchell finally asks.

"The cow was worth five or six dollars."

"No further questions," Mr. Mitchell says as he sits down.

Then, Judge King states, "Defense may cross examine."

This time, Mr. Gettis stands and approaches the witness chair, "Mr. Boyle, isn't it true that you have a grudge against Mr. Atzeroth?"

Now, I think. Finally the truth. Tell everyone how you hate and harass us. Maybe, we will even learn why.

But, Mr. Boyle simply states, "I have no harm to him if he would let my stock alone. I got no harm against him."

Again, Mr. Gettis gives him the opportunity to confess, "Have you done business with Mr. Atzeroth before?"

"I transacted business with him in some cases. I sold him two cows five or six years previous to that, two of my own cattle. I never sold him any of Mrs. Goddard's cattle. It was a yellow brindle cow with Captain Hooker's brand on her. She was in the pen at the time I sold her to him. It was all of five or six years."

Then, Mr. Gettis takes a piece of paper out of his pocket. "Your honor, I would like to enter into evidence this bill of sale dated October 24, 1854 with Mr. Boyle's mark on it."

He hands the bill of sale to Edmund Lee. At last, the judge will see. The judge orders the clerk to enter the bill of sale into evidence and read it aloud for the court. As Edmund Lee reads the bill of sale I wrote so long ago, I remember every word. I know them so well, I can recite them along with him.

Surely now, everyone will know the truth. It cannot be clearer than that. Instead, when Mr. Gettis asks Mr. Boyle if that is the bill of sale for the cows he sold Papa, Mr. Boyle answers, "It was not on the twenty fourth October 1854. I expect it is seven years ago. I never put my mark to a bill of sale. I never touched the pen. The other cow that I sold him was a black white cow in Harvey Lockwood's mark. I did not tell him the mark was not known, the one in Hooker's brand. The cows I sold him were not ordered to writing and signed by my mark."

What? I want to jump up and run to the front of the room screaming. He is lying! He is lying! Can't anyone see? Instead, I sit frozen in disbelief. How can he speak such falsehood so boldly?

Mr. Gettis asks one more question, "Have you sold any more cattle to Mr. Atzeroth?"

Mr. Boyle replies, "I have sold cattle to Mr. Atzeroth since. One cow, a two year old heifer and a year old. I told Miss Eliza Joe to put my name to the first two cows I sold Mr. Atzeroth. I neither wrote the paper I speak of. It was not made to me."

As Mr. Boyle makes his way back to his seat, I feel all the blood rush from my head. I bend over to put my head in my lap. How can he sit there and speak falsely yet appear so calm? Now, what will happen to Papa? Afraid and deep in thought, I miss Mr.

Gettis' next words.

When everyone turns to look my way, I realize that he just called me to the stand. He repeats, "The defense calls Miss Eliza Atzeroth."

Mama pats me on the back as I rise from the bench. I make my way through the crowd, around the three benches set in the middle of the room and between the men who stand in the back and sit on the windowsills. It is so hot that I cannot get a breath. I must not faint. I must go forward. I tell myself over and over all I have to say is the truth. I reach the witness chair where I stay erect waiting for the oath. Reverend Lee rises and walks towards me.

"Raise your right hand."

My hand trembles as I obey. I hope no one can see. The judge tells me I can sit down and I do. I clasp my hands in my lap sure the audience can see my fright.

Mr. Magbee smiles and asks gently, "Miss Atzeroth, have you ever seen the Bill of Sale described earlier and marked Exhibit A?"

The truth, I think. All I have to do is tell the truth, and Papa will be free.

I sit up straight and speak clearly, "I wrote the paper myself marked exhibit A."

At Mr. Magbee's urging, I describe how I told Mr. Boyle that I never wrote a bill of sale before, but he told me what to write. I tell of the search for the missing cow and the instructions for its location given by Jim. I want to say, "We did just as we were told. Mr. Boyle is lying. Can't you see?" But, I respond to Mr. Magbee's questions and focus on the events of those days. I must not leave anything out. When I am finished, Mr. Magbee nods again.

Then, he says, "No further questions, your honor," and sits down.

Now, it will be Mr. Mitchell's turn. What will he ask? My hands tighten. I release their grip and place them at my side. This must be what it feels like to face a wild animal. I think of the bull that Papa faced. If only I had a whip! Relax, Eliza, I think. Just tell the truth. Taking his time, Mr. Mitchell stands and slowly walks towards me.

"Miss Atzeroth," he places great emphasis on my last name, "You wrote the Bill of Sale, presented here as Exhibit A?"

"Yes, I did."

"What is your relation to the accused?"

Oh, here it comes. Just because I am Papa's daughter does not mean I will not tell the truth. In fact, because I am my father's daughter, I am compelled not to lie. Haven't they taught me from a child to be honest and true?

As I practiced with Mr. Magbee, I simply respond, "I am the daughter of Mr. Atzeroth."

Mr. Mitchell turns and faces the jury.

He smiles broadly, then says, "No further questions your honor," and sits down.

I remain in my seat. "You are excused, Miss Atzeroth. Defense may call its next witness."

Wait, there is more I want to say! Papa is innocent. He has done nothing wrong. The charges are false. Yet, here is Mr. Gettis ready to call his next witness. I know he wants me to go as he frowns at me, so I return to the back of the room. Never have I dreamed that I would be reluctant to leave the witness stand. Despite my relief that it is over, I am afraid that I did not do enough.

Mama whispers, "Good."

Judge King turns to the jury and gives them their instructions. All the jurors rise as one and follow Josiah Gates to a small room at the back of the courthouse. Once the last man is inside, Mr. Gates shuts the door and stands in front of it as though to protect the men inside.

"What do we do now?" I whisper to Mama.

"We wait."

Judge King laughs and talks with the clerk and Mr. Mitchell as Papa and his lawyers stay motionless watching the door of the jury room. I stare at the back of Papa's head and wonder what is happening in the closed room. *What are they talking about? Do any of them have any sympathy towards Papa or are they all friends of Mr. Boyle?* Papa must feel my gaze for he turns and catches my eyes before facing forward again. *Did he wink? Isn't he afraid?* The noise in the room grows louder as conversations take place all around me. No doubt they are judging my father's innocence. The temperature increases as well, and I fan myself with my hand. I lose track of time as we wait. It feels like many hours pass, but in reality, it takes less than thirty minutes for the jury to decide my father's fate.

A knock comes from the inside of the jury room door. Mr. Gates opens the door and slips inside. A few minutes later, he returns to the room followed by the members of the jury who file silently back into their seats.

Judge King asks, "Have you reached a verdict?" One man stands. He is the jury foreman. What is his name? I can't recall.

"We have Your Honor. We the jury find the defendant guilty and say that he shall pay a fine of two hundred dollars."

Papa's head droops. Guilty. How can they say he is guilty? Everyone said just tell the truth. I told the truth and look what has happened. Guilty. A two hundred dollar fine for a five dollar cow? Where is the justice here? Mama sees my struggle. She gives me a warning look. Mary is already crying. Mama reaches around me and rubs Mary's shoulder.

Judge King begins to enforce the sentence, but Mr. Gettis is not done. Immediately, he requests a new trial.

"Your Honor, Defense moves that the court establish a new trial on the following grounds: First, because the verdict of the jury was not supported by the evidence given in the case. Second, because the jury should find a verdict for the defendant on the grounds that there was no fraud proven against him. Third, because it was not proven that the Defendant branded or marked the cow."

Judge King refuses to listen, "Motion overruled."

Again, Mr. Gettis speaks, "Your Honor, Defense moves for an appeal to the State Supreme Court."

The Supreme Court. Mr. Gettis will take Papa's case all the way to Tallahassee. He believes in Papa's innocence. *At least someone does.*

"Can your client set a bond for $420.00?" Judge King asks.

Mr. Gettis turns to Papa. Papa looks back at Mama and nods. Mama agrees.

"Yes, Your Honor," Mr. Gettis continues.

Judge King states, "It is ordered that said motion for appeal be granted. Court is adjourned until 9:00 A.M. tomorrow morning."

"What happens now?" I ask my mother.

"I find someone who can loan me $420.00. Then, we go home until tomorrow," Mama says.

Tomorrow? We have to come back tomorrow? *Oh, no.* I remember that Papa still has another charge against him. Harboring a slave. Tomorrow we will be back to do it all over again. I feel like letting go and joining Mary in a crying spell.

"Madam Joe?" We turn.

It is Henry Petersen. "Christian sent me. He could not come, but we wanted you to know we were supporting you."

"It is good to see you, sir. Thank you for coming."

"Madam Joe, is there anything we can do to help?"

Mama smiles, "Yes, there is. Would you care to loan me four hundred and twenty dollars so I can post Joseph's bond and take him home with me tonight?"

Henry Petersen agrees to help. Mama thanks him for his kindness and pledges to repay the two brothers as soon as possible.

"You and your brother are good friends," she adds as we leave the courthouse.

As the crowd disperses, Mama holds back until she can approach Papa and the attorneys.

"I'm sorry, Mrs. Atzeroth," Mr. Gettis says. "We thought we had a good case. I was just telling your husband that I think the

Supreme Court will see the evidence with greater fairness. We will not let this go. It will probably be spring before the justices meet again, but we will be there to present a strong case."

"I know you did your best ,sir. There are many other forces affecting justice in our county these days."

I interrupt, "What about tomorrow? Will Papa be found guilty again tomorrow?"

"Surely not," Mr. Magbee replies. "There is not a shred of evidence to prove that your father knew Henry was a runaway, and as soon as possible, he did the right thing by purchasing him. I hope to settle that case without even taking it to a jury. Go home, get a good night's sleep, and we will see you back here tomorrow."

"Come girls. Joseph?" Mama reaches out and puts her hand on Papa's arm. Lost in thought, Papa jumps, but takes her hand. Arm and arm, they exit the courthouse, and Mary and I follow close behind.

No one speaks as we walk to the river. Papa holds the boat while we all get inside, then, he hoists the sail and we head west. None of us want to disturb him. Once home, we all go about our chores. Papa secures the boat. Mama starts supper. Mary sets the table, and I draw water from the cistern for tea. Other than the sounds of ham frying in the skillet, silverware clinking together and the splash of water pouring into the kettle, the room is silent. Then, we hear Papa's steps, heavy and slow, coming into the kitchen. All three of us turn to look at him. Papa just stands in the doorway. Then, at last, he speaks.

"I am sorry to have put you through this," he says. "I should never have done business with Boyle. Now, I do not question my decision to shelter Henry. It was the right thing to do, but after today, I am not sure what tomorrow will hold."

His shoulders slump in defeat. In an instant, Mama rushes over to hug Papa. Mary and I follow her. I finally give in to my tears.

"It is all my fault. If I had been a better witness, they would have known the truth. They would not have found you guilty! Papa, I am sorry." I feel Papa's strong hands around my back.

"No, no, Eliza. You did exactly right. You have no reason to be sorry. This is all my doing."

Mama says, "No one has anything to be ashamed of. It is the others who will regret this day. Their sins will find them out. It is alright, Joseph. Eliza, Mary, dry your eyes. We will get by."

She turns back to the stove. "Come sit down, let's eat. We will all feel better with something in our belly."

I eat, but the food sits in my stomach like an anchor. None of it makes sense. Mama and Papa believe God will make everything right, but He has not acted on their behalf. Was He even in the courtroom today? I trusted the attorneys and the court, but they failed. My trust was misplaced. *What will happen tomorrow? Is there any justice to be found in this world? Is Mama right? Will the evil done today ever be repaid?*

Despite Mr. Magbee's instruction to rest and Papa's assurance that my testimony did not harm his case, I cannot sleep. I watch the orange harvest moon fill my room with its bright light. I hear Mary's light breathing coming from the other side of the room. How can she sleep when so much of importance is at stake? Now, not only Papa's, but Henry's life will be impacted by the court's decision. The same men will be on the jury. Will they find the guilty verdict again? Why do such bad things happen to good people like Papa, when evil men like Mr. Boyle flourish? Round and round the thoughts go through my mind as the moon travels across the night sky. Finally, exhausted, I sleep, but fitfully.

Mary's persistent prodding pulls me from sleep.

"Liza, get up. Come on. Breakfast is ready." Mary shakes my shoulder, but I don't want to get out of bed. I pull the covers over my head.

"Liza, get up now. We are going to be late for court."

Court. *Oh, no. How could I forget?* I dress so fast that I do not completely tuck my blouse into my skirt. I put a comb in my pocket to use later and grab my shoes and stockings. Running out of the room barefoot, I almost crash into Mama who stands at the front door waiting on me.

"Lazybones, you have no time for breakfast. Take this biscuit and get on down to the river. We will be late for court."

Down at the landing, Papa hoists the boat's sail. It flaps once, and then strains against the morning breeze.

"Morning, sleepyhead," he calls. "Mary says you slept soundly. I'm glad you got some rest."

What does Mary know? Where was she when I tossed and turned all night? Despite my irritation, I know better than to start an argument today of all days. I go to the bow of the boat and sit down before pinning my hair and putting on my shoes. Sensing my bad temper, everyone stays out of my way. If looks could kill, Mary would fall overboard and drown.

Once at Manatee, Papa ties up the boat and again, he walks separately to the courthouse. Today, many of his friends have also been subpoenaed. Nat Hunter, Christian and Henry Petersen, and Samuel Bishop are on the list of witnesses as are his enemies, John Boyle, George Wilson and others that I do not know. As we walk to the courthouse, I keep my head down and shuffle my feet along in the dirt road. I feel a storm cloud filling my heart. If anyone comes near, I may just hit them. I wish for a whip to disperse the crowd. I can feel that it is not going to be a good day. I just know it.

Once again, the courthouse is full. If possible, even more men than yesterday fill the room and stand outside near the windows. Given yesterday's outcome, word must have spread of Papa's second trial. Nat Hunter is not there to greet us today since he has to testify, but he offers a wave to us which I ignore. Henry and Christian smile, but remain aloof. It is better not to appear too friendly.

Papa's case is the first to be heard.

Reverend Lee read the charges, "State of Florida verses Joseph Atzeroth, unlawfully aiding and assisting a slave."

As soon as Reverend Lee sits down, Mr. Gettis rises.

"Your honor, permission to approach the bench."

"Permission granted," Judge King says.

Mr. Gettis walks to the judge's desk with Mr. Mitchell following right behind him. The three men stand in quiet discussion for several minutes. I marvel at the stillness of the courthouse. Despite the noise of men and horses outside the building, inside it is calm. Like the eye of a hurricane. I can hear the floor creak as Mr. Mitchell rocks back and forth on his feet. I watch as a red glow creeps up the back of Mr. Mitchell's neck and around his ears. He is not pleased with what Mr. Gettis says. He shakes his head and whispers back to the judge.

Finally, Judge King nods to Mr. Gettis.

The attorney steps back and then, loudly enough for the entire courtroom to hear, he says, "Defense presents a motion for dismissal due to lack of evidence in this case, your honor."

Sullenly, Mr. Mitchell replies, "No objection, your honor."

Judge King knocks his gavel onto the desk.

"Motion approved. Case dismissed."

Inside the courtroom, conversations immediately begin. The crowd sounds angry. What has happened? Are the men upset that there will be no trial? Mr. Magbee walks quickly to the back of the room and he hustles Mama, Mary and me out of the courthouse. Mr. Gettis does the same with Papa. We rush outside and away from the building. When we have put a safe distance between us and the crowd, Papa turns and shakes the hands of Mr. Gettis and Mr. Magbee. Mama does as well.

"Thank you gentlemen. We appreciate your hard work," she says.

"No need to thank us Madam Joe. The case should have never been brought to court in the first place," Mr. Gettis replies.

"Looks like someone is happy." Mama and Papa join him in relieved laughter as Mary jumps up and down.

"I'm so glad I did not have to testify. Aren't you glad, Liza? I think they were mad that Papa did not go on trial. Don't you think so?"

I cannot respond. What is the matter with me? I stand on the edge of the group, but I do not feel like celebrating. I should be glad. There will be no trial and no new sentence. Papa is free! Maybe now, life can return to normal, but for some reason, anxiety and fear still fills my mind. Something does not feel right. Mr. Gettis and Mr. Magbee return to the courthouse for the other cases that need their attention, and we head for our boat and home.

Chapter Ten

Taking Mama's arm, Papa leads us away from the courthouse.

Mama says, "Oh, Joseph, I am so glad that is finally over. I feel like I could dance."

Papa laughs and twirls Mama around in the middle of the dirt road. Then, out of the shadows of some large oaks, I hear a familiar voice that makes me shudder.

"Atzeroth."

Mr. Boyle. He steps forward into the road. Two of his men who were not in the courtroom stand beside him. *Where did they come from?* Papa and Mama stop their dance, and Papa pushes Mama behind him. Mama beckons to Mary and me. Mary runs to her and hides her face in Mama's shoulder, but I stand my ground. I will not run from a liar and a cheat.

"Looks like someone thinks this is a good place for a party, boys. Wonder why we weren't invited?"

Mr. Boyle's men step forward, but he motions them back.

"You got off light today, Atzeroth. But, it is not over yet. This is the south and we believe in keeping Negroes in their place. That goes for you, too. You'll never be American with your ways and language."

He nods his head towards his men.

"Boys, I wonder if this immigrant knows why his homestead papers haven't come?"

Mr. Boyle laughs, and his men join him.

"Atzeroth, it is time for you to leave this country. Why don't you just pack up and head on back to wherever you come from? We'll be happy to help you along. Won't we boys?"

The three men put their hands on their hips where pistols hang.

No one moves. Then, the rattle of an approaching wagon breaks the silence.

"We'll be seeing you Atzeroth," and Mr. Boyle and his men disappear once again.

With their departure, Mary bursts into tears. Mama holds her fast and rubs her back. Papa clinches his fists together. *What will he do now? Will he file a complaint with the sheriff?*

But, Papa just turns back towards the river and says, "Come, Julia, Mary, Eliza. Let's go home."

The joyful mood replaced by dark foreboding, we start down the road. As we walk, the wagon team overtakes us.

"Good day, Mr. Joe, Madam Joe. Ladies."

I turn to see who is there. As I do, I witness a remarkable transformation. Mary instantly brushes away her tears, dries her eyes and puts a bright smile on her face. If I had not seen it with my own eyes I would not believe that someone could recover so quickly.

"Good day to you, Mr. O'Neil," she sweetly blushes and nods to him.

Who is this man? I have stayed away from the store so long; I do not recognize the customers by face any more.

"Is everything alright, Mr. Joe? You don't look too happy. Didn't you just get a good word at the courthouse?"

"Why yes, William, we did. But, we were just having a discussion with Mr. Boyle is all."

Mama frowns at Papa in warning.

"It is alright, Julia. I sense William is someone to be trusted."

Turning back to William, he continues, "I doubt I will ever know what I have done to create an enemy there, but it must have been something great." He sighs. "But, you are right. We do have much to be thankful for today. What brings you this way, William?"

"I have a load of timber from Mr. Curry's to put aboard the *Ariel*. Mr. Curry wants to send it up to New Orleans. We'll leave tomorrow, I guess. I will miss Manatee. But, I hope to be back on a return voyage soon. This is a beautiful country."

He catches Mary's eye and smiles. So that is it. He is sweet on Mary, and from her adoring gaze, it appears she fancies the Irishman. When did this start?

"Are you headed back to the river?" William asks. "May I give you a ride?"

"Oh, yes, we would welcome it," Papa says.

Why do we need a ride? Haven't we walked this way three times in two days? Isn't the river just around the corner? Papa helps Mama and me into the back of the wagon. Before he can assist Mary, William jumps down from the wagon and offers his hand to her. Blushing again, Mary accepts his help. I cannot help but roll my eyes. This is more than I can bear. *How can Mary go from weeping to simpering in a matter of seconds?*

Mr. Boyle's words still echoed in my ears. There are more important things to consider than romance. Papa and Mama exchange casual conversation with Mr. O'Neil. For once, my talkative cousin is content to just sit quietly. I do the same. What will we do now that Mr. Boyle's threats are out in the open?

At the boat, William again leaves his seat to assist Mary. I think he holds her hand a little longer than necessary, but Mary seems pleased.

As he helps Papa untie the boat, William says, "Upon my return, Mr. Joe, I would like permission to come calling."

He looks in Mary's direction, then adds, "If you do not mind, sir."

I don't think his words are solely directed at my father.

Papa glances back at Mary who dips her head in a slight nod. *When had Mary become so shy?*

Papa claps William on the back and says, "Of course, William, of course. We will welcome you, won't we Julia? Come as soon as you return."

Then, he laughs and shoves the boat away from the dock.

Once we are on the water, Mary finds her tongue again.

"Isn't he handsome, Liza? Such beautiful brown hair. Have you ever seen eyes that color? They change in different light. When he first came into the store, I thought that they were blue, but outside, they turn almost green. And he is so tall."

I try to block out her chatter and am glad when the wind picks up and blows her words away. Too much silliness on such an important day.

Once back at home, we help Mama put together a hasty meal. At dinner, I wait for Papa to speak about the encounter with Mr. Boyle.

When he does not, I venture, "Are we going to do as Mr. Boyle said, Papa?"

"I have been thinking about it. We are so isolated here. I worry about you all. Perhaps it would be safer if we moved."

"Absolutely not," Mama replies. "This is my home. Indians could not run me out, and I refuse to let a bully like Boyle do so. We will stay put. Together, we will stand against him. Girls? Do you agree?"

I nod. Mary does the same.

"Thank you, Julia. Girls. We will stick it out then. Besides, I think the coming months will give Mr. Boyle more things to think about besides an old German Negro lover."

Papa chuckles lightly, but I don't think it funny.

"What, Papa? What could concern him more?"

"Politics, Eliza. If the newspapers can be believed, we may not be living in the United States of America much longer."

"What? I thought you said we were not going back to Germany?"

"No, Eliza. If men of the south have their way, we will not be living in the United States anymore, but another country consisting of only the southern states. A lot depends on who is elected President next year."

"Would they leave because of slavery, Papa? What about us?

We don't believe in slavery. Where will we go?"

"No, Eliza. The fight is over much more than slavery. Even those of us who don't hold slaves can agree. It is over a state's right to make laws and decisions that the federal government cannot overturn. We will just have to wait and see what happens. Don't worry about it or about Boyle, Eliza. Julia, Mary, don't you fret either. We have been through worse, haven't we?"

I remember the hurricanes and the Indian Wars. Mama nods. She does too. But, when I look at Mary, her dreamy expression reveals she is thinking of nothing other than one young Irish mariner.

On the first Monday in March of 1860, Papa sails to Tampa for his hearing before the Florida Supreme Court. The rest of us stay home. The decision will be based on court records and not new testimony. When he returns, Papa shakes his head sadly.

"Mr. Magbee and Mr. Gettis did their best, but the court did not see things our way. They upheld the decision of the Manatee court. We could continue our appeals, but I think I am wasting money and time. The two hundred dollar fine stands, and I have to pay an additional twenty dollars and five cents in court costs. I think I will just leave it be. I need to concentrate on paying back Henry Petersen's loan."

I want to throw myself down on the floor and kick my heels like a baby. It is not fair that everyone will always believe Papa to be guilty.

When I say just that, Papa repeats the same statement he had made last Fall.

"Mark my words, Eliza. The county will have much more to think about than my guilt or innocence soon enough."

Papa is right. Soon, talk of secession captures everyone's attention. I decide even Mr. Boyle's mind must be preoccupied for he does not make good on his threats. Papa continues his mail route, but he tries to come home each night. Once again, Mama tells Mary and me to stay close to the house and not wander off. Months go by with no interference from Mr. Boyle. We all relax.

My twentieth birthday comes and goes and with it the memory of John Boyle's words. News filters into the county from places like Charleston, Richmond and Tallahassee. From newspaper reports, it is clear that should a Republican president be elected, Florida and most of the southern states will no longer be a part of the United States of America. Though some argue that the North would never tolerate division of the Union and war will follow, most do not think that a military conflict will be necessary.

All of this exciting news makes for good conversation at the dinner table. We frequently host guests including William O'Neil who found his way back to Manatee and is already firmly entrenched in Mary's heart. I always know when William is about because Mary turns unusually quiet and bashful. Mary's continued shyness around the man whose affection she seeks surprise and worry me. If such a chatter box turns tongue tied around her beau, what hope will there be for me, shy as I am?

While he continues his work as a sailor, William avoids leaving for any more long voyages. He spends his free time building a palmetto hut on the north side of the river west of our property. Mama is not pleased at the thought of Mary living in a thatch hut. In less than a year, with Mama's encouragement, he begins construction of a log cabin.   About that same time, Florida succeeds from the Union. At first, Papa does not believe that there will be a war, but in March of 1861, the Confederacy calls for Florida to organize an army. In the excitement over succession, many of the men, even those too old to fight sign on with local companies. Mama and Papa disagree over his desire to join.

"You are sixty years old. Too old to be in the army. Besides, we need you here."

Papa insists that he must join one of the volunteer companies.

"They will probably let me stay close to home. They need cattle drivers and blockade runners. Florida will keep the Confederacy fed, and I can help with that."

"Exactly," Mama says. "You can help with that here and on the farm. Grow the food for the soldiers. Keep them strong and fit. That is your job, Joseph."

"Don't you understand? I am already suspect in this county. This is my way to let everyone know where my loyalties lie. I told you already. This war is for all of us. I must take a stand as well," Papa says.

In April, the bombing of Fort Sumter strengthens Papa's resolve, but privately, he confides to me that he will wait one more planting season before deciding which group to join. In between working with Henry to care for the farm, Papa helps to round up the cattle and make salt. Mama is more and more concerned about providing for our family. After the Union Navy blockades the Gulf Coast and the Manatee River, she asks Papa to take her to Terra Ceia to bury a keg of gold coins on the bank somewhere near the spring. She refuses to take Mary or me with her on the trip, stating it will be better for us not to know where it is hidden.

Though I know I can be trusted, it is good that Mary does not know. She will, no doubt, share the secret with William. One afternoon, he arrives as usual just in time for supper. I know of his presence by Mary's sudden start and quick exit out of the kitchen and to the house. *Will the man ever miss a meal?* Frustrated, I set an extra place at the table.

Glancing out the window to see Papa and William talking down by the river, Mama chuckles to herself.

"It won't be long before your cousin will be setting her own table, I believe."

Good riddance, I think. I know I should not be so irritated. I can't figure out what is wrong with me. William is a likable enough man, he loves Mary and it is obvious she loves him as well. Her mind is always on William. It is William this and William that. Isn't William the brightest, the handsomest, the strongest man ever created by God? It is laughable how when William shows up in person, she turns all shades of red whenever he speaks to her. She cannot even carry on a decent conversation. Who could imagine such a thing? All these years I wished for a way to quiet my cousin and all it takes is the arrival of William O'Neil to do it. If you love someone surely you should be able to speak intelligently when they are around!

Oh, what is my problem? I should be happy for Mary. We've had our differences over the years, but surely I can be pleased that my cousin, practically, my sister, will marry such a good, kind man. Still, as I carry the platters of food to the table, something nags at me.

"Eliza! Be more careful. That chicken almost slid right off the plate. What is wrong with you today?"

As I cross back and forth from the house to the kitchen, I ponder that very question. I wish I could ask my mother. Perhaps she knows the answer to my unrest. Then, again, maybe I don't want to share my feelings with Mama today. I bite my tongue and continue to transport bowls of green beans, rice and squash. Reentering the kitchen, I reach around Mama to take a pan of biscuits from the stove.

"Eliza," Mama says gently. "Your time will come. Give Mary this moment of happiness."

As always, Mama knows me better than myself. I have to admit however reluctantly that what I feel is jealousy. Still, I can't respond to my mother's counsel, but the words hang between us in the hot steamy kitchen.

After dinner, William asks Papa's permission to escort Mary for a stroll down by the river. Nodding his head in acquiesce, Papa pushes back from the table, reaches into the pocket of his pants and takes out his pipe. He smiles knowingly at Mama. Blushing, Mary takes her bonnet from a peg by the front door

and walks with William. I stand to began stacking dishes together. In my haste, I drop silverware on the floor. Mama puts
her hand on my arm.

"Slow down, daughter. There is no reason to be hasty. I'll
help you."

The last thing I want is a talk with Mama right now. The
feelings are still too new to speak them out loud.

"No, Mama. I can get this. Why don't you and Papa go sit
outside for a while? It is a nice evening for a change, the air
seems warmer. I will be fine. Go on."

Focus on the work, I think as I scrape the plates and dump
the silverware into a basin for washing. Halfway through my
chores, I realize I still think about Mary's happy face. Surely,
what disturbs me is the fact that she will soon be married and
leaving for her own home. Why else would I be so emotional?
My eyes blur with tears, and I can hardly see the pots I scrub.

Is Mama right? Is there someone out there for me? I am not
smart like Nannie. Or pretty like Mary. I am already twenty one
years old. Girls younger than me have found men to love and
cherish them. *Who is there for me?* Who will want a short dark
haired girl who loves to ride, sail and be out of doors? *Who will
settle for that?*

I hear a commotion coming from the direction of the house.
Dropping the pot back into the dishwater to soak, I wipe my
hands on a dish towel and dry my eyes. I gather my courage
and step outside the kitchen following the sounds to the front of
the house. Mama hugs Mary, and Papa claps William on the
back.

"Eliza!" Papa calls. "Bring us some wine. We will have a celebration. William and Mary are to be married."

I retrace my steps to the kitchen and take my time in opening the bottle and assembling some glasses. Waiting until I rein
in my emotions and stop the flow of tears.

"Oh, Mama," I whisper to the empty room. "I hope you are

right and there is someone out there just for me."

Mary and William choose July 4 for their wedding day. Mama is happy for that day holds special meaning for my parents ever since their arrival in America. What better day to celebrate a wedding as well? Besides, Mama says it will take at least three months to sew Mary's wedding dress, and William needs more time to finish improvements to the cabin.

"I want it to be flawless for my perfect bride," he brags.

The lovebirds are so enthralled with each other it is sickening. I think if I have to listen to any more discussions about wedding cake or lace I will gag. One evening, when I hear Mary and Mama talk about finishing the linens for Mary's trousseau, I offer to mind the store for them so they will have time to sew. As much as I hate clerking, anything is better than listening to the two of them make wedding plans. Mama gladly accepts, and Mary gives me a hug.

"Miss, Miss! Let me see that fabric."

It is only ten o'clock, but already, my head hurts. Flora McLeod and Ellen McNeill arrived not long after I opened the store and want to see every bolt of cloth we have in stock.

"Not that one. There on the top shelf. The green. It should look nice against my skin, don't you think?"

I stand on a stool to reach the plaid taffeta. I hand it down to Flora who pulls it loose from the bolt.

"I can't tell with it all bunched up like that. What do you think Ellen?"

Flora holds it up to her as the cloth unrolls in a heap on the floor. I grab it, as it trails behind Flora in her haste to stand in front of the mirror. It will not do for Mama to return and find her merchandise dirty.

"No, that is not the shade I had hoped for. Where is your cousin? The pretty one?" Flora asks.

Oh, that stings. Do they call me the ugly one?

"She is sewing with Mama today. They are up at the house."

"That is right," Ellen calls from the other side of the store where she inspects some buttons. "I heard there will be a wedding in your family soon."

"Yes, July 4," I say absently, as I brush away the dust and gather the fabric back onto the bolt.

"Isn't she younger than you?"

Flora interrupts and spares me from replying.

"I just don't see anything that suits me here. I am ready to go. Do you want anything?"

"Yes, I will take a yard of this ribbon. It will look nice in Alice's hair don't you think?"

The two women continue talking while I measure the ribbon.

"I was thinking, perhaps I should buy some fabric after all. With the Union blockades who knows when we will get a better selection. I heard Key West has been taken by the Federals. They say that refugees will soon be coming into our area. Those poor souls. To lose everything because they refuse to take an oath of allegiance. Yes, perhaps, I should get that green even if it is not exactly what I had hoped for. And some of that blue as well. One can never have enough dresses, can one?"

I unroll the bolt I just reshelved and a second one as well. Ellen and Flora add thread, needles and buttons to the packet.

"Old Jane isn't quite the seamstress she used to be, but perhaps she can manage with that. I have to go behind her and undo her stitches, sometimes. I wish I had better help," Ellen complains.

I finish writing down the charges just as a stranger walks in the door. Flora and Ellen greet him warmly.

"Michael! How nice to see you!"

Of average height, he still towers over me. His dark wavy hair falls to his shoulders and when he speaks, his speech captivates me. Flora extends her hand, and Michael bends low and presses his lips to it.

"Miss McLeod."

His voice sounds like whipped butter. Ellen offers her hand and giggles as Michael kisses it.

"So, Michael, what is the word from your homeland? Will England join us in the war?"

He is British then. That explains his accent.

"I hope so, Mrs. McNeill. But at any rate, I have decided to take up your cause. I plan on signing up as soon as I am needed."

I cannot get enough of his voice. No matter what he says, it sounds like magic. As though he feels my eyes upon him, Michael turns to face me.

"And who are you?" he asks.

Flora laughs, "Oh, Michael, allow me to introduce Eliza. Eliza Atzeroth. You probably met her sweet cousin, Mary. Eliza does not usually work in the store. What is it you do, Eliza? Keep house?"

I cannot speak. I simply nod.

Flora continues, "Eliza, this is Michael Dickens. He recently came over from England. He is the cousin of Charles Dickens, the novelist."

Turning to Michael, she winks and whispers, "I doubt Eliza has heard of your cousin." Her condescending attitude makes me angry.

Finding my voice, I say, "I know who he is. He wrote *Oliver Twist.* I think *A Christmas Carol* is my favorite of his books, though. Mary read it aloud to us last year."

"Oh, I was wrong. She does know of him. Mary reads the books to her, don't you know."

I blush as Flora and Ellen laugh. Michael does not join them. Oh, he must think me a dolt.

"No, I read them, too. It is just that my, I mean, all of our hands are usually occupied in the evenings, with knitting or sewing, so we take turns reading aloud to each other. To pass the time."

I'm babbling. Shut up Eliza, I think. Ellen doesn't care if I make a fool of myself. Instead, she places her hand on Michael's arm.

"We were just leaving. Would you care to escort us to our boat? I think Archibald is probably done with his business with Mr. Joe and ready to go."

"Of course, I will be happy to walk with you. Miss Atzeroth," Michael nods in my direction.

"Until we meet again. Ladies, after you."

He picks up their packages and follows them out the door, but before he exits, he turns back and winks at me. I think my heart might stop. I am not one for fainting spells, but this must be what the vapors feel like. I sit down. *Oh, my.* Never have I met a man like Michael Dickens. His voice. His hair. Even his manner. He is perfect. Eliza! I caution myself. *Pull yourself together. He is handsome and sophisticated. What would he want with such as me?*

I pick up my broom. Activity. That is what I need. To be busy. To quit daydreaming over someone I will never see again. My mind must be playing tricks on me. Behind me I hear Michael's voice.

"'I should think she would have been a pretty, timid, little, bright-eyed sort of girl. I should have liked to know her.'" I twirl around and almost drop my broom.

"I beg your pardon?"

"From *David Copperfield.* When I saw you standing there, it made me think of it."

He walked closer to me. For a slight man, he fills up the room.

"I should like to get to know you as well, Eliza. May I call on you this evening?"

In all the years, I imagined this moment, I assumed I would be bashful and afraid. Yet, now that it is happening, my heart takes over my tongue.

"Yes, Mr. Dickens. I would be pleased to have you call."

Michael smiles, and I smile back. He has the darkest, deepest eyes I have ever seen. *If I look closer, will I see myself reflected there?*

"Supper is usually on the table by six. Would you care to join us?"

"I am sure I would. But, do I need to ask your father's permission to come calling?"

I laugh. *I can't believe it but I laugh!* When a young man stands before me, I am calm enough to laugh?

"I will take care of my father. Don't be late."

Michael bows low, and I feel like I should curtsey, but I stand my ground.

"Yes, ma'am. I guarantee you that I will not be late." Then, he leaves just as quickly as he arrived.

It is as though his leaving takes all the life from the room. I can barely stand. Once more, I lower myself into a chair. *Does he really like me? Could he seriously want to call? Of all the girls along the river why would he choose me?* I do not know. *Am I dreaming?* Suddenly, it seems the most important thing in the world that he come back. There is so much to do. A meal to fix. A bath to take. Wouldn't I like something pretty to wear? Before now, I had no reason to take an interest in clothes. I hold up the blue silk that is still on the counter. There is no time to sew anything new today, but perhaps I should think about my wardrobe. Why should Flora and Ellen, and Mary for that matter, have all the beautiful things? I fold the cloth back upon its bolt and replace it on the shelf. *Michael is coming to dinner!* Michael Dickens. Cousin of the English author. Mama and Papa will be impressed. Papa! Oh, I need to talk to Papa. What if he is angry that Michael did not ask permission to call? *What time is it?*

Chapter Eleven

It is almost noon! I am inclined to race out of the store and to the house. Then, thinking that Michael might still be in eyesight, I slow my steps and stroll quietly to the kitchen.

"Oh, Eliza. I was just going to send Mary to get you and your father. Did you see him anywhere out there?"

"Mrs. McNeill said he was down by the river. I will go get him."

I retrace my steps and see Papa high up on the mast of the *Mary Nevis* adjusting the rigging. No one else is around. Taking advantage of his solitude, I walk over to the dock, lift my skirt and scoot over the side of the boat.

"Eliza! How's my girl?" Papa has not called me that in a long time. I guess now that I am older, Papa tries to treat me like a grown up, but it feels good to be called his girl once more.

I tip my head back and shade my eyes to look up at him as he continues, "Did Mrs. McLeod and Mrs. McNeill buy out the store? It looked like they carried several packages. *Who was that with them? I did not recognize him.*"

Oh, Papa. If you only knew.

I try to keep my voice casual.

"I met him for the first time today, Papa. Miss McLeod introduced me. His name is Michael Dickens. He is visiting here from England. He is a cousin of Charles Dickens the novelist."

Papa looks down at me and frowns. He shimmies down the mast. Then, reaches out and takes my face in his hand.

"Michael Dickens. Hmm. I think he is more than you say. Your face looks different. Softer, perhaps. Who is this man, Eliza?"

It all comes out in a rush.

"Papa, I don't know. But, I have never met a man who

makes me feel this way. All fluttery inside. I am not afraid of him. It is like I have known him all my life. He says he wants to get to know me better. What if he doesn't like me when he does?"

"And would that be so devastating, daughter?"

I think for a moment, and then reply carefully, "Yes, Papa, I believe it would be."

I sigh. "I do so want him to like me."

"Well, if he is at all a good man, he will not only like you, but love you as well. I knew the day would come, but did not think it would be so soon. So, you met him once and already decide he is the one for you?"

I hold my breath. *If I say it out loud, will it somehow keep my wish from coming true?*

"Papa, he makes me feel good and strong and comfortable. Yes, I think I could spend my life with him. I know it seems silly and odd. We only just met. But, yes, I hope, no, I know he is the one for me."

Now, if only Michael feels the same.

Reading my mind, Papa says, "Then, daughter, I also hope that he feels the same."

Oh, how will I tell Papa I have invited him to dinner? Without giving him a chance to ask my father permission to call? I frown.

"What is wrong, Eliza."

"Papa, he wanted to ask your permission to call, but I told him he did not need to do that."

"What? Now I am confused. I thought you said you liked him. Why did you tell him not to talk to me?"

"Papa," Oh, now I must confess my boldness. "Papa," I start again.

"Yes, daughter."

"Papa, I told him he did not need to ask you. That I would ask you myself."

Papa stares at me for a time, then, flings his head back and roars with laughter.

"Oh, my. Yes, I would say. You must be in love. That's my Eliza. A whirlpool always stirring under the quiet surface. Come, let's go to dinner. We must figure out a way to tell your Mama that a man is coming to call whom your father has never met."

Mama does not take it quite as well as Papa.

"What? You invited a man, a stranger, to dine without asking permission? What will he think of you? Haven't I taught you better manners? Eliza!"

I think I might cry. What to do now? But, something happens to change Mama. Can Papa convince her with just a look? Her face calms. She envelopes me into a hug.

"Oh, my little girls are growing up. First, Mary, now you." Then, she turns back to the stove and takes dinner out of the oven.

"So, what do you think this Englishman would like for supper?"

As the afternoon wears on, I ask myself the same questions Mama and Papa posed. How can I dare to be so fearless and accept Michael's invitation to call? What if I just imagined it all? I've never had a beau. Never known a boy I can talk to so easily. What if Michael turns out to be less than I imagine? Worse, what if he never comes back at all?

By the time six o'clock rolls around, I have worked myself into a frenzy. It is easier to focus on choosing a menu, setting the table, gathering flowers for a bouquet than it has been to select a dress, fix my hair and look into the mirror and analyze my features. Finally, Mary takes me in hand, pins up my hair and adds a flower plucked from the yard to the front of my plain brown dress.

"It spruces it up a bit, but really Eliza, you should let us help you make some new clothes."

I don't confess that just this morning I thought the same

thing, but something happens to me inside. I feel such tenderness towards my cousin.

Compelled, I stand from the dressing table and hug Mary.

"Thank you, Mary. You made the ugly duckling look a little prettier."

"Eliza, you are not ugly! You have lovely hair, so rich and thick. And such a tiny waist. Be proud of who you are. If he is worthy of you, he had better prove it."

Is he? Or am I worthy of him?

"Oh, look!" Mary peaks out the upstairs window. "I think he is here. He is handsome Eliza."

She gives me a shove towards the stairs. "Go down to meet him. He will think you beautiful, I know."

I still can't believe it, but Michael does think me beautiful. He told me that night and has repeated it every day since. Two weeks pass like a whirlwind. From the first day we met, we became constant companions. Michael has many friends, and we make the rounds from house to house in Manatee or to Gamble's Plantation. Amazingly, everyone wants to be my friend now. I have attended more parties, dinners and balls in the last two weeks than I have in my entire life. *Oh and isn't it great fun?* I love being invited to the social events, but it is so enjoyable to go with Michael. Heads turn when he walks into a room. It is like being with royalty. Everyone wants the cousin of Charles Dickens to attend their events. A vivid storyteller who knows the most fashionable games and dances, the people of the river settlements welcome him into their homes. I can't imagine why, but he wants me to go with him! Even Flora McLeod is no longer sarcastic and mocking. She treats me like a little sister. In such contrast to their prior attitudes, Flora and the other women compliment me on everything from my hair to my shoes. I can't believe my good fortune. How good it feels to have friends and to be wanted.

Michael makes me feel so special. He keeps me close by his

side like a rare treasure. When I venture even a short distance away, I can feel his eyes upon me. Pleasing Michael is so important to me now. I want to make him proud of me. I spend what little free time I have concentrating on creating a new wardrobe. My old gowns will not suit for my new standing in the community. Although Michael tells me he likes me just as I am, I do not want to embarrass him. With an unlimited supply of materials, time is my only enemy. I can't win. If I stay up late sewing a new dress for a party, when the event arrives, I am too tired to enjoy it. Despite the excitement of Michael's company, part of me longs for a quiet evening at home. But, Michael prefers going out. I am afraid to say anything to him about my fatigue. *What if he goes to a party alone? He might meet someone else he likes better than me.*

As I put loaves of bread in the oven to bake, I feel a sigh escape. *Where did that come from?* My mind is all mixed up these days. It is a great responsibility to be Michael's companion. When I am with him though, everything is wonderful. It is like being a princess. My feelings for him are so strong and intense. I can't help but be in love with him. I wish I knew if he loved me. I can hardly remember what my life was like before he swept me off my feet, nor do I want to think about spending a day without him. Yet, sometimes, when I am alone, I feel a heaviness that cannot be explained. A weight that will not lift despite the new friends and clothes. It is as though a bell rings somewhere far in the distance warning me of impending disaster. I can't figure out where it hides and why it sounds. I decide it must be my inexperience. Things are just so perfect. My nature is to think something is bound to go wrong soon. I shove my fears from my head and try to remember Michael's face smiling at me.

I'm just tired is all. I just need a minute to rest. I should finish some sewing and dishes soak in the sink, but I have to sit down. There is still some shade on the back steps of the kitchen so I ease myself down on the top step and close my eyes. I lean my head against the doorframe. Brownie comes to me and curls beside me on the step. He rests his head on my knee.

The smell of bread baking drifts past on a breeze. At least that is one chore done for the day. Oh, my entire body aches. My mind whirls in circles. There is just so much to think about. From where I sit, I hear the horses grazing in their pen. In a few moments, Michael will come. Maybe we can go riding. So many people are always around. It would be nice to be alone with him today. I am just so tired.

My eyes stay shut. Is that the sound of Papa's ax? Thoughts of Papa troubled me. I rub my forehead. *Is that a headache coming on?* Since their first meeting with Michael, both Papa and Mama are reserved. Almost reluctant to speak. Even Mary is unusually quiet. Then, there is Nannie. Nannie is never one to hide her feelings. When last I saw her, she didn't hold back.

"Eliza, you need to be careful around that one."

"Why, what do you mean?"

"I can't put my finger on it, but he is not as he seems. Eliza, you know how much I value your friendship, don't you?"

"Yes, Nannie, you have always been a dear friend even in times of trouble."

"Well, then, you need to listen to me. He is not for you."

"How can you say that to me? I love him. He is kind and so sweet to me. He is just the man I have been waiting for all my life."

I cannot believe my friend would be so unkind. I want to cry. Instead of tears, Nannie's next words bring anger.

She repeats, "He is not for you. Wake up and look around you. He runs too fast and hard. How much do you really know about him? He will not last."

I say the first thing that comes to my mind. "You are just jealous. You don't have a man to call your own, and you don't want me to have one either! You may be willing to live your life as an old maid, but I am not. Michael is perfect for me, and I don't plan to let him go just on your say alone."

Nannie doesn't say another word. She looks at me with tears in her eyes, then, turns and walks away. I have not seen her since.

What does Nannie know? I force myself to concentrate on Michael's smile when he first sees me each day. The feel of his hand upon my waist when we dance. His words of affection. His many kindnesses. That is what matters. Mama, Papa, Mary, Nannie. They do not see the Michael that I see. When I am with him, everything is alright. I feel loved and secure. Nothing will change that. Nothing.

I feel a kiss upon my forehead.

"Wake up, sleepyhead. What are you dreaming about?"

Michael! When had he come? I must have fallen asleep. Is my hair a mess? Instinctively, I raise my hands to my head and smooth my bun. My hair has escaped its knot while I dozed.

"Leave it," Michael says. "I like it loose."

He reaches up and pulls the rest out of its confines and wraps a tendril around his finger.

"Beautiful. So," he teases. "You did not tell me what you were dreaming about. It must have been a nightmare; your face was all in knots."

Embarrassed to think that he caught me looking stern, I fumble, "Nothing, I was just resting a minute. We have been out so much that I haven't had much sleep."

Oh, no. He will think me a complainer.

"Not that I haven't enjoyed it," I stammer. "I am just not used to being away from home so much."

Eliza, that sounds even worse, I think. Now, he will know you were such a homebody before he met you. I stop talking, hoping he will not notice my insecurity. If he does, Michael does not let on. I stretch. *Where has Brownie run off to?*

"I know, I have been thoughtless," he confesses. "But, I am

so eager to show you off to all my friends."

Really, he wants to show me off?

"I want them to know that you are my girl."

Am I really? Am I really his girl? Should I pinch myself? Maybe I am still dreaming.

"Would you like a quiet day alone? Why don't we ride over to Terra Ceia? It is time you showed me this island you love so much, don't you think? Since I love you, I should learn to love the things you do as well."

As he traces the outline of my cheek with his finger, my fatigue vanishes. I could fly to the island. Michael loves me. Michael loves me, Eliza Atzeroth. I nod my head and let him take my hand and help me from the step.

I pack a picnic, and we saddle the horses. As we ride the familiar trail north to the south side of the bay and then follow the shore line east and then, north again, I see this land with new eyes as I share it with the man I love. I point out the changes in terrain.

"Pine trees grow in the uplands, but oaks closer to the shore," I instruct.

"I have my own little naturalist," Michael teases.

I am not sure if that is good or bad until he laughs and asks, "What makes those holes high up in the dead pines?"

While I tell him about the woodpeckers that live there, Michael listens carefully. As we pass the Petersen brothers' homesteads, Michael questions me some more. So, I tell him about the men and their families and how they had been such good friends to us. We swim the horses across Terra Ceia River and I tell the story of my first ride over on Niihaasi.

Michael says, "On the way back, I want to try her. I think I would rather ride a wild Indian pony than this plug of your father's."

I have never let anyone else ride my horse. But, I must share her now with Michael. I am willing to share anything of mine with this man. The memory of his words and the knowledge that he loves me fills me with such joy. I laugh aloud as Niihaasi splashes through the water and onto the island.

"Race you!" I called over my shoulder as Niihaasi leaves the beach.

Exhilarated, I kicked her into a gallop on the narrow path leading west to the homestead. With the wind in my hair and Michael's love in my heart, I urge Niihaasi on faster and faster. I hear Michael call to me, but can't stop. These pent up feelings need to make their escape. Michael loves me. And how I love him. All these many years, I never dreamed how wonderful it would be to love and be loved in return. Niihaasi settles into a quick steady gait. Her blowing breath matches the rhythmic motion. It beats in time not only to the hoof beats, but to the steady drumming of my heart. It feels like we are one. Perhaps Niihaasi knows how happy I am today.

I want to continue the pace, but when I reach a clearing I slow Niihaasi to a walk. *Where is Michael? Has he gotten lost?* There are no turns or side paths to confuse him. Soon, he rides into sight bouncing along on Prince's back. The Morgan is not nearly as smooth a ride as my little Indian pony. I better wait for him. Michael looks uncomfortable. Prince stops beside Niihaasi.

"Eliza! What do you think you are doing?"

Michael reaches over and grabs Niihaasi's bridle and holds her fast.

"Riding off like that. You left me alone with no idea where you were headed!"

Michael's harsh tone surprises me. In my exuberance, I did not think he might lose his way.

"I'm sorry, Michael. I did not think."

"Do you ever think?" he snarls.

I drop my head and roll my shoulders forward. I slump down into the saddle withdrawing into myself. He is cross. He has never shown this side until now. *But, isn't it my fault?*

It is all I can do to simply repeat, "I'm sorry. I won't do it again."

"Good, because I would hate to have you ride behind me like a child."

Now, his voice sounds light and teasing. Did I imagine the anger a moment ago? Michael releases Niihaasi.

"Let's ride, but stay with me, will you?"

I keep Niihaasi reined in the rest of the ride. *What just happened? Was Michael upset with me or not? The last thing I want to do is jeopardize his love for me. I will have to be more careful.*

If Michael is irritated, he does not show it again the rest of our ride. Sight of the island cabin cheers me. This place is home.

Some of my fear ease, but, Michael only says, "It is smaller than I thought it would be."

We ride our horses around back and release them into the pen.

Looking at Henry's cabin, Michael asks, "Who lives there?"

"Henry," I reply. "We will probably see him in a minute. He keeps a close watch on the house."

True to my predication, Henry appears almost immediately from the direction of the fields.

"Miss Liza. How you be? Your Mama and Papa? Ain't seen you in a long whil'. Good to see you 'gain."

"Everyone is fine, Henry. I am sure Papa will be out soon."

Gesturing to Michael, I say, "Henry, this is my friend, Michael Dickens. We rode over so I could show him where I grew up."

Henry bows toward Michael. "Mister Dickens. Pleased to meet you."

Michael nods curtly but does not speak.

"Everything looks wonderful Henry. You have been working hard I can see."

"Thank you Miss Liza. I best get back to the field. You take care now. Mister Dickens, watch over Miss Liza. She a right smart girl, but can be a bit headstrong."

Henry laughs, and I join him in the joke. Henry is a good friend.

"I brought a picnic, Henry. Would you care to join us?"

Immediately, I realize I have made a mistake. Michael frowns in disapproval.

"No, thanks, Miss Liza. I got work to do. Come see me 'fore you go, and I give you some vegetables for your Mama though."

As Henry turns and walks away, Michael says, "I will never get used to it. You Floridians treat your slaves with such familiarity that they are quite the upstarts."

"Oh, Henry is not a slave, Michael. He is a freedman. He came to us a long time ago." I bite my lip. Maybe this is not the time to tell about Billy Bowlegs and Henry's escape from the Braden Plantation.

"Papa bought him and set him free. Papa pays him a wage now. He is a great asset to us."

"Why in the world would he do that? He paid to free him and now gives him a salary?" Michael shakes his head. "I didn't know your family was quite that eccentric."

What does he mean by that? Eccentric. Oh, this is not going well. I change the subject.

"Would you like to eat first or see the place?"

"Whatever you want to do. It doesn't look like there is a whole lot to see."

Why is Michael so grumpy and irritable today? Have I done something wrong? As I walk him around the farm, I think back over the morning. It must be that I ran off and left him. Yes, that is what is wrong. He was worried about me and wanted to keep me safe. He mentioned having me ride behind him. I must show him that I can mind. Papa and Mama always tell me to be more obedient. Perhaps this is what annoys him.

I leave the cabin for last. We enter by the front door and into the hall. I set our saddle bags with lunch down on the kitchen table.

"It will just take me a minute, and we can eat," I explain. "I brought some tea, but will need to light a fire to boil the water."

While I work, Michael paces around the small kitchen.

"Michael, would you like to sit down?"

"No."

Will he be angry at me forever?

"Why don't I show you the rest of the house while the water boils?" I suggest.

I lead the way across the hall to Mama and Papa's bedroom. It feels strange to be here with Michael. Is it because Mama and Papa aren't here or because I am alone with him? He walks around the room.

"Very cozy."

I giggle. Stop it Eliza, I think. I sound like a schoolgirl. *Why do I feel so nervous?* There is a tingling in my stomach.

"I used to sleep here too, so in the beginning it was very tight."

I reach down by the bed to show him the little trundle underneath it. As I bend over, Michael steps behind me.

"I don't need to see it, this is all I need."

He pulls me close to him and kisses me. His gesture catches me off guard. This is a different sort of kiss than we have exchanged in the past. Before, he barely brushed my lips with a soft and gentle motion. Now, he holds me tight as his mouth meets mine demanding a response.

What should I do? I stand stiffly in his embrace. *How should I respond? Is this proper? What would Mama think?* Soon, though, I begin to enjoy his attention. It is as though my body has a mind of its own as I relax and submit to his kiss. This is a new experience, but not without pleasure. My heart beats faster than it ever raced even on the wildest horseback ride! Michael draws back and smiles.

"I can feel your heart. It speaks to mine. Now, isn't this better than running off and leaving me on the trail?"

How does he always know what I am thinking?

"Let me show you more, Eliza. I know ways to thrill you even more than a gallop on a wild horse."

Michael kisses me again, and then slowly lowers me down on the bed. My mind goes blank. Nothing is more important than pleasing Michael and having more of him. In the kitchen, the tea kettle whistles. I should get up and take care of it, but it doesn't matter. I care for nothing else but that I am with Michael, and he loves me. He is not angry anymore.

Then, he reaches down and pulls my skirt up over my knees. Wait! This is not right. No, we must not do this. I gain control over my body. Mama would not approve. I try to push Michael away, but he holds my hands down.

"Eliza, just relax. I will take good care of you. Just wait and see."

"No, Michael. We must stop."

"I can't, Eliza. Not now. I love you too much. Just let me show you how much."

Will Michael still love me if I refuse him? What should I do? I need to think. I struggle to pull myself away.

"Michael, we need to think about this."

He refuses to let me go.

"This is not a time for thinking. Do you remember how angry I was when you ran away from me?"

So, he was upset with me.

"Don't try me again, Eliza."

Suddenly, I feel cold and afraid. *Is that a threat?* He says he loves me, but will not listen.

"Michael, please," I cry and turn my head away from his kisses.

He hesitates and then, his tone gentles, "Eliza, run with me, not away from me."

His hand strokes my waist. His soft words and gentle caress

compel me beyond my fear and distrust. God, help me, I think. *Save me from Michael. Save me from myself.*

At once, I hear a voice calling from the back porch.

"Miss Liza? You in there Miss Liza?"

Thank God. Henry.

"Michael, let me up."

Reluctantly he releases me from his grip. I roll off the bed, pull down my skirt, and straighten my hair. Feeling off balance and unsteady, I walk as smoothly as I can out into the hall and to the back door. My hands tremble as I turn the knob. I try to smile.

"Yes, Henry. Is something wrong?"

"Miss Liza, you alright? I hear the tea kettle just a whistlin'. I fear somethin' not right. I think, maybe you just go off and forget about it, so decide to come check jus' in case."

"Everything is fine, Henry, but thank you for coming. I was showing Michael the house and let it get away from me. I will tend to it right now."

Henry lowers his voice, "You sure you fine, Miss Liza? Need Henry to stay close?"

By this time, Michael is behind me in the hall. I say with a bravado I do not feel, "Thank you again, Henry. I will take care of that tea kettle right away. I appreciate you checking on us."

I shut the door and lean against it. *What to do now?* Afraid to look at Michael, I close my eyes. Torn between what I know is right and my desire to please him, I feel like crying. I don't want to show my emotions, but before I can stop it, a tear seeps down my cheek.

Michael steps towards me as I brace myself against the door. *Will he begin again?* He takes my chin in his hand and traces the outline of my cheek.

"Eliza," he says gently. "I am sorry. It is just that I love you so much. Since the first day I saw you, I have loved you. It has been hard these past two weeks to restrain myself. That is why I have kept so busy and stayed with the crowds. I knew that when I got you alone, this might happen. I just love you so very much."

Now, the tears flow at a steady pace.

"Michael, I am sorry, too. It is just that we must wait. I have always been taught that it is wrong to do these things. Oh, Michael, I am so grateful that you love me. I love you, too. I love you enough that my heart may burst at any moment."

I sob with relief.

"Eliza, come with me."

Michael leads me to the kitchen where he pulls out a chair for me to sit down. Then, he kneels before me and tenderly dries my tears with a dishtowel.

"Eliza, I am sorry that I got carried away. I did not mean to frighten you or confuse you. But, what we did. It is not wrong." I start to correct him.

"Hush," Michael puts his hand over my mouth.

"Listen. It is not wrong if we are married. Eliza, will you marry me?"

All of the air flows out of my lungs in a great whoosh. *Marriage! Oh, this is the answer to my prayers. Why have I been so afraid?* Michael's love remains true.

"Yes, Michael. Yes, yes, yes. I will be proud to be your wife. I will marry you."

This time, Michael kisses me with the gentleness that I remember.

"I will always take care of you, my precious Eliza. When the time is right, we will begin again. For now, I will try to be a good boy." He smiles, "But we better have this wedding soon or I may be in trouble with you again."

I laugh and hug him close. *A wedding! Just like Mary, I have a wedding to plan as well!* I can hardly wait to tell Mama and Papa.

Despite my excitement, a seed of doubt takes root as we travel home. I do not like the way that Michael handles Niihaasi.

Since Billy Bowlegs, no one but me has ridden the little Indian pony. She is not pleased to have Michael on her back. She bucks several times and prances anxiously. Michael pulls tightly on her reins and kicks her hard with the toe of his boot. Despite my pleas for gentleness, when Niihaasi still will not mind, he pulls a branch off a nearby oak tree and switches her sternly across the hindquarters until she submits.

"See that's all she needed. Just a reminder of who is boss," he crows.

Is that what Michael wants? To be the boss? For a moment, I wonder if I am making the right choice. *How will he treat me if I do not obey?* Then, he rides up next to me. Reaching across the space, Michael takes my hand.

Smiling, he looks into my eyes. "I love you, Mrs. Soon to be Dickens." Mrs. Dickens. That sounds nice.

"So, when shall we hold the wedding?" he asks.

And I go back to dreaming about the future once more.

Chapter Twelve

Mary surprises me by suggesting a double wedding. Her generous spirit is so unlike the little girl I remember. Maybe, it was there all along but I was too jealous to notice. Even now, I do not think that I could be so liberal. A bride is supposed to be the center of attention at her wedding. Yet, Mary is eager to share the spotlight. After the reaction Michael and I receive to our engagement announcement, we decide it is the most convenient thing to do. Mama and Papa disappoint me with their subdued response to our news. In contrast to the back slapping and toasting when Mary and William announced their engagement, the atmosphere is cautious. Mama sits down heavily in a kitchen chair and frowns.

"So soon? You have only known each other two weeks. Why don't you wait a while?" Papa shakes Michael's hand, and then gives me a hug. He steps back and studies my face.

"Are you sure, daughter?"

I nod my head, but feel like crying. *Why aren't they happy for me? Don't they like Michael? Can't they see how much I love him?* Mary tries her best to be encouraging.

"Liza, I have a wonderful idea! Let's get married on the same day. How much fun it will be. You were going to be my bridesmaid, now you can be a bride as well. We will stand up for each other!"

I look to Michael for support, but he does not say anything. It must be hard for him. Mama and Papa are not being very welcoming.

"Well, we were planning a short engagement," I say and blush. "Michael and I can't wait to start our life together. We love each other so much."

"Good," Mary claps her hands. "Then, it is settled. The four of us can go together to Manatee to get our marriage licenses. Liza, what will you wear? We need to make you a different dress. I think there is some of the same muslin that we used for mine in the store."

She pauses.

"In a different color and pattern though. We don't want to look like twins." Laughing, she continues to share ideas.

"Oh, Mama, you will only have to make one cake at least!"

Dear Mary, she tries to build some enthusiasm in Mama about the double wedding. I feel so guilty for all the ugly things I thought about my cousin over the years. For the first time, I think of Mary as a real sister.

When the arrangements are set, Mama asks, "Eliza, Michael, where will you live?"

Michael remains quiet, so I reply honestly.

"Goodness, things have happened so fast, we haven't even had a chance to talk about it."

"They can move out to the farm for now," Papa declares. "That is if it is agreeable to you, Michael. The house there is just sitting empty. It will be good for it to be lived in again."

I do not think Michael will want to be so far from town. I am pleased when he replies, "Thank you, sir. That is most kind. I confess your daughter swept me off my feet that I neglected to think about where we would live. I will work harder at being a good husband to her. The island will be a nice place to begin our married life."

"Well," sighs Mama. "At least that means we can delay preparing a trousseau for the time being. Everything you need will be out there. We can make more linens when you move to a house of your own later."

"Eliza, Mary, we have work to do. Let's go down to the store and see what fabric we have left that will make a suitable gown for Eliza on her wedding day."

There is not much time to prepare, and I am so busy that I

don't see Michael as much as I did before our engagement. Three days before the wedding, he goes hunting with some of his friends from Manatee. I suspect that there is more to the story, but I comfort myself in knowing that in just a few days, we will be man and wife and together forever. Besides, his absence gives me a chance to talk to Papa alone.

"Papa, I have been thinking. I want to take Niihaasi out to the island with me. If I ride her out and leave her there, would you sail over and pick me up?"

"You would ride all that way alone?" he asks.

"It is not that far. Papa, I have not had one minute to myself in all these weeks. And I would like one last time to ride Niihaasi as well. Just like the old days. Please, Papa. Will you come get me?"

He smiles, "Just like the old days, you have your old man wrapped around your little finger. Of course, I will come get you. But, maybe we better keep this between us. I am sure your mother has some work for you. And she would not look kindly on you riding out by yourself."

Papa tells Mama that he needs my help for a day. I saddle Niihaasi and set off towards the island. As I ride, I scan the horizon. There are no clouds, just a thin haze in the air. It will rain this afternoon. July's intense heat weighs down upon me. Before I ride even fifteen minutes, sweat runs down my forehead and into my eyes. I wipe my face with the edge of my sunbonnet. It is a good thing I brought a canteen of water to quench my thirst. I ride as quickly as I dare in this heat. I don't want to overtax Niihaasi. I am determined to enjoy the ride. This could be my last time on Niihaasi apart from Michael, but there is not much time to savor the moment. It is more important to get to the island before Papa arrives so we can return home together. I click to Niihaasi and hurry down the path.

Papa's timing is perfect. As I ride along the bay towards the cabin, I see him landing on the shore. *Look! Brownie rides in the bow of the boat.* I wave to them. Brownie barks at me.

Papa calls. "Go on up to the house. I need to meet with Henry for a few minutes. I will come by and get you when it is time to leave."

Good. I have time to prepare the house. The next time I come here, it will be on my wedding night. Carefully, I change the sheets on Mama and Papa's bed. I pull the quilt up over them and plump the pillows. Again, that ache in my stomach appears. It must be perfect for my husband. Husband. *Will Michael think I am a good wife?* I dust the dresser, sweep the floor and straighten the rug. Before I leave, I look around the room once more. Three more days, and I will be back. *What will this room hold for me then?* I shudder. From fear or excitement, I do not know. *Where is Papa?* We need to get back home. It is not fair to leave Mary and Mama with all the work.

I walk behind the house. Papa and Henry talk by the horse pen. They lean on the rail. Papa has one foot on the bottom rung. With their backs turned to me, they don't see my approach.

"Henry, keep an eye on her for me. I want her here where I know someone can protect her if need be. I do not trust Dickens. I fear that he will not be kind to her. Eliza deserves more."

"Yes, Mr. Joe. I agree. Somethin' about him tell me he not a good man."

Papa adds, "I wish I could talk her out of this, but you know my Eliza. Once she makes up her mind."

"I know, Mr. Joe. I know. But I watch over her. You know I will."

They are talking about Michael! Neither Henry nor Papa understand how much he loves me. How sad! Two of the most important people in my life do not see how happy he makes me. I cannot convince them. Only Michael, and time, will prove to them that they are wrong. Before they see me, I go back to the house and wait for Papa there.

Papa apologizes for his tardiness.

"Have you waited long? I'm sorry. It is that dog of yours. I can't find Brownie anywhere. I am not sure where he has gotten off to. I finally told Henry that I would leave him here. Henry will care for him until you come back and it will be nice for you to have your dog here with you anyway."

I agree, and we board the boat and sail for home. Neither of us says a word until the boat is once again secured to the landing. As he takes down the sails, Papa finally says what had been unspoken between us the entire trip.

"Eliza, are you sure? Are you sure he is the one for you?"

I struggle with my response and anger that no one believes me. *Why do they keep asking over and over? Why can't they see that I know what I am doing?* But, I cannot bring myself to fuss at sweet, gentle Papa. In only a few days, I will no longer be living in the same house with him. For once, I bite my tongue and simply nod "yes."

On the morning of my wedding day, Mama asks the same question. This time, I am not as confident. I woke this morning and thought, today I marry Michael. But, instead of the thrill that I am supposed to have, I feel sick to my stomach. At breakfast, I cannot keep down more than a little tea and toast even though Mama has prepared a feast. My hands tremble, and I spill my tea. Mary eats a hearty breakfast and runs outside to pick some flowers for our hair.

"Daughter, I can't help but see your nerves this morning," Mama says gently. "Are you sure you want to go through with this? It is not too late to change your mind."

My first thought is of all the people who are coming and the food that has been prepared.

I reply honestly, "Mama, I think it is too late. I can't turn back now. Michael would be so embarrassed in front of all his friends."

"Eliza, listen to me. A little embarrassment now is better

than living the rest of your life with a mistake. If you have any doubts, any doubts at all, we need to stop this. No one needs to know. We will tell them that you are ill. That will give you time to rethink your decisions. Eliza, you have known him only a little while."

"No, Mama. I have known him long enough. He will be a good husband. I know he will. Weren't you nervous on your wedding day?"

"Maybe a little, but I had no reason to think that your Papa would not be a good husband to me."

"Neither do I, Mama," I say as calmly as I can. "I better go and get dressed."

The wedding will begin at eleven o'clock. Mama wanted to hold it in the evening, but with the almost certain arrival of an afternoon thunderstorm, she agreed that it would be best to set it for the morning. By ten forty five, I think I may lose my mind if Mary does not calm down. She bounces back and forth from the dressing table to the window.

"Look Eliza! I see William. Isn't he handsome? I am so lucky. He will make a fine husband."

"Mary, come away from the window. Someone will see you peeking out at them," Mama says. "Liza, stand still. Let me finish pulling your hair back for you. Oh, who in their right mind let me be talked into having both daughters married on the same day? And in July! What is wrong with me? I am all thumbs today."

"Mama, move over. Eliza sit down so I can reach."

Mary deftly places roses in my hair.

"There, that's done. Now can we go downstairs?"

"Not yet," Mama replies. Mary returns to the window.

"Isn't this wonderful, Liza? Didn't I say it would be fun to share our wedding day?"

I can't answer. I don't feel well at all. My chest feels tight, and my head dizzy. If Mary would just stop talking for a minute. Finally, Mama agrees it is time.

"Girls, let me go outside first. Papa will be in to get you in a minute."

We wait inside the front door as Mama gives the final instructions to Ezekiel Glazier who will perform the ceremony. At last, Papa comes inside and offers an arm to each of us.

"My two daughters. All grown up. You two look so beautiful. I love you both." Mary giggles.

"Papa, I'm sorry. We love you too, but let's go. I can't wait to be with William!"

Papa turns and looks at me.

"How about you, little girl? Are you anxious as well?"

I can only nod. I am anxious, but not in the way that Papa means. Mary steps out the door, but my feet will not move. Like an anchor, I pull Papa backwards while Mary propels him forward. He looks at me with compassion. I know he will stay here with me if I only give him the least bit of reason. Then, I look past him and see Michael standing there expectantly. It is now or never. I will myself to remember.

Eliza, just think about seeing him for the first meeting in the store. He was so charming and sweet. And don't you have such fun when you are with him? All the other girls are jealous that he loves you. Of all of them, he chose you. Lucky girl. Any one of them would be satisfied to be in your shoes. It is silly to be so anxious. Look, he is waiting for you now. He loves you. How can you go wrong with such love? No longer hesitating, I match Mary's pace to the altar and take Michael's arm eagerly.

Judge Glazier, acting as justice of the peace, begins the ceremony with a prayer. While he asks God for His blessing on the two marriages, I offer up my own thanks to God. I do not deserve this. He is better than I ever dreamed I could have. *Help me to be worthy of Michael's love. To be a good wife. Thank you for sending him to me, God. Help me, please.*

Besides the prayer, I remember little else about the ceremony. I have so much to think about. Leaving Papa and Mama behind. Becoming Michael's wife. A whole new life ahead of me. Finally, returning to Terra Ceia to live once more. Our wedding night. Just as I begin to be overwhelmed, I feel Michael's hand on my arm to steady me. He always knows what I am thinking. I look into his eyes, and he smiles. Just breathe, Eliza, I think. Everything will be alright. Michael promised. See even now he speaks of love.

Finally, Judge Glazier ends of the ceremony. "I now pronounce you husbands and wives. What God has joined, let no man put asunder."

William puts his arm around Mary and turns her to face the crowd. I am relieved when Michael takes charge as well. The men escort us through the crowd and over to the front porch as Mama instructed earlier. There, we will receive our guests. The line of well wishers seems endless. While Mary, William and Michel enjoy visiting and talking with them, I just want to go sit down somewhere and hide. *Hasn't Michael taught me to set my shyness aside? Where has the confident, brave Eliza gone?*

Before I can slip away, Michael whispers, "Eliza, smile. People are going to think you are unhappy with me."

So, I straighten my shoulders and greet our guests, laughing and chatting as though I have not a care in the world. When instead, it is all I can do to stay rooted to my spot and not run away. There will be no more running away. *Hadn't Michael said to run to him instead?*

When the guests are finally enjoying the refreshments, Mary orders, "Now it is our turn! Let's get something to eat as well."

She walks away holding William's hand. They practically coo like two doves, I think. Michael puts his hand on my waist and pushes me back into the house.

"What is wrong with you?" he demands. "Everyone is watching us. Everyone can see that something is not right."

There it is again. That flash of anger. And on our wedding

day. Disappointment again.

"Michael, I am sorry. I just don't feel well. The heat maybe. I didn't eat much this morning."

"Oh, my poor Eliza. Why didn't you say? Come, let's get you some food and a chair." Will I ever get used to his quick-silver temper and even faster apologies? Michael gently escorts me to a seat under a tree, and then goes to the refreshment table where he fills a plate with food. He hands it to me.

"Here eat this. I will be back in a minute with something for you to drink."

When he doesn't return, I am surprised to find I do not mind. I am grateful for the quiet. I nibble on the sandwiches and cheese he gave me. I close me eyes and let the breeze from the river wash over me. There in the shade, I rest while the party swirls around me. Then, I hear familiar voices coming from be-hind me. They must be on the other side of the tree. *Do they know I am here? No, they must not for they are talking about me.*

"Why in the world did he marry that dumpy little thing?"

It is Flora.

"He could have any of the eligible girls in Manatee, but no, he chooses her!"

"Now, Flora it is their wedding day. Don't spoil it. Let's just enjoy the party."

That is Ellen McNeill. I shrink into my seat. *Oh, don't come around on this side. Don't see me.*

"I won't make a scene, but I just can't figure it out is all. James says Michael is hoping Mr. Joe will give them some land for their wedding present. There are plenty who would like to have that property on Terra Ceia. Michael could sell it quickly and have some cash in his pocket."

"Well, there you may have your answer," Ellen replies.

"Both of you hush. Just stop with your gossip and lies!"

Nannie! *Has she been here all morning?*

"You two are just jealous. It is obvious to all who see them that he is head over heels in love with her. If you can't be nice, then, you shouldn't be here to help them celebrate."

When no reply comes, I guess they must have nothing to say in response to Nannie's reprimand. *Are they gone?*

"Eliza?"

I feel a hand on my shoulder and stand to face Nannie.

"Thank you," I whisper.

"I saw you sitting here all alone. I don't think they knew you were here. Don't let them spoil your day, Eliza. They don't know what they are talking about."

"Did you mean what you said? Does Michael really love me?"

"How could he not? You are a dear girl. Don't forget it. Now, come. Mary sent me to look for you. It is time for the cake pulling."

Before we leave, I put my hand on Nannie's arm.

"Nannie, I am sorry."

"No need to apologize, Eliza. I already forgave you. Let's go, I have been looking forward to your Mama's cake all morning."

Mama worked on the cake for several days. It is four layers high and made of a dense, moist batter like fruitcake but without as many nuts or candied fruit. The icing is made with soft, fine, white sugar so different from the dark sugar produced locally. Mama used only the best for our celebration. Long, thin, white ribbons fan out from beneath the cake. I hold back, but Mary eagerly calls all the single girls forward for the cake pulling. Under the bottom later of the cake are small charms connected to the ribbons. Each single girl present can pull one ribbon from the cake before it is cut. The charm she receives holds meaning for her future.

"Who will be first?" Mary calls.

One by one the single girls in the community step forward. Everyone laughs and talks as they show their prize. A heart means everlasting love; a ring, engagement imminent; clover, good luck; a tiny picture frame, a happy family. A carriage means that she will be blessed with children, but a button signifies an old maid. Finally, it is Nannie's turn. With all my heart, I hope she will not get the button. When Nannie holds up her charm for display, it is a ring! Engagement.

Nannie hugs me and I say, "I hope it comes true, Nannie."

"We are moving to Tampa next week. Perhaps he waits for me there. You have been a good friend. I will miss you."

"I will miss you too, Nannie." We both wipe our eyes.

"This is not a day for crying. Go to your husband, Eliza. The dancing is about to begin."

In the crowd, I cannot find Michael. After asking several people, I finally find him standing with a group of men near the punch table. *Good, I am thirsty.* He must have forgotten about his promise to bring me something to drink. As I approach, Michael slips something into his coat pocket. What is he up to?

"Eliza, are you feeling better?"

He turns to the other men.

"My bride needed to rest a minute. Don't want to wear her out before the day is over, you know."

He winks at his friends. I blush from embarrassment.

"Michael, they are calling us for the dancing."

"Oh, its time for me to do my duty," he laughs again and takes my hand. As we walk, he stumbles slightly.

Now it is my turn to ask. What is wrong with him? When he draws me close to dance, I understand. His breath smells like alcohol. He has been drinking. This is all my fault. If I had not been so nervous and ill, he would have stayed with me and not been driven to his friends and their drink. I resolve to stay close to him the rest of the day.

In the mid afternoon, dark clouds build in the east. It is time to bring the festivities to a close so that guests and wedding party can return home before the daily summer thunderstorm approaches. Mary and I change into traveling clothes.

"Oh, Eliza, I am so excited aren't you? This is the beginning of a new life for each of us. William makes me so happy. Are you happy, too?"

I just nod and wish I had more of Mary's excitement and less of my own fear.

"Liza, are you alright?"

"Yes, Mary, just a little tired. It has been along day, hasn't it?"

"Oh, but everything was perfect." Mary continues to talk about the wedding while she dresses. Then, she hugs me one last time.

"Come, are you ready?" She giggles. "Our husbands wait for us. I am a little nervous, I confess."

I don't reply; just follow Mary back downstairs where once again the well wishers gather to send us off to our new homes. Mama and Papa hug us both.

Papa whispers to me, "Send Henry for me if you need anything. I will be by to check on you in a few days."

William and Mary climb into William's wagon for their short ride overland.

"Good bye, good bye," everyone calls as they drive away.

When it was our turn, the group escorts us to the river and Papa's small sailboat. Michael grumbles about the arrangement so only I can hear.

"How can I steer and get that sail up at the same time. I don't like boats, you know that. Whose idea was this? Everyone is watching, and I will make a fool of myself for sure."

Though he covers it well, I can tell that he is still intoxicated. I must think quickly of a plan or Michael might get angry with me in front of everyone.

"Michael, I will take care of the sail. You just sit down and steer the boat. Head it towards the middle of the river. We'll work together and be fine."

Although Michael's navigation is not quite accurate, we

manage to sail away without anyone suspecting a problem. Once out of sight, Michael slumps in the bow of the boat while I take over the rudder and turn the boat towards Terra Ceia. The wind is chilly. We will be lucky if we get home before the storm. *Home.* I am heading home as Michael's wife. Surely everything will be fine once there.

The cool wind sobers Michael. By the time we reach the island, he is clear headed again. Barking, Brownie meets us at the dock.

"What is he doing here?" Michael complains. "I hate dogs. Don't you know I hate dogs?"

No, I didn't know that. Funny, now that I think about it, Brownie always disappears when Michael is around.

Michael yells at him, "Get out of here!" and Brownie runs off into the bushes.

Flashes of lightening in the distance remind me again of my husband's quick temper.

My husband. But, now, he speaks kindly to me.

"Eliza, go on up to the house. I will be there in a minute. Let me secure the boat."

I do as I am told and wonder as I scurry ahead of the storm, where did Brownie go? And what will this night hold for me? Please God, I pray for the second time that day. *Please God, let everything be alright.*

Chapter Thirteen

My hands tremble as I fasten the buttons on my nightgown. I've never had one so fine. Mama insisted that I have something new for my first night as Michael's wife. Despite the rush of wedding preparations, she made time to sew a beautiful white nightdress for me. I unpin my hair and brush it in the candlelight. I love being here in this cabin on Terra Ceia. I have so many good memories. When Papa suggested that we make our home here, Michael surprised me when he agreed. It probably will not take him long to move back to town. He loves excitement and parties. For now, this will be a familiar place for our beginning as husband and wife. I am comforted that my first night with Michael will be here. Despite their differences, Mama and Papa's marriage is a happy one. Oh, how I hope that the same will be said for ours as many years from now!

I roll my neck and massage my shoulders to ease the tension rising in me. I am both nervous and excited. I take a deep breath and let it out slowly. Who would have thought just six weeks ago that I would be married! Things happened so fast. I love Michael. I am sure of it. I want to be a good wife and perhaps, someday a mother. My stomach hurts. I wish I ate more at the wedding reception. I was too anxious to eat. Where is the box of leftovers Mama packed? Maybe later I can eat. But, not now. *Where is he?* I try not to think of the time ahead. *What will it hold?* Michael will be tender and gentle. I am sure of it. I hope he will. I remember the last time we were here together. I hope he is not as demanding now that we are married. We have a lifetime to learn to love each other.

Thunder rolls in the distance. The storm is approaching. I listen for Michael's footsteps on the porch and when they finally come, ease myself into bed and under the covers. Even with my light weight, the mattress crackles. A nervous giggle escapes at the sound just as Michael enters the room and trips over the doorframe.

"What are you laughing at, Eliza? Not your husband, I hope."

His words are slightly slurred, and in his hand, he holds a flask. That was what was hidden in his pocket. *Is it why he has taken so long? Is he still celebrating? Is he nervous, too?*

"No, not at you. I'm just a little nervous, I confess."

"Get some glasses. I propose a toast to my new bride."

I slide from beneath the security of the sheets across the hall to the kitchen and return with a cup.

"Only one?" Michael asks.

"I don't care for any, thank you."

Michael pours the brown liquid into the mug.

"Here, drink up. It will calm you. I'll use the flask," he says as he turns it up and drinks.

"Go ahead, swallow it. Go on!" he forces it upon me.

I don't want to make him angry so I sip on the alcohol. I shudder at the taste and the burning in my throat. My empty stomach turns queasy. The thunder moves louder and closer. Michael approaches me and strokes the edge of my cheek with his hand.

"So tiny you are, Eliza. Not as beautiful as some, but pretty enough." He runs his fingers through my hair. "You do have beautiful hair, though. I like it down. You should wear it this way more often."

I jump. Is it from the whiskey or from fear? Michael leans forward to kiss me. The taste of alcohol is strong on his lips. I try to relax and enjoy the sensation of his body close to mine. Michael steps back and looks at me for a long time. As if he can read my mind, he asks, "Do you wonder why I chose you?"

I fidget under his scrutiny. *Why am I so uneasy? Why am I embarrassed? I can't even look into his eyes. Is this the way it always is when man and wife came together for the first time?*

Then, Michael laughs, "Oh, yes, you'll do."

Lightening illuminates the night sky outside the bedroom as he raises his hand again as if to caress me. Instead, I feel blinding pain as his fist meets my ribs. He strikes me over and over again until the room is dark, and I collapse onto the hard wooden floor.

The storm is over now, and the sun high. *Just don't think. Don't remember. Focus on your tasks.* My mind races, though outwardly, I am calm. Deliberately and carefully, I work through my morning chores. One thing at a time. Wash the breakfast dishes. Set bread to rise. Put sweet potatoes upon the banked fire to cook for dinner. Make the bed. Sweep the cabin. Keep moving. Empty minded is my goal. When I am done, I escape the cabin. For once, I don't forget my sun bonnet. Grabbing it from a peg by the door, I gingerly cross the porch into the yard. Walking through the clearing between the log cabin and the woods that surround it, I feel the skirt of my new grey work dress soak up the dampness of the grass. Mama would not approve.

Steam rises from the moist, warm earth. It will be another hot day. Although the sun is already high in the cloudless sky, the ground is saturated from last night's thunderstorm. Sweat drips down my back, and I fan my face with my hand both for cooling and to brush away the ever present mosquitoes. I walk to a quiet place near the spring that bubbles and flows into Terra Ceia Bay. A hollow spot between the tangled roots of a towering live oak offers protection. In the past, the water's flow, the rush of the wind between the tree's branches and the patterns of light and darkness have been my solace. Here, even on the darkest days, I never fail to find peace.

Finally, the tears bottled up through the long dark night finally come. Sinking to the ground, great wrenching sobs rise from deep inside me. I clutch my knees and rock back and forth, slowly at first, then faster. I gasp and moan and let go of pent up emotions suppressed for so many hours. Grasping my head between my hands, I squeeze my temples tightly in an effort to stop the thoughts whirling around inside. *How could I have made such a mistake?* It is my own fault. Mama knew and tried to warn me. Papa expressed his concern. Even Nannie questioned, but I was so confident. *What a fool I am. Did he really love me?* Any thoughts of Michael's affection must have been a figment of my own desires and imagination. How could I have thought myself in love with such a monster? If only I could roll the clock back in time. I would take it all back, start over. If only I knew that marriage would transform the charming young Englishman into a brutal sadistic beast.

What did I do to deserve such treatment? Is this punishment for something I have done wrong? Maybe if I am better, someone different, Michael will not act this way? If only I could read his mind and know what he wants from me. *I can change. Whatever he desires, I can do it.* If only we might go back to that first day at the store when I loved him so. But "if onlys" will not change anything. We are legally wed. There is no going back now. My life will never be the same.

Nothing, nothing at all, could have prepared me for the night just passed. I expected some pain. Mama told me about that, but, even Mama could not have known of the terror and the brutality of Michael's ways that lasted throughout much of the night just passed. I rub my wrist remembering when I shrank from him in fear, he pinned me down. When I struggled and cried out, Michael struck me repeatedly. Thinking back, it seems odd. He never hit me in the face where his mark will show. He knew enough to be careful. My reflection in the mirror this morning revealed bruises across my back, chest and thighs. I could not resist his blows. Now, here in this place of beauty, I might believe it a nightmare but for the stiffness and ache I feel. My heart hurts more than my body. Bruises will heal, but my heart is broken forever.

I pray it was just the drink. Surely, sober he will not act that way.

"Eliza!"

I jump at the sound of my name and place a fist in my mouth to stifle my cry. *Michael.* He looks for me. When he left the house after breakfast, I hoped he would be gone all day. *Will he find me? Think, Eliza! Have I shown him this place?* I crouch beneath the spreading tree and tuck myself into a ball. With my face pressed close against my knees, I pray he will not find me. *Will God listen? Or will he abandon me to my choice?* I married almost a complete stranger. Despite hints and warnings, I thought I knew best, thought myself above any harm. Now, I kneel in the damp earth and pray to a God I am not sure will listen.

When I recognize the familiar baying of Brownie, my hopes fall. Michael uses my own dog to flush me out like a rabbit caught in a lure. I hold my breath and squeeze back closer to the tree trunk. Then, I hear the sound of running footsteps and a crash followed by happy barks as Brownie approaches the spring and discovers my presence. I feel the dog's hot panting breath on my neck as I vainly try to quiet him and shoo him away.

Michael appears between the trees. I pull myself upright. I will not to let him know my fear, but one glimpse of my disheveled appearance and tear streaked face betrays the truth.

"Crying, my dear Eliza?" he sneers. "Is that the way for a bride to act on the morning after her wedding night? A man doesn't like to think his beautiful bride is disappointed."

He towers over me. Looking into his glittering black eyes, I wonder how I ever imagined seeing love there. My body tenses in apprehension. Michael senses my wariness. He reaches out and grabs my arm twisting it behind my back. Pain sears through me, and despite my best intention, I cannot hold back a cry.

"Come over here and give your new husband a kiss," he growls.

When I hesitate, Michael tightens his grip and pulls me towards him. My long skirt catches on the uneven tree roots, and I fall at Michael's feet. He laughs.

"I knew you worshipped me my love, but you don't have to bow down at my feet! Do you want a little more of what you got last night?"

At once he is upon me. He rips open the neck of my dress and tears my chemise. I cannot scream, he covers my mouth with his hand. As I struggle to rise, but he pushes me back to the ground and pins me there with his knee. While Michael fumbles with the button on the waist band of his trousers, Brownie growls and rushes at him. Michael strikes my dog with his fist knocking him against the oak with a resounding thump. Brownie whines once and is still. Sickened by my husband's fury, I stop struggling. Will the same thing happen to me? Twigs and stones dig into my back. I feel the cuts begin to bleed as I close my eyes and will my body to be still and my mind to become blank.

When he is finished, Michael rises and stands over me. He brushes the leaves and dirt off his hands. Bits and pieces float down into my face. Like the calm after a storm, even the woods are quiet. For a time, I think even the spring no longer flows.

When Michael finally speaks, he said, "You want to weep? I gave you a reason, now didn't I? Don't ever let me catch you at it again. Understand?"

I tremble in shock while he repeats his words louder this time. He must want an answer from me. Slowly, I nod my head in agreement.

"Pull yourself together and wash your face before you come back to the house."

He straightens his own clothing and then, turns his back. He strides away, and I wonder how that figure could ever excite me. I slowly sit up and see the still body of my beloved dog. I know he is dead. Never again will I hear the thump of his tail against the wooden floor or feel his tongue lick my face. That could have been me. Bile rises into my throat. I cannot hold it back so bend over and vomit. When I have nothing left to expel, I move to Brownie's side and stroke his soft fur.

He is still warm. He did not deserve to die. What did he do wrong? God might punish me, but why did innocent Brownie suffer for my mistake? Loyal to the end, he tried to save me. His eyes are closed, but I remember his deep brown eyes. I crawl far away from the tree roots and the life giving water of the spring. In a clearing near the bank of the bay, I dig his grave with my bare hands.

Fortunately, the ground here is protected from the sun and still moist and damp from the rain. I hollow a deep enough trench, losing track of time as I dig. Feeling the earth between my fingers, something I usually love, gives me little comfort now. How many holes have I dug in this land, to plant and build a home? And all for what? Marrying Michael was a mistake. My punishment will be to live the life I chose. I prayed, but God did not listen. *I will not pray anymore.*

Carrying Brownie to the hole, I cradle his body one last time before gently placing him at its bottom. Crushed, I bury my hopes and dreams along with him. I push the dirt over him, patting it into place. Tears spent, I stagger back to the spring to wash my face as Michael instructed. As I do, I shut my heart to any more hurt and make a silent vow I will never cry again.

If my life centered on Michael before our marriage, it is completely consumed by him now. I learn to gauge his moods and act accordingly. When jovial and happy, he expects me to be the same. When sullen and irritable, I become both invisible and servant like. I try as much as possible to anticipate his needs. When will he want to eat? What foods will be best? Does he want his blue shirt pressed or his brown socks mended? I can never be sure what might bring about his anger, and it is his anger that I want to avoid. What confuses me most is the appearance now and then, of the Michael I first met that day in the store. Some days, he is tender and affectionate. There are just enough of those times to give me hope that life might be alright again, but, they do not last long. I have never felt so sad and alone.

Henry comes by the cabin at least once a day, but Michael always intercepts him. He gives many excuses for my absence.

"Eliza cannot come out now, she is busy ironing. Eliza has something on the stove that she can't leave."

I hear him talking to Henry on the porch, but stay out of the way. I am afraid for Henry's life as well as my own. Michael instructs Henry on how he should work and even suggests clearing additional land to increase the crops. With little knowledge of farm operations, he is still full of ideas. Most of them wrong. Even I know better, but still I keep silent. No need to cross him unnecessarily. On the few times that I actually run into Henry gathering eggs or bringing wood into the house for the stove, I imagine that he has been waiting for me. He tries to talk to me, but I must not engage in conversation. Even if I had not been ashamed to speak openly about my plight, Michael always appears within minutes and in a silent stealthy way as though he is eavesdropping on our talk. I must be so careful. What if Michael loses his temper with Henry? What might he do to the former slave?

It isn't as though Henry doesn't try to get me to talk.

"Good mornin', Miss Liza," he says. "I hate t' bother you. I know you busy with housework and takin' care of your new husband, but is Brownie 'round anywhere? Looks like he go off 'gain."

I hold my breath, then, duck my head so Henry cannot see the fear in my eyes when I remember Brownie's fate. I vowed not to cry again, but the loss of my dog hurts so much, tears come. I just shake my head.

"No, Henry. Maybe he went back to Papa and Mama's."

"Did yo' Papa say when he be comin' out?"

I shake my head again.

"I got somethin' to talk to him 'bout. Maybe, Henry'll take a ride on that lil mare of yourn and go see him. She been itchin' for a ride. You ain't been out to see her since you come home."

Oh, for the days when a ride on my horse could cure all my ills. And Papa. Remember the time when I could run to his arms and know he would take care of me? It is too late for that. I am Michael's wife now.

"Anythin' you want me to tell him, Miss Liza?"

"You can tell him how happy we are, Henry. Isn't that right Eliza?"

Where had Michael come from? His arm encircles my waist, and he pinches my side. That hurts. I struggle to keep my face composed.

"Isn't that right, Eliza?"

I put on a false smile.

"Yes, yes, Henry, do tell them how happy we are."

"Just like two lovebirds. In fact, I miss my wife every moment she is away from me. Come on back to the house, Eliza."

As Michael steers me away, I keep my eyes averted from Henry's. It will not be good to let on things are not right.

"You uns let me know if I can help anyway," Henry calls.

"We will be sure to let you know," replies Michael.

Once in the house, Michael grabs my arm and shakes me. He wrenches it so hard, I wonder, will it come out of its socket?

"Don't let me catch you talking to him again, Eliza. Do I need to watch you every minute?" I am sure he does anyway, but do not say so.

Instead, I reply meekly, "I am sorry, Michael. He stopped to talk to me and I was afraid that if I did not answer, he would see something was wrong."

"What do you mean, see something is wrong? There is nothing wrong here for him to see. Just a husband and wife deeply in love, isn't that right, Eliza? You do still love me don't you?"

This is no time for the truth.

"Oh, yes, Michael, I do."

"Well, you don't act like it these days. Come show me how much you love me."

He kisses me, and as I try to respond in kind. I hope that I am with the gentle, charming Michael and not the hateful, angry one.

On the sixth day of what should have been to have been our honeymoon, Papa sails over on the *Mary Nevis*. He brings a package of spices from Mama. When he reaches to hug me, I struggle not to burst into tears, but Michael is watching me and I must remain calm.

"No crying," he ordered. *If I do, I know I will pay later.*

"I just wanted to stop and say hello," he says. "I am on my way to Tampa to pick up the mail. I thought I would see if you still needed the yawl. If not, I will pick it up on my way back home tomorrow."

"Well, I was thinking of sailing it over to Tampa." *Michael is planning a trip to Tampa? When is he going to go? Would he want me to go with him? He isn't a good enough sailor.*

"But, since you are headed that way, perhaps I will just ride with you."

Turning to me, Michael says, "You will be alright without me for a while, won't you darling? I know you want to stay here and finish your sewing, don't you?"

Ordinarily, I would have enjoyed a sail, even to Tampa, but the thought of some time alone without Michael to worry about sounds even better than an outing. So, I simply nod my head in agreement. Papa does not stay long, and Michael makes sure that we have no time alone. It is just as well. How could I have explained the last few days to my father? What might he have said or done? I left his protection the day I married Michael.

I stand on the front porch and wave good bye, then sit down on the steps in exhaustion. What I wouldn't give for a good long nap. I do not sleep well and wake each morning more tired than when I went to bed. Michael left a list of chores he expected done by the time he returned. I suppose it is to keep me too busy to think about escaping, but I do not want to experience his anger should they not be done by tomorrow. I go right to work. By nightfall, I survey bread set out to rise, a pie cooling on the table, laundry folded, ironing complete and the cabin thoroughly cleaned. I wipe my finger over the dresser in the bedroom as I take the pins out of my hair. Is there even a speck of dust left that he might complain about?

A knock on the back door startles me. *Who is it?* I look out the window and in the fading light, see Henry.

"Miss Liza, I won't come in. Just brought you some milk and cornbread. I'm bettin' you too busy to eat. Didn't want you goin' to bed hungry tonight." I realize that I am hungry.

"Thank you, Henry. Would you come in?"

"No, ma'am. But, if you don' mind steppin' outside, I relish somebody to talk to."

I take the bowl from Henry and walk out onto the porch beside him. Henry pulls a chair around for me, then, settles down on the front step. I ignore the chair and sit beside him on the step. I pull my bare feet up under my skirt and eat.

"Oh, this is so good."

"I figure you be hungry. I member a lil scrap of a girl who brung me food long time ago. It were lot bettern this, I 'fraid."

"This is good Henry. Don't apologize. I don't think my stomach could have taken much more anyway."

"Gotta reason for that ache, Miss Liza?" Henry asks gently.

How much to tell him?

When I hesitate, he continues, "You don need to tell me nothing Miss Liza. Henry's own eyes can see. I seen nuff slavery to know it don't come only to black men." I feel a lump in my throat. I cannot speak.

"Miss Liza, you in a real mess ain't you?"

I start to cry. *No, don't cry.* Michael said no more crying, but with Henry's comforting presence, I cannot stop. Henry pats me on my shoulder.

"Now, now. Miss Liza. Jes left it out. Get it all out. Then, we talk."

Henry waits patiently while I cry. He brings me a towel from the kitchen to dry my eyes. Wasn't it just a few weeks ago, that Michael did the same for me? Oh, why wasn't I more careful? That day was just a warning.

Finally, when I have no more tears left to shed, Henry says, quietly. "So, what you gonna do Miss Liza?"

"I don't know Henry. I am his wife now. There is no getting around it. I am tied to him forever."

"Can you talk to your Papa? He might know a plan. I ain't no lawyer, but gotta be a way round this. Man can't treat his wife this way."

"How can I tell Papa? Henry, he and Mama tried to warn me. Everybody tried to warn me. I was so blind. I am a fool, Henry."

"No, Miss Liza no fool. A firecracker, you are Miss Liza. No, Mister Dickens, he the fool. And a liar. Jus took you in, reeled you right in. Lil sweet talk. Lil charm. Anybody coulda gotten caught in that trap."

"I just don't know why, Henry. Why is he like this? What am I doing wrong? I try and try to be better, but nothing makes him happy. For a time, but then, he gets so angry at me. Henry, he killed Brownie."

"I knowed Miss Liza. Come cross his grave. Spect you dig it alone, too."

I nod and am surprised by more tears. I thought they were spent. It takes less time for me to compose myself now, though.

"Miss Liza. You gotta talk to your Papa when he come next time. I'll do what I can to distract Mister Dickens. And fore you talk to him, you oughtta know, already done tole him what I knew. So, don' be 'fraid to be honest with him."

"Thank you Henry. Thank you for your help. You are a good friend."

"Miss Liza. I goin' to tell you one more thing. Last time, I tole you this, you wouldn't listen to Henry, but you gotta listen this time. Miss Liza, you got someone else sides me and your Papa who wants to help you iffn you just let him."

"Who, Henry. Who wants to help?"

"God. God jus waitin' for you to ask His help."

"Henry, don't you think I've been praying? But, God isn't listening to me! Where was God when Michael killed Brownie? Where is God when I lay in bed and can't sleep for fear of my own husband? I made my choice and God knows it. He isn't going to do anything about it, now, Henry."

"Oh, Miss Liza. How can Henry splain it to you so you understand? God don't want bad things to happn' to you. Sometime he let us have our own way to get our attention, don't you know. But, Miss Liza, God always love you and He still do. Ask Him, Miss Liza. Ask Him to show you how much He love you. Miss Liza, I knowed what it be like to be a slave. I been one. It ain't pretty. But, even all bound up, God gives a man or a woman like you peace. He speaks to the heart. He helps you endure. Don't give up on God Miss Liza. He there. He still there."

I cry once more.

"And when you weep, He weeping too. Just promise me you'll think on it Miss Liza." I sniff and hand Henry the bowl.

"Thank you for the supper, Henry. I will think on it, but I don't expect there is much chance for me anymore."

"Oh, don' be so sure. Good night. And Miss Liza, I be praying even if you won't." Henry disappears in to the darkness. Despite my fatigue, I stay where I am. Henry's words echo in my head. Is there really a chance that God still listens to me? I close my eyes.

"God, Henry says you are there. I don't feel it God. All I feel is empty. But, God if you are there, show me. Because God, I really, really need someone on my side right now."

I open my eyes and look into the night sky. An owl hoots in the distance. I wonder if he is related to the one Mama shot so long ago. Oh, to be a child again and believe that God could save me. What is that? I see a bright light to my left. There, it is again, in the northwestern sky. What is it? Never have I seen such a star. And it moves! From high above my head, a comet races downward. Its tail trails for a long distance behind it.

"God? Is that you? Are you there?" I whisper.

Could Henry be right? Does God still care about me? I watch as the comet makes its way beyond the trees. As it does, I feel a peace wash over me unlike anything I have ever known. I stand and try to catch another glimpse of the light. It is gone, but when I go back into the house, for the first time in weeks, I sleep soundly.

Chapter Fourteen

Henry didn't need to worry about keeping Michael occupied so I could talk to Papa alone. When the *Mary Nevis* sails back into Terra Ceia Bay, Papa is alone. *Will Michael never return then? Am I free from the nightmare?* It takes Papa a long time to come to the cabin. I pace and fret, both dreading and welcoming an opportunity to tell him my troubles. I think he is having some difficulty tying up the boat, until I see him talking to Henry by the horse pen out back. I look twice. My normally quiet and restrained father is red faced and gesturing wildly. Stunned, I watch as he rams his fist into the side of the corral. Whatever could he be so angry at Henry about?

When Papa finally comes to the house, I ask, "Where is Michael?"

"He decided to stay in Tampa. I told him I would look in on you on my way home. I expect he will catch a ride with Captain Sam. Look for him to be along in a few days."

I hesitate.

"Will he be back, Papa?"

"Yes, Eliza. I am sure he will."

Papa rubs his hands together. His knuckles on one hand are raw and bloody.

"Papa, what did you do? Sit down and let me bandage your hand." Having something to do frees my tongue.

"Whatever were you so angry at Henry about?"

"I was not upset with Henry. He was simply helping me understand something that I did not want to hear. Daughter, I know."

I drop my hands. I feel Michael's blows all over again. I look at the floor.

"Eliza," Papa says gently. He reaches to cup my face with

his hand and lifts my head up. "Look at me. Whatever has happened, it is not your fault. But, why did you think you could not come to me with your problems?"

Hot tears fill my eyes.

"Nothing can ever change my love for you, daughter."

"Papa."

With that one word, the dam breaks and I cannot stop weeping. Papa holds me close.

When the tears slow, he says, "We need to make plans. Before Henry told me, I suspected things were not right. He only confirmed what my heart already knew. While in Tampa, I stopped in to see Mr. Gettis. He has joined the army, but Mr. Magbee was available to talk. He remembers you with fondness, Eliza. He will work on freeing you from this sham of a marriage, but it will take time. I hate to say it, but you must stay married to him for a while longer. I believe it is too late for an annulment, am I right?"

I blush and nod my head.

"Mr. Magbee says you cannot leave him. The court does not look favorably on a woman who deserts her husband. Even if we could find an impartial judge, there is no testimony but yours and Henry's. We must wait on Michael to err so he can be charged with unfaithfulness or desertion. It pains me to leave you here with him, Eliza. Be honest with me now, how does he harm you?"

I avoid a direct answer. I do not want to relieve those terrifying moments.

"It is not so bad right now. As long as I obey and keep him happy, he does not hurt me as much."

Papa paces the room.

"I can't bear it," his voice cracks. *Will he cry as well? I cannot stand the thought.*

Then, he rubs my shoulder. When I wince, he drops his hand as though burned.

"I fear for you. Henry will be here, should it get too bad, he will get you away. He will help you get away." Papa clears his voice and speaks stronger. "But, if you can stand it for a little while longer, let us wait until he makes the first mistake." I nod.

"I can wait a little while longer, Papa."

"Oh, Eliza, what kind of a father am I to let you get this way?" I remember Henry's words from the night before.

"Papa, this is not your fault. I would not have listened to you. I think I had a lesson to learn. A hard one. It helps to know you still love me and to see that there may be a way of escape." I stop in thought. "Papa, do you believe God can help me?"

"Absolutely," he replies. "In fact, if we can pull this off without you getting hurt, then, it will be a miracle."

My heart already hurts so bad I may die. *Could a broken bone feel any worse?*

I ask, "Will he come back?"

"Who, God?"

"No, Michael."

"Yes, I am afraid so. Once he has had his fun, he will be back. I did not think he would stay here in this remote place for long. Eliza, you need to know. It pains me to tell you, but the rumor in Manatee is that he married you hoping I would give you this place for a wedding present."

Yes, that is what Flora said as well.

"What he doesn't know is that I still don't even own this land so I could not give it away if I want to. For the first time, I am grateful that the government still has not given me my patent to the homestead."

I wander aimlessly outside after Papa leaves. So many thoughts whirl around in my head, but I feel free even if it is temporary. A few more days without Michael. I lean over the horse pen and scratch Niihaasi on the neck. Henry waves to me from the field and comes over to talk.

"Why don't you take her for a ride?" he asks.

"Oh, I couldn't, Michael would be angry."

"Michael is not here."

"Go on, I will saddle her up for you."

"But, what if he should come home today after all? Perhaps he is trying to trick me?"

Henry speaks over his shoulder as he saddles the horse.

"Go west and stay along the shore. As soon as his boat comes into the bay, you will see it and you will have time to get home before he does."

He reaches for my hand, and then lifts me up on Niihaasi's back.

"Go on now. You know how much a ride makes you feel better. Clear your head so you can think."

It does feel good to be atop my horse again. We follow the line of the bay to the west. I stop and look around me. Papa's claim must end about here. This wide expanse of land is still available. I wish the Homestead Act was still in force. I would claim this as my own. If women could make claims in their own name. Maybe someday, I will figure out a way to buy it. *Wouldn't it be nice to have a place of my own? Something no one else can take from me?* Fearing I have been gone too long, I study the land around me. Remember this Eliza, I think. *Here is something you can live for.* I make my way back to the cabin. Back to my present, but dreaming of my future.

Whether it is the ride or the comfort offered by Papa and Henry, I do not know, but I feel better. Less fragile, more sturdy. I have people who love me and will help keep me safe. All I have to do is to be careful and stay out of Michael's way. Someday, maybe I will be free and an independent woman again. The thought gives me courage and strength.

I am free of Michael for almost a week. Every night, I sit outside and watch the comet make its way across the sky. I pray. *Thank you God. I know you are here.* When I see Captain Sam's boat sail into the bay, I know Michael will be aboard. I pray that this time of healing will last through whatever may come. I may appear weak and frail on the outside, but I vow to remain strong and resilient on the inside. He came close, but he will not break me. When Michael comes to the house, he is in a jolly mood.

"Tampa is a wonderful town. It is going to be a big city someday. I think we should move. There is much more to do there than on this island."

I cautiously agree, but nothing comes of his proposal. I continue to work hard not to offend him. To stay on his good side. And it appears to work. Though the light in the sky no longer shines, its brilliance remains in my heart. I console myself with the thought that with Michael at home, he would not allow me outside to see it anyway.

By mid August, the game gets harder and harder to play. Michael's mood still rises and falls almost as frequently as the tides. A fatigue so great that I can hardly get out of bed in the mornings overcomes me. Nausea is my constant companion. Though I manage to cook Michael's meals, I cannot eat more than weak tea and toast, and often, that will not stay down. I make frequent trips to the outhouse when I can make it that far. *What is wrong with me?* Worse, are me fluctuating emotions. Though determined to be strong, I feel like crying at the least little thing. Try as I might, I cannot not hide my illness from Michael. Instead of being concerned, he is annoyed.

"I hope you don't have anything contagious,"

By seven o'clock each evening, I can no longer keep my eyes open.

"I may as well still be in Tampa," Michael says. "You are no company. You might as well go on to bed."

I am grateful to finally lie down at the end of each day, but it feels as though I rest on a mattress floating on the sea. I feel so dizzy, and my stomach rolls all night long.

One afternoon, while cleaning rugs, I try to gather the energy to lift the metal beater to loosen the dirt when the world suddenly goes dark and I collapse to the floor. Henry's face swims before me.

"Miss Liza, Miss Liza, you alright?"

Michael's face replaces the black man's features.

"Get away from my wife. Don't touch her. Eliza, get up this minute."

I struggle to my feet, then off the porch towards the out-house.

"I think I will be sick."

Returning to the house, I cross paths with Henry

"Take this Miss Liza. Put somethin' back in yore stomach."

He hands me a pot of chicken broth. I change into a clean nightgown, eat some broth and go to bed. Though I want to sleep, I cannot rest. Michael stands in the doorway eating the rest of the soup, staring at me.

"I do not know what is wrong with you, but you better straighten up. I didn't take on a sickly wife."

First thing the next morning, before I can even get out of bed, Mama walks in the front door. Bless him. Henry must have gone for her.

Addressing Michael, she demands, "How long has she been like this? Why didn't you send for me sooner?"

Michael just shrugs his shoulders, but does not leave.

"Go, away, Mr. Dickens. I need to talk to my daughter."

"She doesn't have anything to say to you that she cannot say in front of me."

That does it. Mama draws herself up to her full height. Michael is a tall man, but in that moment, I think Mama is the taller of the two.

"Mr. Dickens, I would have a moment alone with my daughter. Unless you have something to hide from me?"

"No, no. I will leave you alone. Eliza, I am taking the yawl. Since your mother is here to care for you now, I will be in Tampa for a few days."

Without even packing a bag, Michael leaves the house.

"Mama, it is not good to anger him so."

"I know what kind of a man he is, Eliza. Your father told me everything. I am sorry for your trouble. We will try to help. But, now we must figure out why you are so ill."

"Mama, I do not know what is wrong with me. When I stand up, the room spins around me. My stomach is so upset, I cannot eat. I am tired and sad all the time."

"Eliza, when was your last monthly cycle?" I think for a few seconds.

"I don't remember. So much has happened. Sometime before the wedding, I guess. I have been so afraid and worried, I did not think much about it."

"Well, Eliza, I think you are pregnant. Perhaps something good will come out of your situation. Think! I am going to be a grandmother. Twice, for your cousin Mary is also expecting."

Pregnant! A baby. How can I bring a baby into this world? Will this be what it will take for Michael to love me again?

"What do I do now, Mama?"

"We work on getting your strength up and finding something you can eat. You have someone else to nourish now so must take care of yourself. If we can get something to stay in your belly, you should feel better all the way around. But you will have to be careful not to overdo. And no more horseback riding for you young lady!"

Mama stays for a few days to help me around the house. With Mama cooking my favorite foods, I start feeling better. When Michael returns, he notices that there is more color in my cheeks.

"You look better. What did your mother do for you anyway? Are you cured?"

How will he take my news? Will this cause him to treat me more kindly?

"There is nothing wrong with me that time will not take care of. Michael, I am pregnant. You are going to be a father."

"A baby. That's the last thing we need right now. What use are you to me anymore?"

I do not know whether to be happy or to cry when Michael leaves without another word and returns to Tampa. At least I no longer have to worry about pleasing him. But, will my child grow up without a father?

He does not stay away permanently and returns home frequently. His surprise appearances keep me off guard and afraid. While he does not touch me again, I wonder if he knows that I am hoping to find a valid reason for divorce or if he does not want to hurt the baby.

While the physical abuse stops, he is just as harsh with his words. Whenever he comes home in some half hearted attempt to continue our marriage, he spends most of his time criticizing my cooking, my housekeeping and my appearance. Nothing misses his eyes. Even the things on which he used to compliment me on no longer bring him pleasure. One morning, I try to break the silence at the breakfast table by telling of a flock of Great Blue Herons I saw rise out of the bay early that morning.

"Michael, they were so beautiful! They completely filled the sky. The sun was just rising, and it tipped their blue wings with pink so that they looked lavender."

Michael quells my enthusiasm. "Why did you wait so long to tell me? Next time you see them, get me right away. There is a rich market for the feathers of those birds. I could have made a lot of money if they were as thick as you say."

It makes me sick to think about shooting any of them. *Where has the man who I once loved gone?* His attitude is not the only thing that makes me ill. Though I now understand the reasons for my nausea, fatigue and dizziness and under Mama's tutelage how to combat them, a month later, a whole new set of symptoms erupt that I fear do not relate to my pregnancy. I am embarrassed to mention them to anyone, but soon the pain I feel whenever I use the outhouse is constantly with me. I know I must seek some help.

I wait until a day that Michael is gone to ask Henry to take me to visit my mother.

"You alright Miss Liza? You look a little peaked."

"I don't know Henry. I still don't feel very good. Mama says in time, my condition will improve, but I never knew having a baby was so hard."

"Oh, Miss Liza, don't you know. It all be worth it when you hol' that babe in your arms the first time."

"I hope so Henry. Right now, it seems a long, long time away."

"Be here for you know it. You need to see your momma. That will make you feel better. Henry'll get the boat and take you over. Jus' hol up a minute."

"I'm sorry. I know you have work to do."

"No problem atall. I'm needing to do some fishin'. I can do it while you visit."

The air is too still to sail, so Henry rows the boat around the southwestern point of the island, through the narrow inlets around the smaller islands along the shore and through the narrow cut into the Manatee River. As he rows, Henry sings in time to his strokes. Each line is punctuated by the splash of the oar in the water:

Canaan land is the land for me,
And let God's saints come in.
Canaan land is the land for me,
And let God's saints come in.

Come down, angel, and trouble the water,
Come down, angel, and trouble the water,
And let God's saints come in.

There was a wicked man,
He kept them children in Egypt land.

There was a wicked man,
He kept them children in Egypt land.

Come down, angel, and trouble the water,
Come down, angel, and trouble the water,
And let God's saints come in. "

The song goes on for many verses all telling about the Children of Israel's escape from Pharaoh. I enjoy the brisk rhythm and the lively tune.

It doesn't take me long to learn the chorus and I join him in song. "Come down, angel, and trouble the water, Come down, angel, and trouble the water, And let God's saints come in."

When we finish, I applaud.

"I like that song, Henry. Where did you learn it?"

"Don' rightly know, Miss Liza. Seems like I always knowed it. Maybe sometime long ago, my Mama sung it to me."

"Do you remember your mother, Henry?"

"Only lil bits and pieces." Then, he sighs, "My babies, now. Them I member."

"You have children, Henry? I didn't know."

"Had me a wife, too."

"Where are they?"

"Don' know. Miss Liza." Henry shakes his head and repeats softer this time. "Don' know. But I find them someday."

How sad not to have his family here with him.

"How will you know where they are?"

"God know. He show me. If not here. Someday in Heaven. Someday, I rock those babies again."

I cradle my stomach. My little one doesn't even show yet, but I make it a promise. I will never leave you. My marriage might be a mistake, but you will be cherished. By the time, we round Hooker's Point, the wind picks up, so Henry hosts the sail. In no time, I climb out of the boat and meet my parents halfway to the store.

"Well, look at you," Mama says. "Where did you come from?"

Papa smiles and shakes Henry's hand. "Now, Mama, don't worry. It looks like Henry is taking good care of her."

"Yes, sir, Mr. Joe. I don' let nothin' bad happen to Miss Liza. Look, I done brought some fish for you."

"Guess I know what we will be having for dinner, Julia."

The two men stay behind to clean the fish. Mama and I walk to the house.

"What are you thinking, Eliza? You have the baby to take care of now, you know. You shouldn't be so careless."

"Mama, it was alright. I am careful. Henry did all the work. I just sat there."

"So, what brings you home?"

Home. Once upon a time, I thought the cabin on Terra Ceia would be home. How things have changed.

"I need to ask you a question about something." Better to just plunge in. "Mama, when you were pregnant, did you ever have any other troubles?'

"Like what?" Mama asks.

I describe my symptoms. Mama frowns.

"Eliza that does not sound normal. It worries me a great deal. Something could be very wrong. I think we better ask a doctor."

"Mama, I don't need a doctor. I am sure I will get well. Don't you know some remedies I can use?"

"No, nothing that I could be sure would not harm the baby. We better get to a doctor and soon."

Mama has never been one for procrastination. While Henry takes me back to the island later that day, only two days go by before my parents come to pick me up in the *Mary Nevis*. I sail across Tampa Bay for the first time in years. *Will we run into Michael while we are there? Will he be angry that I did not ask permission to come? What will the doctor say? Worse, what might the doctor do?* I have always loved sailing, but today, I cannot enjoy the ride. In fact, I feel a little seasick. Papa notices my discomfort.

"Eliza, there is a blanket and a bed in the cabin. Why don't you go down below and take a little nap?"

A nap sounds fine. So, I go below deck, curl up on the bunk and sleep all the way to Tampa. Once there, Mama takes me directly to the doctor's office. Several other patients are ahead of us so we settle into chairs to wait our turn. Despite my long nap, I feel so fatigued that my head droops on my chest, and I doze once more. I jump when Mama pats my arm, and I hear my name.

"Do you want me to go back with you?" Mama asks.

I do, but will I seem like a weakling to ask? Dr. Branch settles the question for us.

"Madam Joe? How good to see you again. I had forgotten that Eliza was now married. Come back. Both of you."

I imagine it will be embarrassing to tell Dr. Branch my problems, but Mama saves me the trouble. Immediately, Mama begins explaining about my pregnancy and these new symptoms that plague me.

Dr. Branch frowns, then, says, "Young lady, I must have your honesty now. Even though your mother is sitting here do not lie to me." *Whatever could he want to know?*

"Have you been with any other man but your husband?"

"No, no sir. No one. Only Michael."

"You were a virgin when you married?"

I blush too mortified to speak and nod.

"Well, then, you had better send your husband round for treatment. I am reluctant to tell you this, Mrs. Dickens, but you have a venereal disease. Gonorrhea, to be exact."

A venereal disease? What does that mean? Mama's face grows red. *Is she angry with me? What did I do wrong? Michael has these symptoms, too?*

"I do not know about this pregnancy. We will do our best to

treat you and save the baby."

Save the baby? What is wrong with the baby? My frayed emotions give way, and I begin to cry. *Why is the baby in danger?*

"Now, now, Mrs. Dickens. I am sure that your husband will have an explanation for his unfaithfulness. Perhaps he got this disease before he even met you. He could have had it and not even known about it."

Michael gave this to me? It is because he has been unfaithful to me. Now, the truth filters through the fear and fatigue to fill my mind. No wonder Mama is angry.

Chapter Fifteen

Mama asks, "What treatment will you prescribe, Dr. Branch?"

"First and foremost, a lot of rest. You must live life at a slower pace until the disease is completely gone. That means longer than just until the symptoms have subsided."

How am I to take it easy? There are so many things to do around the house. With Michael gone most of the time, it all falls upon me.

"Avoid salted or highly seasoned meats. Absolutely, no liquor. Stay as cool as possible. Avoid being near a fire or out in the sun. Every day, you are to bathe with lukewarm water. You may apply a poultice of oatmeal moistened with vinegar. I have a prescription for you to take to the druggist. Take it regularly and do not stop even though your symptoms disappear. Purchase some Perry's Purifying Specific Pills while you are there as well as some Cordial Balm of Siriacum. Take two of the pills at night and two in the morning. Mix the medicine the druggist will give you with a tablespoon of the cordial balm."

I can hardly keep all the directions straight. I hope Mama is paying attention. For now, I reeling from the disclosure that Michael did this to me. I could lose the baby. Just when I start to believe that things will truly be alright. *Am I to be punished for my mistake in marrying Michael time and time again?* Mama listens to the doctor as he describes a potion I must drink every other day to keep my bowels clear. My head starts to spin again, and my stomach rolls.

"I'm sorry," I whisper both to my baby as well as Mama and Dr. Branch. "But, I think I am going to be sick."

After vomiting into the basin Dr. Branch hurriedly thrusts my way, I feel a little better, but not much. Still, I rise when Mama does.

"Thank you Dr. Branch," Mama says. "We appreciate your time and wisdom. I trust we can keep this visit confidential? I am sure Mr. Dickens would prefer to hear this diagnosis in private rather than on the street." Dr. Branch frowns.

"Why Madam Joe, of course I respect my patient's privacy. I am sure that Mrs. Dickens would not want everyone to know as well."

Yes, I think. Mrs. Dickens would prefer that no one know this and many other things that her husband does to her.

"Congratulations on your pregnancy, Mrs. Dickens. If I may be of service in any other way, please fell free to contact me. Oh, I forgot to add. If the medicines and treatment I have prescribed do not stop the course of the disease, we have several other options. Bleeding, leeches or lead injections could help as well. But, only after the baby is born, of course."

Bleeding, leeches, or injections of lead? The room spins again. Mama notices my discomfort and grabs me by the arm leading me from the room.

"What now, Mama?" I manage to stammer.

"First, the pharmacy. Then, we go straight to Mr. Magbee's office. You have your grounds for divorce now, Eliza. And heaven help Michael Dickens if I get hold of him first."

After a visit to the pharmacist which is almost as embarrassing as the one to the doctor, we walk to Mr. Magbee's law office. Unfortunately, he is not available. I hoped that he would take my case for I remember his kindness at Papa's trial. Besides, Papa told him the details of my marriage to Michael so I won't have to repeat the tale. I almost back right out of the office when I see Henry Mitchell's name listed as a partner in the firm. How can I trust the man with the personal details of my life when he worked so hard to convict Papa of a crime he did not commit? Surely there are other lawyers in Tampa. Before I can leave, Mr. Gettis, home on furlough from the army, comes out of his office and greets us.

"Madam Joe, Eliza. How are you today? Is this a social visit or do you need my assistance?"

Mama answers so bluntly I wince.

"Eliza's husband, Michael Dickens is a scoundrel and determined to kill her, either by his own hand or sharing his dirty disease with her. He is rotten through and through. Yes, Mr. Gettis, I would say we need an attorney."

If a hole opened up in the floor and dropped me through it I would be satisfied. Nothing like having all my secrets laid bare for anyone to hear. Mr. Gettis ushers us into his office and peppers me with questions. I squirm under his inquisition. His frank discussion of my suffering distresses me. At times, a lump rises in my throat so great, I cannot speak. When I hesitate, Mama speaks for me. Finally, the lopsided interview is over. Mr. Gettis puts down his pen and shuffles the papers upon which he had taken notes.

"Well, Madam Joe, Eliza, I believe we can help you. While we could not win this case on the defense of abuse, if Dr. Branch will testify, we should be able to prove your husband's unfaithfulness. And I expect there are plenty of witnesses here in Tampa who will testify to his activities while he is in town. Let me do some investigating, and I will see what a case I can prepare."

I nod. Can we just go home now?

Mr. Gettis continues, "But, I must say, Eliza. If we are to take this case before a judge, you will have to be less reticent to speak of personal matters on the stand. Your mother will not be able to testify for you. Good day, ladies. "

On the way home, I fret over his parting words. When the time comes, will I be able to speak openly of all that has happened to me. *What will other people think when they hear the details of the last few months? Will they believe me or trust the man whom many call friend? Will Dr. Branch be willing to testify?*

Over the next few weeks, the treatment Dr. Branch prescribed both relieves and compounds my discomfort. The baths and the poultice help ease some of the pain, and I take the medicines prescribed for me every day as instructed. At Mama's insistence, I now live with my parents at the river house. I help with the meals and cleaning when I can, but mostly, stay in bed and rest as the doctor instructed. I do not want to take any chances with this baby. Despite how he or she was conceived, I love my child dearly already.

I was reluctant to go home, fearing to face those in the settlement, but after my first dose of the cleansing potion made of senna leaves, epsom salts, coriander seeds, caraway seeds and ginger, I am grateful to be with my mother. If I thought the morning sickness bad, this is even worse. The potion works so quickly that it is all I can do to swallow the mixture that tastes so terrible before having to run to the outhouse. The coriander, caraway and ginger do not conceal the strong flavor of senna leaves. Mama patiently nurses me through the bouts of sickness. It is more than I deserve to have a mother who loves me so and treats me so kindly.

Though I wish for a quick cure, the medicine doesn't seem to be working. Mama wants to take me back to see Dr. Branch, but I beg for more time.

"Please Mama. Let's see if this works before we let Dr. Branch try anything stronger. Remember the baby, Mama."

I think about the baby all the time. Every time I pick up a spoonful of medicine or swallow a pill, I pray, God please don't let this hurt the baby. Even though I am only three months along, my waist is already thick. With my small stature, my pregnancy is quite apparent. Sometimes, after my daily bath, I stand naked in front of the mirror and stare at my stomach. *Is there really a baby inside of me? Will he or she be born alright?*

I hide within the house, avoiding the other settlers. Mary comes to visit. She pats her stomach and then, mine in turn.

"Oh, Eliza, won't it be wonderful if we both have girls and they can grow up together. They will be almost like twins. Just like us, they will have a cousin for a sister!"

Mary's happy chatter and talk of William and her home are painful for me to hear. Mary was always the good girl, and she made a wise choice. She found love and peace. *What did I get? Unfulfilled longings and regret fill my future.*

With my inner turmoil, it is easy to forget that there is a war going on. Still, I hear bits and pieces about the war as Mama and Papa discuss it at mealtimes. When supplies in the store grow low, Papa plans to use the *Mary Nevis* to run the blockades and bring merchandise in for sale. Mama argues against it.

"Governor Milton opposes blockade running," she states. "The items brought in come from the north. You contribute to their economy and risk your life to do it."

Papa counters, "The Confederate government wants us to keep our nation and our army strong. Without factories here, we cannot do that unless we buy our goods somewhere else."

They never reach a compromise satisfactory to both of them.

Mama settles the disagreement, however, "Joseph, leave the blockade running to the men with bigger and faster boats. Don't tempt fate. We have enough troubles right now."

Indeed we do. In late October, Mr. Gettis sails down from Tampa and brings the divorce petition for my signature. In them, he refers to me as an affectionate, chaste and obedient wife and asks Judge King to demand that Michael appear before the court and explain his actions. In seven statements, Mr. Gettis outlines the reasons that the Judge should grant me a divorce from Michael. He accurately describes the pain both in body and mind that I suffer at Michael's hand. My eyes well up with tears as I read. Then, I flinch when I see the fourth reason and the words, the Gonorrhea, underlined so that they stand out boldly on the page. Oh, the shame of it all. I remember Mama's words so long ago when she tried to convince me to delay the wedding.

Hadn't she said, "A little embarrassment now is better than

living the rest of your life with a mistake?"

Oh, if only I had listened, then. But, now though I will be mortified for my neighbors to know the cause of my troubles, if I only endure for a time, I will be free to make a fresh start. Still, I am glad that I do not have to go with Mr. Gettis to file the paper with the court. He submits the petition to Judge King on October 28, and that same day, the judge issues a subpoena for Michael to appear in court on November 18.

When he is served, Michael comes to the house. He argues with Papa and demands to see me, while I hide in my room. I feel guilty for leaving Papa to deal with him, but at the same time, am grateful that he bears the brunt of Michael's anger. I watch through the window as Papa escorts him away from the house. It reminds me of my wedding day when I peeked outside the front door and saw him standing there, waiting on me. But, this time, instead of smiling so sweetly, Michael rages and curses at Papa. My father stands his ground. He never raises his voice so I do not know what he says, but soon Michael turns to go. *How could I ever have thought myself in love with him?*

Later, Mama asks, "Joseph, how did you convince him to leave?"

"I told him he would have his day in court to tell his side. Then, I suggested he might want to get back to Tampa and see Dr. Branch. I simply reminded him of what happens to a man when gonorrhea goes unchecked."

Mama smiles and says evilly, "What I wouldn't give if it were too late for him to get help."

I just feel wistful and sad. Seeing Michael brings up all the old feelings. Until that very moment, I did not realize that all this time, even with all his abuse, I still hold onto the hope that something might happen to change him back into the man I first met. What might it have been like if Michael were true to what he appeared that day in the store last spring? *Would he have been a good father?*

"Did he ask about the baby, Papa?"

Papa shakes his head, "No, daughter, I am sorry, he did not."

"Sorry?" Mama says. "Good riddance. Now you can raise this baby as you like and not have to worry about that monster influencing your child."

Mixed with my wonderings of what might have been, I dread the upcoming trial. I wish it is as easy as Mama thinks to be rid of my husband and that there is some other way to end the heartache without having to appear in court. But, if that is the only way to be free, I will just somehow find the courage to do it.

A week later, I learn just how hard it will be. After dinner, Ezekiel Glazier calls. I have not seen him since my wedding day. I am grateful that Papa is home to intercede. My parents do not leave me alone with the justice of the peace. After polite conversation, Judge Glazier turns his attention upon me.

"Mrs. Dickens, upon hearing of your request for a divorce, I was compelled to come and see you. I must remind you of the promises that you made on your wedding day in front of me, witnesses and most importantly God." Judge Glazier stands and walks towards me. "Do you recall your vows that day, Mrs. Dickens?"

His piercing blue eyes drill into mine, and I shrink back into my chair.

"Yes, sir," I whisper.

His voice rises, "Then, you must know that you promised to love and obey in sickness and in health? A disease, even one as shameful as you carry, is not a reason to leave your husband, Mrs. Dickens. You were legally wed. No matter that a piece of paper may be granted to you, you will always be married and no one, no one can change that. I see you are expecting? Do you want your child to grow up fatherless?"

Mama stands.

"Judge Glazier, I thank you for your visit. There are many things that you do not know. Perhaps after the trial, you will understand better. Joseph, will you see Judge Glazier to the door?"

He turns to follow Papa outside, but looking back over his shoulder, says, "Madam Joe, there is only one thing I need to know. Your daughter made a vow, and she would seek to break that vow. May God pass judgment upon her for her unfaithfulness."

Unfaithful? Michael was unfaithful, not me. What did I do wrong except to believe a man who said he loved me? I bolt from my chair, taking the steps two at a time, and throw myself on the bed weeping.

"Eliza, you must not cry so," Mama follows me upstairs and pats my back. "Think of the baby. This is not good for your child."

As much as I cherish the infant I carry, I cannot stop. *God does not love me.* How can I think that a wicked sinner, disobedient and deceitful like me can ever be loved by God? Try as I might, I will never be good enough for God. Hadn't I known that all along? Then, in the midst of my wailing, I feel a cramping down low in my belly.

"Oh," I moan and roll over on my side to clutch at my abdomen.

"Eliza, I told you. This is not good. You have to stop crying." Mama says again, more harshly this time "Do you want this baby?"

Despite the cloud of grief, I think, yes, yes I do. Though I cannot speak it aloud, Mama responds.

"Then, quit your crying. Focus on the baby, Eliza. Forget everything else. Breathe and lay still."

Mama dries my tears and helps me to undress and put on my nightgown. Then, I curl back down upon the bed. The pain in my body eases, but my heart still hurts. Exhausted by my weeping, I drift off to sleep, but not before praying.

"God, I know I have done wrong. But, please, do not punish my child for my sins. Judge me, punish me, but let my child live."

God's answer to my prayer comes in a letter informing me that all court cases for the fall term are canceled until further notice. The message blames the war, but I know this is to be my fate. I will be married to Michael Dickens for the rest of my life. Hell on earth, it might prove to be, but I will endure, if only God allows my baby to live.

By Christmas and Mama's birthday, Dr. Branch's treatments seem a success, but I do not feel much like celebrating. Michael comes and goes, while I remain at my parents' house on the river. He visits often enough to remind me of my inadequacies. I never know when he will show up or how long he will stay. Almost six months pregnant, I do not feel comfortable being alone on the island for long periods of time. Besides, by staying with my parents, not only can I remain under their protection but I have Mama to help when my illness makes me tired. Though my symptoms ease, I still feel fatigued and sometimes nauseated. Mama says I will feel better soon, but I have no hope that I will.

Papa and Mama try to make Christmas special. Papa brings in a cedar tree. Like she has ever since I can remember, Mama decorates it with candles and her precious glass ornaments brought from Germany. Normally, I love looking at each one as I help hang them on the tree. This year, I can only sit and watch from a distance. Everything seems like a dream as though I am watching myself watch the others. Among the gifts for me under the tree are some baby clothes that Mama made. I smooth them with my hands. So sweet and delicate. Yet, they hardly even hold my attention. I am not interested in anything these days. Mary and William come for Christmas dinner, and we feast on wild turkey Papa killed the day before.

During the meal, Mama observes, "Next year, we will have two little ones at the table. Do you think St. Nicholas will come?"

Mary laughs and claps her hands. "I can hardly wait. Oh, what do you think we will have, Liza? William wants a boy, but I dearly hope it is a girl."

I do not answer. It takes every bit of effort to even lift the fork to my mouth.

As always, there is concern about the approaching war. In the back of everyone's minds is the thought that though the babies might be present next year, their fathers and grandfather might be at war. After dinner, when the dishes are clean, we adjourn to the parlor to visit. Mary and William sit upon the loveseat. Mary leans her head against William's chest, and absentmindedly rubs her belly. William bends forward and kisses her on the top of her head. Watching them tenderly interact, I feel so listless and alone. *Why is everything so easy for Mary?* She looks just as lovely as ever despite the extra weight of pregnancy. She has not been sick at all and glows with happiness while I hardly recognize myself in the mirror. I am gaunt and pale. No wonder Michael does not want to be around me. William will be a good father. Unlike Michael who is not the least bit interested in my ordeal. *Will he even be around to watch our child grow up?* Michael might as well go ahead and enlist. He is never around anyway. Today, even Mama and Papa seem closer than usual. Papa stands behind Mama's chair and massages her shoulders. I cannot stand it anymore.

"I think I will go take a nap." I try to smile and pat my extended belly. "Too much Christmas dinner. I can barely keep my eyes open."

I climb the stairs slowly, and then stop as I hear my name spoken.

"Poor Eliza," Mary says. "I wish she could be happy again."

Mama sighs. "I do not know how she can as long as Michael

is in her life. If only court would have held one more session. No matter what Judge Glazier said, I feel sure Mr. Gettis would have won the case. Surely, no one would expect a woman to live with such a man. Who knows how long until she can be free of him?"

Papa comes to my defense. "Now, now, don't worry about her so much. Eliza is a tough one. Give her time. She will be fine. When the baby comes and she regains her health, she will be back to her old self. Just wait and see."

I have heard enough. I force myself to place one foot in front of each other. Keep moving though my feet felt like they are anchored to the floor. *Is Papa right? Will I ever feel normal again? I lie down on my bed but cannot sleep. Where is Michael today? Who does he celebrate Christmas with? Is he with another woman? How will I raise this baby alone?* Perhaps it had not been so bad to live with him. Over time, maybe I could have grown used to his ways. The thoughts whirl around in my head, and I cannot rest.

I stare at the ceiling. *What might it be like to quietly slip downstairs? To walk to the river's edge and wade into the water?* I can imagine myself drifting under its depths the green sea lulling me to sleep. I would float there, under the water, free from suffering. No one would hear my cries. It would be so easy, but something holds me to my bed and keeps me from my plans.

For a week, I hide in my bedroom as much as I can. I feign sleep and make excuses for my fatigue. In reality, I just don't care anymore. *Why get up? What does life hold for me anyway?* Only pain and heartache. *Where is the reason to live?* Now I understand Henry's longing for heaven. There has to be something better than this life. If only I could be found good enough to go there.

On New Year's morning, I help Mama prepare another holiday meal. Mary and William will come over again. I wish I had an excuse and somewhere else to go. Maybe, I should go back to the island. The prospect of being alone is appealing. If I could just shut myself away. Everyone means well, but I am tired of being the center of their concern. Oh, to just lie down and never wake up. I think I would be better off dead than sick and expecting a baby who has no father's love.

What was that? A sharp pain in my lower abdomen takes my breath away. I am afraid. *After all of this, will I lose this baby after all?* There it is again. I put my hand against my belly and feel something push back. *Is that the baby?*

Mama looks around from the stove.

"Eliza, what is wrong? You look white as a sheet."

I gasp again. "Mama, put your hand right here. Feel that?"

Mama reaches over and presses her hand against my stomach. There, I feel the pressure again.

Mama laughs, "Eliza you have a feisty one there. Is that the first time he has kicked you?"

I nod. "Looks like he is trying to get your attention. Just giving you a reminder he's still in there."

I sit down and hold my hand on my stomach. *Does my baby know that I feel sad enough to wish I were dead? I'm sorry baby. I have been so busy thinking about myself, I almost forgot about you. I did make you a promise didn't I? I will try to be a better mother. I do want to live so I can see your face and kiss it. I will tell you over and over how much I love you.* The baby kicks me again. For the first time in months, I laugh. Mama smiles as well.

"Happiness suits you, Eliza. You don't look so peaked already. Laugh some more. Your baby can hear you, I believe."

Mama is right for I am rewarded with another punch and then, a wave of motion as the baby rolls over to the other side. I laugh again at the feel and the sight of my belly moving on its own. Mama joins me.

Just as dinner is served, I hear someone calling for Papa.

"Mister Joe, Mister Joe! Where you be Mister Joe?"

Henry. *What does he want?* It must be something urgent to bring him off the island. With emotions running so high over secession and slavery being one of the excuses for war, Papa warned Henry to stay close to the farm and away from the mainland. We all gather at the window as Papa goes outside to talk to Henry. He rides Dan. Despite the winter chill, the mule is lathered in white foam between his legs and on his chest. Henry rode him hard and fast. Papa motions for him to dismount and the two men led Dan to the horse pens. Papa throws several buckets of water over the mule to wash the sweat off of him, and then, turns him lose in the pen to cool down. The two men walk back to the house together.

"Julia, set another place at the table. Henry, join us for dinner."

"Oh, no, Mister Joe. I can't do that."

"Henry, you must be hungry," Mama says.

"That I am Misses Joe, but if you jess fix me a plate, I can eat it outside."

"Henry, I insist that you eat here with us. William move over and get Henry a chair," Papa orders.

Mama nods, "Yes, Henry, we welcome you to our table."

Always curious, Mary asks, "What brings you here in such a hurry, Henry?" He looks at Papa for guidance.

"Henry wanted to tell me something. We'll talk more about it after dinner. Right now, let's eat. I am famished," Papa says.

I wonder what news Henry brings. *Does it involve me?* But, I hardly have time to think about it, so intrigued am I with these new sensations as my stomach continues to move and gyrate. Every once in a while, the baby kicks so hard it hurts. I cannot help but grimace and reach for my belly.

After a particularly painful jab, I say aloud, "Ouch!"

Everyone turns and looks at me.

"Eliza, look at your stomach. Oh, is that your baby moving?" Mary exclaims. I blush.

"How long has he been doing that?"

"It just started today."

"My goodness, I can't wait for our baby to do that. Look William, have you ever seen something so wondrous?"

William looks embarrassed. So, does Henry. I guess they do not know what to do. It really isn't proper for a man to be staring at my middle.

"It is alright gentlemen. You can look. I don't know how you can miss it. He is bound and determined to be the center of attention today."

I laugh. *Isn't that just like my luck?* To wish that everyone would quit worrying over me and then, to have my belly heave and roll like storm tossed waves in front of everyone? And yet, I feel strangely comforted by each jab and poke. I know you are in there, little one. I promise to be both mother and father to you. I can do it with your help.

Seeking to take the attention off my body, I ask, "Henry, can you tell us now what you came to say?"

Once more, Henry looks to Papa for advice. This time, Papa nods.

Henry opens his mouth, but Papa interrupts him. "Eliza, I am glad to hear you laugh again. This baby will be good for you, I know he will. I want you to remember how much you have to live for."

Papa knows how sad I have been. *Did he know about the times I wished I would die?*

He continues, "Henry has brought some bad news that may upset you. You need to be strong. Remember your baby, Eliza."

What is it? What has happened that would cause Papa to be so concerned for me?

Henry begins, "Miss Liza, I don't rightly know how to tell you. Mister Dickens, he come to the island yesterday. I knowed somethin' was up. He were in fine spirits. But, I couldn't figure out what he had up his sleeve. He don't usually talk to me, but he say that he goin' away. 'I won't see you for a while' he say. 'Goin' off and fight. Gonna kill me some Yankees,' he say. He got to talkin' some more and he tell me he joinin' the cavalry in Tampa. Miss Liza, I wish I thought more clearer. I jus' glad to be rid of him. I know how bad he treat you. But, Miss Liza, I jus' didn't think 'bout what he might do next. Otherwise, I woulda done somethin' to stop him."

"What Henry? Tell me. What did Michael do?"

"Oh, Miss Liza, I so shamed to tell you. I shoulda stopped him. But, when I got up this mornin' he were already gone. Miss Liza, he done rode off on Niihaasi. He done took your horse and joined the cavalry."

I feel like I am falling. To go from such joy to such sorrow so quickly. One moment, I laugh over my baby's antics; the next my heart breaks over the loss of my sweet little Indian pony. Worse than the thought that Niihaasi is now subject to Michael's firm hand is the image of my little mare in the midst of battle. It is more than I can bear. From somewhere, I hear the sound of someone weeping. *Who is it? As though waking from a dream, I feel drops of water falling on my chest. Is it me? Am I crying?*

"Eliza, Eliza!" Mama shouts at me. "Eliza pull yourself to-gether. The baby. Think of the baby."

At that moment, the baby kicks again. I grab my waist once more. *Oh, baby. Will you break my heart someday just as your father has broken it now?* My crying eases into hiccups. Amazingly, the baby hiccups as well, and my stomach jerks in a soft rhythm.

"Miss Liza, I so sorry," Henry says.

Pull yourself together Eliza, I remind myself. Think of the baby.

I manage to reply, "Henry, it is not your fault. It is all mine. I made the mistake. I am paying the price."

Then, Mama helps me back to house and upstairs to my room. I try to rest with memories of my proud Indian pony and all the pleasure she has brought over the years. How long will I pay for choosing Michael? What more can he take from me? He stole my dignity, crushed my spirit and now, takes the one thing

I love most in this world.

Once more I feel the baby move, but this is not the violent motion of the last few hours. It feels like a gentle caress. *Thank you little one. Thank you for understanding how much I need you.* I cry myself to sleep and dream that I ride like the wind over the moon and among the stars upon a silver horse. It is a dream I have had before, but this time, I ride, with a baby strapped to my back, and in my ears is the unmistakable sound of a child's high pitched, clear and sweet laughter.

.

Chapter Sixteen

Like climbing out of a deep, dark pit, I think I have come to terms with my grief and am ready to face a fresh start, then, some simple occurrence and down I slide into depression again. Seeing William and Mary so happy together. Thoughts of my carefree girlhood. Time spent upon Nihaasi's back. My body's reminder of Michael's unfaithfulness. They all serve as triggers to bring on sadness once more. Papa watches me with tender eyes. He tries to entertain and comfort me, but it does not help. His gentleness only reminds me of what my baby will lack because of my mistakes. Mama believes work will solve my ills. She keeps me busy with as many chores as my body will handle hoping that I will forget my problems and sleep soundly at night. Despite the tasks, my dreams remain vivid. Sometimes, I ride on Niihaasi; other times, I relive the sweetness of Michael's courtship. Frequently, I wake in fear enduring the surprise of his brutality once more.

No matter what the night brings, each day, before I open my eyes, melancholy washes over me again. I think I cannot go on. I cannot endure another day. Then, the baby moves reminding me of my responsibility. I get up, dress and go to work. One day, no, one moment, at a time, I move through life. Some days, I feel at peace and others, restless and agitated. Most days, I just get by.

It does not help that the war finally comes to the Manatee River settlements. Two weeks into the new year, Captain Sam stumbles into the yard. I am surprised to see him so early in the morning. Out of breath and looking around him in fear, he asks to speak to Papa. While Mama takes him to the kitchen for some tea, I search for my father. Pulling my shawl around me as I walk, I cannot find him easily. A thick fog hangs over the river. I finally locate him in the woods behind the house felling trees for lumber. While I wait for him to finish his work, I smell the cedar chips left from his labors. I love that smell. It reminds me of our first little cabin on Terra Ceia. From there, my mind drifts to my wedding night. No, don't think about it. I gather some of the fragrant pieces in my apron. Mama will be happy. She scatters the flakes around the house to repel bugs. I walk in silence back to the kitchen with Papa. He slows his steps to match mine.

Papa reaches to give me a hug. "I miss my chatterbox," he says simply.

My eyes fill with tears.

"I'm sorry, daughter; I do not want you to be sad. If there is something I can do to make it better, please tell me."

I know he would go to Tampa and bring Niihaasi back if only I ask. I cannot bring myself to do it. When I married Michael everything I owned became his. Legally, there is nothing that I can do. Niihaasi belongs to Michael now. If Papa goes to get her, Michael could bring charges against him. Papa has already been through enough with the courts. No, I will not ask him to bring back Niihaasi as much as I want to do so.

"It is alright Papa. I will be fine. Everything makes me cry these days. Mama says it is the baby and when, he is born, I will be fine."

"Ah, yes. And then, we shall hear crying all hours of the day and night," Papa predicts. "I remember those days. It will be good to have a little one in the house again. I wonder what is wrong with Captain Sam. I was pleased when he offered to take over the mail run for me. With things as they are, I need to be closer to home."

He is staying home because of me. I hate that my situation makes it difficult for everyone. I wish that they would just resume their lives and quit trying to protect me.

When we enter the kitchen, Captain Sam is calmer, but now, Mama is upset.

"Joseph, they have taken the *Mary Nevis*."

"Who, who took her?" Papa asks.

"The Federals."

Captain Sam explains, "Joseph, I am so sorry. I had the mail from Manatee and was on my way to Tampa. Amelia Sawyer and her boy, Theodore, were with me. She wanted to go to Tampa to check on her husband, Samuel. We left early this morning in hopes of making it out of the river and around into the bay before daylight so to avoid the blockaders. I was staying close to shore, thinking I could get out into the bay unnoticed, but, as I made the turn past Shaw's Point, I could see lights near Passage Key. They must have caught the moonlight off my sail, and they had the wind behind them. It was not long before I knew that they would soon overtake us. All I could think about was keeping the mail from them. I did not know what information might be held in those envelopes. So, I ran the *Mary Nevis* as close to the sand flats as I could, launched the dingy and made for shore. There were six cutters coming in so fast, I did not have time to bring Mrs. Sawyer or her boy with me. There was not room in the boat, nor could I take a chance on the extra load slowing me down. I could only hope that the Federals will not harm a woman and child left alone like that. I told them to be quiet, but the child would not listen. I do not know if his wailing distracted the sailors, but one boat stopped and took them aboard. The other five chased me, but I managed to escape by hiding in the mangroves. I waited until they were gone and came straight here. I have the mail, safe and sound, but I am sorry for the loss of your boat."

"Where is Mrs. Sawyer now, Captain?" Papa asks.

"I do not know. I hoped that they might have brought her here."

"No, we have not heard anything until now." By this time, Mama is pacing back and forth in the kitchen.

"And what I am supposed to do now, Captain? I had a lot of

money invested in that boat. And how will we fulfill our contract to keep the mail running?"

"Julia," Papa leaves his seat and places his hand on Mama's arm.

"There is no need to fret. What is done is done. I am sure that Captain Sam did not want to leave the boat behind. He had no choice."

Captain Sam nods, "I am sorry, Madam Joe. If there had been any other way."

Mama sits down at the table. With her head in her hands, she moans.

"Joseph, this war will bring us no good."

"This war will bring no good to any of us," Papa agrees. "But, we are in the midst of it now, so there is no turning back.

While Captain Sam's news makes Mama angry, Papa determines to join the war effort.

After the captain leaves, Papa says, "Julia, I must volunteer you know. After this, the fight becomes personal. I cannot sit back and let those Yankees destroy everything we have built here."

"Joseph, we have been through this before. You are too old to fight."

Papa shakes his head. "Get used to the idea, Julia. I will go."

His words provoke Mama even more. She redirects her fury over the lost boat at Papa. I do not like the tension in the house as the two of them treat each other civilly, but with coldness instead of the warmth they usually show towards each other. Their conflict becomes even worse when news reaches us that the Union Navy destroyed the *Mary Nevis*. My father's resolve strengthens, while Mama despairs over losing Papa as well as her boat. I know he will serve. The question is only when will he leave.

Because of our prominent location on the edge of the river, we know that it will not be long before Federal troops pay us a visit. After they seized the *Mary Nevis,* Mama empties the store and hides everything, but a few items. She leaves just enough so that the store will not appear abandoned and instead, simply low on supplies. When four sailors and their captain appear in the store one day, there is hardly anything for them to take, and no reason for a search of the rest of the property. Thankfully, Papa is not home when they arrive, or the men will surely take him captive. While Mama keeps them occupied in the store, I walk as calmly as I can with a basket of clothes out to the line. Hanging a blue towel at its end, I pray Papa will remember our warning signal and stay away. As the men leave, they walk right by me. One man tips his cap in my direction.

Then, I hear him say to the captain, "Such poverty stricken, wretched women. What will become of them when all their men are captured and gone?"

I cannot help but wonder the same thing myself.

It is not long before the Confederate troops find their way to our store as well. This time, Mama makes sure that they get the supplies they need. Private Robert Watson comes first, sailing to the store before daylight from the camp at Shaw's Point.

"Ma'am, I'd be obliged if you could spare some beef. We have sixty hungry men guarding the entrance of the river and nothing to feed them."

Papa butchers a cow, and Private Watson returns to camp with over two hundred pounds of meat. The next day, he brings his commander, Captain Mulrennan. Mama invites them into the parlor and offers them weak coffee made of parched corn.

"Julia," Papa requests. "Bring out the whiskey. These men need more to fortify them than that."

Mama does so reluctantly. Some day, that might be all the medicine we have. Why squander it in drink now? When the men down their glasses so eagerly, she cannot deny them a second round.

"Is there anything else we can do for you gentlemen?" she

asks as they leave.

"Pray for us, Mother Jose," Private Watson requests. "We leave for Tampa tonight and from there, who knows where we will be sent."

"That I will do, Private Watson," Mama replies. "I will not forget."

I see the sadness in my mother's eyes and know she thinks of the day coming soon, when she will send her own husband off to war. When Captain Mulrennan's men leave for Tampa, we feel the presence of the Federal troops even more. They seize a barge full of molasses from Archibald McNeill and the schooner *Ariel* from Mr. Curry. William is lucky that he is not aboard that day. Now, with the ship on which he made his living gone, there is nothing standing in his way to join the army but the birth of his child. On March 5, over Mary's protests, he joins a group of other Manatee men on a trip to Tampa to enlist. They become part of the Fourth Florida Regiment under General Braxton Bragg and pledge to serve for three years or the duration of the war.

Though Papa wants to go with him, I suspect he is waiting for his grandchildren to be born before he enlists. When he learns of William's impending fatherhood, Captain Robert Smith sends him home on leave. Mary is so grateful to see him that she clings to him and weeps. He also brings news of Michael.

"He was sent to Tallahassee for training."

A lump in my throat prevents me from asking, but William knows what I want to hear.

Kindly he adds, "No word on Niihaasi. I had hoped that he might have sold her in Tampa and gotten a different mount." He shakes his head. "But, no one has seen her so he must have taken her with him."

I resign myself to the fact that I will never see Niihaasi again. I take solace in the coming baby though I grow anxious and weary as my body expands. I cannot rest during the night and am uncomfortable during the day. It seems like my stomach gets in my way every time I try to do anything. According to Mama, it will be any day before I feel the pangs of labor.

"I think the baby has dropped," she adds.

I wonder when my child will choose to make its entry into this world. At night, I lie awake and feel it move within my belly. I try not to fret, but cannot help but remember a childhood memory. The day Mary's mother gave birth. And the day that Mary's mother died.

I was only four when Aunt Monica, Uncle Franz and Mary came to live with us. Monica was pregnant and unused to living in the wilderness of Florida. It fell to me to take care of Mary and help Mama while Uncle Franz and Papa went to the Land Office in Newnansville to file homestead papers. Mama was teaching me to milk the cow, and when we returned to the house we found Aunt Monica sprawled across the hallway arms clenched around her belly. Red liquid seeped from beneath her nightgown. In the corner, Mary huddled in fear, clutching a blanket.

"Eliza! Listen to me! You must take Mary outside. Get a loaf of bread and some butter. Take a mug of milk and give her something to eat. Do not come back to the house until I come to get you!"

When I protested, Mama shouted, "Now Eliza! Go now!"

I scrambled past where Aunt Monica lay on the floor moaning in pain. "The baby, the baby is coming early."

I ducked into the kitchen, grabbed the supplies Mama told me to retrieve and took Mary by the hand. Practically dragging her out the front door, I looked back to see Mama picking up Aunt Monica and helping her back to the bedroom. Aunt Monica's nightgown was soaked with blood, and she doubled over in pain.

"Mama? What else can I do Mama?" I asked.

"Pray Eliza. Pray like you have never prayed before."

"Julia, oh Julia. What will become of my baby?" Aunt Monica sobbed.

Mary's hysteria drew my attention. I couldn't help Aunt Monica give birth to the new baby, but I could at least help take care of this one. I pulled Mary away from the house. Afraid and confused, she refused to cooperate. Over one of my arms dangled a cloth sack filled with a loaf of bread and bacon Mama fried for the breakfast. In that same hand, I held a mug of milk. While wrestling with Mary, I spilled some on my dress. The bag smacked against my leg when I walked. Finally, I quit battling Mary and left her sitting with her blanket in the middle of the path crying while I ran to the spring, put down my burdens and went back for my still sobbing cousin. Taking her to the edge of the spring, I used my apron as a towel, dipping it the cool water and washing Mary's tear streaked face. Intrigued by the water, she calmed.

I worried that Mama would forget about us. Would she remember with the excitement of the new baby's arrival? Hours passed until Mama came. For a time, the shadows hid her face, but as she came closer, I realized she was crying.

"Is everything alright, Mama? Is the new baby here?"

"Yes, Eliza. She has come. But, I need your help some more. I need you to be a big girl. Can you do that Eliza?" Mama sounded very sad.

I was afraid.

"Mama, what's wrong?"

"I have something I need to do outside. Eliza, bring Mary back to the house. I need you to sit with Aunt Monica and come get me if she needs me."

"What are you going to do Mama?"

Mama did not answer, but beckoned for me to follow bringing Mary with me. Eager to return to the house, Mary did not fight me this time, but Mama's footsteps were slow. I did not know what to think.

"Is Aunt Monica alright, Mama?"

"I think so. I don't know for sure. It was a long difficult birth. I have done my best to make her comfortable. Come inside. Give Mary to me for a moment."

Mama allowed Mary a peek inside the bedroom. The little girl strained for her mother, but Mama held her tightly.

"Your mama's sleeping, Mary. Now it is time for Mary to sleep, too. Be a good girl and go upstairs with Eliza. When you wake up, you shall see your Mama."

I looked around the doorway, as well and could see my aunt lying quietly on the bed. Her face was pale, and her hands were still.

"Is she sleeping?" I whispered.

"Yes, Eliza. Now take Mary upstairs. When she falls asleep, come back downstairs and sit with Aunt Monica. I will be out back, call me if she wakes up."

"But, Mama, where is the baby?"

"She is sleeping, too Eliza. Now, go do what I said."

I pulled and prodded a reluctant Mary up the stairs and put her on her pallet. She refused to lie down calling for her Mama instead. I tried to quiet her.

"Don't wake your mother," I begged. Finally, I bribed Mary by letting her hold my rag doll. I patted her back until she went to sleep just like Papa often rubbed mine. All the while, I wished Papa would come home. Something wasn't right. Mama was too sad, but I knew Papa would make everything better. Papa could fix anything.

With Mary finally asleep, I tiptoed back downstairs. Aunt Monica was still under the covers. I looked around the room for the baby. There she was in the little cradle beside the bed. Papa made that cradle long before I was born. He told stories of my three older brothers who had used it as did I. I never knew my brothers. They all died of smallpox before I was born and we left

Germany. Mama said they were in heaven now.

This little baby looked just like a china doll that I saw once in a store in Fort Brooke. What would they name her? Perfectly formed. What a tiny little nose and sweet mouth. Her eyes were closed, and little black curls covered her head. Her skin was tinged a faint bluish color. I reached out and touched the baby's face ever so gently. She was cold. Perhaps, she needed another blanket.

Behind me, I heard a faint gasp as Mama entered the room.

"Eliza," she murmured and placed her hands on my shoulders.

"She's cold, Mama. She needs another blanket."

"No, Eliza. She is not cold. She is nice and warm and in heaven with the angels."

Heaven? Heaven was for dead people. *Wasn't the baby just sleeping?*

Mama continued, "The baby died, Eliza."

I felt the air escape out of me in a rush. *Dead! How? God let this sweet little baby die? Hadn't I prayed that everything would be alright? What would Aunt Monica do without her baby?*

"Is Aunt Monica dead too?" I asked.

"No Aunt Monica is alive. She is exhausted and needs to sleep. She does not yet know that her daughter is dead."

No wonder Mama was so distressed. Tears welled up in my eyes as Mama picked up the baby and held her close. She wrapped her tightly in a blanket covering her all over even her little face. Then, she turned to leave the room.

"Where are you going, Mama? Where are you taking the baby?"

"I must bury her, Eliza. In this heat, she will not last."

"Bury her? In the ground?"

"Yes, now stay here with Aunt Monica until I return."

"Did you dig a hole, Mama?"

Mama did not turn around. She kept walking with careful,

measured steps. I thought Mama could hardly pick her feet up and set them down again. Her back stooped as she cradled the baby.

"Yes, Eliza. Now no more questions. I will be back soon." Numb and frightened, I sat down in a chair next to Aunt Monica's bedside and wept silently for the cousin I never knew and for my mother as she buried the baby in the dark, damp ground.

Aunt Monica did not wake up the rest of the day nor the next. Though Mama stayed close beside her bathing her face and talking to her, she never again opened her eyes. Uncle Franz and Papa arrived home just in time to save Mama from burying her own sister alone.

I held Papa's hand as we stood next to a mound of dirt that marked Aunt Monica's grave. Next to it was a smaller mound already covered in a thin layer of grass. Uncle Franz wept while little Mary, exhausted from sorrow, rested her head on her father's shoulder and went to sleep. Soon, after, Uncle Franz died of a fever, and Mary became an orphan.

I remember those days as though they were yesterday. As I wait for my own child's arrival, I wonder what might happen and imagine my parents once again standing next to a tiny grave and a larger one that could be mine.

My labor begins on the morning of April 18. At first, I think I must have slept wrong for when I wake, my back aches. As I set the table for breakfast, I absentmindedly rub my spine.

Mama notices. "Is your back sore this morning?" I nod. I am surprised when Mama smiles.

"We might be getting a baby today."

"Today? I'm not ready. I still have to finish knitting that blanket."

"Mmm, then, you better get to it. I think you are going into labor."

I feel restless and out of sorts.

"What do I do?"

"Just keep working. That's the best thing for you. Keeping your body active and moving will make the delivery come faster and easier."

Mama just doesn't want me to take it easy today. I have been lazy lately, but that doesn't mean I won't help when I am needed. I doubt a little backache signals the beginning of labor. Two hours later, when I bend over to put a chicken in the oven to roast, I feel a trickle of liquid run down my leg. Startled, I look down just as a rush of water falls to the kitchen floor.

"See, I was right," Mama says matter of factly, while I remain rooted in the same spot. What should I do now?

"That baby's coming. You're going to be a mama, today."

A mama. Suddenly I feel panic. The image of that sweet still face of Aunt Monica's baby comes to my mind. *What will this day hold for me? Will my baby be alright? Will tomorrow find me holding my own child or standing by a little grave? Please God, please let my baby live.* Mama sees the stricken expression on my face.

She says gently, "You will be fine and so will your baby. He's a fighter and so are you."

She takes me by the arm.

"Now, go put on some clean clothes and we will walk. That is the best thing for you right now."

We stroll down to the river to where Papa stands on the landing. The sail is up on the yawl.

"And what brings you lovely ladies down this way? Did you know I was about to leave and come to see me off?"

He reaches down to untie the lines.

"I'm going across the river to Manatee to pick up a load of shingles from Reverend Lee. Henry will need them before long to replace the roof of the Terra Ceia cabin. Soon, they will be impossible to find."

The thought lies unspoken between us all. There will be no more shingles because any day there will be no men left in the settlement to cut them.

"Joseph," Mama says softly. "I would prefer you go over to Shaw's Point instead of Manatee today."

Papa frowns.

"Reverend Lee said he would sell me 1,000 shingles for $10.00. I'm surprised that he will let them go that cheaply, the old skinflint. I need to get them today before he changes his mind."

"The shingles will have to wait. We need you to go to Shaw's Point. It is time to fetch Granny Tinsley."

The blood drains out of Papa's face.

"Granny Tinsley? It is time?"

At that precise moment, my first real labor pain arrives.

"Oh," I groan and grab my stomach bending forward. "Oh!"

"Now, Joseph," Mama says calmly.

As Papa scrambles into the boat, she turns to me.

"Breathe, Eliza. Take a breath. The pain will be gone in a moment." When it eases, Mama takes my arm again. "Come, let's walk some more."

We walk back and forth between the river's edge and the house until the pains come harder and faster. I long to rest and beg Mama to let me go to bed.

Finally, when the midwife, Granny Tinsley, arrives, she orders me to Mama's bedroom where I will give birth. She sends Mama to the kitchen for hot water and soap. I am grateful for Granny Tinsley's presence. As she helps me bathe, she chats about some of the births she has attended.

Once clean, I curl up on the bed. The pains come one right after each other now. There is hardly time to recover before another one hits. I writhe in agony. *When will it be over?*

"Almost time, Eliza," Granny Tinsley strokes my forehead.

I am so hot.

"Do I have a fever?"

So many women have died from childbed fever.

"Eliza, don't borrow trouble. The heat is to be expected.

Nothing unusual," she wipes my head with a cool cloth. "You are doing fine. It won't be long before you hold your little one."

Mama paces anxiously about the room.

"Madam Joe. Settle down, settle down. Don't get your daughter upset. I will tell you when you can help. In the meantime, go get more hot water for me, please."

When Mama leaves, Granny Tinsley smiles. "It is hardest on the grandma's I do believe. We know what you are going through and don't we wish we could take the work for you?"

I cannot help but arch off the bed when the most intense wave I have felt so far grips my insides. It feels like someone reaches through my skin twisting my belly in two. I think I may die. Visions of Aunt Monica's death flood my mind.

"Tell my parents I love them. Tell them to raise my baby," I moan.

"Eliza, don't be silly. You are a strong girl. Nothing is going to happen to you," reassures Granny Tinsley.

Please God, let my baby be alright.

A mind reader, Granny Tinsley adds, "Your baby will be fine as well. Now, I think it is time for you to begin pushing."

Mama reenters the room with a basin and the kettle as I scream with pain.

"Just in time, Madam Joe. I think your grandbaby is ready to come into the world."

Granny Tinsley pushes up my nightdress as Mama places thick pads of soft cotton quilts underneath me. Granny urges me down to the lower part of the bed, then, pulls my legs apart. I fight her and push her hands away.

"No, I can't do this."

"Yes, Eliza, you can," say Mama and Granny Tinsley in unison. Granny Tinsley spreads my legs apart again and stands between them.

"Now, Eliza, push. Push with all your might. You shall see your child. Now, push."

Then my brain stops thinking, and my body takes over with a desire too strong to ignore. All I can do is bear down and expel this hurt from between my legs.

I push and groan. I clinch my fists and beat against the mattress. Sometimes, I scream with anguish, but with Granny's encouragement I do as my body wills.

"I see him, I see his head," Granny cries. "Come on, Eliza. One more push and he will be out."

Then, sweet release as I feel the pressure ease and a rush of fluid between my legs.

"It's a girl!" Mama and Granny Tinsley say as one.

A girl. A daughter. A newborn's thin wail fills the room. And she lives. My eyes flood with tears. I weep in joy and relief. *My baby lives.* As Mama cleans my daughter and wraps her snuggly in a blanket, Granny Tinsley presses on my stomach.

"Oh," I groan. I thought the pain was over. "That hurts."

"I'm sorry, Eliza, but we need to get the afterbirth from you. We don't want any chance of fever." Something slimy touches my legs. "There, now you are done."

As Mama places my baby upon my chest, Granny Tinsley says, "And wasn't she worth all that pain?"

I gaze upon my tiny dark haired daughter for the first time and think, yes all the pain, all of it, even at the hands of my husband, it was all worth it. This will be Michael's only gift to me. I touch my daughter's nose. She puckers her lips and tries to suck. She begins to cry. *I will cherish you and keep you safe, I promise. You will never suffer like I have.* The baby quits crying as I cradle her in my arms. For the first time in months, I feel whole and complete. Here is the love for which I have longed.

Chapter Seventeen

Once I am presentable, Mama goes to find Papa. She ushers him into the room and over to the bed where I sit propped against the pillows.

"Come, Papa. Come meet your granddaughter."

"A girl? Julia, I was right." Turning to Mama, he says, "Grandmamma, you were wrong." He winked at me. "She was convinced it would be a boy. A girl, I said. I'm glad."

"So, what is her name to be?" Granny Tinsley asks.

I have dreamed of this day. This will make my parents so proud. I look first at Papa. "Josephine." Papa beams.

Then, I add, "Josephine Louise."

My daughter will share Mama's middle name. Mama smiles as Papa takes the baby from me.

"Well, Miss Josephine Louise," he grins down into my daughter's face. "You and I are going to get along just fine." Cradling the baby, he proclaims. "You did good, Eliza. Real good. She's a dandy."

Mama nods in agreement, and then puts her arms around Papa as he holds his namesake fast. Josephine opens her mouth in a sleepy yawn as her grandparents proudly waltz her around the room. Granny Tinsley and I laugh at the trio.

Their dance is interrupted by a loud knocking on the door.

"Madam Joe! Mr. Joe! Are you home?"

It sounds like William. Papa hands Josephine back to me, and then goes to the door. Mama hurries after him.

"Is Granny Tinsley here? They said she would be here."

"Yes, William. Calm down. She is here," Mama says.

"Mary is in labor. We need her now! I don't think we have much time."

I can't help but think. *It is just like Mary to upstage me and have her baby on the same day. Oh, how can I be so ugly to my cousin? I should be praying for Mary's safe delivery.*

Granny Tinsley goes to him. I can hear them talking outside my door.

"How great are her pains?"

"Oh, they are terrible. You must come now," William begs.

"How long has she been having them?" she asks again.

"They just started. I came right away."

"Has her water broke?"

"What? What do you mean?"

Granny laughs.

"I think we have time. Let me just tell Eliza good bye and then, I will go with you."

I know Mama is torn between staying with me and going to help Mary. I give her permission to leave.

"Mama, you go with Granny. Papa can stay here with me. We will be fine."

"Joseph, I left a chicken on the stove to cool. There is bread as well. Make sure Eliza gets something to eat. I will be back as soon as I can. Come William, lead the way."

Mama and Granny Tinsley leave with the father to be.

Despite my overwhelming love for Josephine, I feel let down and alone. *William is so excited about his baby. Oh, Josephine. I am sorry that you do not have a father to fret over you. I don't even know where your father is today.* As though he can read my thoughts, Papa takes Josephine from me. He stands in front of the mirror and holds the baby up as though she can see.

He states solemnly like a pledge, "Hello there, granddaughter. Can you see your grandpapa? We have the same name you know. I will always be here for you. You can count on me."

He kisses her on the head, and then settles down in the rocking chair.

"Eliza, I know you are tired. Get some rest. Josephine and I will be right here when you wake up."

Papa takes such good care of us. When I wake from my nap, Papa prepares supper. I eat a little, but Josephine begins to cry.

"Daughter, I think she is hungry."

"Give her to me, Papa."

I unbuttoned my nightgown and place the baby at my breast. Papa blushes and averts his eyes. Immediately, Josephine latches on and begins to nurse.

I wince. No one warned me that it would hurt so much.

"Are you alright?" Papa asks worriedly.

"Yes, this will just take some getting used to." I smile. "But Josephine seems to like it so I will learn to as well."

"Yes, daughter, she will expect a lot from you, but the first thing you will learn is that none of them will be a chore because they are done in love."

I know just what he means.

Mama does not return until the next morning. She checks on us immediately. I can see the weariness on her face.

"Is Mary alright, Mama?"

"Yes, she had a hard delivery, but she is alright."

Once again, I remember my aunt. Mary's mother. *Will the same fate await the daughter?*

"Are you sure Mama?"

"Yes, I am sure. She will need some nursing for a few days. Granny Tinsley will stay with her. I was anxious about you. It is hard to have two daughters giving birth in two days!"

So, Josephine will not share her birthday with a cousin after all.

Mama continues, "What was I thinking when I let you be married on the same day!" She laughs, "I am more worried about William. The man was beside himself with worry." Yet, my own baby has no father. I change the subject.

"And the baby?"

"Another little girl. She is tiny, but should be fine. Granny Tinsley will watch out for her. They named her Louisa. Imagine, both my girls named their babies after me."

I frown. *That is the name I chose. How can they share a name?* But, Mama is pleased, so I must not complain. Josephine stirs in her cradle next to the bed.

"Let me see this granddaughter of mine. I hardly got to hold her I left in such a rush. She is beautiful, Eliza."

Despite my love for my own daughter, I feel contrary. I want to ask if she is prettier than Mary's baby, but I do not want to upset Mama.

Instead I say, 'Why don't you go lay down? Papa has been taking good care of us. Get some rest."

"If you don't mind, I think I will. The next few days will be hectic as you girls regain your strength. I guess I will be cooking for all of us for a while."

I feel guilty. If I hadn't rushed into the marriage with Michael, I would be up and about and helping to take care of Mary. Perhaps it is I who has taken away from Mary's special day. I will try not to be a burden.

"Go get some rest, Mama," I say as I reach for my daughter. "We will be just fine."

Soon, Mama has two less plates to prepare. Despite Papa's promise to Josephine to always be there for her, he must fulfill his obligation first. When the babies are a week old, Papa goes to Tampa and enlists in the Fourth Florida Regiment. He enters as a private receiving fifty dollars and a clothing allowance every two months. I am already out of bed and helping around the house between times spent caring for Josephine.

Mary remains bedridden. Louisa's difficult birth left tears that must heal before she resumes her activities. Compounding Mary's troubles, Louisa is a difficult baby. She requires more attention than Mary can give her. Mama spends most of her day at Mary's. I understand the need, but it only fuels my jealousy. Mary always demands more than her portion of Mama's love. It is especially difficult to be left alone now that Papa is gone.

Reluctantly, William travels to Tampa as well. The regiment moves north to the battlefields of Tennessee. Even with his wife so ill, he can wait no longer. Mama promises to provide for his wife and daughter.

"Eliza, I'm sorry," she says. "I'm glad that you are so strong and able to take care of yourself. I wish I had the luxury to pamper you, but Mary needs me more."

I just keep on kneading the bread dough. Better not to say what I really feel.

"At least we are past the three days where she might get childbed fever. I think she will be alright once she becomes accustomed to William's absence."

Unlike, me, I think. I have no husband to worry over. Though still married, I have heard nothing from Michael in the four months since he rode away on Niihaasi. I wonder if he has killed any Yankees as he boasted he would to Henry. The war saddens me. To think of Papa at sixty years old drilling and preparing to shoot men that, in another time, he might welcome into his home makes me shudder. It just does not seem right. I figure I am not the only one to think so. Any mother with a son will feel the depths of the sacrifice. Some of the boys who muster into service are little more than children. Nobody asks the women though.

Looking into Josephine's face as I nurse, I am glad that my baby is a girl. The way things are going, this war might not be over for a very long time. With most of the men gone, the Federal navy tightens the blockade even more. Ships keep the river settlements from receiving anything that cannot be produced locally. I am amazed at what that means. No paper, rope, ammunition, fabrics, medicine, or manufactured goods. Rumors that the Yankees burn homes and outbuildings circulate about the area. Before he left for war, Mama asks Papa to dig a deep hole. She transferred the stock from the store there and buried it beneath the earth hoping to keep it from being stolen. Even the barrel of flour and bolts of cloth are lowered underground for safekeeping.

Once Mary can travel, Mama brings her and Louisa to the river house. That makes Mama's job easier, but does not please me. Louisa screams almost all the time. She disturbs the entire household as Mary struggles in vain to sooth her. She acts like she is hungry, but when offered the breast refuses to take it. Mama tries to feed her from a makeshift bottle. Nothing works. Not patting, rocking or walking. Louisa cannot be satisfied. Lack of sleep and the incessant crying makes everyone tense. It is bad enough that I have to wake to feed my own baby, but when Louisa wakes screaming no one can rest. I think of leaving Mary and Mama to deal with the wailing, taking Josephine and going back to Mary's house to live.

Finally, Mama consults Granny Tinsley who recommends a dose of ginger and soda in hot water. That provides some relief, but Louisa remains irritable and demanding. Josephine, however, is the perfect baby. *At least I think so.* She only cries when she is hungry. She nurses well and sleeps at regular intervals. When she wakes, she stays quiet in her crib until someone comes to care for her. *Why can't Mary teach her own daughter to do the same?*

By August, we settle into a routine. Henry comes once a week to bring fresh vegetables and meat. We are better off than many of the settlers, especially those who live in Tampa and must feed the rebel soldiers. Still, there is always the worry over the safety of Papa and William, and the question of when a company of Yankee soldiers will show up at our porch. One rainy night, just as they prepare for bed, someone hammers on the front door. The noise wakes Louisa who begins to scream.

"Shh, shh, baby," Mary begs as she jiggles her daughter and paces up and down the hall.

"Mary, take her to your room," Mama commands.

"Eliza, you and Josephine go to mine."

When we hesitate, Mama snaps, "Now, girls."

I look through a crack in the bedroom door as Mama opens the exterior one. On the porch are five Yankee soldiers.

"Yes, may I help you," she asks politely.

I marvel at her calm. She speaks as though it is neighbors come to call. A young man steps forward. The way the other soldiers treat him, he must have some rank, but I cannot tell by his uniform what it is. He takes off his hat as he enters the house.

"Ma'am, we seek shelter for the night. It is too wet for us to sleep outdoors. We would much appreciate a room and a hot meal."

"Sirs, as you can hear, we have a cranky baby in the house. I doubt you would get much rest here. However, I can offer you our store as lodging. It is quite empty these days as you are most effective at keeping any goods from reaching our home. There are no beds, but you are welcome to it if you do not mind sleeping on the floor."

The soldiers look at one another. I suspect this is not what they have in mind. Surely, they will not force us to sleep in the store.

Finally, the young man clears his throat and says, "The sound of a baby crying does not trouble me. I left my own son at home. I have not seen him or his mother in months."

"I am sorry," Mama replies. "Would you stay here in this house then?"

"No," he answers. "Perhaps, the little one will quiet if we leave. If you will be so kind as to show us the store, we can make do there. We will need something to eat, however, and a place to wash. It has been a long day."

Mama takes them to the store. Then, she returns to the house.

"Mary, for once we can be thankful that Louisa was unhappy. Eliza, is Josephine asleep?"

I nod.

"Then, come help me in the kitchen. Mary will keep an eye on the babies. We must fix them something to eat. Do we have any beef for stew?"

We work late to prepare a meal for the men. Mama will not let me serve them, but insists on carrying the food to them alone.

"Stay here. I prefer that they not see you girls at all."

When we finally blow out the last candle and go to bed, everyone sleeps soundly. Even Louisa is exhausted. Since the birth of the babies, Mary and I live downstairs to save climbing upstairs to tend to the children. Because Louisa is so sensitive, she and Mary share the spare room. I share my parents' bed with my mother. Josephine's cradle rests beside the bed where it has been since her birth.

Sometime before dawn, I wake with a start. *What is that? Someone is in the house!* I am afraid to move. *Is it the soldiers? Are they coming to steal? Are they coming for us? What should I do?* Mama reaches over to put her hand on my shoulder. She is awake. *Does she hear it too?* A gentle pat of reassurance and then, Mama lies still. She must be telling me to be quiet and not to move. The figure of a man steps quietly in the room. In the dim light, I can barely see as he tiptoes to the cradle. *Josephine! Will he harm my baby?* Again, a gentle nudge from Mama. I will myself rigid feigning sleep. *What are his plans?* With my eyes slightly opened, I watch as he bends over the cradle. He places something beside my sleeping child. Josephine, don't wake up, baby. Then, he bends down, tucks the blanket in tighter and kisses the infant on her head. Once done, he eases back out of the room.

As he turns, I can see his face. It is the young soldier who spoke for the group last night. My heart beats so fast I am sure he can hear it. He will know I am awake. He does not seem to notice, however, and moves into the hall.

I hear the door shut softly, but am afraid to move until Mama whispers. "Stay here. I will see where they are."

She rolls out of bed and slides along the wall to the window.

Peering around its edge, she says, "They are leaving. Just a few more minutes and they should be gone."

We keep our voices low.

"Mama, I was so frightened. Why do you think he came in here?"

"I am not sure, but I think that he just wanted to be near a child and give her a kiss. Perhaps he craved the sweet scent of a baby. Maybe he was pretending it was his own boy that slept in that cradle."

Yes, I suspect Mama is right. He must miss his own child dearly. Oh, if only Michael thought the same way.

When the sun finally rises and we are sure that the men were gone, I venture to see what he left in Josephine's cradle. There, tucked under the blankets, I find a five dollar gold piece. *Was it payment for their lodging? Or a father's thank you for a moment of pretense, a longing temporarily satisfied?* Even odder, when I check on the store later that morning, I discover a bolt of china silk. The beautiful colors catch my eye immediately upon entering the building. *Where did it come from?* Mama never carried such exorbitant fabric in her store. The soldiers left it, but why? I take it to the house.

"What do you suppose it means?" I ask Mama.

"Who knows with a Yankee?" Mama shrugs.

"I suppose they meant it for us, but it is too fine for clothing around here."

Mary agrees, "It is not like we will be invited to any balls."

"What shall we do with it?" I wonder.

"I don't know," Mama replies. "You found it, so you decide."

I leave the cloth in the parlor for several days. Every time I pass it, I touch its soft surface. I love the bright colors of red, green and blue. It makes me feel good to have something so pretty in the midst of this bleak time.

Mary will not leave me alone. "Have you decided yet? Perhaps we should make dresses. It would be nice to have something new."

Finally, I think of a way to use the cloth so it will be on display all the time as a reminder of the soldier's kindness. I sew curtains for the parlor and have enough left over to use in my room upstairs. It doesn't make any sense at all that curtains should give me so much pleasure, but they do. Oddly, seeing them hanging there gives me a sense of hope. Someday, life will return to normal.

In late September, word of Papa and William comes to Electa Lee through a letter from her husband. She delivers the news in person. William is now a 4th Sergeant. Papa is in a hospital in Knoxville. The doctors do not know what is wrong with him, but as soon as she hears, Mama pronounces a diagnosis.

"I told him he was too old to fight," she fumes. "Now, how will we get him home?"

For two months, he is too ill to report for duty. Finally, November 7, the army gives him discharge papers and sends him home against his will. It takes him almost another month to reach the Manatee River. A train brings him to south Georgia. From there, he walks or catches rides as he can to Cedar Key. He books passage on a small sailboat that skirts the coast and avoids the blockaders. When, he finally arrives home, I almost do not recognize him. Where has my spry, fun loving Papa gone? As he hobbles up the steps to the house, I wonder what has changed him so.

Papa does not talk about it. All he will tell us is that the surgeon, a Dr. Robards, was wrong to send him home.

"I might not have been able to withstand the marches and the battles, but I could have stayed to help. There was no need to send me all the way home," he argues.

Privately, Mama disagrees.

"It will take a lot to heal him and bring him round to his old self," she tells me, but to his face, for once, Mama holds her tongue and does not argue. Mary has many questions about William. *What is he wearing? How does he live? What is his company like?* Papa tells her as much as he can, but Mary wants to know more.

"I wish I were with him. I will go mad with curiosity. And I miss him so."

Under Mama's care, Papa becomes his old self again. Though he continues to protest his discharge, I suspect it is because he feels guilty at being home with his loved ones when most of the other men of the community are still at war. I make sure he spends plenty of time with Josephine as a reminder of his obligations at home.

Christmas is right around the corner. So much has changed since last year. I can hardly remember what life was like without the baby. There is only one baby in the house now. Mary insists on going to her own place for Christmas.

Papa sings a German Christmas carol outside the window as he sharpens his ax. I glance across the kitchen where Josephine sleeps in the cradle. Papa moved it to the kitchen this morning so I can work and keep an eye on her. It is warmer here by the stove. So far, Papa's exuberance has not awakened the eight month old. Papa always abandons his usual reserve during the Christmas season. Each year, he looks forward to the holiday with as much excitement as a child. Mama does too because of her Christmas birthday. Last year, I drifted through the season sad and alone. This year, I join in my parent's enthusiasm. It will be Josephine's first Christmas. Though the baby is too young to understand, I want it to be a special one.

With the war all around us, it seems even more important to have something to look forward to. Every day is precious, even poignant. Papa is going to do his favorite holiday task, bringing home the Christmas tree. This year, he will cut two trees. One for Mary's house and one for ours. He must find just the right ones. Mama is particular. She scoffs at the red cedars found in the Florida landscape. Even after years of living on the Florida coast, they still compare unfavorably to the sturdy pines and firs of Germany. When Papa announces his plans to seek the trees, Mama snorts and mutters under her breath about the pitiful example he is sure to bring home. I laugh. It is a game they play every year. I am sure Papa will be gone a long time in an effort to prove Mama wrong. The singing grows faint as he leaves to find an evergreen strong enough to support the candle stubs Mama saves all year long.

I hum the carol softly, check the fire in the stove and slide the last pan of gingerbread cookies in the oven. The treats will double as tree decorations along with Mama's old glass balls. I cannot bake as many as we used to in years past. The flour in the barrel that Mama buried is dry and moldy. I scrape it off the sides and then, sift through it to find enough to use. Sugar is hard to find. The Federal troops destroyed all the cane mills including Gamble's large one. All I have is the rough brown sugar that we make at home in our own kettle. None of the fine white sugar is available this year for baking. Not that anyone really cares. Life and death seem to be all anyone really thinks about these days.

News of the war trickles into Manatee slowly. It will be harder to win than anyone thought a year ago. The fighting takes place far from home in places of which I never heard. Pea Ridge, Arkansas. Shiloh, Tennessee. Bull Run, Virginia. Fredericksburg, Virginia. Every time I hear of a battle, I wonder. *Is Michael there? What about Niihaasi? Is my little mare even still alive?* Some of the men in the Confederate Army manage to slip home for visits occasionally. The war news that they bring with them circulates through the community in whispers until it is hard to separate fact from fiction.

I recall a conversation I overheard outside the store just a week ago. Though we do not have much to sell, people still come in hopes of finding supplies and news. I dust the flour from my hands as if to shake off the words spoken so loudly it was obvious that they were meant for me to hear.

"She filed for divorce, you know. Accused him of unfaithfulness. But, he says he was disappointed in her. She wasn't much of a wife to him. Sick all the time, you know."

"I heard he is back in Tampa. Came home on leave. Says he wants to see that baby girl and make sure it is his."

Over the past few days, the humiliation of that moment has turned to anger. I pull the cookies from the oven and shut the stove with such a vengeance that the smokestack rattles. *What kind of a man would say that about his wife?* Then, the anger gives way to fear for I know just what sort of soul my husband possesses. The thought that he might be in the area fills me with dread. *Please God, don't let it be true. Keep him away from me. And Josephine as well. Keep us both safe. Please God.*

The sound of footsteps on the path outside of the kitchen interrupt my prayer. In an effort to recapture the holiday sprit, I rush to the door to welcome Papa inside.

"Did you forget something? You're back so soon!" I call before stopping in horror. Michael stands on the steps.

"Soon? Has the year gone by so fast for you then, dear Eliza? I assure you that it seemed like an eternity to me."

He leans against the doorframe blocking the only way of escape. I eye him warily and glance around the room looking for some means of defense. The cradle is hidden in the shadows. I must keep Josephine's presence a secret.

"Michael, Merry Christmas!" I insert a false note of gaiety in my voice, but Michael frowns.

"I saw your father leave. And your mother is at your cousin's as well. Anyone else around?"

I back away. He watched me and waited for a chance to catch me alone. I knock over a chair as I scramble out of his way. The noise wakes Josephine who begins to cry. Michael startles.

With a few long strides, he reaches the cradle before I can stop him. He grabs his daughter and lifts her into the light.

"Well, what do we have here? Whose brat is this?"

Michael prevents me from rescuing Josephine by holding her out of reach. I know not to let Michael see my tears. Pleading only fuels his anger.

With calm I do not feel, I say, "Michael, let me introduce you to your daughter. This is Josephine. Hand her to me so I can show you."

The baby's frightened wails drown out my words. With his child dangling in the air from one hand, Michael reaches for a knife he wears at his belt.

"Quiet!" he yells. "Be quiet now!"

In one frantic move, I leap forward and wrestle the baby from Michael's grasp. From the cradle, I grab a piece of cheesecloth wrapped around a lump of sugar and thrust one end in Josephine's mouth. Immediately, the pacifier calms her. Her screaming stops. The kitchen is silent.

"Put her down," Michael orders in a low voice.

Afraid to refuse, I obey and gently placed my daughter back in the cradle. Please God keep her safe. Please God, I pray. Take me if you must, but save her. Michael waves the knife in my face.

"Such a good mother you are, Eliza. How about showing me some of that affection? It has been a long time, hasn't it, dear?"

He spits out the words. Dear. Has he ever held me dear? Michael presses the knife against my throat. I feel its sharp edge cut into my flesh, but I ignore the pain. I must divert Michael's attention away from Josephine. My legs feel like jelly, but I have to protect my baby. I stand rigid and unyielding when Michael reaches out to stroke my hair. I refuse to look at him or respond. Michael slaps me. Still, I will not cry. I have been here before. I know what is expected. Take me, Michael, I think. Take me, but leave the baby alone. He strikes me again and again. I can no longer stand and fall in a heap on the rough floor. The taste of iron fills my mouth as blood drips from my nose down my face. My left eye swells shut, and my ears ring from the impact of the blows. I finally understand, this time, Michael will not stop until he kills me.

Then, the beating ends. What is he doing now? Has he changed his mind? Through my one good eye, I see Michael unbuttoning his pants. I know what he plans to do. Involuntarily, I flinch as he comes towards me.

"I've dreamed of this for a year. I vowed to make you pay for your accusations. I was the laughingstock of Manatee and Tampa. If you thought I mistreated you before, you were sorely wrong. I will show you pain now."

His fist smashes the side of my head, slamming it into the floor, and the world goes blissfully dark as I retreat into unconsciousness.

I wake to smell burning gingerbread. Then, a baby's cries followed by a shout from outdoors. Michael stands and reaches for his knife. He turns towards the door. I summon my last ounce of strength and kick him in the back. As he loses his balance, Michael steadies himself placing his palm on the top of the hot stove. His screams blend with Josephine's.

Papa enters the room and aims his gun at Michael who is doubled over with pain. I struggle to rise and pull my skirt around me as I stumble to the cradle. With a bloody hand, I gently rock the baby.

"I should have killed you over a year ago," Papa says quietly. "I did not, and I will not today. But, I warn you. If you ever come here again. If you ever touch my daughter or my granddaughter again, I will not hesitate. You will be a dead man, Dickens."

With his gun, he motions for Michael to go.

When Michael attempts to retrieve his belongings, Papa commands him, "Leave it! Now go!"

Cradling his injured hand, Michael turns and glares at me.

"You and I aren't finished yet!" he growls.

"Go, before I shoot!" Papa shouts.

With one last look, Michael exits the kitchen. I will never forget the hatred in his eyes. *Where is the love that used to shine there for me?* I collapse into a chair, put my head on the table and weep.

"Liza," Papa's quiet voice calms me. "Eliza, look here. Let me clean your face."

Papa takes a rag and dips it into a basin of warm water. Gently, he dabs at my nose, mouth and eye wiping away the blood. Then, he applies a paste of flour and salt to my cheek.

"This will sting, daughter. I am sorry, but it will stop the bleeding."

I cry out as the concoction burns my wounds. He rummages for herbs on Mama's shelves and makes a poultice for my eye.

"Hold this tight to ease the swelling," he instructs.

I notice that his hands tremble. I take one in my own.

"Papa, thank you for saving me." Tears flow down his cheeks.

"Did you get the trees so soon? Why did you come?"

"Daughter," Papa chokes on his words. "I do not know what prompted me. I was only thinking of finding the right tree. Then, a wave of anxiety washed over me. I could not get you out of my mind. Something did not feel right. I came as fast as I could. I'm sorry that I was too late to protect you."

"He would have killed me." I am surprised I can say it so calmly. "And Josephine as well. Papa, I prayed. God sent you. I know He did."

"I am sure of that as well. Come, let's go to the house. You need to rest, and I need to sit down and hold my granddaughter for a moment."

Papa lifts Josephine out of the cradle, holds her in one arm and with his other, helps me up and out of the kitchen. As I limp down the steps towards the house, I think about what just happened. Nothing has changed. I am right back where I started from, broken and bleeding from Michael's hand. *Is it possible that he will crush my heart again? Yes, he has.* Then, I think. There is one difference. This time, I know for a fact. *God saved me.* I don't know why, but He did.

Two months later, I ponder God's plan. Henry told me over and over that God loves me, but, now, I wonder if instead He is mocking me. As I rock Josephine to sleep, I know what I have suspected for some time. For a reason that I cannot fathom, God chose once again to give me a gift forced in violence. Sometime in the fall, Josephine will have a little brother or a sister. Instead of a husband's tenderness, I will have another child to love. *But, why, oh, why must I always look upon my children and ever be reminded of my failures?*

Chapter Eighteen

As I wait on the birth of my second child, I find some comfort in the fact that I do not feel so ill this time. Perhaps some of my problems with Josephine related to the disease Michael shared with me. If difficult pregnancies are related to anxiety, I should be flat on my back again. My nose heals with only a small bump to mark Michael's latest beating, but the attack disturbs the peace I feel since Josephine's birth. I never feel safe anymore and live with the fear that Michael will return at any moment. Then again, maybe my good health comes from the fact that I am just too busy to be sick.

By the winter of 1863, Federal troops control the coastal areas of southwest Florida. Though Floridians refuse to admit it, the Confederacy's power is gone. With the Union soldiers and sailors stationed at Fort Myers to the south, nothing goes in or out of the Manatee River without their knowledge. Many of the other settlers are hungry. I am grateful that Papa and Henry work so hard to care for our family. I have mixed feelings towards the Federal troops.

While they are bent upon their work of crippling the south's economy, my encounters with the individual solders are often pleasant. On May 24, a Captain of the Union forces stationed at the river brings a wooden box to our house. I assume he expects us to fill it with supplies and begin making a list in my head of what we can spare. It will not be much. With five adults and two children to feed, there is never enough to go around. I am glad that Papa is out on the island helping Henry with the crops. The soldier could force him to take the oath of loyalty to the United States or go to jail. Mama cautiously greets him at the door.

"Ma'am," he says as he sets the box down on the porch steps

and removes his hat. I see that instead of being empty, the box is full of packages.

"Today is my wife's birthday. It is easy to remember because it is Queen Victoria's as well." *What did that have to do with us?*

"I miss my wife and wish I were with her to give her a present today. It struck me that there were other women here in this area who might substitute. I know there is much need because of the work that we are required to do."

Mama nods in agreement.

"So, I brought this gift for you. Will you accept it in place of my wife? It would ease my longing a bit to know that I could help you."

"Why thank you sir. That is most kind. I would be honored to take it. But, I must give you a gift in return. I am sure that it has been a long time since you had any fresh meat or vegetables. Perhaps some chicken and potatoes to take with you as you go?"

After Mama repays his courtesy, the Captain bows and returns to his ship.

I am curious about the exchange. "Why did you return his favor, Mama? Isn't a gift something given with no need to reciprocate?"

"In this case, I did not feel comfortable taking something for nothing. Even though he offered, I could not in good conscience take something from a Yankee when they have brought such harm to our community." Mama bends to pick up the box. "Besides how do you think your father would feel if I accepted such a gift?"

I did not think of Papa's feelings.

Mama smiles, "Still, let us see what our northern friend brought us."

As we unwrap the parcels, I feel as though he has given us diamonds and jewels. Bacon, cheese, sugar, flour and spices are luxuries unavailable to us because of the blockade. It has been so long since we had cake. Oh, how nice it will be to bake again. I am glad for such a wise mother. How sad it would have been to refuse such a gift.

We use the extra supplies sparingly. In September, we still have enough sugar saved to sweeten Granny Tinsley's tea while she coaches me through childbirth once again. But, we need not have set it aside, for when my pains begin, there is no time to fetch the midwife. Even though this is my second baby, the intensity of the contractions is surprising. This time, there is no building through the day. One moment I am fine, hanging clothes on the line while Josephine plays in the grass at my feet, and the next, pain rips through me so gripping that I cannot breathe. Fortunately, Mama is nearby in the kitchen.

Once the cramping eases, I call, "Mama!"

Josephine mimics me. "Mama, mama."

Mama sticks her head out the window and comes outside.

Scooping Josephine up in her arms, she says, "It is time then?"

"Yes," I pant. "Mama, this is odd. My labor just started, yet I feel the need to push already. Oh," I moan again as another wave washes over me. "I may have this baby out here in the yard."

Papa is not near the house, and I beg Mama not to go and look for him.

"The kitchen, Eliza. If the baby is coming as fast as you say, we should go to the kitchen. I have some water on the stove. Hurry."

As much as I want to, I cannot rush. For every step, I take the pressure builds. Mama goes ahead of me and settles Josephine in her high chair with a spoon and bread crusts to amuse her. Then, she races back to assist me. With her arm around my waist, she almost carries me into the kitchen. There is no time for a bath or conversation as when Josephine was born. Instead, Mama sweeps everything off the table in an instant.

"Pull up your skirt and stretch out on the table, Eliza. I am sorry there is no time to get you to the house. I wish there were a mattress or pillow for your head."

I don't care. I just want to bring this baby into the world. I want it now. Mama reaches down between my legs.

"Oh, my! Eliza, his head is almost out. Push now. God help us. This baby will not wait."

After only one excruciatingly long contraction while I bear down with all my might, the baby drops into Mama's hands.

"Another girl, Eliza. The spitting image of Josephine."

But this baby does not cry like Josephine had. Mama pats her on the back, holds her upside down and still she does not breathe. I know it is seconds, but it seems like hours pass.

Somewhere in the background, Josephine bangs her spoon and says, "Mama, mama." Then, in desperation, Mama reaches into the baby's mouth and with one finger sweeps the back of her throat. The baby coughs once, and then makes a tiny bleat.

"She lives, Eliza."

Exhausted, I put my head back onto the table. As the fear eases, I begin to tremble violently.

"You will catch a chill. Just a minute, let me wrap her up in a towel."

Mama swaddles the baby and places her on the table. Then, she pulls me to a sitting position and helps me to stand. The afterbirth slides down my leg and puddles on the floor.

"Can you walk to the house?" I nod but my teeth chatter together. *Why am I so cold?* It is not winter.

Mama struggles to carry the baby and encourages Josephine to walk beside her. She begs to be carried as well and cannot understand why this newcomer takes her place in Mama's arms. Once settled into bed with two quilts pulled around me, my tremors ease. Josephine insists on getting into the bed with me and curls up under the covers at my side. The baby is very quiet even as Mama bathes her and wraps her in a clean blanket.

"Is she still breathing?" I ask afraid of what Mama may say.

"Yes, she seems healthy enough." Mama smiles and hands her to me.

"Perhaps she knows what an ordeal she just put you through. She was in an awfully big hurry to get into this world. Now that she has had her way, she is content."

I stare at my new daughter as I hold her close. Yes, she does seem perfect. At times during my pregnancy, I wondered how I could have enough love to share with two children. Now, I know there is no limit to a mother's love as my heart swells with affection for this tiny one.

Josephine reaches across and pats her sister on her head.

"Baby," she says.

"What will her name be?" Mama asks.

"Julia. Julia Ellen. For her grandmother who brought her into the world. What would I do without you, Mama? Thank you."

"No, it is I who must thank you, Eliza. As well as God who is responsible for that first breath she took. I did not think it would happen for a while." Mama places her hand upon the baby's head.

"Welcome Julia. Welcome to our family."

Once more, I escape the threat of childbed fever. In less than a week, I leave my bed and resume my housework. I have two healthy babies and much to be thankful for when Thanksgiving arrives. Yet, the holidays hold a touch of melancholy for me. In the last two years, Christmas has been a time of anguish and remembering Michael's cruelty. After Josephine's birth, I wondered how I would raise a baby without a father. Now, I pray that neither of my daughters will ever come to know him.

Just before Christmas, I receive word that my prayers may have been answered. Last I heard, Michael served with the First Florida Cavalry. In intense fighting on November 23 at the Battle of Missionary Ridge, his unit voluntarily dismounts and joins with the infantry in the worst of the battle. Over 6,000 Confederate soldiers are dead, wounded or missing when the battle ends. Likely Michael is one of them. I don't know how to feel. *Relief or sorrow?* Instead of focusing on Michael's whereabouts, I grieve more for the loss of my little grey mare and wonder if she survived the battle. Yet, no word comes about either of them.

Christmas of 1863 is subdued. Only Josephine is excited about the arrival of St. Nicholas. News of a skirmish at Myakka the week before brings the threat of fighting closer to home. Provisions are low. While we have plenty of meat and vegetables, the last of the Captain's gift are finally gone. The girls outgrow their dresses but the fabric buried in the yard is too ruined for clothing. Added to the mix is Mary's frantic worrying over William. He, too, was at Missionary Ridge, and Mary has heard nothing from him. When she arrives for Christmas dinner with Louisa, I am shocked by her appearance. Thin and pale, she is not taking care of her hair or clothing. *How could the once pretty and vivacious girl have come to this ghost like appearance?*

"Mama," I whisper as we carry food from the kitchen to the house. "I think we had best ask Mary to move back in with us. I do not think she is taking care of herself."

Mama agrees, but Mary refuses to stay the night.

"I want to be at home. That is where William will come when he returns. I do not want to miss him."

No amount of arguing can convince her that William will know to come for her at the river house.

After dinner, Mama tells Papa to take Josephine and Louisa out of the house for a while. I help Mama light the candles on the tree while Mary sits stone-faced in a chair. This kind of behavior I understand. *Wasn't that me just two years before?* I urge my cousin to participate in the preparations but she sits lifeless staring out the window. A few packages are scattered under the tree for the children. Mama opens the door and calls them.

"Josephine, Louisa, come see! St. Nicholas was here."

The girls run into the room with their grandfather not far behind. Josephine takes one look at the decorations, puts her hands on her hips and bursts into tears.

"Why is she crying?" Mama asks in surprise.

I hand Julia to Mama and pick up Josephine.

Holding my daughter on my hip, I say, "Look, Josey, see the lights and the gifts?"

But, she only cries louder.

"What is wrong darling?" I ask and smooth her hair out of her eyes.

"Sanic? Where sanic?"

Papa laughs, "She is looking for St. Nicholas. I told her he would come." He reaches out and takes her from me.

"We missed him, baby. Maybe next year. Now, let's see what pretty things he left for you."

Papa takes her to the base of the tree where he hands out the few packages. Louisa joins them, and the threesome laugh together in merriment. Mama passes Julia back to me, and I snuggle her close. These are happy memories for a change. I remember Mary still sitting unsmiling in the chair. Well, happy for most of us. Because I remember how deeply the hurt runs on this day when you are lonely and afraid, I cross the room to Mary, put my hand on her back and pat her gently. Perhaps the new year will be a better one.

Not until February does Mary finally hear from William. He sends her a letter telling of his decision to transfer from the Army to the Navy. Along with him is Robert Watson, the young private who came for beef on that early morning so long ago. They are assigned to the Savannah Squadron and will serve on the ironclad *CSS Savannah*. Mary is relieved.

"William will be safer on the boats. He knows how to be a sailor. This is good."

Almost immediately, her appearance improves. She looks

better and color returns to her cheeks.

"I still miss him, Eliza," she confides. "Sometimes, I think I will burst for the longing. I don't know why he has not been able to get some leave to come home. But, as long as he is safe, I will get by."

What if something happens to William? I fear Mary might lose her mind. I know what anxiety and dread can do to a woman. There is much to fear even in our own backyard. The babies, now almost two and six months wear clothes made over from some of my blouses. I have only one dress still of any service. I wince when I think of the soldier's comments about our wretched and poverty stricken appearance at the beginning of the war. *What would he think of us now?*

The Union forces are victorious at least on the coast of Florida. Egmont Key is their stronghold. While the Confederates take the lens from the lighthouse, its location is still key to control of Tampa Bay. By May, the Federals capture Tampa. They require all men still in the town to take the oath of loyalty or face imprisonment. Papa stays longer and longer at the farm on Terra Ceia. At least there, he is isolated and has some measure of security. The Yankees look more kindly on a woman alone anyway.

In an effort to lower morale among settlers, the Union commanders place a troop of black soldiers at Manatee. More and more runaway slaves join the Union army. To Eliza and my family, their presence makes little difference until one afternoon in August when Henry comes to see Papa. It rains, a hard blowing storm, but as always, Henry is uncomfortable in the house. Even when Papa insists he come into the parlor, he prefers to remain on the porch. The girls take their naps, while I sit with Papa and Henry as they talk. Mist from the rain feels good on the hot summer afternoon.

"Mister Joe, I come to say good bye."

Oh, no. Where will he go? Henry is a good friend and wise

counselor. I cannot imagine my life without him.

"I suspected you would be going soon, Henry. I do not blame you for leaving us."

"I promised to stay an' help the women while you was gone. I promised to keep Miss Liza safe. But, you home now. Mister Dickens, he gone. I been true to my word, but it time to move on."

I long to beg him to stay, but Henry is right. He fulfilled his obligations to our family long ago. Perhaps, he will find his own family now. That thought comforts me.

"Where will you go, Henry?" I ask.

"First, I'm goin' off to war. Now that you be home, Mister Joe and Mister William in the navy, I can fight with good conscience. I don' have to fear comin' 'cross you on the battlefield."

"Oh, Henry. Be safe, will you?"

"Yesm' Miss Liza. I gots lots to live for. You know that by now, don't you?"

I think of my girls.

"Yes, Henry, I do. Now, I do. What about your family? Will you go look for them?"

"Onest I finish the job makin' sure my people are free, then, I go huntin' them down."

Mama comes out on the porch with a fussy Julia.

Henry nods towards the child, "Got some babies of my own need rocking."

"Mama, Henry is leaving. He is going off to fight."

"Then, we cannot send you off empty handed. I will pack you some food to take. It is only fair that you should share in the bounty you helped to give us all these years."

Mama hands the still groggy Julia to me.

"I will go and gather a few tools for you to take as well. Some rope and an ax. I think I have a knife to spare as well," says Papa.

He pulls his hat over his head and darts out into the rain.

"Miss Liza, I been prayin' God'd provide a chance to talk 'lone with you. Looks like He done answer me." His eyes fall on Julia. The baby is back asleep. "She's a beauty Miss Liza."

"Would you like to hold her, Henry?"

"Yesm' what a blessin' that would be." I hand Julia to him, and he cradles her gently.

"What was it you wanted to tell me, Henry?"

"Miss Liza, I prolly will not see you gain. At least in this world. But, I want you to remember all I tole you. Remember God. How much He love you. Teach those baby girls to love Him, too."

"Oh, Henry. I know you say God loves me. Sometimes I feel it too. When He protects me or when I call out to Him, He is so close to me. But, mostly, I don't know. I don't see how He could love me. When I look for Him like you told me to, I don't find Him. I don't think He is listening, Henry."

A big crash of thunder rattles the porch. I jump, and Henry laughs.

"Oh, He be speaking Miss Liza. Sometimes, he just don't talk in a shout. Just cause God's silent, don't mean He's absent, Miss Liza."

"But, why can't I feel Him? If He is as strong and as powerful as you say. Surely I should feel Him. All I feel is lost and alone most times."

I didn't add, I wish I felt like He loved me, but Henry knows me well.

"Feelins don' mean nothin'. They come and go. But, God, now He always, always the same. He there, whether you feel Him or not. Like I say, He always love you."

"But if He's there, then why do so many bad things happen to me? Not just to me, but other people too? How can God really be there when so much evil takes place?"

"Miss Liza, I know you been hurt. I see it. There loads of wicked folk in this worl'. Just cause bad happen don't mean there ain't a God. Hurtin' just be part of this worl'. Sometime it rain and sometime the sun do shine. God in it all."

Thinking of Judge Glazier, I ask, "But why are even the people who say they love Him mean?"

"God ain't the same as us, Miss Liza. He a different matter altogether."

"I don't know Henry. I've made too many mistakes. I don't think God can ever make it right."

"Gotta take your eyes off your problems and let them go. God know what you go through, Miss Liza. The past don' matter no more. Look to future and these two little blessings He done give you."

I feel tears well up in my eyes.

"Won't you come back to see us again, Henry?"

"Don' rightly know. But, if not here, then, I see you in heaven."

I ask Henry the question I have pondered for so long.

"But how do I get to heaven, Henry? I'm not good enough."

Henry laughs, "Ain't none of us good enough Miss Liza. That why God sent His Son, Jesus to die in our places. He take our sin and make us clean again. Just like when you do your laundry and hang it on the line. All those stains gone, clean as can be. Sometime, it just take a little scrubbing is all. When we be stubborn, he gotta work a little harder to clean us up."

Smiling, he adds kindly, "God can do that to your heart, ifn you just ask. Then, someday, He take you to heaven, too."

I shake my head.

"You always make it sound so easy, Henry."

"How many times I gotta tell you? Let go and trust Him. He there even when you don' think so. He love you. He want you to be His chile'"

"I'll try Henry. I really will. But, I just don't have your faith."

"Ain't my faith, Miss Liza. Tis His. Whatever I got, He give me. He'll keep hammerin' away at your heart, jus' like He done mine. The only answer to bein' at peace is to open the door and let Him walk on in and make Himself at home. All He waitin' on is for you to make up your mind. Make a choice, Miss Liza. Don't wait no longer."

Papa and Mama return to the porch both hold packages of supplies. My stomach knots when I see what Papa holds. It is Michael's old duffle that he left behind the last time he came. Papa saved it all this time. He looks at me with a question in his eyes. I nod. Better to break the ties with the past as Henry advises. Henry hands Julia back to me. I reach for the baby, and then catch Henry in an embrace. Julia wakes wiggling and squirming against us.

"Good bye, Henry. I will never forget you."

"Forget me, Miss Liza. Just don' forget the One I come to tell you 'bout."

Papa shakes Henry's hand. Mama does the same. Then, he turns and steps towards the river. I am not sure, because his back is to me as he walks and the rain makes it hard to hear, but I think that as he leaves, he sings a song about heaven.

That night, I cannot sleep. Everything Henry said echoes in my mind. The one thing I can always depend upon is Henry's sure faith. He never wavers in reminding me of God's love. His message is always clear and the same. *Is God as constant?* I listen to Josephine's easy breathing. Oh to be a child again with no cares or concerns. Josephine does not worry about tomorrow. She trusts that she will be cared for. When I hold her fast and whisper. "I love you," she has no reason to doubt. *So, why can't I do the same? God loves me. He sent Henry to tell me. But, others fail me.* Michael said he loved me and then, look what he did. *People can't be trusted.*

What did Henry say, "God ain't the same as us, Miss Liza. He a different matter altogether."

Am I judging God by the people I encounter?

I get up out of bed and go to my wash stand. I am thirsty, so

I pour a glass of water from the pitcher there. The water does not satisfy me. I long for something else. *What am I missing?* Henry said I need to make a choice.

Again, it reminds me of Josephine. She loves to stand on one of the steps in the middle of the stairs. From her small size, it looks like a lofty perch.

Papa crouches on the floor below her and cajoles, "Come on Josey, jump to Grandpapa."

Laughing, Josephine says, "I'm coming, Grandpapa," and launches herself into space. She always lands safely in her grandfather's arms. Even in her youth, she knows that Papa will not fail to catch her.

Henry is gone, but he leaves behind a testimony of faith. I want what he had. It is time. Time to let go and trust. My heart beats fast as walk back to bed and kneel on the floor beside it. *What should I say? A voice whispers in my heart, Jump to Papa.*

So, I pray. *God, I'm coming. I feel you hammering away on my heart. So, I'm opening the door. There's a lot of ugliness there, God. A lot of hurt. I'm sorry for the bad I've done. Henry says you can scrub it all away and make me clean. Help me to remember you are there, even when I don't feel like you are. I want to be your child. I want to be like Henry and have faith and peace. I'm tired of being lonely and afraid, God. And when it is time, take me to heaven. I won't be in a rush about it. I have the girls now. But, help me remember when life gets hard that there is something better waiting on me. Thank you for listening. Amen.*

When I stand to get back into bed, I feel lighter. As though I held one of Papa's heavy anchors and dropped it overboard into the sea. Until that moment, I did not realize how much of a burden I carried around. *Is that all it takes to get rid of the weight? As simple as making a leap of faith and deciding to trust God to care for me?* Time will tell, but for now, I feel free. As I put my head on my pillow once more, I think I just might float to the ceiling. Instead, I smile, curl up under the covers and roll over into a sound and dreamless sleep.

Chapter Nineteen

When I wake the next morning, the war still rages, chores need to be done and somewhere Michael lurks waiting to hurt me again. However, the feeling of freedom lasts, despite the circumstances around me. I shake my head and wonder, *can I continue this way?* But, I also wonder, *what took me so long to follow Henry's advice?*

Henry is not the only one we say good bye to that month. William finally receives leave and comes home only long enough to pack up Mary and Louisa and take them back to Savannah with him. Mama is angry at their decision and refuses to tell Mary good-bye. I feel sorry for my cousin, especially when news arrives that General Sherman captures Savannah and presents it to President Lincoln as a Christmas gift. I beg God to keep William, Mary and Louisa safe.

She reasons to Mama, "With the city intact, there should be some shelter for Mary and Louisa there even if William left with his boat."

Mama spits out, "What kind of a life is that? And where do you think they will live with thousands and thousands of soldiers rushing into the city looting and taking food and shelter away from the civilians? I warned her, but she wouldn't listen. We will most likely never see them again."

I am afraid to say more, but I keep praying. I remember Henry's teaching. God is in control. He can be trusted to care for Mary and her family.

I believe even despite more bad news filtering into the settlement. After being surrounded by Grant's forces, on April 9, 1865, General Lee surrenders at Appomattox Court House. The other Confederate armies follow suit. The war is finally over. Although a peace treaty is signed, vestiges of war remain in the

Manatee region. Federal troops control the area, and their gun-boats patrol the river. Even as the men who served in the rebel forces slowly make their way home, tensions run high.

One day in late May, Papa decides he will sail to the island to check on the farm. Since Henry left, it is increasingly difficult to keep up both places. Mama and Papa talk about giving up the river house or the Terra Ceia land. Papa still does not have his homestead papers and cannot sell the farm. Mama refuses to consider leaving the store. At breakfast, Papa urges us to go to the island with him.

"Let's just lock up the store and house and spend a few days on the island. There is nothing to sell anyway. Come on, Julia, I have some things to do there and you and Eliza can help me."

It is a beautiful day. *I want to be on the water.* When was the last time I went sailing? Not since Josephine was born. Though I have not been back to the island to stay since I lived there with Michael, this is as good a time as any to face down my past. I feel stronger now that I have God to rely upon. I am happy when Mama agrees to go, so we pack some bags and load them on the boat. It is Josephine's first trip on the sailboat, and she is thrilled with the adventure. She wants to hang over the edge and watch the waves go by. Mama holds Julia who sleeps through the excitement while I keep a firm grip on Josephine's skirt to prevent her from falling overboard.

"She comes by her enthusiasm honestly," Papa smiles. "I remember doing the same thing to you."

As we sail out of the mouth of the river and into Tampa Bay, we see the *Kingfisher* in the distance. Part of the Union navy, the ship helped to keep the blockade in force during the war. I watch it as we sail. Is it coming towards us?

"Papa, are they coming at us?" I call over the wind.

"I was just thinking the same thing myself. What would they want with us?"

Soon, we see that the *Kingfisher* indeed plans on intercepting our much smaller yawl. In order to keep from colliding with the boat, Papa lowers his sails in a gesture of submission. From the larger boat, three smaller boats are lowered that soon surround us.

"Where are you headed, sir?" calls a young officer on the Union boat.

Papa replies, "Taking my family for a sail. We are going to our farm on Terra Ceia."

"And what would be your names?"

"I am Joseph Atzeroth; this is my wife, Julia, my daughter, Eliza and our two granddaughters. May I ask why you are keeping us from our journey?"

The officer ignores his question.

"I am going to have to ask you to follow me back to the *Kingfisher* sir. Or you can board our boat, and we will tow yours behind us."

Again, Papa asks, "For what reason?"

"Our captain needs to talk to you."

Mama speaks, "We have done nothing wrong. What do you want with us?"

"You will see in good time. Will we board your boat or will you follow us?"

"I will follow you."

As Papa hoists the sails, I wonder, what do they want with us? I feel afraid, then, remember to pray. God, I do not know what is happening here, but you do. I choose to trust you. Please keep us safe.

Upon reaching the *Kingfisher*, the sailors lower a ladder down to the yawl. A sailor gets into the boat with us and motions to the children and me.

"They may stay here." But, he points to Mama and Papa, "You two need to come with us."

"I will not leave my daughter and her children here alone. They will come with us."

"As you wish," he says.

He assists Mama and me up the rope, and then hands Julia and Josephine to us. Papa follows, but looks back. The sailor nods him ahead.

"I am to stay here and guard your boat."

A sailor escorts us to the forward deck of the boat. Looking back at the yawl, I notice that instead of guarding the boat, the sailor who remained aboard searches it from top to bottom. Sometime is wrong.

As we move forward, a small cluster of sailors break into two groups making a way for us to pass. Before us, stands the captain who brought Mama the box of gifts on his wife's birthday.

"Thank God," Mama whispers.

Yes, thank God. Our fate lies in the hands of this kind man.

"Ma'am," he tips his hat towards Mama. "Don't I know you?"

"Yes, sir," she replies. "We met on May 24 almost exactly two years ago. I remember because it was your wife's birthday, and she shares it with Queen Victoria. You brought a package of gifts to our house in honor of her special day. How is she by the way?"

"My wife is fine, thank you for asking."

Then, the captain tilts his head back and begins to laugh. We stand dumbfounded. What is there to laugh at today? Josephine whines and squirms in my arms.

"I want to get down and play," she says, while Julia starts to cry.

"I am sorry to disturb you and your family," the Captain says. "You see we have heard that Judah P. Benjamin, the former Confederate Secretary of State is in the area. We have been given the mission of finding him. I believe I will send my men out to be fitted for glasses. I beg your apology Ma'am, but they thought perhaps you were him."

Mama sputters in indignation at being confused with a man, but Papa and I see the absurdity of the situation. We join the captain in relieved laughter. After he entertains Josephine by allowing her to turn the ship's wheel and wear his hat, the captain loads us with gifts, and orders his men to help us back onto the yawl.

"Be sure to give my regards to your wife," Mama calls. "Should you ever bring her to this area, we would be happy to provide you with lodging."

Everyone waves good bye, and Josephine blows the captain a kiss as we sail away.

"What a nice man," Mama says as she looks through the packages he sent.

"Julia, I believe you could be sent to the moon and make some friends there," Papa shakes his head in wonder. "When were you going to tell me about his first visit?"

Mama and I laugh. I remember my prayers and spend a few moments thanking God for his provision once again. *You have a funny sense of humor, God.* Who would have thought Mama could be the Secretary of State? As I feel the wind blowing in my hair and the sun on my face, I laugh again.

The war officially ends on June 23, 1865, and three more months later William, Mary and Louisa finally return home to their house on the north side of the river. Still angry, Mama refuses to go to see Mary. Mama insists she is just too busy. We are in the midst of some demanding days. With the war's end and the passage of another homestead act, new settlers pour into Florida. While some are Yankees looking for free land, many are southerners with homes and property destroyed by the war. They hope for a fresh start. No matter what side they took in the recent war, the new arrivals need a place to stay while they scout for prospective land claims. Mama, always hospitable as well as quick to identify a business venture, opens up the house to lodgers to supplement our income.

One day in November, Papa sits down at the kitchen table for dinner. Josephine scrambles out of her chair to sit in his lap. How my three and a half year old loves her Papa. At least, she has a man in her life to cherish her. Not one word from Michael in all this time. I wonder what happened to him? Is he still alive? One year old Julia bangs her spoon on her high chair. The sound and the memory of Josephine in that same spot flashes through my mind. Almost two years ago, I stood immobile right here as Michael came in through the kitchen door. Don't think about it, Eliza. I try to block it out of my mind, but can't help but wonder does he even know he has two daughters now?

Papa interrupts my thoughts. "Going to be a storm this afternoon. I think it will be a big one. Better bring everything in from the yard that might blow."

After so many years of living on the water, Mama and I trust his judgment.

As though to reinforce his predication, he adds, "I can feel it in my bones. This will be a bad one. I'd hate to be out at sea today." We rush through the meal in order to prepare the house. Papa heads back down to the river to secure the yawl farther out into the river away from land. He reinforces its mooring with two anchors.

Inside, while the girls nap, I bring all the washtubs and basins from the porch into the house. When Papa returns, he helps Mama secure the shutters on the windows. As the interior of the house darkens, I fill all the oil lamps. Mama brings food into the house so that we will not have to walk out to the kitchen in the storm. Then, we wait. For a time, I watch the river from the front porch. As the wind increases, whitecaps race across the normally placid water. The sky turns black. Soon, flashes of lightning light up the sky, and the rain falls in torrents. At times, it blows sideways. Lost in my thoughts, I realize my skirt is wet. The girls are awake. Frightened, Josephine curls up in Papa's lap. I go back into the house, secure the front door, and get Julia out of her crib. We join my parents in the parlor. The rain drums against the house while I listen as Papa tells Josephine about the storms we have endured on the island.

"Will our house blow down, Grandpapa?" she cries.

"Joseph, stop scaring her. No, Josey," says Mama. "This is big strong house, and it is a little storm. We will be fine. Come over to grandmamma and I will give you a cookie."

Not even the thought of a sweet can lure Josephine out of her grandpa's arms.

The storm rages around us throughout the night, but as Mama promised, the house stands. When the sun appears the next morning, fluffy white clouds fill a vivid blue sky. The yard is laced with palm fronds and tree limbs, but the yawl still floats at its mooring in the river. Papa stands on the landing and peers down the river with his spyglass. As always, Josephine wants to be with her grandfather, so I take her down to join him.

"What are you looking at Grandpapa?" she asks.

"There is a little boat making its way down the river," he says. "It appears that a schooner took refuge at the mouth of the river last night. I suppose they are coming from it." Josephine opens her mouth wide.

"Does a river have a tongue?"

For a moment, Papa looks confused. Then, he laughs.

"No, Josey. A river has a mouth, but no tongue. The mouth of the river is where it opens out into the bay. Remember when we went to see the big ship a little while ago? When the captain let you spin the wheel and wear his hat?" Josephine still doesn't quite understand Papa's language.

"I didn't know we were in the mouth. I would have looked for teeth," she says. Papa hands his spyglass to me and swings Josephine up over his head.

"You are a funny little girl," he says as he puts her on his shoulders. I glance through the spyglass. "It doesn't look like they are coming this way. I guess they will go on to Manatee.

Come on you two. Mama should have breakfast ready by now."

Papa takes off at a gallop with Josephine riding on his shoulders shrieking with glee. Once again, I think of my girls growing up fatherless, but decide, aren't they really better off without Michael in their lives? I sigh and then, pray, thank you God for Papa.

Though I remain alert anticipating Michael's return at any moment, when people ask about him, I reply, "He was at Missionary Ridge."

Everyone knows how devastating that battle was and how many losses the Confederacy sustained that day. They presume he is dead. I can only pray that is true, but still, I watch and wait. Mama still refuses to visit Mary, but she does not begrudge me from going. She never asks about Mary, but I make sure to keep Mama informed about her in hopes that someday my mother will give in.

Papa also visits Mary and learns to know his third granddaughter, Louisa. Papa always has enough love for everyone. *I wonder why I didn't recognize that when I was younger?* Josephine and Louisa are fast friends now. They sometimes gang up against Julia and reluctantly allow her to participate in their games.

"She's a baby," they protest.

I remember caring for Mary when we were little, so have some sympathy for their complaint. But, I also know how it feels to be the odd one out. That is not going to happen to my children if I can help it. Soon, my girls look upon William and Mary's house as their second home. Mary is a kind and doting aunt, and William teases and laughs with them. Everything will be wonderful, if only Mama could relent and join the fun.

Josephine feels the same way. One day as we walk home from Mary's, she asks about her birthday which is a week away.

"Louisa is going to have a birthday party. Can I have one, too?"

"Yes, I think that would be fun," I agree. I shift Julia to my other arm. The baby is getting too heavy to carry, but she is sleepy and ready for a nap. I know it will not do to set her down. She will just sit in the road and cry.

"What kind of cake do you want to have?"

"Spice cake. I love Grandmamma's spice cake. Do you think she will make me one?"

"I am sure she will," I reply, but I am not really paying much attention thinking of all the chores I still had left to do that day.

Josephine's next statement catches me by surprise.

"Louisa has a Papa, but I don't have a Papa, but, I have a Grandmamma and she doesn't. Could we share?"

"What do you mean?"

"Could I give her my Grandmamma, and she could let me have her Papa?"

"Why don't you ask your grandmamma?"

"I don't think Louisa will share her Papa though."

At Josephine's next question, I think my heart will crack in two.

"Do I have a Papa?"

I can only choke, "Yes, honey, you do."

"Well, where is he then? I want him to push me in the swing like Uncle William does for Louisa."

"That is what Grandpapa is for," I hope to placate my daughter, but it does not work.

"That's not the same. I want a Papa. Where is mine?"

"He went to fight the war. He hasn't come home yet."

"Well, when will he come home? Will he be here for my birthday?"

"I don't think so, Josey."

Then, in an effort to change the subject, I ask, "What do you want for your birthday present?"

Josephine kicks at a stone in the path and says, "Just a Papa."

How to respond to that? I cannot bring Josephine's father home, nor do I wish to, but I can try to give Louisa a Grandmother.

While I help clean up the kitchen after supper, I say to Mama, "Josephine wants to have a birthday party. She asked if you would make her a spice cake."

"Anything for my granddaughter. Can you believe she will be four years old already?"

Mama shakes her head in disbelief. "Time has gone by fast. Now that we have sugar again, I can make her a really nice cake."

"Mama, that is not all she wants. She wants to have Mary and her family here as well." Mama stops drying the pot that she works on.

"Mama, Louisa is her best friend. She should be here for the celebration."

Mama does not say anything. I try one more time.

"Mary had a hard time in Savannah. She won't talk about it, but I know she did."

Then, I let Mama be. Better not to press her.

A few minutes later, Mama sighs. "Do what you think best, daughter."

On the day of Josephine's birthday, a beautiful tall cake rests on the kitchen table. Mama busies herself in the kitchen as I insert four tiny candles in the white icing. *Is she nervous about seeing Mary again?* Soon, I hear excited laughter. They are here. I look at Mama. She stands at the kitchen window watching as Josephine excitedly greets her cousin.

"She has grown so tall," Mama says softly.

I look behind her. There in the doorway stands Mary.

"Mama?" she asks hesitantly.

My mother turns around and faces her. Wordlessly, she stares at Mary. *What will she do?* Then, she smiles and opens up her arms.

"Mary, welcome home, child." Mary rushes over and the two women embrace.

"I'm sorry, Mama. Sorry for leaving you. Sorry to upset you and worry you. You were right. I shouldn't have gone."

Mama shushes her.

"That is in the past, let's leave it be now."

They break apart.

Mama smoothes Mary's hair, and then says, "Go call the birthday girls. I think that we have two birthdays to celebrate today, don't we?"

So, Louisa will get a grandmother for a birthday gift, I think. I just hope Josephine does not wish for her father to come home.

While Michael still does not return, more and more new settlers arrive into the Manatee lands. A week after the girls' birthday, I look out the front window of the house and see two strangers talking to Papa on the shore. Their beautiful boat is tied up to the landing. It is a small sailboat a little bigger than the yawl. They must be discussing boats, because Papa waves in the direction of their vessel. Soon, he brings them up to the house.

"Eliza," he calls. "Make us some coffee, please. These are our new neighbors. Well, as close to neighbors as you can get with a river separating you. Eliza, meet John Fogarty and his brother, Tole."

"Welcome, gentlemen. Papa, I will just be a moment."

I walk to the kitchen. Mama is there with the girls making cookies.

"Oh, that is good timing. Papa has company and has asked for coffee. Can you spare some cookies as well?"

Josephine puts her hands on her hips.

"These are my cookies, so you should be asking me if I can spare some."

"Little miss, don't talk back to your mother," Mama says

sternly. "These are for all of us, and we can certainly share them."

Then, she smiles, "Why don't you arrange them on a pretty plate and go back with your mother to serve them to the men?"

Excited by the prospect of playing hostess, Josephine does just that. I watch as she eats one cookie for every three that she puts on the plate.

"That is enough cookies for you, daughter. Let's save some to eat with our company. Come on now."

I carry the coffee pot and some mugs, while Mama brings the cream and sugar. We slow our steps to wait on Julia who toddles behind and Josephine who balances the plate very carefully on a tray.

When we arrive, the men are deep in conversation about boats and their design. Papa introduces John and Tole to Mama.

Then, he adds, "They are ship captains and boat builders. They plan on starting a business across the river from us."

John replies, "There is so much beautiful wood here to work with. I cleared some land to claim as my own and I almost hate to cut down the trees to build the house. I keep thinking of what nice boats they will make."

"Are you married, Mr. Fogarty?" Mama asks of John. "No, not yet."

Mama! *How embarrassing.* Surely Mama is not hinting that he might take an interest in me? After all, I still do not know for sure I am a widow.

John continues, "My brother here is though. He has three children as well, two boys and a girl."

"Well, let me give you some advice. If you plan to bring your women here to the Manatee, you best finish your house before you build any boats. It is a rare woman who will consent to live in this wilderness without a roof over her head."

Papa laughs and tells the men the story of our arrival on Terra Ceia and Mama's refusal to live in a tent.

"I will take your recommendation seriously," Tole tells Mama. "I am anxious to bring my family to Florida. They are still in New York."

"I wish you well, then," Mama says. "I know how hard it is for your wife to be separated from you for so long."

Inspired by Mama's speech, they take their leave and sail back across the river to return to their work. Before they leave, they tip their hats to us and say thank you for the refreshments. Josephine bows to them in a sweet curtsey that makes me smile.

They shake hands with Papa and John says, "Should you ever need the help of a neighbor, be sure to let us know. We will be happy to provide you with a new boat or boat repairs as well. Come see us."

Turning to Mama, he adds, "Madam Joe, I will be glad to bring you any supplies you need for your store. Before we leave to go back to Key West, I will stop by and get a list if you would like."

"That would be lovely. Thank you for thinking of it."

"Such nice men," Mama says as we clean up the dishes.

I only hope she isn't planning on doing any matchmaking. The last thing I need is another husband.

Chapter Twenty

Another visitor arrives less than a month after the Fogartys. This time, it is a Catholic priest who lands on our doorstep seeking lodging. Father Clavreul travels around Florida from his home base in St. Augustine, ministering to the Catholics in the isolated communities along the coast. Though a Lutheran, Mama welcomes him into our home.

She confides to me as we prepare a meal, "It will do your father good to talk to the priest. Sometimes, I worry about his spiritual welfare."

"Mama, how can you think that? There is no one kinder or gentler than Papa."

"I know, I know. But, your father never talks about what he believes. Perhaps the priest can get it out of him."

I think that there can be no doubt about what Papa believes about God. He lives his life so that God will be happy with him. In fact, I believe that God has some of the same characteristics as my father.

Father Clavreul offers to say mass before he leaves on the next leg of his journey. Mama sends me to bring William and Mary for the service. William is delighted to meet the priest. Mary greets him politely as well. I hang back. I know nothing about the Catholic faith. As the priest prepares for the service, I see that Mama intends to participate so I feel more comfortable. That is until Father Clavreul announces before he holds communion there will be an opportunity for confession. Each member of our family waits in the hall while Father Clavreul speaks to us one at a time. *What should I say to the priest when it is my turn? Should I tell him all my sins?* Henry taught me to go directly to God. *Why then do I need to repeat them all again to this man?* Mary comes from the parlor dabbing at her eyes.

"Go on in Eliza. It is your turn."

What should I say?

I say the first thing that blurts into my mouth, "I am not Catholic."

Father Clavreul smiles. "That does not matter. I am here to help anyone who wants to come to God."

"I go to God all the time," I say. "I could not live without Him. He saved my life."

The priest nods his head.

"And do you confess your sins?"

"All the time. I have many," I add sheepishly.

"And they would be?" he prompts.

"I used to be jealous of my cousin, but I am not any more. I love her like a sister now."

"That is good. Anything else?"

I hesitate.

The priest seems kind enough so I venture, "I lie sometimes."

"About what?"

"About my husband. When people ask about him, I tell them he is dead."

"And he is alive? Where is he?"

"I do not know. He was in the war. He never came home."

"I do not hear regret in your voice. You do not seem sad about his absence. Were you a good wife to him?"

I sigh.

"Once I loved him. But he was not kind to me, Father."

"It does not matter if he was kind to you. You were his wife, were you not?"

I cannot speak. Will I find condemnation from the church again?

"Until you know for certain that he is dead, you are still married to him," Father Clavreul says sternly.

I nod. He does not say anything I did not already know. Unless I seek divorce again. But, best not to mention that to the priest. He dismisses me with a reminder of my marriage vows. I leave the room with a heavy heart. *Where then is forgiveness that Henry professed?* After administering communion to all of us, Father Clavreul takes his leave. I am glad to see him go. His visit only muddles up my brain. I felt so at peace about my relationship with God. Now, I am not so sure.

I fret about Father Clavreul's words. The thought consumes me for two days after the priest sails away. I cannot sleep, and by the third day, my mind is numb and my body exhausted.

Papa notices and asks, "Daughter, are you unwell? You looked peaked."

"I have not been sleeping well, Papa."

"Is there a reason for your unrest?"

"Ever since the priest was here, I feel unsettled. He told me that I will always be married to Michael until I have proof that he is really dead." I shiver. "What do you think Papa?"

"I think that you should not rely on a man to tell you what is right. Only God knows the truth. He knows what happened to you and what is in your heart. And Michael's, as well. Let Him be the judge. I have my opinion, but you should ask God what to do."

"But, what do you think I should do?"

"I don't want to cloud your judgment with my advice. You ask God; spend some time waiting on His answer. Let me know what He says and then, we will talk again."

I nod and turn to go.

Papa says, softly, "Eliza."

I look back.

"Don't fret. You will make yourself ill. God has a plan."

God has a plan. That is what Henry said. For the rest of the day, even through my fatigue, I comfort myself with that thought. I hope for a few moments alone so I can pray, but new lodgers arrive and I am too busy. By the end of the day, I can hardly hold my eyes open. As I put the girls to bed, Josephine stops and kneels by her bedside to say her prayers. I feel guilty. I force myself to pray. It is as though I feel Mama on my shoulder urging me to my knees each night. Now, I do the same to my daughter, and in the past, Josephine also talked to God out of duress.

The priest inspired Josephine to pray. *What did he say to motivate her?* I remember Henry's charge to teach my girls about God's love. I haven't done a very good job. I will have to do better in the future. Still and all, somewhere Josephine learns for as she clasps her hands, she talks to God as though He is a friend. She chats about her day, thanks Him for this or that.

Then, she states the crux of her desires, "God please bring me a Papa. If not my real one, then, somebody else. It doesn't have to be my real Papa. But, make him jolly and someone who will love me. Most of all, God, give him a sailboat so he can teach me how to sail."

Where did that come from? I just shake my head and tuck my daughster into bed.

"Mama, am I a good little girl?"

"Why do you ask," I say as I pick up Josephine's dress from the floor and hang it on a hook.

"Father Clavreul said God answers good little girls' prayers. Am I good?"

How should I answer? I don't want to mess this up, God.

"Sometimes you are good like when you play nicely with your sister and sometimes you are bad when you disobey me. But, Josephine, God doesn't answer our prayers based on what we do. He does listen and wants us to be happy, but He gives us what is best for us. He answers our prayers based on His love for us. Sometimes, He gives us exactly what we ask for because He knows that it will be good for us. But, sometimes, He doesn't, because we ask for things that will harm us."

"A Papa couldn't be bad for me, could he, Mama?"

I think of Michael.

"It depends on the man, Josephine, just depends on the man." I stroke her hair. "Now roll over and go to sleep. It has been a long day."

As I prepare for bed, my own words to Josephine echo in my head along with Papa's admonition to ask God for direction.

God what should I do? Should I wait on word about Michael? What if he comes home again? How can I keep my girls safe from his wickedness? Should I get a divorce? Isn't divorce wrong?

Before I gain any answers, I fall asleep for the first time in days. But, I wake in the middle of the night. My heart races. *What was I dreaming about?* As the silence of the house calms my spirit, I remember. I dreamed of Michael's courtship. The sweetness of his love and his kind attention. *But, wait, had that been Michael?* As I think more, I realize that my dreams were not about my husband. *Who was the man in the dream?* The man who smiled at me was almost as small as I am. He stood just a few inches above me. He had a mustache so blond it was almost white. And bright blue eyes. There was someone with him. *Who was it?*

Remember, Eliza. Think. Then the vision becomes clearer. In the background, Tole Fogarty ties a boat to the landing. But, the man I saw in my dream was not John Fogarty. *Who was he?*

I feel strangely comforted by the dream. As I listen to my daughters' even breathing, I pray again, God, it would be nice for them to have a father. A kind man who will love them and cherish them like Papa treats me. *If he is out there, God, bring Him to us. I will keep trusting you. I will wait for you to tell me what to do. Send me some sign. Let me know if I should seek a divorce or just stay the way I am.* I think of Henry's teaching. God is not absent just because He is silent. *Even if I have to wait a lifetime, God. I would rather do what you want me to do than mess things up again by rushing in where I shouldn't go.*

I remember Josephine's prayer and smile. God, if you are

working on Josephine's request, I'd like a little warning before you send him around. Then, I roll over and drift back to sleep.

I wait on God as I promise. Most days, I am too busy to think about my future. It is only a matter of getting through the day. Boarders come and go as they either find a place to call their own or decide to move on somewhere else. One day in November, Mr. and Mrs. Campbell of Clarke County, Mississippi come to stay with us. They search for land for several days. Mr. Campbell is very quiet. His lung ailment can only be cured by moving to a warmer climate. I wonder if he does not speak because it hurts too much to breathe. His wife, Sarah, is just his opposite. Each evening at supper, she talks and talks. She tells us every detail of their day and speaks discouragingly of what available land they see.

"If only I could find a place just like yours," she sighs. "It is so beautiful here with all the trees and the flowers you planted. I just love sitting on your porch and looking out over the river." She turns to her husband, "Wouldn't it be nice to live somewhere like this? I would pay $1,000 in gold for a place like this! Don't you agree, dear?"

Mama puts her fork down. She looks at Papa. He raises his eyebrows.

"Sarah, as a matter of fact, our place is for sale. At least one half of it is. We plan on keeping a portion along the river, but this house and store and about forty acres are available if you are really interested."

I about fall out of my chair. *When did they decide this?* Mama always refused to leave even though Papa begged her to move back to Terra Ceia. My head spins. *How can this happen so fast?* Ordinarily, I do not like change, but a chance to move back to the island sounds wonderful.

"Really! Oh, my. That would be perfect. Wouldn't it, honey?" Mr. Campbell does not have a chance to reply. "We will be so happy here. I would love a chance to run a store."

She babbles on while Papa stares at Mama. He is just as surprised as I am. Mama nods her head as Sarah outlines her dreams. On November 27, 1866, Sarah Campbell becomes the proud owner of the Atzeroth Store, house and thirty-eight acres of land for which she pays Mama $1,000 in gold coins. Mama holds back forty six and a half acres for the future. I suspect it is insurance in case Papa never gets his land grant, and they are forced to move from the island.

That year, we spend our first Christmas back on the island in eighteen years. How life changes, I muse. Once I dreamed of raising a family here on the island. Now, that comes true, but I am both mother and father to my girls. At least Papa and Mama support me. Just as I did when I was their age, Josephine and Julia love island life. They miss Louisa, but Mary promises to bring her over regularly. Josephine's only concern is whether St. Nicholas will find us in the new house. When he delivers Christmas gifts on schedule, she is content.

With the sale of the river house and our move to Terra Ceia, it is even more important to secure the deed for the island property. I listen as Mama and Papa discuss their dilemma.

"With the homestead law and new people coming into the area every day, if word gets out that we still do not have our patent, someone might try to claim our place," Papa worries.

Although Mr. Boyle remained eerily silent during the war years, I wonder how long it will take for him to be up to his old tricks. He now lives farther east, but one never knows. In June, Papa sends a letter to his old friend and employer, John Jackson. In it, he asks the surveyor for help in obtaining his patent.

Papa says, "If anyone can make sense of the system, it will be John Jackson. He knows the right people. I hope he will help us."

It does not take long for Mr. Jackson to reply. Though he now lives in Tampa and runs a general store, he takes the time to sail to Terra Ceia and deliver the news in person.

"When I received your letter, I thought to myself, it is high time I came and visited with my old friend," he says upon settling down at the table for dinner.

It never fails to amaze me how quickly Mama can prepare a meal even when she has no advance warning that company is coming.

"Besides, I kept thinking about your wife's wonderful cooking." He laughs, "Perhaps it was more my stomach than my heart that brought me here."

Mama says, "You are always welcome at my table, Mr. Jackson. I enjoy cooking for a man who knows good food. How is your wife?"

"Doing well, thank you for asking. Now that this infernal warring is over, we hope to enjoy some time of peace. Ellen is glad to have me at home and not running around 'like all the young men' as she puts it. Joe, why is it that a woman always tells you to act your age no matter how old you are?" I wonder if he is complaining about his wife, until he smiles.

"Even though the Federals would continue to interfere in telling us how to run our lives, I am in hopes that we are now on the verge of great prosperity in our region," he adds.

Papa nods in agreement.

"What I really came for, was to apologize to you. I feel at fault for the problems in getting your paperwork straightened out. I was in this area in 1858 and redid your survey, but the Land Office would not accept it." He frowns, "They said that the starting point was not sufficiently clear because I used a blazed tree bearing northwest as a corner stake." He shakes his head, "Since when is a tree not a clear enough boundary marker?"

Mr. Jackson continues, "Your case was turned over to the Tampa Land Office for further work, but the War Between the States took precedent. I am afraid that those orders went up into flames during the war." Mama moans.

"Never fear Madam Joe. I fully intend to rattle all the cages I need to to make sure your family gets their rightful claim. I have already sent a letter to Hugh Corley, Register of State Lands, asking him to look into the grant. I told him how you are one of our best citizens, Joe, and how it is of great harm to you not to have your patent. I am confident that something will come through soon." He pushes back from the table and sighs, "Madam Joe, you are still the best cook in the area."

I take advantage of the lull in conversation to ask, "Mr. Jackson in your opinion, can a woman file for land under the new homestead act?"

"The law says anyone who is head of a household can make a claim, so I do not see why not. Why? Were you thinking of choosing some land of your own?"

Papa and Mama wait for my response. *What will they think of such an idea?* Then, Papa slowly nods his head.

Mama agrees, "I think that is a fine idea, Eliza."

Papa asks, "John, what would it take for her to make a claim?"

"Only choosing some unclaimed land, filing for a patent and paying a small fee. Then, you have five years to live on it, as well as clear, plow and fence a portion of it." He frowns. "But, you must clearly be head of your own household. I have heard rumors about your husband, Michael. Whatever happened to him? Have you heard?"

"No, not a word."

I look at three year old Julia playing quietly with her sister in the corner of the room. She is a constant reminder of my last contact with Michael.

I lower my voice so Josephine will not hear, "He has been gone over four years, and I have not had any contact with him."

Mr. Jackson replies, "Sounds like you have grounds for abandonment then. He is probably dead, but without a death certificate it will be hard to proof. I recommend you file for divorce then."

Divorce. There it is again. *I pray, God, is this the sign I asked for? Is this the path I should follow?*

Before he leaves for Tampa, Mr. Jackson speaks to me alone.

"I know some may have condemned you for setting aside your marriage vows, but do not be ashamed to do what you need to do to provide for your girls. Those of us who truly know you and your circumstances understand the necessity. Besides, there are many women in your shoes these days. You cannot believe how many divorces are being filed because of the war. So many women thought their husband was dead, so they re-married. If you had not had your father's protection, I am sure you would have done the same thing. What else is there for a single woman in these wilderness lands? But, once they remar-ried and in some cases had more children, their first husband reappeared home from the war. Why it took them so long to make it home or regain their memory of their responsibilities, I do not know. The state is charging these women and their new husbands with adultery until either they go back to their first husband or divorce him and remarry. Think about how many families have been torn asunder by the uncertainty of the war. You won't be alone in your quest to straighten out your marital situation."

I appreciate Mr. Jackson's encouragement and candor, but I am still reluctant to face the court in Manatee. Besides my desire for a divorce began long before Michael went off to war. While I feel sorry for those other women, it is not circumstances that propel me towards divorce, but my own choices.

The next morning as we clean up from breakfast, Mama says, "I have been thinking. What if you filed your divorce in Hillsborough County? We could argue that that was Michael's last address therefore we chose to file there. Perhaps that might keep some of the wagging tongues silent." I rarely hug my mother anymore, but impulsively I turn and embrace her. That idea just might work.

"I wonder when Papa can take me to Tampa? Do you think Mr. Magbee is still practicing law there?"

"I took the liberty of asking Mr. Jackson while he was here. Mr. Magbee is still practicing as an attorney although he is farming as well. As for Papa, he is as anxious as you are to get this cleared up. He said he would take you anytime you are ready. I will stay home with the girls. I think it will be easier on you if you don't have them along." I hug her again.

"Thank you, Mama. You have thought of everything." Mama hugs me back, and then pushes me away.

"Now go on and get your chores done. If you are leaving with your father, I am going to have my hands full taking care of those granddaughters of mine."

I spend some time in prayer that night and feel at peace with the decision to go to Tampa and file for divorce. Papa and I leave the next morning. Josephine cries when I get aboard the boat. Not because she is afraid to stay behind, but because she cannot go along.

"But, my whole life, I have always wanted to go to Tampa," she wails.

When I hesitate, Mama rolls her eyes.

"Go on now and leave our young actress with me."

I laugh. Yes, Josephine is certainly putting on a show.

I sit in the bow of the boat as Papa steers it out of Terra Ceia Bay, around the point and into Tampa Bay. Despite my turmoil over this decision in the past, today, I feel free. This is the right thing to do. If Mr. Jackson and Mama and Papa understand, perhaps the other settlers will as well. I do not know about Judge Glazier or Father Clavreul, but it no longer matters what they think. This seems to be the direction God wants me to head. *If it is not the right thing to do, God, You better stop me now, I pray.*

After I talk to Mr. Magbee, I knew God's Hand must be in this. Why else would things go so smoothly? Not only is Mr.

Magbee the attorney I prefer, because of his gentle manner and kindness to me so long ago, but he is willing to take my case. While I feel I would have the courage to tell him my whole story, he still has Mr. Gettis' notes from my original testimony so I do not need to go through it all again. He also possesses all of the papers from Mr. Gettis' original petition.

"I hid them in my house for safekeeping during the war," he says. "I was afraid that the Yankees might confiscate or burn the office. I felt an obligation to keep my files protected."

I am grateful for his foresight. Mr. Magbee also agrees with Mama's idea that the new case will best be filled in Hillsborough County and supports Mr. Jackson's stance that this is a different era. A woman need not fear to seek relief from the court by way of divorce.

"Not only do we have new judges on the bench, but there are so many women just like you. Who would have thought what havoc a war could play on families?"

The best news of all, Mr. Magbee saves for last.

"Eliza, I do not see any problems in having your petition granted this time. In fact, I do not even think you need to appear. I have your testimony should I need it, but we are not trying to prove who is at fault here. Michael's absence is enough evidence in itself. The choice should be clearly seen by the judge."

Oh, what wonderful news! Mr. Magbee sends me home with greetings for Papa and Mama. As I walk back to meet Papa at the boat, I feel like my feet do not even meet the shell road. In fact, if not for the dust on the bottom of my skirt, I might wonder if I floated above the ground.

"Mrs. Dickens."

A gruff greeting from behind stops me in my tracks. I recognize that voice. *Can it* be? Today of all days how can he ruin my happiness? I turn round and face John Boyle. It has been many years since I have seen the man. They have not been good to him. I am shocked by how time has ravaged his features. Perhaps it was the war.

"Mr. Boyle." I try to keep my voice even.

"I hoped to come across you someday. I just thought it would be in Manatee, not here in Tampa. What brings you here?"

Oh, no. I am not going to tell you anything. Eliza, keep your mouth shut. I refuse to speak. Mr. Boyle takes a step closer to me, and I back away. All I can think of is the evil he wrought on Henry and my family.

"Wait, don't go. I want to tell you something."

Run, Eliza. Run, fast, I think, but I stand my ground. God, please help me. Please, don't let him hurt me.

"Mrs. Dickens, I want to apologize to you and your family for the harm I brought you in the community."

What? What does he say? If he sprouted three heads I would not have been more surprised. *He is apologizing?*

"I had a lot of time to think during the war. Almost got killed many times. And all I could remember was how mean I'd been. I promised God that if he got me through the war, I would be a changed man. I hope you can forgive me. And your mother and father too."

Dumbfounded, I can hardly think. *What should I say? How can He expect me just to say alright? After all he did to us?* Then, the most amazing thing happens. My heart tenders towards this man. I see him in an entirely new light. *What has changed?*

I do not quite understand it, but somehow, I manage to stammer, "You are forgiven Mr. Boyle. I will pass your request along to my parents as well. God bless you Mr. Boyle."

"He already has Mrs. Dickens."

As we sail away from Tampa, I think how much has changed. If God can touch Mr. Boyle's heart and my own for that matter, surely He can do anything.

On the way home, I share with Papa the good news from

Mr. Magbee and the incredible encounter with Mr. Boyle.

Papa agrees I did the right thing. "How can we withhold forgiveness when God has done so much for us?"

I just shake my head in wonder. Things are changing so fast.

One thing stays the same. Papa still does not have a deed to his land. In October, Mr. Jackson writes another letter to the land office. This time, he emphasizes the old reason why Papa may have been prevented from obtaining his patent.

Mr. Jackson states, "Interested parties have long been trying to oust them from their land in order to take over their claim."

That argument catches the attention of the new government workers set in place to keep the old rebel regime from taking hold again. In an effort to keep the once powerful Manatee settlers squashed, they move the county seat far out east to Pine Level. As a result of Mr. Jackson's carefully placed suspicion, Papa hopes that finally, someone will listen to his request.

While Papa waits for a decision regarding his land, I receive my divorce papers with surprising speed. They arrive in the mail delivered by Captain Sam. When I see the return address is Mr. Magbee's office, I suspect what is inside. Still, my hands shake as I open the envelope. There inside are the papers that finally release me from Michael forever. Relief, sadness and regret all wash over me at the same time. Once, I had such high hopes. I brush away a tear as I release that desire once and for all. *Well, I still have dreams don't I?* Though none involve a man, now with this document, I can file a claim for a place of my own. A place to raise my little girls free of fear.

"Thank you, God," I whisper even as I weep tears of sorrow for what could have been. Then, the doubts set in. *What will become of me now? How can I farm alone?* A divorcee will not be accepted in proper circles no matter what the circumstances. I second guess my decision. *Was I right? Is this what God wants me to do? Why does it feel so wrong all of a sudden?* Once again, I turn to prayer.

"If I was wrong, please forgive me. I need a fresh start. Help me to have faith."

An image forms in my mind. I imagine hammering a post into the ground and all around it is my land. *God, someday, I will drive a stake in the earth that you will give me, but for now, I claim this moment for you. You brought me to this place. I will choose to trust you.*

Chapter Twenty-one

I come to see that Henry was right a long time ago when he said that God will use the bad things in my life to make me a better person. If anything, my difficulties have taught me compassion. In February, when I hear Mr. Campbell succumbed to his lung ailment, I ask Papa to take me back to the river house to express my condolences. Though I do not know what it is like to lose a husband that you dearly loved, I do know the taste of grief. And the despair that comes from thinking you are alone. Mary is already there doing her best to comfort Sarah. Though it is a nice sunny day, the house is closed up. I open the doors and windows to let the breeze blow through. Perhaps that will rid the house of the smell of death and sickness which is still so strong. Mary nods in gratitude for the effort.

"Oh, why oh why did I bring him here? He should have died at home with his loved ones around him instead of so far away from Mississippi. It was just too much on him to make the move."

I know all about self blame. I place my hand on Sarah's and say, "Sarah, listen to me. You cannot blame yourself. You did what the doctor told you to do to keep him well. You did not know that he would die."

Sarah grasps my hand so tightly that it hurts.

I continue, "Don't look back at the past and second guess yourself, Sarah. What is done is done. Look ahead. What will you do now?"

"I cannot live here alone. Nor do I want to. The memory of his suffering fills this place. My daughters want me to come home. To think I once thought this place could be home. I will go back to Mississippi. I will go back alone."

Sarah breaks down and weeps some more. I can only sit and hold her hand until the crying eases.

"What can we do to help?" I ask.

Mary and I make sure that Sarah eats and begin to help her pack her belongings. As I walk through the rooms that were once my home, I wonder what Sarah will do with the house and the store. Sarah does not wait long for a buyer. Samuel Sparks Lamb, a man from her hometown, is in the area looking for land to purchase. When he hears about Mr. Campbell's death, he calls on Sarah. She agrees to sell him her land, and he returns to Mississippi as the owner of our former home.

"Isn't it good the way God works?" I say to Mary. "To send a buyer and not just anyone but someone that Sarah knew and could feel comfortable that he would not take advantage of her."

Another newcomer to the area helps us as we minister to Sarah. Ann Fogarty, John's new wife, catches a ride in one of her family's boats across the river to see if there is anything she can do. I like Ann right away and am happy to know that Mr. Fogarty found himself such a nice girl to marry. They are still newlyweds, having just come to the Manatee lands a few weeks before. She jumps right in and helps me with the packing in the kitchen. Mary finally convinces Sarah to lie down and rest while she works on boxing up the household items.

"How will you get back across the river?"

"My brother in law, Bill, will come back for me after he has a load of wood," she replies.

I think of my dream and blush. I take a breath and then, ask, "Is there another brother, then?"

"Yes, two more. Bill and Jerry. Jerry has a family and decided to stay in Key West. But, Bill came here shortly after John and I did. We are all living together until we can build more houses."

We. Then, Bill must be married as well. So much for that odd dream.

As we work side by side, I ask, "Is he gathering wood for the houses?'

"No, for a boat that they want to build. These Fogarty men. They love their ship building. They have done the basic framework of the house, but could not wait to build their first boat. Bill's job is to travel the rivers and bays looking for sticks along the shoreline."

"Sticks? They build their vessels of sticks?"

Ann laughs, "Not just any sticks, but huge logs cut from the oaks, cypress and cedars along the water. They choose the trees as close to the water's edge so that the wood can be easily loaded onto the boats and taken back to our place. Sometimes, they pile them six high. They are having good success in finding what they need. Hopefully, they will lay the keel next month. After that, he will go out searching for knees to create the bends."

Lay the keel? Knees. Bends. Ann uses a lot of language that I do not understand.

"So they can start building the smack," Ann tries to simplify.

Smack? Now I am even more mixed up. Seeing the confusion on my face, Ann laughs.

"Come over next month and we will show you what it is all about. You have to see it to understand, I guess."

As soon as I can, I ask Papa to take the girls and me over to the Fogarty's house. The size of their house is surprising. Two stories with eight rooms, the large house has a passageway ten foot wide to connect it to the kitchen. Porches on both floors protect the interior from the sun as well as provide a place to visit or rest in the cool breezes that come off the river. Ann welcomes us in and introduces us to her family. Ellen, Tole's wife is pregnant and their two year old daughter, Elizabeth, plays at their feet. Right away, Julia and Elizabeth begin to chatter baby talk to each other. Ellen explains that her three sons are out with the men working on the smack. I laugh again at the name of the boat. *What in the world is a smack?*

Ann leads the way to the new boatyard. The smack is much bigger than I imagined it to be. Over forty feet long and seventeen feet wide, the boat has a seven foot deep hold for storing fish or cargo. With its square back, it looks like it will be a steady work boat. John comes forward to shake Papa's hand.

"Welcome to Fogarty Ship Builders. We are off to a great start. I am glad you could come and see us at work."

Tole waves but continues sanding as his three sons climb in and out of the boat. Josephine holds back, but I can see that she wants to join them. Papa notices, too, so he takes her over to the boat and sets her inside while he talks to Tole. Josephine joins right in the conversation as though she is a grown up asking questions about each part of the boat. I watch her proudly. She is growing into a fine young woman. I start when John speaks to me again.

"Mrs. Dickens," he begins.

"Oh, please call me Eliza."

"Eliza, I would like to introduce you to my brother, Bill."

I turn to greet this third Fogarty brother and feel my cheeks turn pink. *Here is the man about whom I dreamed! How odd.* I feel as though I have known him a long time. If he notices my blush, Bill is too polite to say.

I stammer, "Pleased to meet you," and he does the same. Then, he resumes his work.

"Can you stay for dinner?" Ann asks "We are having turtle stew. Bill is a marvelous turtle catcher."

"I don't believe I have ever had turtle stew before," I say.

"Really?" Ann exclaims. "We eat it all the time in the Keys. Then, that settles it. You must stay and dine with us."

As we walk back to the house, I can't get Bill's face off my mind. *How could I dream of a man that I never met and yet, have all of his features so firmly embedded into my thoughts?* I want to ask about him, but am afraid to draw any attention to myself. I am glad when Ann keeps talking. I am still too surprised to say anything, but oh how I want to know if he is married. Finally, Ann speaks of him. It is as though she knows exactly what I hope to hear.

"Now, Bill, he is the bachelor of the bunch. The only one without a family so he sleeps on a pallet in the kitchen. When mother came for a visit, he gave her his room and moved out there. I think he looks forward to a few minutes peace each night. The boys can be a handful and love to roughhouse with their Uncle Bill."

I do not need to hear anything else. Bill is not married. *What does that mean for me?* Still confused over his appearance in my dream, I pray.

What are you up to, God? I am not looking for anyone to take care of me. I will be fine on my own.

Then, I remember Josephine's prayer, "God, bring me a Papa who can teach me to sail."

Oh, my goodness. Bill is a sailor! *Might he be willing to take on someone else's children to raise? What am I thinking?* The last time I jumped into a relationship with a man, it turned out badly. *No, God, I don't need a man. You can just ignore Josephine's request, if you please.*

After a delicious meal of turtle stew which if I had not known its contents, I could have sworn was beef, Papa steers the yawl towards home. Julia sleeps in my arms, but Josephine talks nonstop to Papa about the boat, its parts and how they work. My, she learned a lot listening to the men. She is very bright. She really ought to be in school. When I remember my unhappy years in the classroom, though, I decide to let her be a while longer. There are just as many things she can learn working on the farm and spending time with her grandfather.

That night, Josephine once again reminds God of her desire for a father.

As I tuck her into bed, Josephine says, "Mama, does Robert's

Uncle Bill have any little girls?"

"No, Josey, he does not."

"Well, I think he would make a good papa and he loves sailing."

I sigh. "Josey, you just wait on God. Don't get ahead of Him. If He wants you to have a father, He will send one your way."

"How can I get ahead of God, Mama? He is everywhere. How can He be everywhere?"

After a lengthy discussion of God's omnipresence with my six year old, I am exhausted. The child is a lot smarter than me, I do believe, but at least she forgets about her prayer.

I cannot. In my own talk with God, I argue against remarriage. *I don't care who you send my way, God. I am not looking for another husband.* Then, it dawns on me. *Who says that Josephine's request means I must remarry?* If God is willing, He can send a kindly man to be like a father to Josephine, but that does not mean I have to marry him. What if we just stay friends and spent time together with the girls? He could be someone to influence them and teach them the kinds of things a father should. That would fulfill Josephine's longings without forcing me to take on a husband. *Now, that, God, I would be amenable to, I think as I close my eyes confident the matter is settled.*

God and Bill Fogarty seem to agree to it as well. Over the next year, he visits more and more frequently. In the beginning, he just stops by with one of his brothers on his way up and down the coastline hauling timber. They pause in their travels to talk to Papa and ask where they might find the sort of tree that they seek to harvest. Mama always invites them in for a cup of coffee and some kind of sweet. Josephine will not leave them alone, always pestering them with questions about whatever turn the conversation takes. The men are great teases, but particularly Tole. When he puts on his Irish accent and tells wild tales of the sea, Josephine and Julia hang on every word. They look forward to the visits by the brothers they now call Uncle

Tole, Uncle John and Uncle Bill.

Then, Bill starts to come alone for a visit. He says he misses his little friends, Josephine and Julia. What a thrill it is for Josephine to hear that he comes specifically to see her. He always stays long enough to play with both girls. He hangs a swing for them in the same oak tree where I once had mine and pushes them for a long time while Josephine talks of flying like a bird. Bill teaches them to fish and is ever patient with them, baiting their hooks and taking their catch off the line while they squeal and shout with excitement. Much to Josephine's joy, he also teaches her to sail, but first both girls learn how to swim.

"A sailor must be able to keep their head above water should they land overboard," he argues.

Josephine swims like a dolphin. Julia learns how, but does not enjoy it as much. She prefers to wade along the beach and pick up shells. One day as I watch their lessons from the shore, Bill emerges from the water and threatens to throw me in. He shakes his wet head like a dog and sprays water droplets all over my skirt. The girls giggle from the shallows.

"Mama does not know how to swim," Josephine declares. "You better teach her how before you throw her in here with us."

"You don't know how to swim?" Bill asks incredulously. "Then, we must schedule a swimming lesson."

As he advanced towards me, I laugh and run away from him and up the bank.

"What do you think I am, a fish? This is one prize you cannot catch!"

"Oh, don't be so sure of that," Bill teases.

The girls think him wonderful, and so do Mama and Papa.

"That Bill Fogarty," Mama says. "He is a good man. One you can trust."

Papa likes having him around. Bill can always find something that needs fixing or making. There is nothing he cannot build. I have to admit that I like his company, too. He is a good friend. He knows when to speak and when just to listen. I find myself talking to him about things I never dreamed I could discuss with a man.

One day, as we sail on the bay with the girls hanging over the bow dangling their hands in the foam tipped waves, he asks, "Tell me about your husband."

Though I do not plan to speak so frankly, I reveal all the details of my awful marriage and the troubles I overcame to seek my divorce.

"I am so sorry, Eliza. There had to be something deeply wrong with him to have treated you so poorly. You deserve much better."

Bill is like that, simple and direct. He says things plainly and means what he says, but he is compassionate as well. I wonder what it would be like to marry a man of his word. A gentle and tender man. Then, I remember. Michael seemed to be something he was not. After we married, the truth emerged. So, when my heart tempts me to run wild, I hold it in check. It could be easy to look to the future.

Especially when I enjoy spending time with his family. I catch their eyes on us together. They know he visits Terra Ceia much more frequently than necessary. They know he has come to love my girls like they are his own. Yet, I hold back and keep a guard on my emotions. No need to take this relationship any farther than just friends.

It is Bill who encourages me to follow through on my dream of land ownership. He files a claim for land near his brothers' on the south side of the river.

"Eliza," he says. "It is a simple process. Just a form to fill out. If you like, I can help you with yours. Your father says that there are still some unclaimed parcels here on the island next to his. You should stake your claim."

I remember that day long ago when I decided to trust God

even if I wasn't sure what the future might bring. Now, here I am alive and happy. Just a few years ago, I did not think it possible, yet this dear man and his family are my friends. Mama and Papa still live with me, and I have two lovely daughters. *What more do I need?*

Thinking back to the past, I recall a time when life seemed hopeless and worthless. On that day, I vowed that if I could, I would have my own land claim. Now, is the time, even if just to show myself it can be done. I send a letter for the papers and fill them out claiming two lots on Terra Ceia Bay to the west of Papa's land totaling sixty-six acres.

I would have been content to let life continue on at this comfortable pace, but Bill interferes. In early October, Julia and Josephine race around the yard in the cool crisp air pretending to be dogs. They jump and yip rolling around growling at each other while Bill and I laugh at them. He tells them that John's dog has puppies and that they can have one if I say it is alright.

"Bill, how can I say no after that? Who would be so heartless! You spoil them you know."

He reaches over to take my hand. I almost jerk it away he surprises me so. As he traces my knuckles gently with one finger, he says, "I know, but they are so easy to spoil. You would be too, Eliza, if you would let me."

I sigh. *Why can't we just stay friends?* Bill is so sweet. I might even be able to love him, but, the thought of marriage again scares me. Once, I felt a love so intense for a man that it overtook my better judgment. *No, I will continue to hold myself back. I can never let myself fall in love again.*

I withdraw my hand from Bill's.

"You are a dear man. But, you know my past. I am not ready for more than friendship."

"Is it possible to hate a man I have never met? Has he so spoiled the thought of love for you that you will not even consider letting me court you?"

"I cannot think of any other man, I would rather spend my life with than you. But, I don't know. Will you give me time?"

"How long, Eliza? How long must I wait?"

I think for a moment. *What if he decides to give up on me altogether?* I couldn't bear to lose him, yet. Even though I cannot think of marrying him either. And the girls. The girls would be heartbroken.

"Give me six months. Then, ask me again."

"I will not speak of it until March then. But, on the first day of March, be prepared to give me an answer, Eliza. I will give you the time you ask, but I am a determined man. I promise you I will ask you again."

All through the fall and winter I watch and listen. If Bill has any flaws, any secrets, I cannot find them. *Who am I to say though? I was blind to Michael's.* I discover a difference between Michael and Bill. Everyone who knows Bill loves him. Both families are anxious for me to give him a favorable answer. Every night, I pray for clarity. I know that Josephine prays because she is no longer content for Bill to be a surrogate father. She lets God and me know her wishes as often as possible. If only my daughter would be as content to wait as Bill.

On March 1, I shade my eyes and scan the horizon. Regretting I left my cape in the cabin, I hug my shawl closer around my shoulders. Standing on the landing, I remember that hot summer day when Bill threatened to teach me to swim. What would it be like to have him so close as he helped me float on the water's surface? I shiver. Up at the cabin, a group of live oaks prevent the north wind's full force. Here at the water's edge I feel its icy grip. March comes in like a raging lion. A cold front brings plunging temperatures and a strong steady gale that whips Terra Ceia Bay into a froth of creamy white caps. No one will venture out on the water today. Not even seamen as skilled as the Fogarty brothers. When Bill pledged to ask me again on March 1, he did not know the weather would be so sour. No, not even a promise will tempt him to risk losing a boat or even his life.

I move into the protection of some palm trees. High in the sky, the sun weakly offers a little warmth as well. Feathered white clouds streaked across the bright sky. It is more than the wind that causes my chill. *What will I do? Why do I wait? He will not come today.* Despite the cold, my palms grow damp. I wipe them on my blue wool dress, and nervously dig the toe of my leather boot into the sand. I still do not like wearing shoes, but it is too cold today to go without. I smooth my hair. The wind pulls tendrils lose from my braid. Go back in the house, Eliza. You have better things to do than stand here and wait. Once again, I squint as I stare into the distance. A glimpse of white catches my eye, but it is only a snowy egret taking flight. A cold nose brushes my hand, and I reach down to fondle the head of a young black dog. Bill made good on his promise to the girls, and they now have Blackie to cherish.

"Hello, little boy. Why aren't you home in front of the fire?"

My mind drifts back to another dog. In another time. *No, don't go there.* Today of all days, don't think about that. Six months ago, I begged for more time to sort out my feelings about love and marriage. No, today, I will not, I cannot think of Michael. An hour passes. Still I wait and watch. Blackie leaves my side to join his young mistresses by the kitchen stove where they learn to bake bread from their grandmother. I know I should return to the cabin to start dinner, but hope forces me to wait.

Then, I see it. A white sail in the distance. By now, I can recognize the characteristic design of a Fogarty built boat. At last, the vessel moves closer to shore, and I glimpse the familiar heads of Bill and Tole. Tole cups his hands around his mouth and calls to me. His voice carries clearly across the water despite the wind.

"Eliza me girl. Is it me or me cargo you await so eagerly?"

I blush. At least if the men can see it, they will blame the color of my cheeks on the wind and cold. Tole does love to tease. Even from the shore, I can see Bill cuff his brother's shoulder. I smile. He's come, just as he promised. I think of home. The noon meal is already being prepared. Mama should know that there will be two more at the table. I call back to the men as the boat shifts and darts between the waves.

"Come to the house when you dock. Dinner will be ready when you are!"

Then, with one last look and a wave, I head to the kitchen.

No doubt the men will be colder, even than me, and will welcome a hot drink before dinner. Fortunately, as always, Mama is prepared for company. When the men come clattering into the kitchen with Papa, all is ready. Josephine jumps up from her place to greet Bill and Tole with a hug. Even Julia raises her hands to be lifted up for a kiss.

"Ah, this little lass knows who is the best uncle on the planet," Tole proclaims.

Josephine clings to Bill making it clear who her choice is.

"Sit down, sit down everyone," Mama says. "Josephine, will you say grace?"

I almost interrupt her. Perhaps that is not a good choice for today. I do not need my daughter reminding God of her desire for a father right now in front of Bill. I breathe a sigh of relief, when Josey simply says, "Thank you God for all our blessings." Then, my daughter raises her eyes and pointedly look at Bill and smiles.

Mama and I serve a thick hearty stew of dried beef, potatoes and carrots. The girls show off the bread that they baked. I pour steaming cups of coffee, then sit down to my meal. The men talk of the weather and its effects on the spring planting season. Though born into an ocean going family, Bill confesses that he truly wants to be a farmer. He is always eager to garner more wisdom from Papa about crops and the land. Tole describes the latest boat they are building, and Josephine hangs on his every word. Where has this thirst for sailing come from in my daughter?

I hear little of the conversation. I keep my outer demeanor calm, but all the while, my mind races through my options. Bill will expect an answer today. *What will I tell him?*

The sound of chairs scraping across the wooden floor startles me. I blink once, and then rise to clear the dishes. I feel Bill's eyes follow me as I move back and forth between the table and the dishpan beside the stove. The men continue their conversation until I dry the last pot and pick up the dish pan. Bill intercepts me and carries it outdoors.

I take my shawl from a hook by the door and follow him outside. Emptying the pan on the ground, he turns to face me. He clears his throat, but hesitates.

Finally, he says "I ran into Grief Johnson the other day. You know he is a surveyor, but he is a Justice of the Peace as well. I asked him if he'd be around this month. He said he would. He's even got a job that will be bringing him out this way."

The concern in his eyes does not match his even and light tone. Bill's hand trembles as he reaches for mine. He grows quiet. I understand his worry. It seems impossible, but this confident man loves me so much that he is shaking. An overwhelming sense of gratefulness and love overcomes me. Bill promises love. Until now, fate denied me in that regard. I decide once and for all to forget the past and take a chance. Oh, Bill, ask me. Go ahead and ask me.

"Eliza, will you marry me?"

I nod my head slowly. A light floods Bill's eyes and erases the fear that once was there.

"Hey, brother!" Tole sticks his head out the kitchen doorway. "Did she say yes?"

Bill whoops. "She did indeed!"

Then, he hugs me as the girls race out the doorway to join in the embrace. At least they are happy. *I think I am too.* Even still, in the midst of their gaiety, I pray, *please God, don't let me regret my answer.*

Chapter Twenty-two

A little less than four weeks later, amid a chorus of good byes and kisses, we board John's smack, the *Grover King*. For a few moments, Bill disappears through the open hatch to place my bag in the small cabin below. Then, he joins me on the deck. When he reaches for my hand, I jump. Sensing my nervousness, Bill squeezes it tightly, and then places it on the wheel.

"I'll hoist the sails. You steer," he says.

The tallest mast is behind the wheel so I cannot see him as he works. Yet, I feel his presence closely and my stomach clinches at the nearness. Guiding the boat keeps my mind occupied for several minutes as Bill hoists the main sail and then, the smaller one at the aft of the boat. By the time, he rejoins me, the gentle beating of the wind in the sails and the rush of water against the boat's hull calm me. I feel the tension leave my body. There is still tonight to consider, but for now, I am content to concentrate on our afternoon sail.

"It was a lovely ceremony, Bill. Grief was a good choice to officiate."

"Not to mention your Mama's cooking." Bill rubs his stomach. "I won't need to eat for days."

There it is again, that nervous feeling in the pit of mine. I leave Bill to guide the small craft out of Terra Ceia Bay and sit on a smooth wooden bench in the stern. From my vantage point, I watch Papa's dock disappear from view. The girls were reluctant to stay behind, but Bill promised to take them on a trip of their own soon. I turn my attention to the many small islands guarding the bay's opening. They are really only oyster beds covered in mangroves. The small bushy trees anchor themselves in the shells and take their nourishment from the salty water. Thousands of birds make their homes within the shelter and feast on the fish that swim among the tree roots. I laugh with delight as a flock of bright pink roseate spoonbills soar over- head.

Bill knows these waters well and carefully negotiates our way through the shallows. As the boat leaves Terra Ceia Bay and enters Tampa Bay, the winds grow stronger, and the little craft races towards its destination. In the distance, I can see Eg- mont Key. Bill says that there are plans to rebuild the lighthouse on the island. Since the war's end five years ago, the light is still tended, but the building itself stands neglected. The narrow passages on each end of the island are treacherous to captains unfamiliar with the area. Not like my husband who knows eve- ry square inch of these waters. *My husband.* I shake myself. It is hard to believe that once again I am married.

Bill adjusts the sails to take us west towards Anna Maria Is- land where we will spend the first night of our brief honey- moon. Bill promises a longer trip at another time, when we can take the girls with us. For now, it is impossible to be gone too long. The reputation of the Fogarty Brothers boat building com- pany is widespread. Residents depend on water travel for their main method of transportation. With all the new settlers coming into the area, someone has to supply them with boats. The Fogarty Brothers intend it to be them and the demand for Fogarty built boats is high. Bill and his brothers work almost night and day to keep up with the orders.

Secretly, I am glad. I am reluctant to leave the girls behind for long, but I am also relieved that my time alone with Bill will be brief. When we return home, we will live in Henry's old cab- in behind my parents. I remember those first weeks alone with Michael and shudder. It will be better this way. I try in vain to block out the memories, but they still come. Even though my marriage to him was almost a decade ago and I have not seen him in seven years, he continues to threaten my happiness. I cringe when I recall that first frightening night as his wife. *Oh,*

God, please let this night hold no such surprises. Surely there will not be any. Haven't I taken longer to get to know this man?

Bill's shout interrupts my unpleasant memories. At his excited gesture, I look behind me to the rear of the boat where a school of dolphins play in the wake. I stand to see them better. Their slick grey bodies dive effortlessly through the waves as they slide in and out of the water. One leaps high in the air and makes a graceful arc before plunging beneath the water once more. A sudden gust of wind pitches the boat forward. I start to fall, but Bill reaches out to catch me.

This time, I welcome his embrace. Kissing my cheek, he pulls me forward to sit beside him at the wheel. There, nestled against his side, I relax and, for the first time, realize my weariness. The emotional events of the preceding days have taken their toil. I rest my head on Bill's shoulder and fall into a troubled sleep.

I dream someone is chasing me. *I run through the woods dodging branches and limbs. My heart races and my breath comes in ragged snatches. A dog howls in the distance. I trip and fall to the damp, hard ground. I try to get up, but something holds me down. Trapped, I fight against my attacker. I wake with a start. I claw at the blanket that covers me and jerk upright from the wooden bench grown cold with the sun's descent. I take deep gulps of the cool night air and shiver in terror. Slowly, my breathing returns to normal as I take in my surrounding and try to set aside the vivid dream. It is dusk, and I can hear the squeal of the anchor chain as Bill secures the boat for the night.*

"Wake up sleepyhead!" Bill calls from the bow. "Are you going to make me cook my own supper?"

I steady myself. Bill must not see my fear. After all, it was just a dream, wasn't it? Bill is not Michael. At least, I hope not. With that thought, I rise from my seat and meet my new husband. After supper of cold meat and cheese, I still feel jumpy. I am not ready to go below, so entice Bill into teaching me about the stars which he uses for navigation. He points out a variety of constellations and tells me stories about their shapes.

"See there, that's the bear," or "Can you see the stars pouring out of the big dipper?" With his help, I can trace each one. Then, we grow quiet.

"Eliza."

"Bill."

We both say each others name at the same time.

"You go first," I say.

"I just wanted to say, I am not Michael. You don't have to fear me."

"I know. I really do. It is just I have all these old memories to fight back."

"Eliza," he traces his finger along my neck. I shiver.

"Whatever you want to do. If you want to wait, we can wait. It is up to you."

I think of his kindness. I have nothing to fear. Bill is not Michael. I turn towards him and reach for his face.

Cupping his cheek in my hand, I say, "No. I am ready. I want to replace those bad times with something better. Help me forget, Bill."

He kisses me tenderly, and then together, we go down into the cabin.

The next morning, I wake next to my new husband. The sailboat rocks and sways gently at its mooring. In the dim light inside the cabin, I watch Bill as he sleeps. *Such peace. Thank you God for this gift.* I never knew that love could be so wonderful. Bill opens his eyes. Before I can close mine and pretend to sleep, he sees me staring at him.

"Good morning, my love. Did you sleep well?"

Overcome with emotion, I nod. Yes, I have never known such joy. *Please God, let it always be this way, I pray.*

We take three more days for ourselves before sailing back to Terra Ceia. Each day we fish and sail. Once, we row in the dingy to the shore of Anna Maria and dig for clams. Bill builds a fire on the beach, and I cook clam chowder for supper. Every night, we sleep locked in each others arms and each morning awake to the gentle sway of the boat. Every day, I feel my heart melt a little more as I learn the ways of my gentle husband. My fear drifts farther and farther away. Always, Bill remains true to the man I befriended before we were lovers. I am confident that he will not change, that there are no surprises in his nature kept secret from me. The specter of Michael fades and slips away.

On the morning that we journey home, Bill says, "Mrs. Fogarty, I declare, you grow lovelier every day."

Mrs. Fogarty.

"That is what love will do for you," I tell Bill as I reach up and give him a kiss. "It takes all the rough edges away."

I am reluctant to end our time together, but at the same time, I long to see the girls again. *How have they fared in the four days since we left?* Bill is also eager to see them again.

"How about we get on home and see our daughters?" he asks.

He pulls up the anchor and soon, we fly towards home. I think the girls will probably be waiting on us. We promised to be back in four days, but, when we reach the bay, no one is there. While Bill ties up the boat, I go on ahead. I miss my girls. In the front yard, I stop for a moment. Something is not right. Someone is weeping. *Mama? Josephine? Julia? Who is crying?* Bill catches up with me.

"What is it?"

"Someone is crying. I don't know who it is."

We follow the sound of the noise. Under a large oak tree, Josephine is curled into a ball with her head buried in her skirt.

"Josey, what's wrong."

I drop down to the ground beside her.

"Mama," Josephine cries even harder.

"Tell me, what is wrong. Mama will fix it. Papa's here too."

"Mama, you can't fix it. I killed her, Mama. I didn't mean to, but I killed her. She's dead."

"Who, Josey? Who is dead?"

"Julia. She died. And it is all my fault, but I didn't mean too."

Julia, dead? *My baby?* I can't breathe. There is no air. Nothing. I choke and gasp. Mama and Papa stand before me. Tears run down their cheeks. I can barely speak,

"Julia. Dead?"

Mama nods her head slowly in assent. *How? Why?* This must be some joke. *I just find happiness only to be denied it? Who are you God to play such tricks on me?*

Julia and Josephine were playing ball. Josephine threw it and it hit Julia in the chest knocking her to the ground. By the time Papa arrived, she was dead. Though everyone assures me that there was nothing I could have done, I cannot get over the fact that while I sailed across the bay with such freedom and joy, one daughter lay dead and the other crying, convinced she killed her sister. *Is God punishing me for choosing to marry Bill? Am I expected to exchange one love for another?* The night before Bill's loving arms wrapped around me. Now, he holds me as I weep.

The next day, I stand beside my daughter's graveside as the little coffin Bill carefully constructed is lowered into the ground. While he labored, Papa sailed to Mary's to let her know. In turn, William went to Fogartyville. The same crowd who just days before joined in the celebration of our marriage gather once again. This time, we mourn. Even with Bill's arm around me and Josephine close beside, I can hardly stay erect. I feel like crumpling into the dirt. Bury me with her. Bury me instead of her. I want my daughter back. I close my eyes and try to remember her face, but the thump, thump of dirt hitting the wooden box reminds me she is gone. Perhaps no one can hear the crash of my heart breaking over the sound. Bill practically carries me back to the house where I sit quietly as the crowd mills around me. Someone is always talking, saying how sorry they are. I nod to each one, but really do not hear what they say. I eat when someone puts a plate into my hand, but do not taste the food. Nothing, nothing matters anymore.

Except Josephine. How to help my daughter cope with my grief and anguish when I can barely consider my own? That night, when all the family and friends are gone, Josephine refuses to sleep in her own bed. So, Bill and I take her into ours. The normally vibrant and talkative child lies between us stiff and still. I pull her close to me. Bill pats Josephine's back, but she pushes him away. She begins to cry. When, the tears come again, all three of us weep together. *Will they ever run dry?*

"I hate Louisa," Josephine manages to say.

"Why do you hate Louisa? She is your cousin."

"She told me that she would be my sister now. But, I had a sister. I don't want Louisa to be my sister. I just want Julia to come back. I was mean to Julia, Mama. Sometimes I told her to go away and not come back, but I didn't mean it. Really, I didn't. I am a bad girl, Mama."

"No, no Josey, you are not a bad girl. Why would you say that?"

"I prayed for a Papa. I wanted one so much, I told God I would do anything for a Papa. I got a Papa, but I lost my sister."

"Oh, Josey." I hear myself in my daughter's words. *Isn't that exactly what I was thinking all day? Why is my first instinct when anything bad happens to think I am being punished?* Now, my daughter feels the same way. Hearing it spoken aloud helps me realize how wrong that line of reasoning is. It is time to stop this way of thinking once and for all.

There in the dark, I console my daughter and as I do, I comfort myself as well.

"No, no, Josey. That is not the way God works. He didn't want Julia to die."

"I heard Mrs. Bethel say, 'God needed another angel in heaven.' He took Julia, I know he did."

"No, Julia, you heard wrong. God has plenty of angels. People die. It is the way our bodies are made. We are not meant to live on this earth forever. Julia did not die because someone did something wrong or because God took her from us."

"No, she died because I killed her." Josephine says solemnly.

"Josephine, did you say to yourself, I am going to kill Julia as you threw that ball?"

"No, I just wanted her to catch it so she could throw it back to me."

"See there, you even wanted her to play. You did not want her to die. You didn't kill her, Josey."

Josephine contemplates my words.

Finally, she asks, "Where is she now, Mama?"

"She is in heaven. And I know she is happy," I say with confidence I don't feel.

"What do you think she is doing, Mama?"

But, before I can answer, I hear Josephine's soft breathing and know that at last, she sleeps.

Bill reaches around my child and softly strokes my hair.

"I love you, Eliza. Try to sleep as well." Amazingly, I do.

The next morning, Josephine wakes us early.

"Mama, Mama, get up. I saw Julia."

Julia. *Where is Julia? Why was Josephine in our bed?* Then, I remember. Julia is dead. Though I have cried so many tears, more spring to my eyes.

"No, Mama, listen. I saw Julia." I cannot speak.

"Where did you see her?" Bill asks.

"I saw her in heaven. You are right Mama, she is happy. She was laughing. A man was holding her. I think it was Jesus. He was all bright and shiny. Julia loves him. I can tell."

She tugs on the sleeve of me nightdress.

"Mama, the man told me something. He said we don't have to worry about Julia anymore. He will take care of her. Mama, he told me something else. He said, someday, I will be with him, too. That I would die and go to heaven. He told me not to be afraid. He said to tell you not to be afraid either."

In her excitement, Josephine kneels in the middle of the bed and continues, "The man said we will see Julia again. Someday, I will play with my sister again. Then, he went off with Julia. I could see trees and there was a river. I bet they were going to find a swing. Maybe they were going swimming. Mama, heaven looks like a wonderful place. It is going to be alright, Mama."

I listen to my daughter describe heaven. *Thank you God for comforting her in a way that she can understand. And thank you for helping her share that vision with me.*

Josephine's bright outlook spills over on me. Though some days are a struggle just to get out of bed, I cling to the fact that Julia is in a better place and someday, I will hold my daughter in heaven again.

Two weeks after Julia's funeral, Papa finally receives good news. On April 14, he receives the papers confirming his land grant. After twenty seven years of waiting, he legally owns our land. At supper that night, he shows the papers almost reverently.

"I must get to Manatee to record these soon."

He turns and kisses Mama.

"Julia, can you believe it? I am a landowner now. We will finally have our deed. I must let John Jackson know and thank him for his help."

I am happy for Papa. I know how good it feels to own a piece of land. But, I would trade all of mine if only Julia was alive again.

Spring turns into summer. Blindingly hot weather arrives, sapping me of all my strength. It is too hot to eat. Even when the afternoon rainstorms come through to cool off the steaming earth, I still cannot enjoy my supper. Food no longer sits well with me. I am still grieving, I think.

Sometimes, the sight of Julia's empty bed, or a seeing a seashell along the beach reminds me of my daughter's absence. Even though I chose to trust that God is in control, it still hurts so much. One morning as I bend over the laundry tub, I feel faint. Slowly, I ease down onto the porch steps and put my head between my knees.

"Eliza, are you alright?" Mama asks.

"I just don't feel well. Sometimes, my grief catches me a little off guard is all. I will be fine in a minute."

"Are you sure it is grief that makes you this way? You look different, but it is not sorrow that makes you so. When was your last monthly cycle?"

Funny, I wonder the same thing, but I credit the halt of my menses to my loss.

"I really can't remember. I think it was before the wedding."

"Eliza." Mama draws out my name in a single breath.

"I know, Mama. But, I cannot imagine that it could be true."

"What are your other symptoms?"

"I don't feel like eating, yet I am gaining weight. I feel so lethargic and tired. But, all of that could be a result of Julia's death."

"And they also could be a result of new life. Do you want to see a doctor? There is one in Manatee now, a Dr. Pelot."

"No, let's just see where this leads," I reply. "I could be wrong."

"When will you tell Bill?"

"When the time is right. Let's just keep it a secret for now."

Mama agrees, and then adds, "I wouldn't keep it from him for long, though. The man is going to be over the moon with happiness when you tell him. And we could all use some more happiness right about now."

I think about Mama's comment later on that month, when Bill invites me to go for an evening sail.

"Where is Josephine?" I ask. "She will want to come."

"I bribed your mother into keeping her occupied for me. It

has been a long time since we have been alone together. I just wanted a few minutes to have my wife all to myself."

A feeling of contentment floods my soul. *He loves me so.* In spite of all the hardship we have encountered, that is the one thing I can count on. I climb aboard Papa's yawl as Bill unties the lines and raises the sail. Soon, we skip across the bay waters in the moonlight. It feels good just to sit here next to him on the seat as he steers the boat by its rudder. I nestle beside him, and he puts his arm around me. His hand absently rubs my waist. *Can he feel the thickening there?* Perhaps this is a good time to share my secret.

"Bill," I whisper. He cannot hear me over the sound of the wind and waves.

"Bill!" I say louder this time. He looks down, smiles and raises his eyebrows in question.

"Bill, what would you like for Christmas?"

"For Christmas? It is mid summer. Why do you ask such a question?"

"I just wondered. Would you like a boy or a girl for Christmas?"

"A what? A boy or a girl what?"

Then, the answer dawns on him.

"A baby? We are going to have a baby?"

I nod.

Bill shouts. "A baby! I am going to be a father!"

I look up and see a full moon shining down on us. Mama is right. If it were possible, Bill Fogarty would jump right over the moon if he could.

My stomach continues to grow as the seasons change. Fall arrives and with it the baby's first kicks. Bill loves putting his hand on my belly to feel the movements there. He is learning about farming from Papa. He vows he will be a farmer one day and set aside his work as a shipbuilder.

"I already know how to grow children," he teases me as he

plays with Josephine and waits for our baby's birth. Mixed with my happiness is a growing concern about Josephine's health. The rainy season ends, but leaves Josephine with a bad cough. Sometimes, she cannot catch her breath and chokes. It is particularly bad at night. Then, none of us can sleep for Josephine's wheezing. The high pitched bark alarms me, and I take her to Manatee to see Dr. Pelot.

"Rain Fever," he pronounces and gives me some medicine for Josephine to swallow and another one to place in a saucer and burn.

"The vapor should open up her lungs," he says.

Instead of getting better, Josephine grows worse. Lying flat increases the coughing, so I spend many nights in the rocking chair, holding Josephine in my lap as she sleeps fitfully. I pray a lot. *Please God, spare my daughter. I can not bear to lose this one as well.*

Then, a fever comes. Josephine alternates between chills and sweating. When she is hot, I bath her in a tub of water. When she is cold, I bundle her in blankets. All the while, Bill hovers over us both, helping where he can. Even though she loves the Papa for whom she prayed, when she is ill, Josephine wants her Mama. One night as I sway back and forth in the rocking chair holding my daughter fast as she labors to breathe, I pray in time to my rocking. *God, I am so weary. Listen to her little chest as it rattles. Please God, heal my little girl. Make her strong and whole again so she can play and do the things she loves so much.*

Josephine stirs and whispers, "Mama?"

"Yes, Josey."

"Mama, don't worry about me. Remember the man, Mama? Don't be sad. The man is here. I am going sailing."

I think she must be dreaming. I am so tired. My head nods to my chest, and the rocker is still. I dream of Josephine at the helm of Papa's yawl. *She sails away out of sight of land. I stand on the shore. Come back, Josey. Don't leave Mama, I cry.*

I jerk awake. Josephine is quiet, and her body cool. *Has God answered my prayers? Is the fever gone? Is she healed?*

Wait. I feel of Josephine's chest. It does not rise and fall.

I cry, "No, God, no!"

Bill wakes from where he sleeps nearby.

"Eliza, what is it? What is wrong?"

I choke on my words.

"Josephine. Josephine is dead."

"Are you sure? Perhaps she just sleeps."

He takes Josephine's limp body from me and places her on the bed, but he cannot rouse her. I remember my dream.

"Come back, Josey. Don't leave Mama."

I fall over my daughter's lifeless body.

Chapter Twenty-three

All night, I keep vigil with Josephine. Mama sits beside me saying nothing. What can anyone say that will comfort me? By lamplight, Bill and Papa construct the second little coffin in six months. I cannot go through another funeral. *God, help me.* I visualize another hole in the ground, another child being lowered down into the earth's depth. *God give me strength.*

I feel a familiar cramping in my abdomen. The baby, *no, God. It is too early.* A gush of blood, and I know that it is too late for a miracle. With Josephine's body beside me, I give birth to a perfectly formed, but tiny stillborn boy. I hold him in my arms for just a moment until Mama takes him from me. Bill wipes away tears, as he cradles his firstborn child and kisses his soft little head. Then, he searches for wood for another tiny box.

Fine God, take all my children. Take them all at once. What do you care? I rage against God and His failure to keep my children safe and secure. *What do you want from me? Am I an unfit mother that you would do such a thing?*

By morning, I am too sick to get up for the funerals. Both Josephine and the new baby are buried without their mother's presence. *Didn't I say that I could not go through another funeral? Now He chooses to answer my prayers?* I picture God laughing at me. That will fix her, He probably says. She doesn't want to go to the burial, then, I will keep her from it. I no longer expect a response to my prayers.

For two days, I remain in bed in a darkened room. Even if I want to, I cannot get up. My body has a mind of its own. My legs will not hold me, my arms are empty and weak. I do not have the strength. I wish to die.

I recall a time so long ago when I was pregnant with dear sweet Josey. Then, too, the darkness flooded my soul. It would have been so easy to wade into the water and drown my sorrows under the waves. Maybe, I should have. Maybe it would have been better not to have known them at all than to have lost them this way. Perhaps, it is not too late. Something kept me from it then, the love of my child. But, now, there are no children to hold me to this earth so full of sorrow and pain. If only I had the strength. I would walk down to the water and never hurt again.

"May I come in?" Ann Fogarty knocks on the door of the cabin. "Bill said you might be sleeping, but I hoped you would be awake. I brought you something."

Ann offers me a book, but my hand will not open to take it. She sets it on the bed beside me.

"It is a Bible. It was mine as a girl. I thought it might bring you comfort. Oh, Eliza, I do not know what to say to you. I cannot imagine the depths of your grief. But, from the time I first met you, I could tell that you believed in God. Even in the darkness, Eliza, He is there."

Tears seep from my eyes and down my cheeks. I thought it impossible to cry anymore. *How does Ann know the depths of my despair?* Try as I might, I cannot summon the words to tell her how lost and alone I feel. God might be a loving God, but it does not feel like that right now. I know I should have faith even when I can't understand, but in the darkness, I do not have the power within myself to choose to trust.

Ann continues, "When I am lonely or afraid, I read the Psalms. Did you know that some of them were written by a man who was sad because his child died? He knew how you felt Eliza. He was surrounded by his enemies and did not feel like he could go on, but still God was with him. Would you mind if I read some aloud to you?"

When I don't respond, Ann picks up the Bible and reads.

I hardly listen.

"'Bless the Lord, O my soul: and all that is within me, bless his holy name.' Even when we feel like our soul is empty and dry, if we look deep within ourselves, we can still find something to thank God for," Ann explains. "'Bless the Lord, O my soul, and forget not all his benefits.' I know how easy it is for me to get distracted from the good things that God has done for me in the past when I focus only on my present circumstances."

She asks, "Is it the same with you?"

Yes, it is the same with me, I guess. In my sorrow and grief I can hardly remember when life was good and full. I pay closer attention.

"'Who forgiveth all thine iniquities; who healeth all thy diseases; Who redeemeth thy life from destruction.'"

That sounds like me. My life is totally destroyed.

"'Who crowneth thee with lovingkindness and tender mercies; Who satisfieth thy mouth with good things; so that thy youth is renewed like the eagle's.'"

Is that really possible? The last few days have not held love or mercy. I am exhausted, completely alone and unloved. Yet, if what Ann reads is true, God can bring something good out of this time. *Can He really bring renewal?* I think of the eagles that soar over the prairie. What would it be like to fly so high and free away from my sorrow?

"'The Lord executeth righteousness and judgment for all that are oppressed.'"

Oppressed is a good word to describe how I feel right now.

"'He made known his ways unto Moses, his acts unto the children of Israel. The Lord is merciful and gracious, slow to anger, and plenteous in mercy.'"

Mercy again, where is His mercy towards me now?

"'He will not always chide: neither will he keep his anger for ever. He hath not dealt with us after our sins; nor rewarded us according to our iniquities. For as the heaven is high above the earth, so great is his mercy toward them that fear him.'"

I think of a clear blue sky on a crisp fall day when it seems like you can see all the way to heaven. *Is God's love for me really that high? I do not feel loved right now.*

"'As far as the east is from the west, so far hath he removed our transgressions from us. Like as a father pitieth his children, so the Lord pitieth them that fear him.'"

Do you really pity me, God? Are you thinking of me right now as I am beside myself with grief?

"'For he knoweth our frame; he remembereth that we are dust. As for man, his days are as grass: as a flower of the field, so he flourisheth. For the wind passeth over it, and it is gone; and the place thereof shall know it no more.'"

My children. My children will be dust. My heart breaks at the thought.

"'But the mercy of the Lord is from everlasting to everlasting upon them that fear him, and his righteousness unto children's children.'"

Is that a promise God? Was Josephine right? Do you really hold my three babies in your arms right now?

Ann continues on with the Psalm. The words comfort me even if I do not understand all that they mean.

"'To such as keep his covenant, and to those that remember his commandments to do them. The Lord hath prepared his throne in the heavens; and his kingdom ruleth over all. Bless the Lord, ye his angels, that excel in strength, that do his commandments, hearkening unto the voice of his word. Bless ye the Lord, all ye his hosts; ye ministers of his, that do his pleasure. Bless the Lord, all his works in all places of his dominion: bless the Lord, O my soul.'"

Bless the Lord, O my soul. I like the way that sounds. Perhaps someday, I will feel like blessing God again.

"Where are those verses found?" I startle myself with my own voice. I thought I would never speak again. I am hoarse and weak from crying.

"That is Psalm 103. Here I will mark it for you." Ann takes a ribbon from her hair and places it within the pages.

"Would you like for me to read more?"

I shake my head.

"No, not now. But, thank you for coming."

"I will leave the Bible here in case you want to read those verses again," Ann says.

"Eliza, know that I am praying for you. I cannot comfort you, but God can. Remember how it said, 'God's love is everlasting?' Even when you can't feel Him. Even when the future seems uncertain. God still loves you."

Ann stands to go. She puts the Bible back beside me. Slowly, I move my hand towards it until my fingers can touch it. I never had a Bible of my own before. Always, Mama's thick German Bible rests in the parlor, but, I cannot read German. I am not much of a scholar, but perhaps, if there are more words of comfort in this book, I will read it for myself.

God still loves you. Wasn't that what Henry always said? I recall that day long ago when I was pregnant with Josephine and Henry took me to visit Mama. We talked about his babies. How he longed to rock them again, but that he might not be able to until he went to heaven. *Did Henry know then what the future would hold for me? Did God?*

How did Henry know that I would need his words so desperately some day? And Josephine's dream, so vivid and clear. *What did the man tell her?* That she would die and go to heaven. Not to be afraid, he said. Not to be sad. I stay in bed for another week, thinking of my babies, all three of them carried by Jesus until I can join them. Gradually, instead of visualizing my own death, I can only think of life.

Over and over in me, echo the words from long ago, "Come to Papa." That day when I jumped and put my trust in God, there were no guarantees that life would be perfect. Henry's life was certainly an example of that. He suffered slavery, separation from this family, beatings and attack. Yet, he remained steadfast to his belief that God loved him Henry said that God promised to keep me close. So, I imagine myself crawling up into my Heavenly Father's lap.

Sometimes I feel comfortable and secure. Sometimes, I weep and wail. I beat my head against the pillow and tell God of my anger and disappointment. Still, He holds me fast and will not let me go. No matter my frame of mind, God does not abandon me. Sweet memories of my little girls fill my mind keeping me from drowning in my sorrow. God's love is everlasting and so will my love be for my children, even the little boy I did not have the opportunity to know. Perhaps there are some things I can be thankful for. *If I look hard enough.* I can start with Bill who grows sadder and sadder each day I refuse to get up. Like God, he loves me and will not let me go.

Finally at peace, I rise and dress. My insides still shake, but at least on the outside, I am calm. For now, I will choose to trust even if I don't know why there are three little graves behind the house with my children's names on them. One day at a time, I moved forward. Some days are more painful than others. Some days bring glimpses of joy. As time passes, my faith grows fueled by reading the Bible Ann brought. It is still so hard.

I miss my children desperately. Not only the three first lost, but two more miscarried. I never get used to the loss. To be so filled with happiness one day and have it stolen from me the next. By the last pregnancy, I barely allow myself to dream, so sure am I that the baby will not live full term. That little one is another girl. She even looks a little like Julia and Josephine. Five babies dead now. Five resting in Jesus' arms. Or climbing trees in heaven if Josephine can be believed. It doesn't make it any easier, though I found some comfort in knowing like Henry one day I will rock my babies again.

Through it all, I develop a love for Bible Study and prayer. I can't believe it, but I crave God's Word. Reading the Bible that Ann gave me helps me to understand more about God. It keeps me from sinking into darkness. Every day, I find that I am a little stronger.

Ann and I often meet to discuss what I am learning and to share passages of scripture. I still love Psalms the best, but we read the stories about Jesus' life, too. I especially like Matthew 19:14 where Jesus says, "Suffer little children, and forbid them not, to come unto me: for of such is the kingdom of heaven." It helps to know that Jesus himself called the children to Him. Josephine was right. Julia loved the man.

Like my daughters, I am also learning to love God, but I do not care for the church. Though Ann often asks, I refuse to attend church with her. Every Sunday, John rows Ann and their son, Robert, down the river to the church at Manatee. Too many hurt feelings still plague my heart for me to be able to join them. I might be loved by God, but His followers prove to be another matter entirely. All except for Ann and Bill's family, in my opinion, God's earthly followers leave much to be desired. They excluded me once, falsely accused my family twice and accused me of sin. No, I can live without the church. People may disappoint and fail me, but God, as Ann showed me in the Psalms on that dark, dark day, never changes and remains always faithful and true.

In August of 1871, I feel the now familiar symptoms of pregnancy. Despite my growing beliefs, pessimism fills my heart. *Another loss to endure, God?* You must think I'm stronger than I am. I do not even bother to tell anyone. *Why dash their hopes again?* It is almost more than I can endure. I can at least spare Bill the pain. It saddens me to see him playing with his nieces and nephews. They love their Uncle Bill. Josephine and Julia once loved him as well. He would be such a good father. My heart breaks more for his loss than mine. *Does he regret marrying me?*

While I plan to keep my pregnancy a secret, my body gives me away almost from the start. Oddly, this pregnancy takes me back to the symptoms of my first. Just as when I carried Josephine, nausea plagues me as do dizziness and fainting. I try not to let my illness show, but it is impossible.

One noon, I walk into the kitchen where Mama fries fish. Papa and Bill sit at the table discussing the latest crop. The smell immediately assaults me as I step through the doorway. My stomach rolls, and I back out of the room and flee to the outhouse. When my heaves finish, I wash my hands with water from the basin on the porch. I splash some onto my face as well. Returning to the kitchen, I find Papa, Mama and Bill sitting at the table, plates untouched staring at me.

"Sit down, Eliza," Mama says kindly.

But the odor in the room is still too strong. Once again, I rush outside. I rest on the steps of the porch breathing deeply willing my stomach to settle. *Why me God? What is it about me that causes You to plague me so?* I am too weak to even rise. Not only because my body feels so frail, but at the thought of losing another child. *I cannot bear this God. Go ahead and take him now. Don't make me wait and hope and think that maybe this time everything will be alright.*

Bill joins me where I sit, head between my knees. How long have I cried? My skirt is soaked with tears.

"Eliza," he says softly, as he lowers himself to the step beside me.

"Don't cry. It will be alright."

"No, it won't." I rub my hand across my nose. I must look miserable with my eyes swollen.

"That is always what I think and then, my baby dies and I am left with only heartache."

Bill puts his arm around me.

"I'm sorry. I know you have been disappointed before, but maybe this time."

Poor Bill, he has suffered, too. *How to tell him I would just as soon miscarry today and get it over with?* I don't feel like trying anymore. No, I cannot tell him that. He will think me heartless.

I lean against him and sigh.

"Your parents and I have been talking. I want to take you to see Dr. Pelot in Manatee. There must be something he can do."

"No." I regret the sharpness of my tone, but he must understand. "I will not go to Manatee."

"Then, Tampa, there must be a doctor in Tampa. Eliza, I cannot stand back and do nothing. Let's try. Go with me, please?"

Does he think I lost my babies for lack of trying? My face gets red. *Does he think that another woman, a better woman, might have a houseful of children underfoot?* As hard as I try to remember about God's love and faithfulness, in times like these, it is so hard.

"Please, Eliza," Bill rarely asks me for anything.

This is his child, too. I can at least give him this, but I will not go to Manatee.

Instead, we sail to Tampa. My spirits lift out on the water. The salt air gives me strength. Maybe this time, things will be different. I remember the first time I sailed to Tampa. How I hated to leave my home on the island to live at Fort Brooke. I tell Bill about the move.

"I have lived in Tampa, and on the river. But, I never could imagine being happy anywhere but Terra Ceia." I frown.

"And now?" Bill prompts.

"And now, I know that no matter where I go, this world holds both joy and pain. I won't ever be truly content until I am in my heavenly home."

"So, are you unhappy with me, then as well?"

"Oh, no." I reach over and take his hand and squeeze it.

"I am so blessed to have you as my husband. You have taught me about love. I learn much about God through your kindness and consistency. No, Bill, you do not make me unhappy. In fact, what joy I have is from knowing you and being your wife."

I tilt my head back and scan the sky.

"It is just so hard. So much bad happens not just to me, but everyone. My head knows that God is in control, but sometimes, my heart hurts so deeply that I forget. It is like being torn in two. One foot set firmly on knowing God is in charge and loves me, but the other is rooted in sorrow and grief."

Bill nods. He feels it, too. I think for a moment.

"Did you know that Ann and I are studying Abraham?"

"I know that you two are the most unusual women I have met. What do you find to talk about out of those dusty books, I will never understand."

"It's not boring at all, Bill. I thought it would be, but there are so many stories in there of how God blesses His people. He made a promise to Abraham that he would be the father of many nations. Abraham did not think that it could happen because his wife was old and so was he. They didn't even have a home. They just wandered around from place to place dodging enemies and looking for the land that God had promised them. Abraham made a lot of mistakes and everything did not go well for him, but God was still there, watching out for him, making a way for him when he listened and obeyed."

"I still don't understand how you can say that you can't be happy here, with me," Bill says.

"I can be happy. It is just that part of me knows that there is something better somewhere. I just don't feel complete. I am longing for something, somewhere else."

Bill offers, "Maybe if you had a baby, you would feel better."

"A baby would be nice, a child to love, but even then, that can be taken away."

I think of the little graves behind the house. Bill knows it, too.

"I can be content here, but I will never be satisfied."

That doesn't sound right, will Bill think I am complaining about him?

"Bill, I wish I could explain it so you would understand. It is like this boat. You are a good sailor, you know how to maneuver the sails to help them catch the wind and when the seas are calm and the wind is just the right speed, we go flying over the water. But, everything has to be in place. If the rudder breaks or a storm comes or the wind stops blowing, we flounder along or come to a dead stop. I'm happy, but not as happy as I will be when the conditions are perfect. And they won't be perfect until I get to heaven."

"I guess that makes sense. But, Eliza, I love you and want you to be as happy as you can here and now, with me."

"I know, Bill, and I want the same for you. That is why I agreed to go and see the doctor. It would be so easy to give up. But, for you, I will fight to keep this baby."

Something new occurs to me. I feel a stirring of excitement I have not felt for a long time.

"Bill, I never thought of it until now, but if God could give Abraham a baby, maybe, He will give us one, too."

Bill smiles at me. "I hope so. Not just for me, but for you, too."

Dr. Branch remembers me.

After hearing about my miscarriages and the strains of the last few years, he says, "I don't know any physical reason why you should not be able to carry a child full term, Mrs. Fogarty. You had healthy babies. You can again. Perhaps, you are working too hard or worrying too much."

I squirm in my seat. *Is he blaming me then?*

Dr. Branch is quick to correct himself, "I did not mean that it was your fault. This is a tough place to be a woman. There are many demands on you, I know. As much as I wish I could say for sure what would help, medicine is not advanced enough to predict who lives and who dies. Only God knows what the future holds for you. My best advice is to go to bed. Don't overdo, get plenty of rest. Let others wait on you. That still may not be enough, but at least you did the best you could."

Dr. Branch does not give me the magic potion I long for. Instead, he turns me back full circle. Medicine cannot help me, but God can. If He chooses to do so. *Will He?* As we sail home in silence, I watch the sunlight dance upon the waves and the white puffy clouds that filled the blue sky above us. I remember the illustration I used earlier to try and help Bill understand how I feel about this world and my longing for a heavenly home. The words seem inadequate now.

It sounds like I have no reason to live. That isn't true. There is still good in the life that God gives me. Bill is one. I am grateful for his love. *How can I put into words the mix of grief and contentment I feel?* The world is full of sorrow, yet God remains in control. All I have to do is trust that somehow in all of the hardships that I have faced and will endure, God can be trusted to make things right. *I hardly understand it myself, so how can I share it with Bill?*

The beauty of my surroundings reminds me of a hymn that Mama often sings, "Commit Whatever Grieves Thee." I hear her strong alto voice in my mind.

Commit whatever grieves thee
Into the gracious hands
Of Him who never leaves thee,
Who heaven and earth commands.
Who points the clouds their courses,
Whom winds and waves obey,
He will direct thy footsteps
And find for thee a way.

On Him place thy reliance
If thou wouldst be secure;
His work thou must consider
If thine is to endure.
By anxious sighs and grieving

And self-tormenting care
God is not moved to giving;
All must be gained by prayer.

Thy hand is never shortened,
All things must serve Thy might;
Thine every act is blessing,
Thy path is purest light.
Thy work no man can hinder,
Thy purpose none can stay,
Since Thou to bless Thy children
Wilt always find a way.

As Bill pilots the little boat back to Terra Ceia, I pray, God help me to quit fretting and worrying. Help me to remember that you control the wind and the sea and that you will find a way to help me get through this. *God, if it is your will, please grant us this baby. Not just for me, but for Bill. Find a way, God.* I remember long ago that Henry said the faith I saw him in was only there because God gave it to him. So, I add, *give me faith as well, God. Faith no matter what happens.*

When we arrive home, Mama and Papa wait anxiously. God must be listening, for I feel calmer than when we left.

After Bill explains what Dr. Branch said, I add, "It is all in God's Hands. We will wait and see. But, I promise to do as Dr. Branch has said, if you don't mind doing without me. I feel very selfish to ask for you all to pamper me so."

"Nonsense!" Mama replies. "We will all do what we can to help."

Papa nods, "You concentrate on growing that little one and the rest of us will take care of everything else. And we will all be praying as well."

"Now, off to bed, Eliza," Mama says. "Bill, see that she stays there!"

Though I don't feel at all funny, I have to laugh and make light of it.

"Yes, Ma'am. I'm going, but you will miss me come dinnertime."

"Oh, we'll be round to keep you company. You'll be sick of us before this is all over."

Papa smiles and hugs me. Then, I follow Bill to the cabin and to bed.

Papa is true to his word. Most days, Bill sails to Fogartyville to help his brothers with the shipyard. So, every day, Papa brings me dinner and sits with me while I eat. He spends an hour or so as we talk about the past and make plans for the future. "Remember when", becomes a favorite game as we talk about old times. I learn things I did not know about my father's childhood, and gain a different perspective on our pioneer life.

"Oh, how I hated to go off and leave you and your Mama here alone all those times. I never knew when I sailed back into the bay if you would still be here."

"Were you worried that something might harm us?"

"Yes, but I was more worried that your mother might be so fed up with life in the wilderness that she would take the first boat out of here." Papa laughs.

"She stuck with me through thick and thin though. I have been a blessed man to have her love."

"Remember when she shot the owl, Papa?" We laugh together at the memory. Somehow, looking back, it does not seem as scary as it once did. Good comes even out of the bad.

I speak my thoughts aloud.

"God has blessed us. When we were in the midst of it, sometimes it was hard to see. But, He has. Papa, remember when that priest came, and Mama made you go to mass?"

"Yes," he answers.

"I failed to share with her completely what I believed. She was worried about my relationship with God." He laughs. "I have taken care to rectify that. I learned not to be afraid to tell people about God. I used to think if I just lived my life as a good man that they would know Who I served. But, I realized you have to speak up as well. Otherwise, they think you just live under a lucky star."

Chapter Twenty-four

Weeks go by, and I stay in bed. Other than short walks to the outhouse, I remain flat on my back for so long I feel weak. My head spins when I stand. But, every day, my stomach gets a little bigger. *The baby lives.* Although everyone comes to visit frequently, situated as I am in the cabin away from the house, I feel isolated and often out of sorts. I don't mean to be. I can't control my irritation. Poor Bill takes the brunt of it. He comes in from a day at the shipyard full of stories about his brothers, their wives, and children. He tells of their work and the customers. The ports that John visits in his role as ship captain, and it just makes me aggravated. People play, work and enjoy the outdoors while I lie here as the season turns with nothing to do but think. It is worse than those long ago days stuck at school. I do not want to hear his tales. I interrupt to complain. The pillows are flat. The mattress is lumpy. The cabin is hot. Can he open a window? Now, the sun is in my eyes. Shut the drapes. As soon as Bill leaves to get his supper or help Papa with chores, I feel great remorse. I know I should not treat him that way. It is not his fault that my body does not bear children well. As soon as he comes back, I plan to apologize, but upon his return, I forget and start in again with my list of woes.

One day, Mama brings an armful of fresh linens as Bill stands quietly under the latest onslaught.

Mama says, "Bill, I think Joseph is looking for you out in the garden. He wanted to show you how the peppers have grown."

Bill barely makes his escape, before Mama turns to me and says, "Eliza, I know how difficult this is for you, but you must stop this harping. Do you realize how you sound? So ungrateful. The man has done nothing wrong, but try and make you happy. How do you reward him? Sounding like a spoiled princess. We want to help you, but you don't make it easy on your husband. I realize that there is not much you can do in bed, but why don't you spend some time figuring out how you can help others and be kind instead of griping every minute of the day. For Heaven's sake, make a list of all you have to be grateful for at least."

Then, Mama flounces from the room leaving me alone to contemplate her words. Spoiled princess. Yes, that is what I have become. *When was the last time I said please or thank you?* I do have much to be grateful for, but neglect to show it. Not only to my family, but to God as well.

Vowing that I will not let another moment go by without starting that list, I begin at once. Bill. Mama. Papa. So far, the baby lives. A place to live. Family. Friends. Before I am done, Bill comes back into the room. I have been so self centered, I have not noticed how sad and tired he looks. Another thing to be thankful for, that Mama did not let me continue wallowing in my misery while Bill's troubles went unnoticed. I pat the bed.

"Come sit down for a minute."

Bill approaches the bed cautiously. Poor dear. Have I been so mean that he is wary of approaching me? He sits down gingerly.

"Bill, I am sorry for being so rotten. I have been behaving like a spoiled princess. I shouldn't complain so much. I really do have a lot to be grateful for starting with a very dear husband who wants to please me. I love you. Will you forgive me?"

Bill strokes my cheek.

"Of course, I will. I know how hard this is for you. I wish I could do more to make it easier."

"I will be fine," I say honestly. "I have just been thinking of everything I cannot do. But, I am going to change that and make a list of all I can do."

Bill smiles. "There you go, Mrs. Fogarty. I like that spirit."

My list turns out to be quite long. I can knit and began a blanket. If for some reason, I can't use it for the baby, I will just make it big enough for a bed. I take on the mending and darn socks as well. Mama lets me help with some of the food preparation. I can shell peas or snap beans lying down. I read my Bible for hours on end, and most of all, I can pray. Not just for myself and the baby, but for others as I hear of their needs.

In that role, I feel most useful. I did not realize what joy can be found in bringing other people's problems to God. When people come to visit, I ask them if there is something I can pray about for them. My time of idleness turns into a time of great privilege as I go to God day after day interceding for my family, friends and neighbors in prayer.

One morning as I pray, I cannot get Michael out of my mind. Normally, thoughts of my former husband bring forth a wide range of emotions, fear, anxiety, hurt, anger and betrayal. I cannot even think that name without my stomach knotting. It is odd, but now, I feel God speaking directly to me.

Forgive Michael. Forgive him? How can I ever pardon him for the wickedness he did to me? Let me count all the hurts, God. Physical, mental, emotional. How many lies did I believe? How many beatings did I take? How many illnesses did I suffer? How much embarrassment did I endure? How much anguish did I feel? All because of him. And you are asking me to forgive?

Let it go, Eliza. *No, God. I cannot let it go.* I try to ignore God's calling. Trying to drown Him out, I open my Bible to read. That is a mistake for my eyes immediately fall upon Matthew 18:21-22, "Then, came Peter to him, and said, Lord, how oft shall my brother sin against me, and I forgive him? till seven times? Jesus saith unto him, I say not unto thee, Until seven times: but, Until seventy times seven."

No, God. You have asked me to do too much. Yet, the longer I think about those words, the more I know that I have to obey. *God, I said I cannot do it, but if you will help me, I will try.* I remember Michael's face and imagine talking to him.

"I forgive you. I forgive you for the lies, the pain, and the fear. I forgive you for taking something precious from me, the love I gave, and throwing it back in my face. I forgive you for cheating my daughters of knowing their father. I forgive you not because you deserve it but because I choose to forgive."

In all of my wildest dreams, I could never have imagined that the act of forgiveness would be so freeing. *Have I been carrying such a load all these years without realizing it? What a weight off my shoulders!* Now forgive the others, God says to me. And so, one by one, I begin recalling past hurts and slights and pardoning those offenders as well.

When Papa comes to share dinner, he looks at me strangely.

"What have you been up to this morning?" he asks.

"Not much," I hedge. "Why do you ask?"

"There is a light in your eyes that I have not seen before. I can't put my finger on it exactly. Not happiness, but almost a peace. Is something different then?"

And so, I tell him everything as he nods and witnesses the power of forgiveness.

When I am done, he says, "Daughter, you inspire me. There are some for whom I have held a grudge. Perhaps, I need to make my own list as well. And let some of that ugliness go."

He kisses the top of my head as he leaves.

"I love you Liza, dear. I always will."

One person who does not come to see me is Mary.

When I ask Mama why, she confesses, "She is afraid to come. She feels guilty that Louisa still lives and does not want to hurt you by bringing her daughter or speaking of her to you."

"Tell her to come, Mama. Tell her I need to see her."

A few days later, Mary arrives.

"I am sorry that I have not been by sooner."

"I understand," I assure her. "This has been a difficult time. I was not a nice person for a while. But, I am better now. Tell me how is Louisa?"

Mary cautiously begins speaking of her daughter. Even

though it hurts, I ask questions to draw her out.

"Where is Louisa now?" I ask.

"She is in the kitchen with Mama. I left her there."

"Go and get her, won't you? I would love to see how she has grown."

So, Mary fetches Louisa, and though it is hard, I greet her warmly.

After they leave, I realize that there is she still one thing I need to deal with. It takes me a few days to figure it out, but on October 19, I know. No one else says anything, perhaps they hope I do not remember as there are no calendars in the cabin, but I will never forget the day.

Josephine died one year ago. Thinking about that horrible night, I wonder, is it possible that I need to forgive God? *Could one do such a thing?* No matter how much I speak piously of God's will and God's timing, deep down I hold a seed of bitterness. Recognizing the resentment is easier than doing something about it. Again I wrestle with God. *Am I wrong to bring this up? Am I lacking in faith because I must ask?*

Still I feel Him whispering, "Go ahead and ask. Give it to me. I can take it."

I am afraid. *How can I speak to God this way?* I feel like He is giving me the invitation to lay it all bare.

So, I whisper, "I am angry with you God. Why me? Why my children? Will you ever tell me the reason why?" Then, cautiously I take another step.

"I am willing to give up this anger if you will just take it from me."

I look down. My hands are clinched. I open them palms up and feel the anger slip away, and I move closer towards finding true peace.

I remember that moment of peace eleven days later, when I wake one morning to the sound of Mama's cries. Bill jumps out of bed, pulling his pants on as he dashes out the cabin door.

"Stay here," he orders.

But, it is hard to wait. *Whatever can be wrong with Mama?* After what seems like an eternity, Bill reenters the cabin. His head is down as he rubs his hand through his hair. Then, he looks me in the eyes. Something terrible has happened. I can see it reflected there.

"Bill, what is it? Tell me?"

He sits down beside me on the bed and takes my hand.

"Eliza, I am afraid to tell you. We have worked so hard to have this baby. I do not know how you can bear this."

"Bill, what is it? Is Mama hurt?"

"Yes, your mother is hurting. But, not in the way you think. Eliza, oh, how can I say it? Eliza, your father is dead."

Papa? Papa dead. *He was just here last night!* He teased me about coming to tuck me in, just like he used to when I was little. *No, Papa cannot be dead.*

"No, you don't know what you are talking about. Papa can't be dead."

"Yes, Eliza, he is. He must have died in his sleep. Your mother did not realize until he would not wake up this morning. Eliza, I have to see to her. I have to send word to Mary. I am sorry. I must leave you here alone with this news fresh in your mind."

I can scarcely take in what he has said, but I try to stay calm. Remember the baby.

"What can I do to help?" I ask.

Bill kisses me on the cheek. "Do what you do best. Pray."

So, I pray. *It isn't that I have not prayed when my children died. I did. I prayed with deep desperation, but, something is different about the situation this time.* Something within me opens to a feeling of peace and calm that covers me in a way I have never felt it before. My heart feels no anger or resentment. It makes no sense at all. I love my father and will miss him terribly. *Thank you God for the time we had together in the last few months. Thank you for the vis-*

its and the talks as I lay here in this bed. Forgive me for my unrest and resentment. For in that time, I got to know my father in a way I never knew him before. I smile. Not just my earthly father, but You, my Heavenly Father as well.

Many people come to pay their respects to Papa over the coming days. Several of the women visit me, too. Everyone talks about the death of Josiah Gates, founder of Manatee a few weeks before. His service was an elaborate rite complete with a large metal coffin and a procession of pall bearers. I am glad when Mama chooses to keep Papa's funeral a simple affair. A wooden coffin made by Bill and his brothers. A few dear friends, Captain Sam, Asa Bishop, Captain Tresca, and family, William, Bill, his brothers, all carry the casket to the graveyard behind the house. I do not go. Though I believe God will protect my baby, I stay in bed so as not to give Bill any other reasons to worry. He has enough on his mind. He loved Papa dearly as well, and now, he has the responsibility for Mama's care. Despite my grief, I chuckle. That will not be an easy task. I would not wish that on anyone.

I do not realize how much of a problem Mama can be until Bill makes a surprising announcement. After Papa's death, he and Mama take to bringing their plates to the cabin to eat with me. Mama says it is so that I do not have to eat alone, but I suspect it is because the kitchen is too empty and lonely without Papa there. Bill pulls a little table closer to the bed for the two of them, but I giggle and proclaim, "I have my own table. Look!" Everyone laughs as I balance my plate upon my large belly. The baby still lives and now, he plays within my extended abdomen. Once again, my stomach rolls and pitches with a baby's movements providing entertainment for all to see.

I do not miscarry, despite our time of mourning. Seven months along. We make it through our first Christmas and Mama's birthday without Papa. Soon, Bill and I will celebrate our second anniversary. Julia died almost two years before. Jose-

phine would have been ten in April. It comforts me to think that
now, my girls and the three others I lost have their grandfather
to play with them and hold them close. I imagine them playing
horsie among the clouds.

"Keep them safe until I get there, Papa," I sometimes whisper as though he can still hear.

One night at supper, Bill says, "I have kept a secret from you
ladies far too long. Joe knew and we had talked a lot about it,
but the time never seemed right to tell you two."

He shrugs his shoulders.

"The timing is probably not right today either, but I better
confess."

I lean forward. *A secret, what can it be?* Bill is not the type to
be underhanded, so it must be a something good. Mama also
looks expectant.

"I have been building a house in Fogartyville."

A house! Why did he keep such an important thing from me?

"It is near my brother, Tole's, on Fogarty Point. The house is
very near the river so you can see the water from all three
sides."

Still stunned, I see how proud he is of his work.

"The house has a double porch across the front. It is quite
lovely even if I do say so myself. Ellen and Ann say that you
will like it."

I am surprised, but not angry. Mama, though, has a sour
look on her face.

Bill continues, "It has plenty of room for all of us. I think we
should move right away before the baby comes, Eliza. I will feel
more comfortable if you are close to a doctor and my family to
help take care of you."

Uh, oh. Now Mama will really be angry.

"And I suppose you do not think that I can take care of my
own daughter when this baby comes? Perhaps you think that I
did not do a good enough job with the last ones?" she says as

she rises and carries her plate from the room.

Bill stands in confusion, "No, no ma'am. That is not what I thought at all. I just want to make sure Eliza and the baby are safe."

"Near your family, you said," Mama continues out the door.

"Well, her family will not be going. I am staying here. This is my home. You can do as you wish."

I reach out my hand towards Bill. He leaves the table and comes to sit on the edge of my bed.

"That did not go very well," he says.

"No, had I known I might have advised you to present it differently," I laugh. "You sure did give us both a surprise."

"Are you angry, too?"

I smile. "No, just a little taken aback. Why didn't you tell me earlier?"

"I originally intended for it to be a surprise. Then, everything happened with your father and well, I just wasn't sure anymore."

Bill's voice cracks. "I miss him so. He always knew just what to say."

I lean forward and kiss Bill softly.

"I miss him, too. But, sometimes, it is like he is still here, and I can hear him talking to me."

Bill nods. "So, what shall we do about your mother?"

"The question is, what will she do about us? You might as well get it in your head that Julia Atzeroth will never do anything that she does not want to do." I shake my head.

"She will go or she will stay, and we will work around it. Now, Mr. Fogarty, what do you have planned for me?"

Bill describes the house some more. When he is done, he says, "I think you will be happy there, Eliza. Ellen and Ann cannot wait for you to come. I know you still have a ways to go before our child is born. We have been so careful up until now, but do you think you could travel to Fogartyville? I would like my son to be born there."

"Fogartyville is it now? And what of Manatee or the new town Mr. Lamb is creating called Palmetto. What is wrong with being born on Terra Ceia for that matter?"

"Fogartyville is closer to the doctor. Just in case. Please, Eliza. Do you think it will be safe to travel?"

I repeat the advice Dr Branch gave us, "Only God knows Bill. Let's pray about it and see what He says."

"Well, ask Him to convince your mother into going along while you are talking to Him won't you?"

I laugh, "If she goes, it will definitely be because God is at work."

I pray, and so does Bill for that matter. We agree to go as long as it is a very calm day and no chance of a bumpy ride. Bill fashions a bed in the bottom of the yawl so I can rest on the journey. While God has given us approval to go, He obviously did not get through to Mama for she steadfastly refuses to budge.

"This is my home," she repeats. "Don't worry about leaving me here alone, I will be fine."

But, I worry about abandoning her. When Bill finds an Irish woman who is willing to come and stay on the island with Mama, we are both relieved. This time, Bill asked for my advice in approaching my mother.

"Don't tell her the woman is here to help her. Tell her the woman needs a place to stay and ask if Mama is willing to help her."

That is the way Bill states his case, and Mama is quite willing to help the "old lady" out.

"I will be back regularly to help with the farm, too," he tells her, only to be informed that she will not need his help.

I roll my eyes. "I told you," I mouth to my husband.

The first clear day, with just the right amount of wind, Bill helps me walk slowly towards the bay. For seven months, I have only been as far as the outhouse, so it takes great effort to go so far. We stop several times along the way so I can catch my breath. Finally, we reach the boat. Bill picks me up and carries me on board where I settle on the pallet he placed there.

"Are you alright," he asks.

I know he is concerned. I struggle with anxiety as well. *How will this affect the baby?*

Now, I say with confidence, "Trust God, Bill. We will be fine."

He places his hand on my abdomen.

"Rest easy, little one," he says.

At that moment, the baby kicks so hard, Bill's hand bounces away.

"Oh," I groan. "That hurt."

"Are you sure you are alright?" Bill's face twists in concern.

"Yes, I am fine, but I think the baby is saying he is ready to go for a ride. Hoist the sail, Papa and let's get going."

So far, there is no sign of Mama. I do not expect one. I remember how she treated Mary when she left to join William. Though I was married to Michael over ten years, I never really lived away from my parents. Mama attended the birth of each of my babies living and dead. This change cannot be easy on her.

As the boat leaves the shoreline, Bill says, "Well, look there."

"What, look where?"

"You cannot see from down there, but don't get up. Your mother is waving to us."

"Really? Wave back to her."

"I am," he replies. "I'm waving as hard as I can."

Thank you, God that she bids us goodbye, I pray. That is something anyway. Keep her safe and bring her around to coming and living in Fogartyville with us soon. This little one will need a grandma to take care of him.

To shorten the distance, Bill takes us through the cut off between the mainland and the island that separates Terra Ceia Bay and the Manatee River. It is too shallow and narrow to sail through, so he poles the boat along. At least this way, we will not have to venture into Tampa Bay where the waves maybe choppy. From the channel, it is just a short sail across the river to the dock at the new town of Fogartyville. It has been so long since I visited the Fogartys. I lean up on one arm to see over the side of the boat. There is a new road and a large dock extending almost to the middle of the river. Bill does not steer for the dock, but straight to the river bank.

"Look, there is our home."

"Oh, Bill, it is beautiful. I never saw such a fine place."

The house is clearly visible from the river. A double porch runs its length, and all the front doors and windows open onto it. Up under the peak of the roof is a big window.

"Is there a third floor, too?"

"Yes, for now, we can use it as an attic. But, I thought it would be a good place for the children to sleep eventually."

Children. Oh, my husband is an optimist.

"Now, let's get you through this greeting party and up to the house," he says.

A mass of Fogartys gather on the lawn in front of the house waiting for us. I can see Ann standing next to John who holds Robert. Then, there is Ellen with Tole and their family. The boys jump up and down with excitement to see Uncle Bill. *My! Haven't they all grown?*

Bill carries me to shore. It is a little embarrassing to be treated like such an invalid. Ann comes forward and kisses my cheek.

"Welcome, Eliza. Welcome to Fogartyville. We are so glad to have you on this side of the river!" She laughs. "I hope you don't tire of me, now we can visit every day!"

"Oh, no, I cannot imagine getting tired of any of you. This is very exciting for me. I have been cooped up in the wilderness for so long now."

"Well, you are going to think this is a wildness rather than a wilderness with all these Fogartys in and out, but come on. I can't wait for you to see your new house. The men worked so hard on it. I have to say, I am a little jealous of all the things they thought to do to yours that I do not have. I am going to have them come around and do some improvements to my place now that they are done with yours," she confides with a wink in her husband's direction.

"Bill, you can put me down now," I protest.

"No, I have been waiting for a long time to carry my bride over the threshold of our home," he replies.

Everyone laughs, and one of the boys runs ahead to open the door. With all the doors and windows to catch the breeze from the river, the house is nice and cool inside. The front door centers a large parlor which takes up the middle third of the downstairs.

"Bill, we prepared the bedroom on the left," Ellen instructs.

Bill turns that direction and carries me through another door into a lovely room with windows on each wall.

"Oh, this is so pretty. It looks like a garden."

Bright flowered curtains hang from the windows, and a beautiful pastel quilt stretches across the bed. Ann pulls the quilt and sheets down so that Bill can put me upon the bed. He gently removes my shoes, then, I pull my feet up and tuck them under the covers.

"This is lovely. I know I will rest easy here. Thank you all."

I stretch out on the bed and put my head on the pillows. It has been a long day, and I am tired already.

"We'll go so you can take a nap. One of us will be back at noon with your dinner. We will make sure that you do not have to do anything but care for that baby until he gets here," Ann says.

One at a time, all the family members give me a hug and say that they will see me later. When the last one leaves, I cannot keep my eyes open another minute.

"Thank you, Bill. It is a beautiful home."

"I cannot wait to show you the rest of it. But, now, you need to sleep. Are you sure you are alright?"

"I am fine. It will be nice having you so close by now. I don't have to worry about you going back and forth to Fogartyville anymore every day."

"No, but I will need to be going back and forth to Terra Ceia to check on your mother. I wish she would have come with us."

"In time Bill, in time. Once the baby is here, you will not be able to keep her away."

I yawn and stretch again. The baby kicks me hard, and I wince.

"I'm alright," I say before Bill can ask.

"Just another punch is all. I hope he settles down so I can take a nap."

I am so tired that it does not matter if the baby rolls and squirms all day. The salt air combines with all the exercise to work like magic. In just a moment, I am fast asleep.

The days speed by as I wait for the birth of my child. Either Ellen or Ann arrives at every meal to bring me food and check on me. Whoever comes usually stays to chat. I like them both, but have more to talk about with Ann. Or perhaps it is that Ann has more time with only one child to care for instead of Ellen's five.

"Does it hurt you to see our little ones," Ann asks one day.

"No, not anymore," I say as I rub my stomach.

The baby moves and kicks all the time now, and it is hard to rest. I have taken to referring to the baby as he since all the Fogartys are convinced it will be a boy.

"He is active and for that I am very grateful. There is no doubt that he is alive and ready to take on the world."

"I don't think I will ever get a chance to feel that," Ann says wistfully. "I love my little Robert, but it would be nice to know what it is like to carry one myself."

I remember that Robert is adopted. His mother died from yellow fever.

"It is not too late. There may be one yet," I say.

"We have been married five years and nothing. You would think by now."

Ann stops. "I shouldn't complain. Look at all you have been through. I am just blessed to have my one."

"It is alright Ann. I know the longing you feel. At one time, I thought it would have been better to have never given birth than to have lost them so young. I still do not understand, but I have come to believe that I don't need to. All I have to do is trust that God knows best, that He loves me and is in control. Everything else, I leave up to Him."

Ann nods.

"But, that is the hard part, leaving it up to Him. I want what I want and I want it now."

I laugh, "I know that impatience. It got me in a whole heap of trouble one time."

I laugh again. "Well, more than one time. I still have difficulty waiting, but I am getting better at it." I pat my stomach. "This baby sure has taught me that. Being in bed for so long will teach you a lot." Then, I flinch, "Oh, I wish someone would teach him to wait. Oh, baby, that hurt."

I continue, "You know what I wish I knew though. I wish I knew why I am here. Do you remember when we studied Esther? She knew that God had placed her in the palace to save her people and though it was hard, she did what He called her to do."

"Yes, I remember," Ann says. "What was it her uncle said to her?"

"For such a time as this," I answer. "All these months I have been in bed, I have been thinking. What time is this for me? What do you think He has called me to do?"

Ann thinks a moment.

"Did you know that John takes care of the lighthouses and tends the buoys that guard the entrance to the river and the bay? He has to make sure that all of them light properly because without one of them doing its job, a ship could end up in shallow waters and sink."

I did not know that John has that responsibility, but I know of the importance of the guiding lights.

"John took me up to the top of the Egmont Key lighthouse with him once. You could see for a long way from up there. I imagined how many boats pass by and see that light even from a far distance away. The most interesting thing was that the light is just a tiny flame. But, it rests in the center of a huge piece of glass. That lens is cut and shaped in just the right way to reflect the light and magnify it. That is what makes the lighthouse so visible even from a long way away."

What is Ann talking about? What does this have to do with finding purpose in life?

Then, my friend concludes, "We are like that lighthouse, Eliza. It is our job to reflect God. We might be just a tiny flame warning people about danger and guiding them towards home. But, if we are set in the middle of God's will for us, He uses us frail as we are to do that work. I have watched you cope with all the hardship you have faced. I do not know how you have survived the losses. I know your life has not been easy. But, yet, you stand here," she corrects herself, "Well, today, you lie here."

I laugh.

"But even lying here in this bed, you are a beacon, a witness to everyone who knows you of what a life committed to God and willing to let Him be in control can be like. You give me and everyone else a little glimpse of heaven, Eliza. We can see the peace and contentment you express and know that there is something better out there, someday waiting on us. That, my friend, is your purpose and my purpose, too."

Tears come to my eyes. When Ann puts it that way, it sounds like something really special. *Can my ordinary life make such a difference to someone?*

I do not know what to say. So I say simply, "Thank you. That helps. I guess if even one person can learn from what I have been through, it will be worth it."

"Well," Ann states, "This one person has, so I think you can say it was."

She turns to go. "I'll be back in a little while. Why don't you get some rest? It won't be long before your baby will be keeping you up all night long with his crying."

Please God, let it be so, I pray. Then, I continue, *Thank you God for Ann. For sending her to be a lighthouse to me and help me understand. I want to be a beacon, too, God. No matter what happens, let me continue to show people to You.*

The next day, I feel lazy and listless. When Bill kisses me good bye, I can't even open my eyes.

"Hey, sleepyhead, going to tell me to have a good day?" he asks.

I don't answer. Something isn't right.

Still with my eyes closed, I ask, "What are you doing today?"

"I was going to head over to Terra Ceia and check on your mother. Why?"

I hate to worry him, but neither do I want my husband far away from me today.

"Bill, I don't feel very well. I don't think you should go far."

Instantly, he is concerned.

"Why what is wrong?"

"It is probably nothing, but I just want you to stay close."

"Do you need the doctor?"

I keep my eyes closed so can't see him, but can tell by his voice he is getting anxious.

"I don't know. I don't think so. I have just never felt this way

371

before. It is probably nothing. I haven't been sleeping very well at night. With so little activity, I am not very sleepy and the baby rolls around so. I am probably just tired is all."

"I am not going anywhere today. I will stay here. I am sending Tole for the doctor and John for your mother. This scares me Eliza."

"Don't be frightened," I murmur. "But I would like to see Mama."

I pull my hand from under the covers to reach for Bill's.

"Eliza, your hand is so swollen. Let me see the other one."

He pulls down the covers.

"That one is swollen, too. Now that I look closer at your face, it seems like it is puffy."

"I have just been in bed for so long. I will be alright when the baby comes, and I can get up again."

"I'm sending for the doctor. Stay still, I will be right back."

I laugh to myself. *Where does he think I will go?* I feel like I am floating and drift back to sleep.

I wake to hear lots of voices around me. I try to open my eyes, but the light is blinding. I put my hand over my eyes.

"Could you close the drapes, please? The light hurts my eyes."

"Eliza," it is Ann. "The drapes are closed."

What is wrong with my head? It aches so.

"I don't feel good."

"I know, daughter."

Mama is here, too.

"Dr. Pelot is on his way."

I just want to sleep. Everyone should go away and let me sleep. When the doctor arrives, I wake again. He clears everyone but Mama and Bill out of the room.

"I do not know what is wrong with her, but she needs to give birth right away. Why is she lying in bed?"

"She had three miscarriages," Bill explains.

"Dr. Branch told her to stay in bed. She has been here almost the entire pregnancy."

"Well, Dr. Branch may have given you sound advice, but not for now. She needs to get up and walk around. We need her labor to start right away. If she doesn't begin on her own, I will have to break her water and try that."

"Eliza, Eliza, come on now. We need to walk. Open your eyes."

Bill wants me to get up, but I cannot open my eyes.

"Her face is so swollen, I don't think that she can open her eyes," Mama says.

"Eliza, hold onto me. Let's walk. I will keep you from falling."

"No, go away, I just want to sleep."

"Eliza, listen to me. Get up and walk, now."

Mama means business. I feel like a little girl again. If Mama says walk, I better walk. I slip out of bed and let Bill take me by the waist. Around and around the bedroom, we pace.

"Eliza," the doctor says, "Can you still feel your baby move?"

When did I last feel him kick? Last night? This morning?

"I don't remember."

"Keep walking," Mama says.

Where am I? Am I by the river? Is it time for Josey to be born? No, Josey is dead. Which baby is this? There have been so many. Then, I feel a rush of water between my legs.

"Good, good, that's what we want," Dr. Pelot says.

"Keep walking, Eliza," encourages Mama.

The pains come. Not as fast as Julia's, but building like Josephine's. Finally, the swelling begins to go down in my face and hands. The headache eases, as well. I can see now. Bill's expression is sad. *Has he been crying? His eyes look swollen, too.* Finally, the urge to push. As always, my body takes over to do its work. Mama lets me lie down. Dr. Pelot examines me.

"Almost time, Eliza. Give me some good pushes."

I am tired. Tired of walking. Tired of hurting. Tired of all the people telling me what to do. But, the contractions keep on coming and the baby bears down the birth canal, and there is nothing to do but push and scream and push some more.

"I can feel his head," Dr. Pelot says. "One more good push, come on Eliza."

Bill cannot speak. I hardly have time to glance his way. He is crying again. I grip his hand and with one yell from deep inside me, the baby slides out into Dr. Pelot's hands.

"It's a boy!" he calls.

"Is he alright?" Bill asks.

Dr. Pelot does not answer. Instead, I hear the lusty cry of my son.

"Take him, Madam Joe," Dr. Pelot says. "I need to attend to mother."

"That is a lot of blood," I hear Bill whisper. "Is there usually that much blood?"

It is then that it dawns on me. Bill is still in the room. *Why is he here? Aren't fathers supposed to be outside? I am glad he is here. Glad I can say goodbye. It is time to go.*

I can hear Josey calling me. And Papa.

"Come to Papa," he says. Look there is Julia. She holds a baby girl. And two little boys stand beside her like stair steps. Time to go. I am so tired, but, something holds me back. I cannot move towards them. Behind me, the cry of a baby. *He needs me. They are safe and sound. With Jesus. My baby needs me more.*

"Eliza! Eliza! Can you hear me? What should we name the baby, Eliza?"

"William," I whisper. "William Joseph Fogarty."

"I think we turned the corner," I hear Dr. Pelot say. "I was worried there for a moment. She's had a lot of bleeding, but I think it has stopped now. You want to get some fluids in her. Water, tea, broth. Whatever she can take. I don't think I will leave quite yet. I want to stay and keep a close eye on her. We still have to watch for fever. "

I open my eyes.

"Where's my baby?"

Relief floods Bill's face. Mama lifts my son so I can see.

"Let me have him."

William Joseph Fogarty nuzzles against my breast where two little girls once sought nourishment. *I will live. Not just for him. But to be that lighthouse. I have to tell others what I have seen. But, not now.*

I reached my hand out and draw Bill close. This time is for William and for Bill. My family. For as long as God gives them to me.

Author's Note

If you are reading this, then, you have finished Eliza's Story. Thank you for coming along on this tale I have woven from her life. If you are like me and read Author's Notes, you may want to know how this book came to be. It started a long, long time ago when I was a preteen. I was a voracious reader and took to reading some romance novels of which my Sunday School teacher did not approve. Instead of forbidding me to read them, she put something better in my hands, the historical fiction of Eugenia Price. Until that time, I had little interest in learning about the past. My school teachers taught history as a list of dates and names. In Miss Price's books, history was not as boring.

My parents, seeing my interest in her stories, took me to visit St. Simon's Island, Georgia. There, in the cemetery of Christ Church, it dawned on me that the people she wrote about were real. I vowed then and there to become a historian and grow up to show people that history was not solely about facts, but a collection of true stories of the people who came before us. That decision led me to the history departments of two fine universities where I learned to do research in primary sources, the information produced during whatever time period I studied. While at Furman University, my parents moved to Terra Ceia Island and built a house near the foundation stones of the Atzeroth family's log cabin. I wrote my undergraduate thesis on the Atzeroths which was later published in Tampa Bay History, a journal produced by the University of South Florida's history department where I finished my Master's Degree. Over time, not only did I become a better researcher, but other historians, knowing of my interest in the Atzeroths, sent me bits and pieces of information that they discovered while working on their own projects. The novel that you hold in your hand today is based on over twenty five years worth of poking here and there and uncovering the skeleton of Eliza's life.

I have many people to thank who helped me in this project. First, is the staff of the Manatee County Clerk of Circuit Court's Historical Resources Department who work so hard to protect and preserve Manatee County's history, as well as Manatee County Teen Court who look out for our community's children. They are wonderful people who are serious about their work and have all been encouraging in my position as their supervisor. Honestly, they do not need a supervisor. They can manage just fine on their own. I must single out Cindy Russell, the world's best genealogist who took the hints I dropped about needing help and searched the Internet for "my people", and Lu Rupert, who kept everyone's finances in line so I didn't have to worry about museums going broke while I had my head in the clouds musing over where Eliza would end up next. My bosses, Manatee County Clerk of Circuit Court, R.B. "Chips" Shore, who hired me over two decades ago even when he didn't have a job opening for a historian, and Christine Clyne, have also been supportive. Fellow historians, Joe Knetsch, Pam Gibson, and Ron Prouty sent me things that they found in the Florida and National Archives. Joe was of particular help, uncovering the discord between the Atzeroths and the other settlers.

My friends, Patty, Bethany, Vera Jo, Christina, Di, Julie, Penny and Ola kept telling me I could do it while my mom and Patty's mom, Claire, called after each set of chapters were finished to say how much they enjoyed the story. Some of these chapters were written in a writing class taught by Carol Crawford at the John C. Campbell Folk School in Brasstown, North Carolina. If you ever get a chance to take any of the classes offered there, do so. It is an inspiring place whether you are a writer, an artist, a crafter or a musician. There, I learned to just write and fix it later. I hope I've done enough fixing, Carol! While at school, I stayed at the beautiful home of friends, Peg and Jack Shoemake.

I am sorry that Jack did not live long enough to see this book published, but many times while writing, I felt Jack's spirit perched on my shoulder egging me on. In addition, there is a group of people who I have never met, but without whom this tale could not have been told. Each chapter was posted on my blog on the Internet. Fellow bloggers, Sophie, Suze, Vicki, Danielle and Ray helped me stay motivated and disciplined. Cherie Hill of Write Source Publishing Services made the book look so beautiful, I cried with joy!

The scenes on horseback were fleshed out during rides upon my Morgan horse, Trucker, (not Prince) with my friend, Andrea, who rides a Paso Fino, one of the ancestors of the Florida Cracker horse. As we rode around Terra Ceia and at Little Manatee and Alafia State Parks, I could easily imagine what Eliza's rides might have been like as well.

Of course, there is my family who stood behind me through the long year of writing this tale. My parents who started this whole thing with the trip to St. Simons encouraged me and chauffeured children around while I typed. I need to apologize to my in-laws for one very late dinner. I can confess now that I forgot to put the rice in the oven because I was writing and lost track of time. Housework and laundry also got sidetracked when I had a thought I needed to write down. I should also apologize to my husband, Glen and my boys, Robby and Timothy, and to Timothy's wife, Miranda, for the many times when they were talking to me, but I wasn't listening because I was thinking of Eliza's tale. I couldn't have done this without you guys! Glen even took me back to St. Simon's to visit Eugenia Price's grave and pay my respects to a woman whose gift I admire greatly.

Finally, I must give all praise to my Heavenly Father who offers me grace I do not deserve and gave me the gift of words. I hope most of all that you see Him in Eliza's Story and that He has been glorified throughout these pages.

ABOUT THE AUTHOR

Cathy Slusser is a second generation Floridian who grew up in St. Petersburg, but spent holidays and vacations with her grandparents who lived in Manatee County. She moved to Terra Ceia Island in northwest Manatee County in 1979. Cathy fell in love with history upon reading Eugenia Price novels in Middle School. When she traveled to St. Simons Island, Georgia and saw the places those characters lived, she knew that the subject of history could be alive and exciting. Ever since that time, she has made it her goal to share that message with others.

She has a bachelor's degree in history from Furman University and a master's degree in history from the University of South Florida. She has worked for the Manatee County Clerk of Circuit Court's Office for twenty-nine years and is Director of Historical Resource. In this role, she supervises five historical sites, the Manatee Village Historical Park, the Manatee County Historical Records Library, the Florida Maritime Museum at Cortez, the Palmetto Historical Park, and the Manatee County Agricultural Museum, as well as Manatee County Teen Court. Cathy has two grown sons, Rob and Tim, a fabulous daughter in law, Miranda, and a daughter of the heart, Christina. She married her husband, Glen, a third generation Floridian in 1981. She enjoys horseback riding, fusing glass, felting and writing. Cathy is passionate about preserving Manatee County's past and telling its stories to residents and visitors of all ages.

Made in the USA
Charleston, SC
19 November 2013